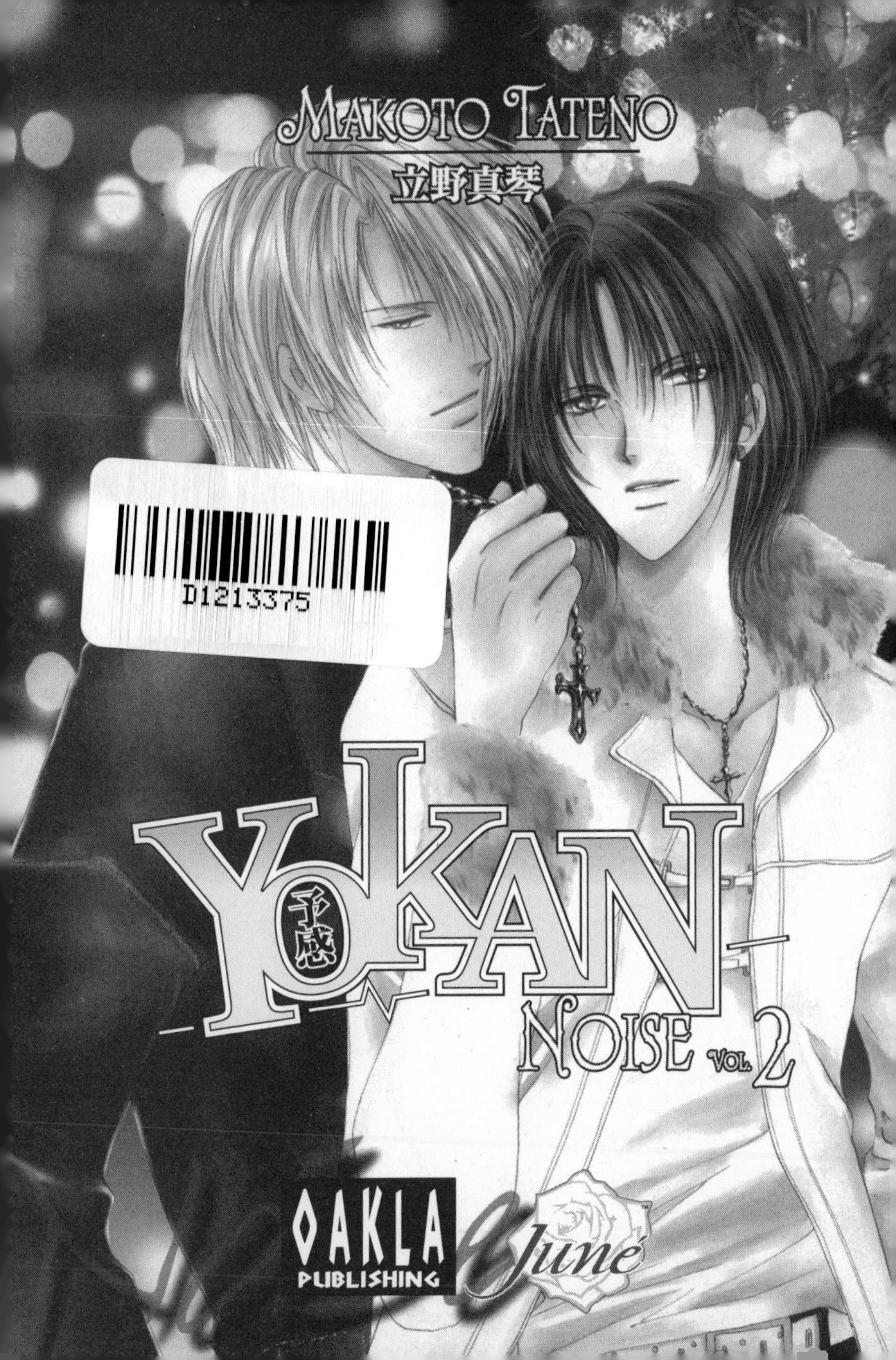
MAKOTO TATENO
立野真琴
YOKAN
予感
NOISE VOL. 2
OAKLA PUBLISHING
June

YOKAN NOISE VOL. 2

Co-Publishers
Masahiro Nagashima
Oakla Publishing

Hikaru Sasahara
Digital Manga, Inc.

Translation	Sachiko Sato
Lettering	Replibooks
Editing	Bambi Eloriaga
Japan Relations	Shinri Matsuoka
Graphic Design/Layout	Michelle Mauk/Matt Akuginow
Editor In Chief	Fred Lui

English Edition Co-Published by

OAKLA PUBLISHING
1-18-6 Kamimeguro
Meguro-ku, Tokyo 153-0051
Japan

www.oakla.com

DIGITAL MANGA PUBLISHING
A division of DIGITAL MANGA, Inc.
1487 W 178th Street, Suite 300
Gardena, CA 90248 USA

www.dmpbooks.com

First Edition: September 2010
ISBN-10: 1-56970-161-X
ISBN-13: 978-1-56970-161-4

1 3 5 7 9 10 8 6 4 2

Printed in Canada

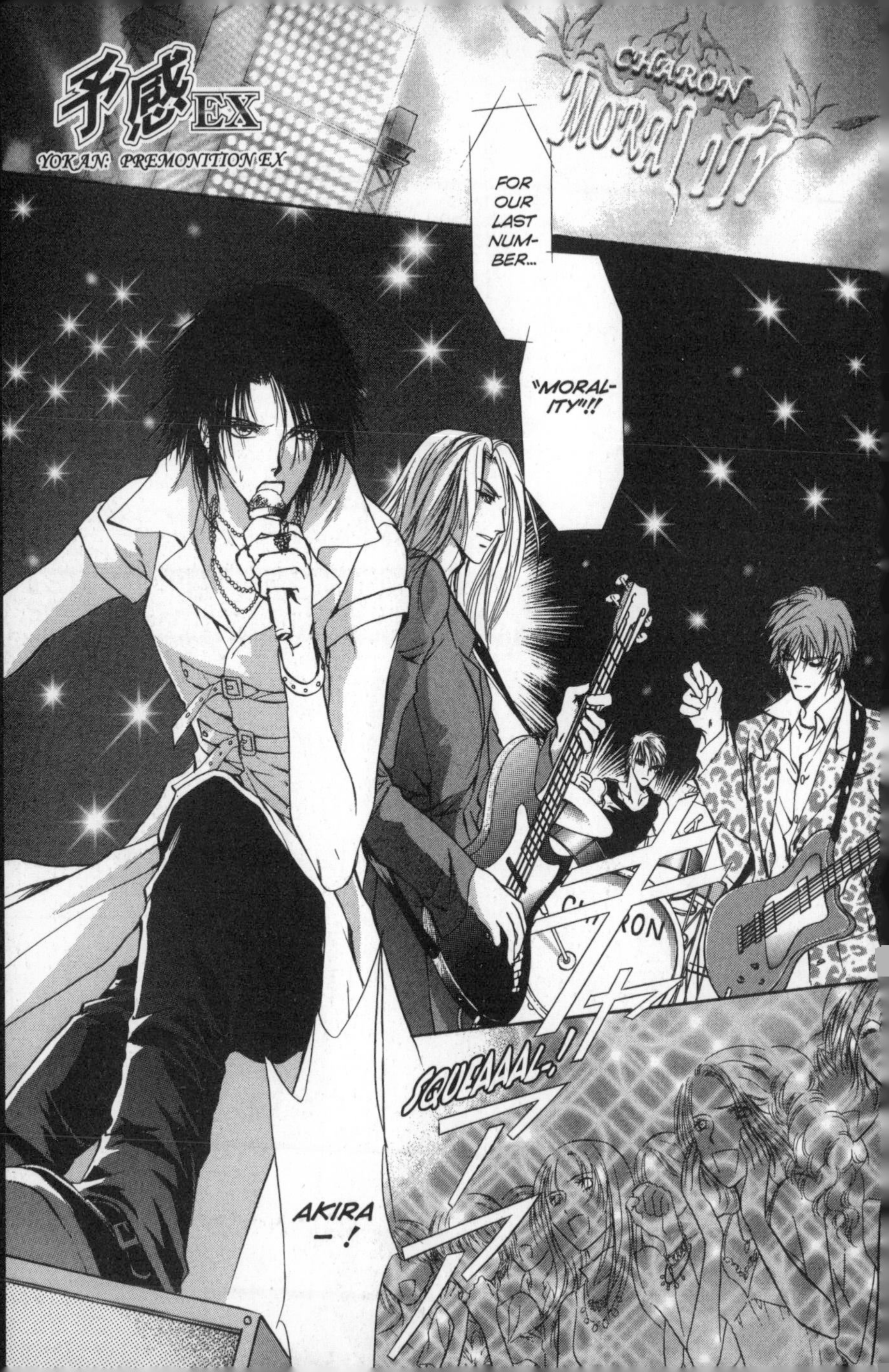

予感EX
YOKAN: PREMONITION EX
CHARON
MORALITY
FOR OUR LAST NUM-BER...
"MORAL-ITY"!!
SQUEAAAL-!
AKIRA —!

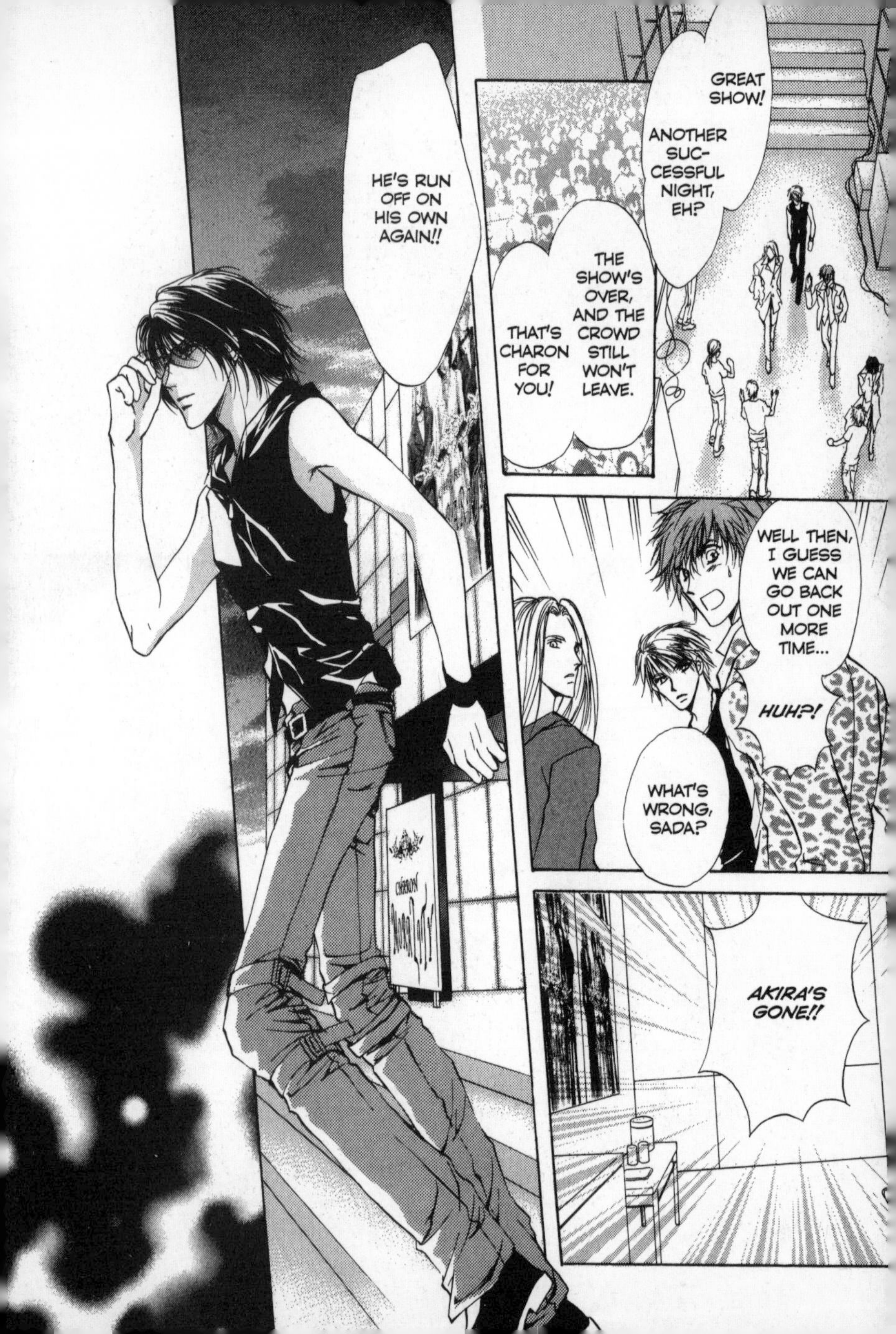
GREAT SHOW!
ANOTHER SUCCESSFUL NIGHT, EH?
THE SHOW'S OVER, AND THE CROWD STILL WON'T LEAVE.
THAT'S CHARON FOR YOU!
WELL THEN, I GUESS WE CAN GO BACK OUT ONE MORE TIME...
HUH?!
WHAT'S WRONG, SADA?
AKIRA'S GONE!!
HE'S RUN OFF ON HIS OWN AGAIN!!

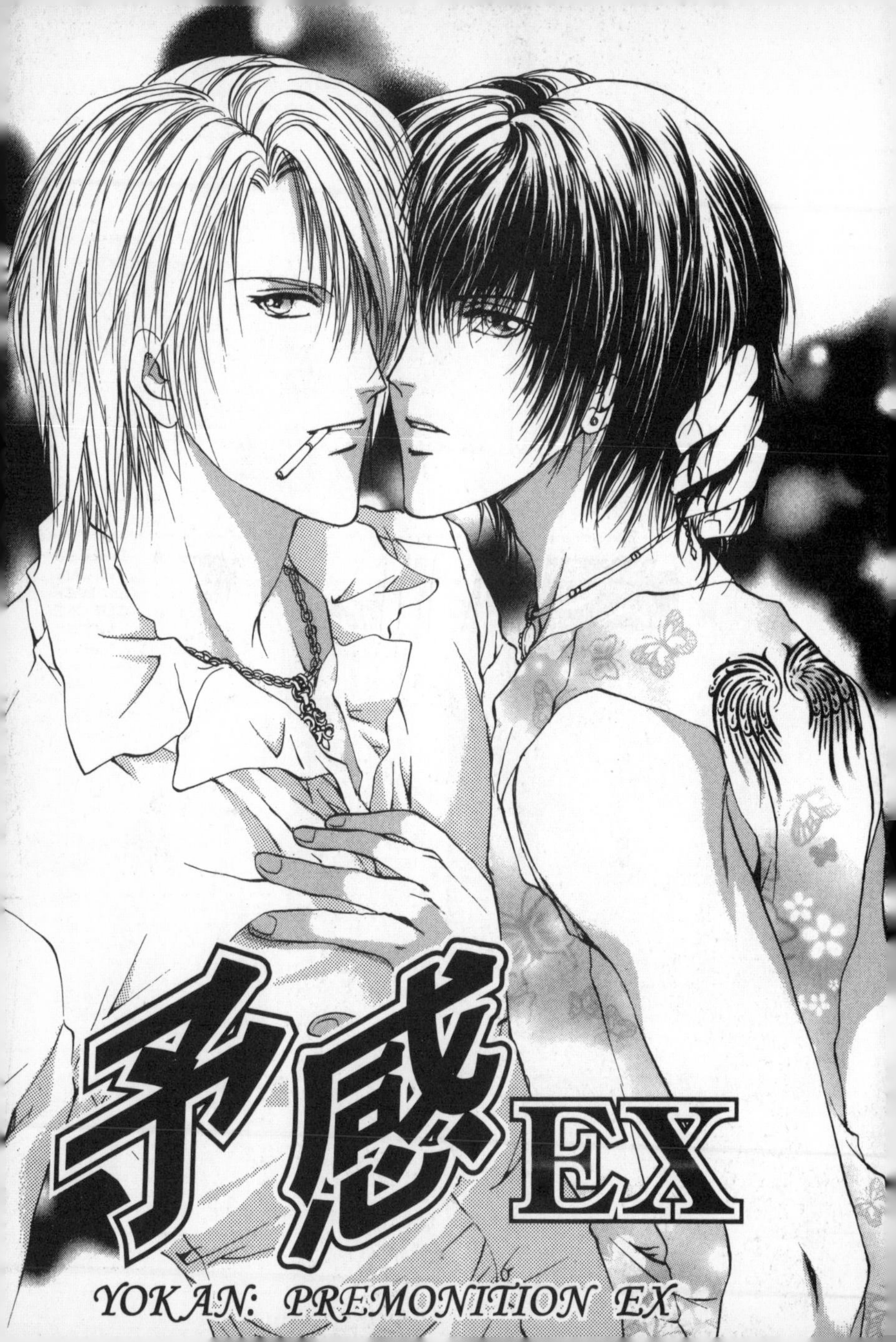
予感 EX
YOKAN: PREMONITION EX

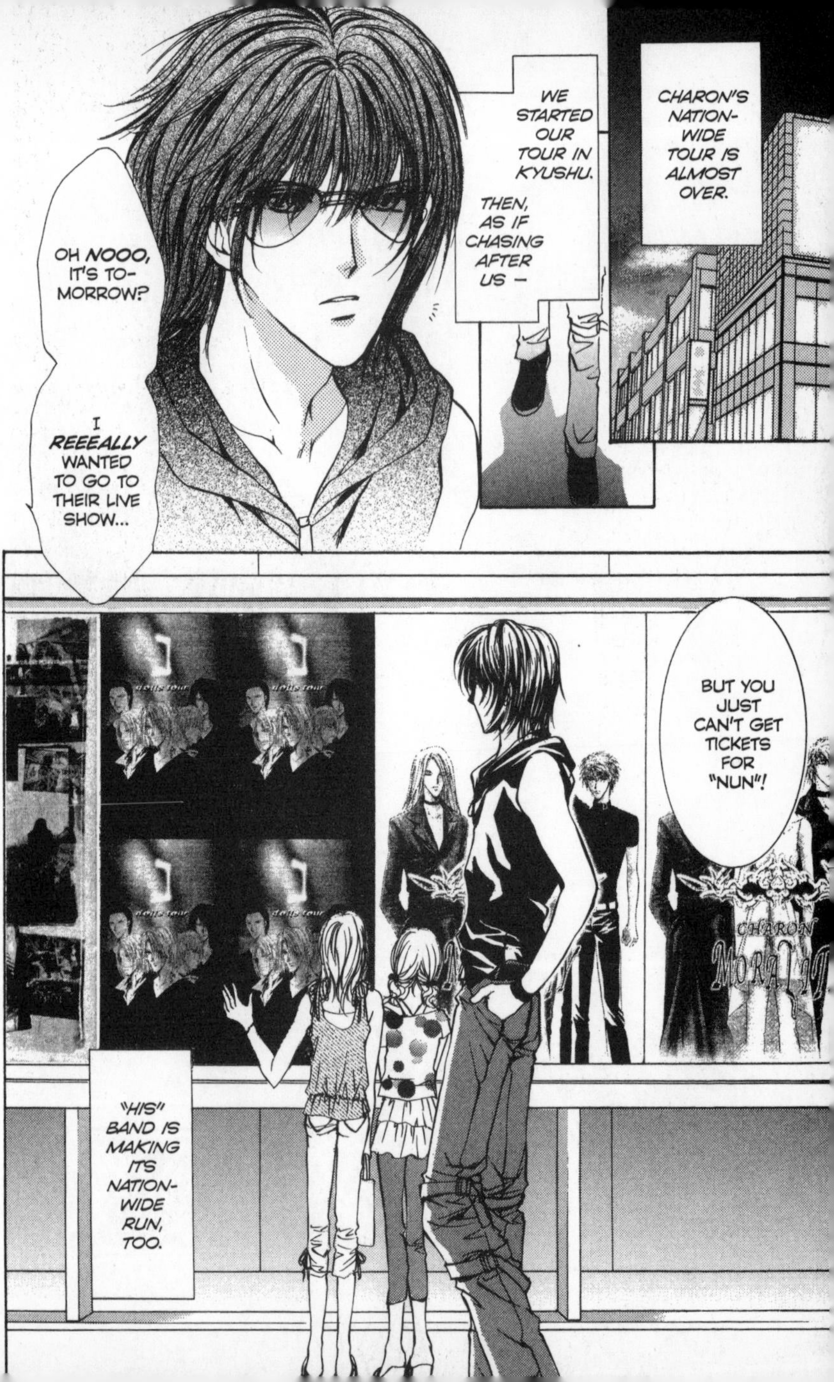
CHARON'S NATION-WIDE TOUR IS ALMOST OVER.
WE STARTED OUR TOUR IN KYUSHU.
THEN, AS IF CHASING AFTER US –
OH NOOO, IT'S TO-MORROW?
I REEEALLY WANTED TO GO TO THEIR LIVE SHOW...
BUT YOU JUST CAN'T GET TICKETS FOR "NUN"!
CHARON
"HIS" BAND IS MAKING ITS NATION-WIDE RUN, TOO.

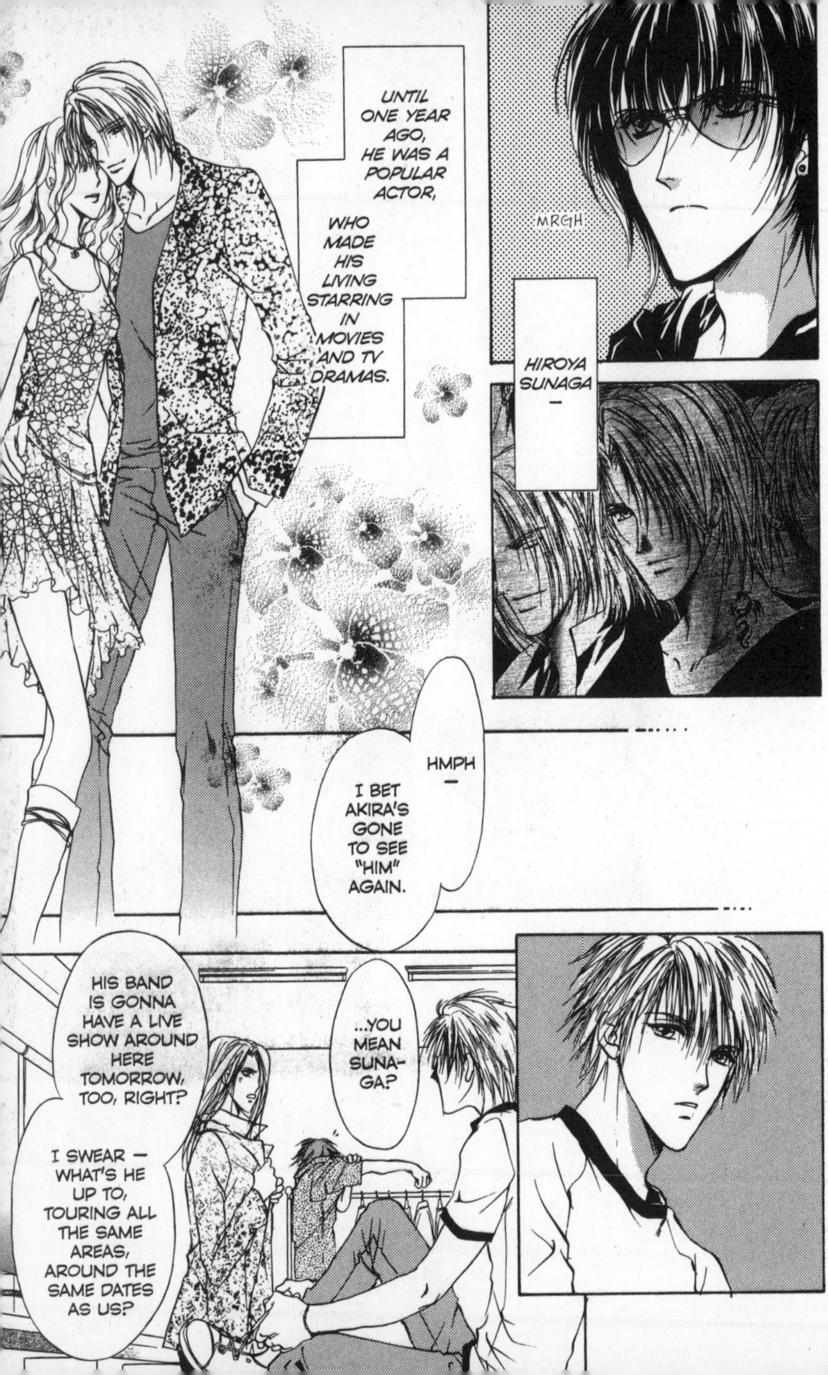
MRGH
HIROYA SUNAGA —
UNTIL ONE YEAR AGO, HE WAS A POPULAR ACTOR,
WHO MADE HIS LIVING STARRING IN MOVIES AND TV DRAMAS.
HMPH — I BET AKIRA'S GONE TO SEE "HIM" AGAIN.
...YOU MEAN SUNAGA?
HIS BAND IS GONNA HAVE A LIVE SHOW AROUND HERE TOMORROW, TOO, RIGHT?
I SWEAR — WHAT'S HE UP TO, TOURING ALL THE SAME AREAS, AROUND THE SAME DATES AS US?

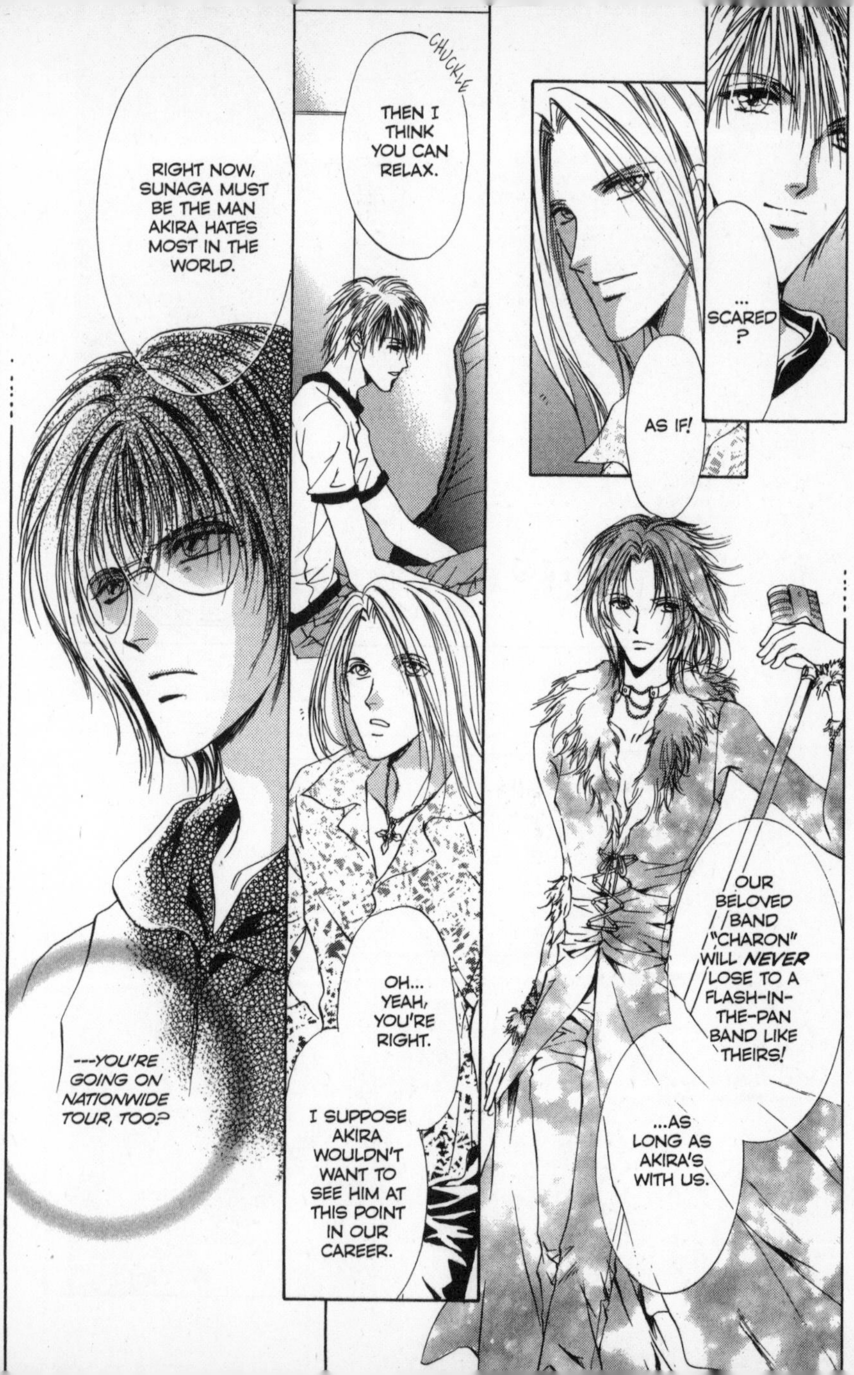
...SCARED?
AS IF!
OUR BELOVED BAND "CHARON" WILL ***NEVER*** LOSE TO A FLASH-IN-THE-PAN BAND LIKE THEIRS!
...AS LONG AS AKIRA'S WITH US.
CHUCKLE
THEN I THINK YOU CAN RELAX.
OH... YEAH, YOU'RE RIGHT.
I SUPPOSE AKIRA WOULDN'T WANT TO SEE HIM AT THIS POINT IN OUR CAREER.
RIGHT NOW, SUNAGA MUST BE THE MAN AKIRA HATES MOST IN THE WORLD.
---YOU'RE GOING ON NATIONWIDE TOUR, TOO?

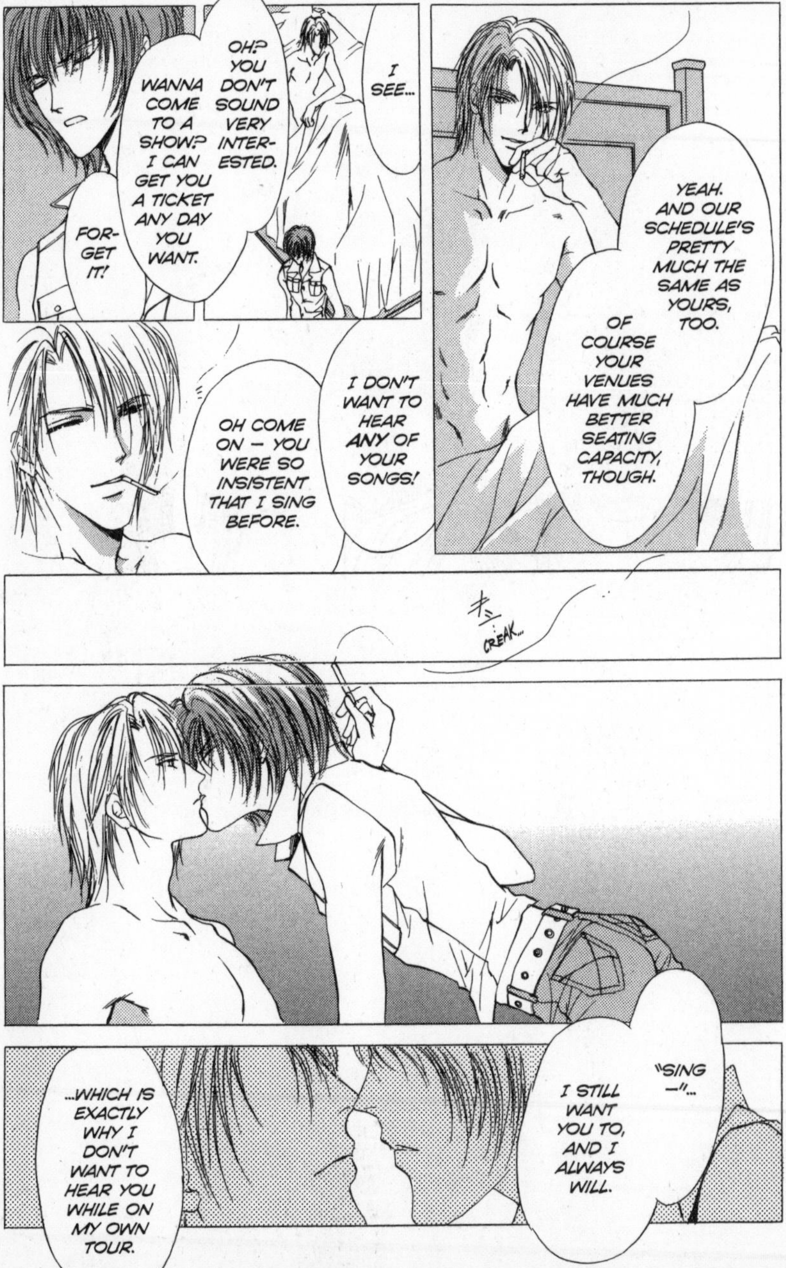
YEAH. AND OUR SCHEDULE'S PRETTY MUCH THE SAME AS YOURS, TOO.
OF COURSE YOUR VENUES HAVE MUCH BETTER SEATING CAPACITY, THOUGH.
I SEE...
OH? YOU DON'T SOUND VERY INTERESTED.
WANNA COME TO A SHOW? I CAN GET YOU A TICKET ANY DAY YOU WANT.
FORGET IT!
I DON'T WANT TO HEAR *ANY* OF YOUR SONGS!
OH COME ON – YOU WERE SO INSISTENT THAT I SING BEFORE.
CREAK...
"SING—"...
I STILL WANT YOU TO, AND I ALWAYS WILL.
...WHICH IS EXACTLY WHY I DON'T WANT TO HEAR YOU WHILE ON MY OWN TOUR.

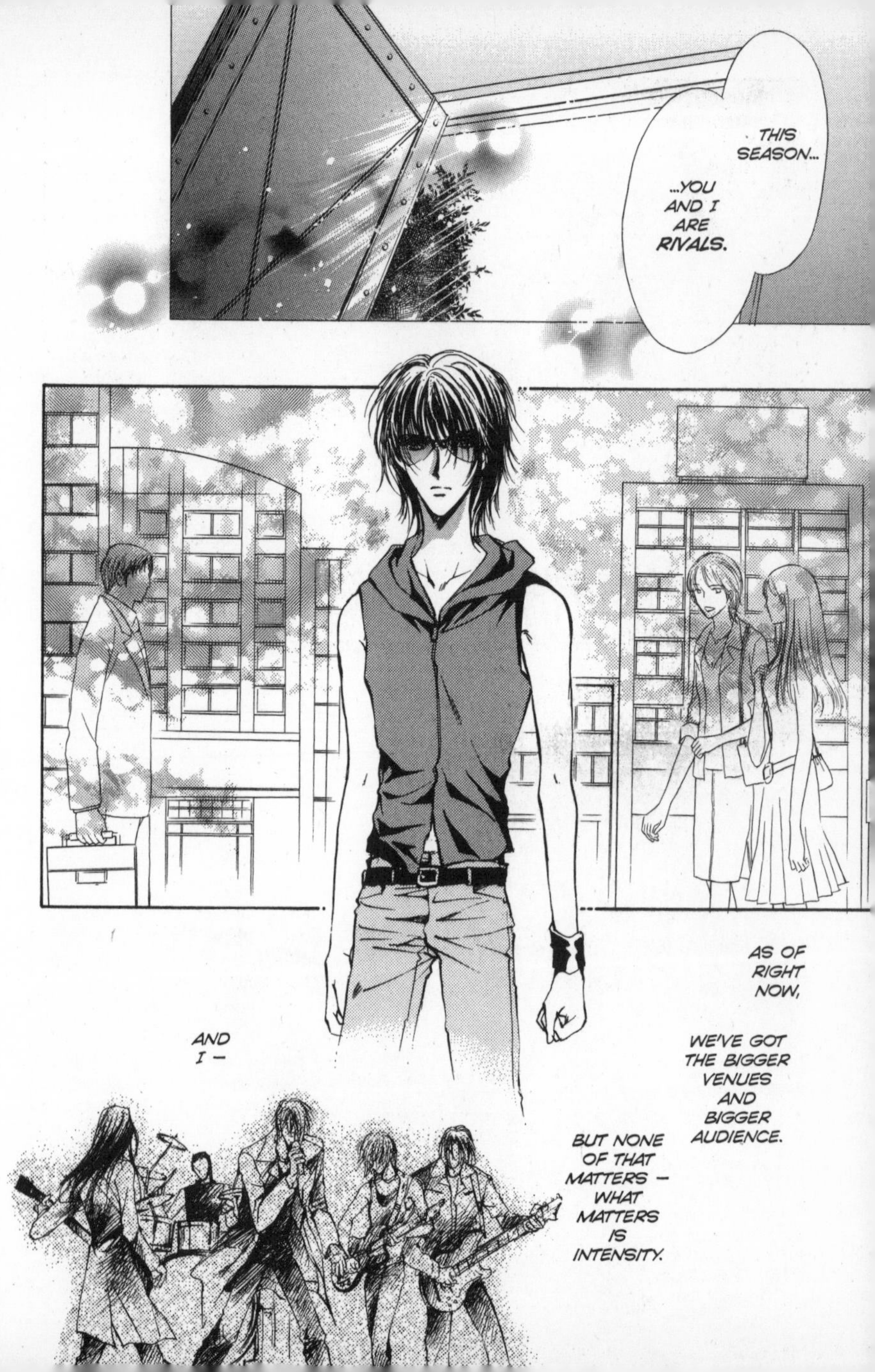
THIS SEASON...
...YOU AND I ARE RIVALS.
AS OF RIGHT NOW,
WE'VE GOT THE BIGGER VENUES AND BIGGER AUDIENCE.
BUT NONE OF THAT MATTERS — WHAT MATTERS IS INTENSITY.
AND I —

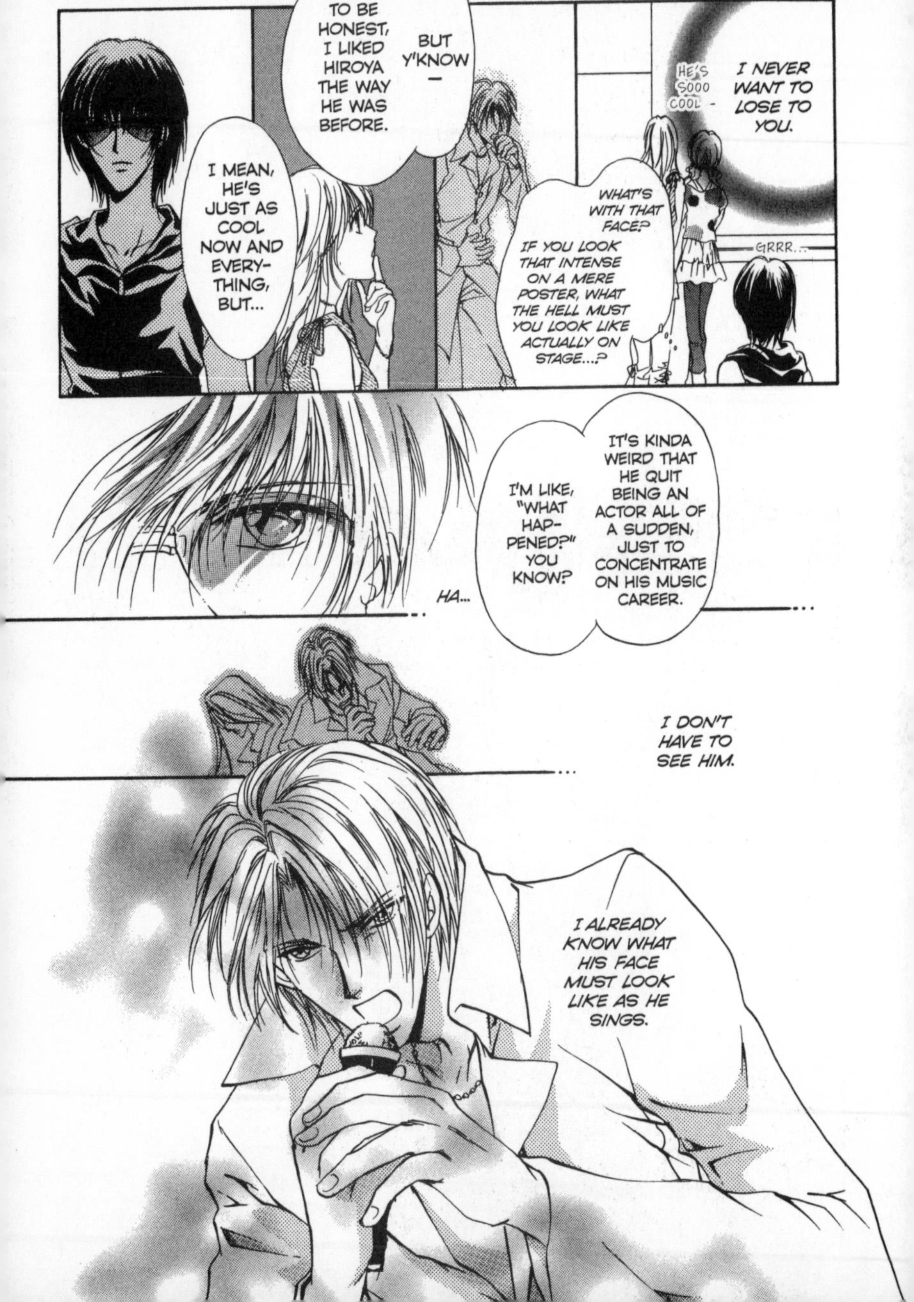
I NEVER WANT TO LOSE TO YOU.
HE'S SOOO COOL -
GRRR...
WHAT'S WITH THAT FACE?
IF YOU LOOK THAT INTENSE ON A MERE POSTER, WHAT THE HELL MUST YOU LOOK LIKE ACTUALLY ON STAGE...?
TO BE HONEST, I LIKED HIROYA THE WAY HE WAS BEFORE.
BUT Y'KNOW —
I MEAN, HE'S JUST AS COOL NOW AND EVERY-THING, BUT...
IT'S KINDA WEIRD THAT HE QUIT BEING AN ACTOR ALL OF A SUDDEN, JUST TO CONCENTRATE ON HIS MUSIC CAREER.
I'M LIKE, "WHAT HAP-PENED?" YOU KNOW?
HA...
I DON'T HAVE TO SEE HIM.
I ALREADY KNOW WHAT HIS FACE MUST LOOK LIKE AS HE SINGS.

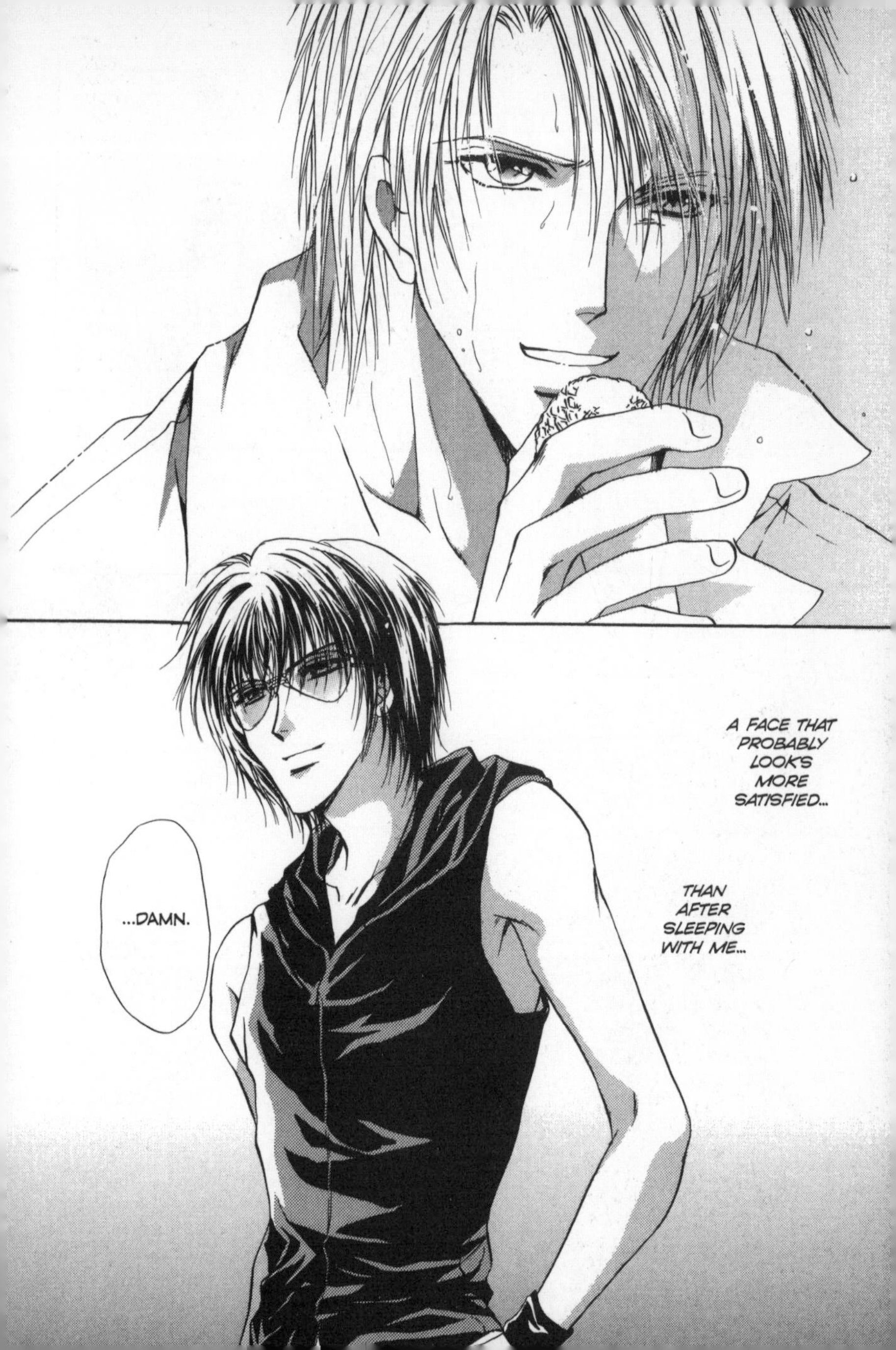
A FACE THAT PROBABLY LOOKS MORE SATISFIED...
THAN AFTER SLEEPING WITH ME...
...DAMN.

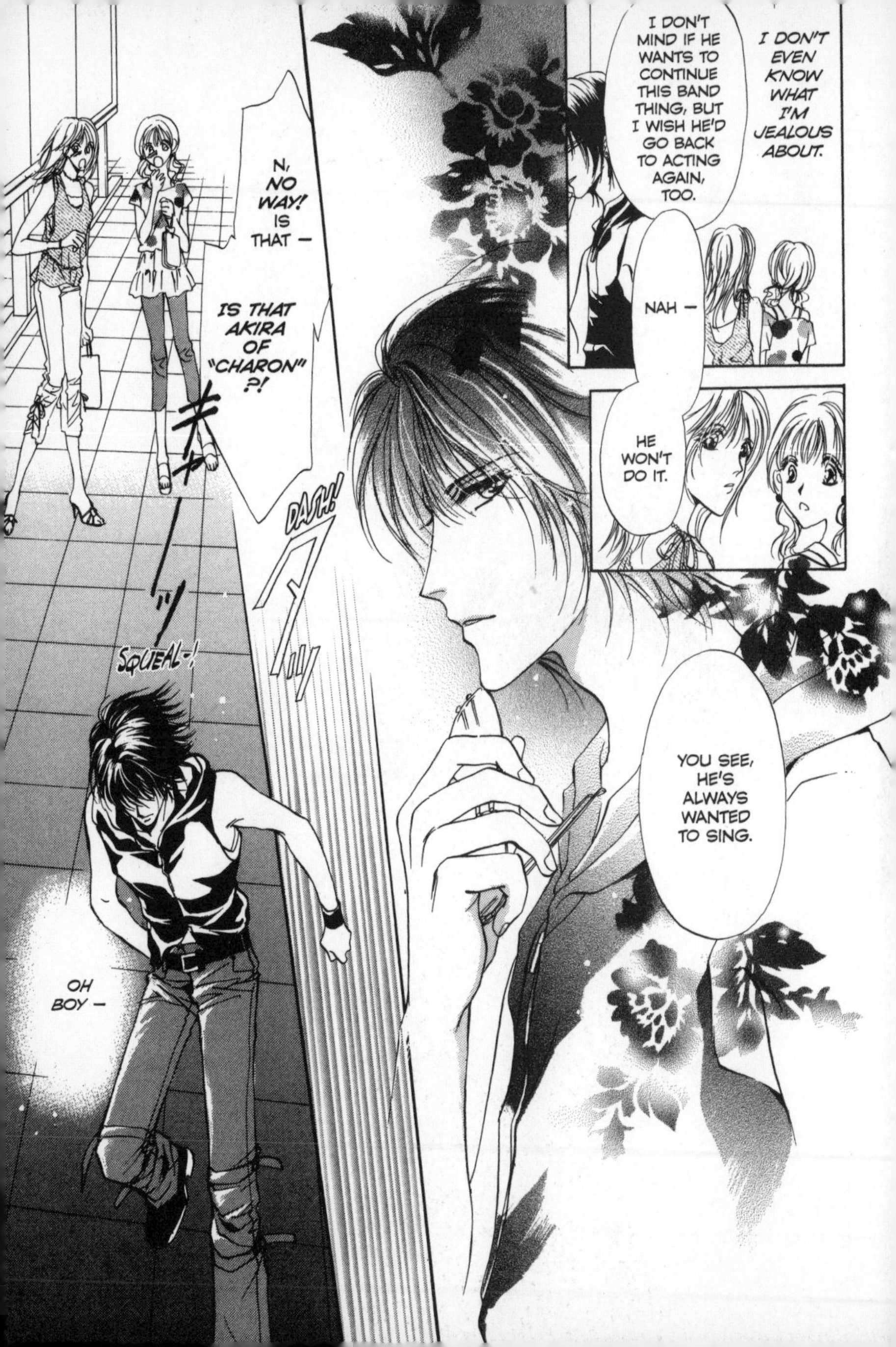
I DON'T EVEN KNOW WHAT I'M JEALOUS ABOUT.
I DON'T MIND IF HE WANTS TO CONTINUE THIS BAND THING, BUT I WISH HE'D GO BACK TO ACTING AGAIN, TOO.
NAH —
HE WON'T DO IT.
YOU SEE, HE'S ALWAYS WANTED TO SING.
N, NO WAY! IS THAT —
IS THAT AKIRA OF "CHARON" ?!
DASH!
SQUEAL—!
OH BOY —

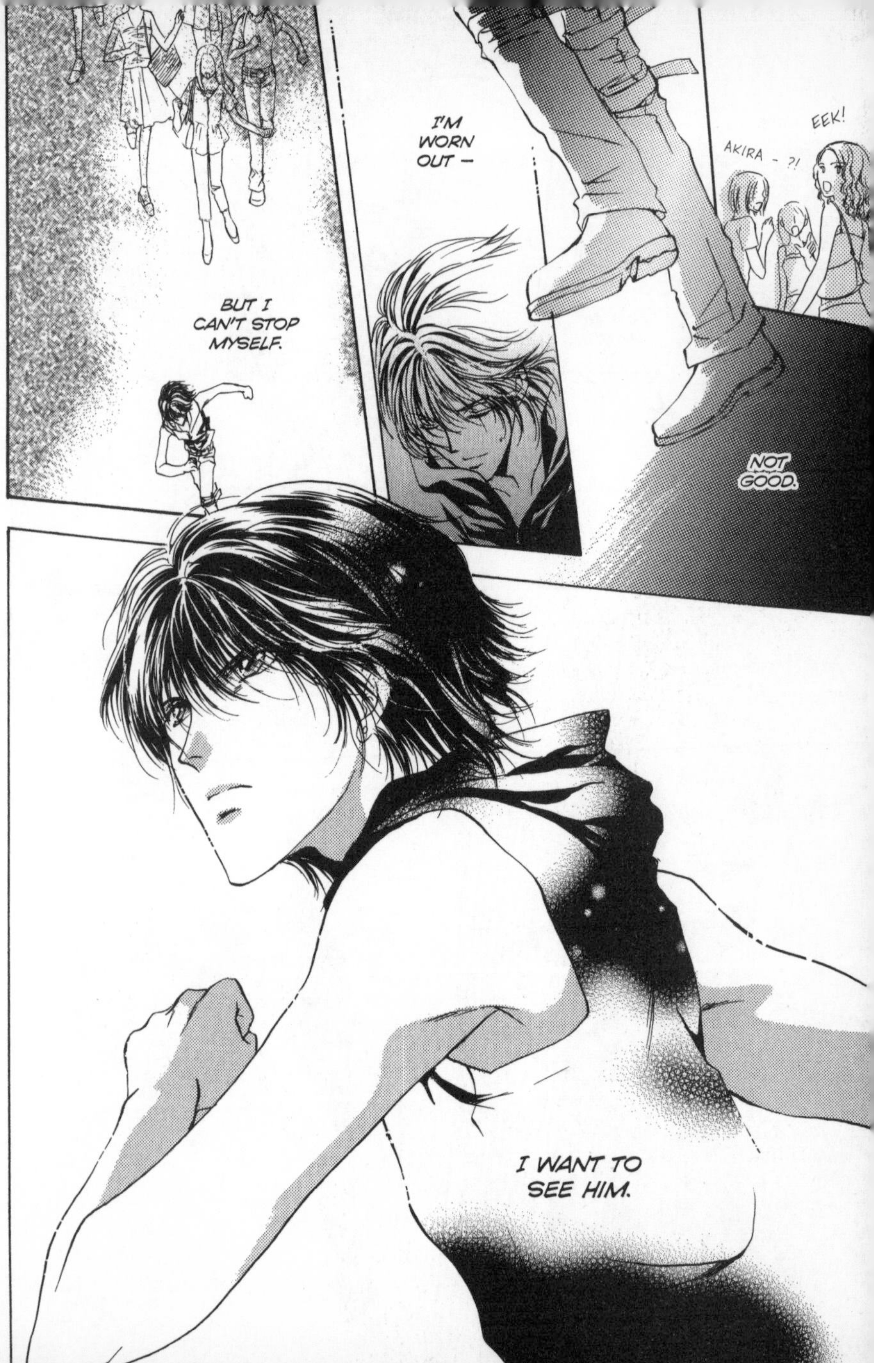
EEK!
AKIRA - ?!
NOT GOOD.
I'M WORN OUT -
BUT I CAN'T STOP MYSELF.
I WANT TO SEE HIM.

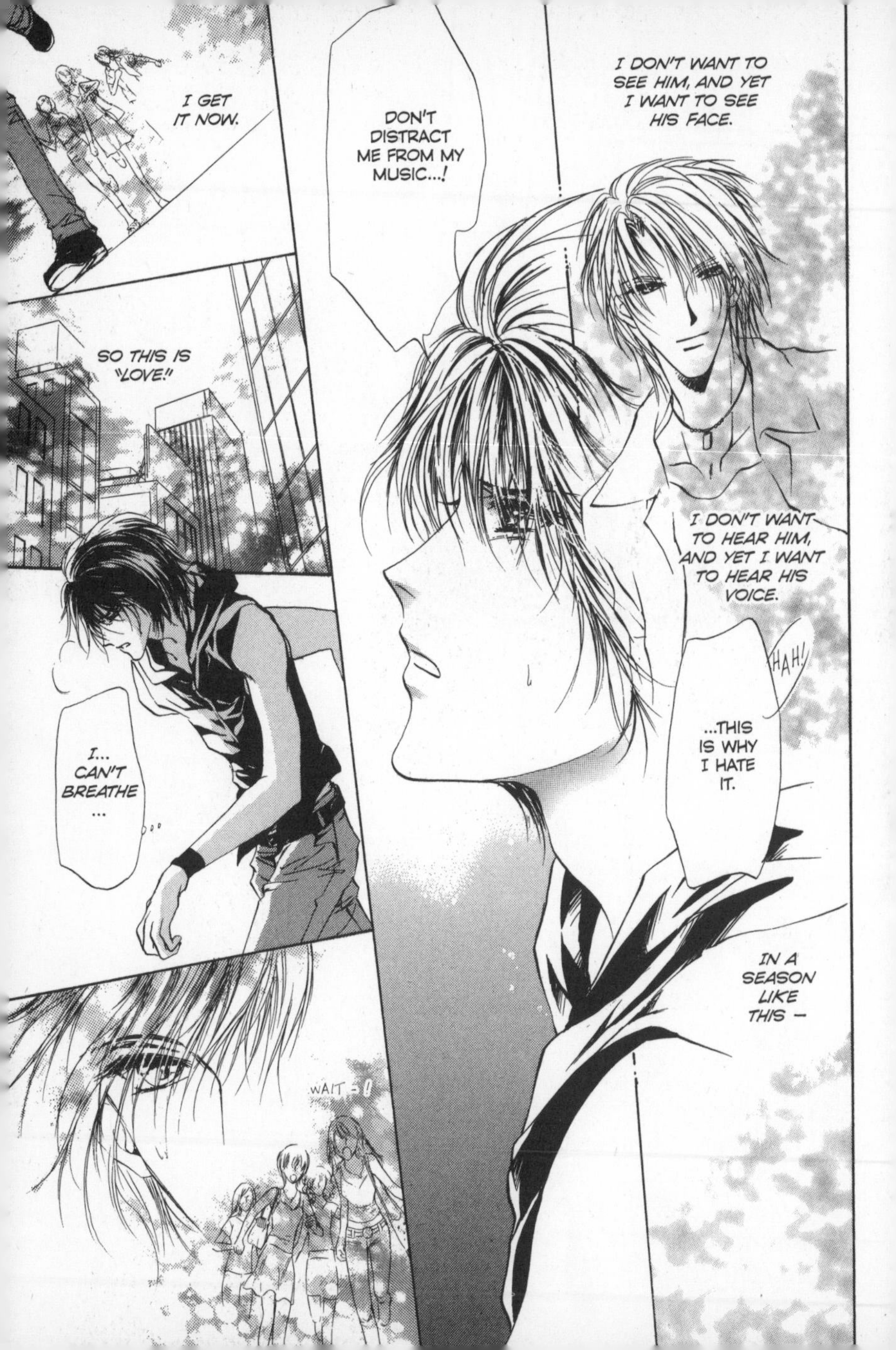
I DON'T WANT TO SEE HIM, AND YET I WANT TO SEE HIS FACE.
DON'T DISTRACT ME FROM MY MUSIC...!
I DON'T WANT TO HEAR HIM, AND YET I WANT TO HEAR HIS VOICE.
HAH!
...THIS IS WHY I HATE IT.
IN A SEASON LIKE THIS —
I GET IT NOW.
SO THIS IS "LOVE."
I... CAN'T BREATHE ...
WAIT —!

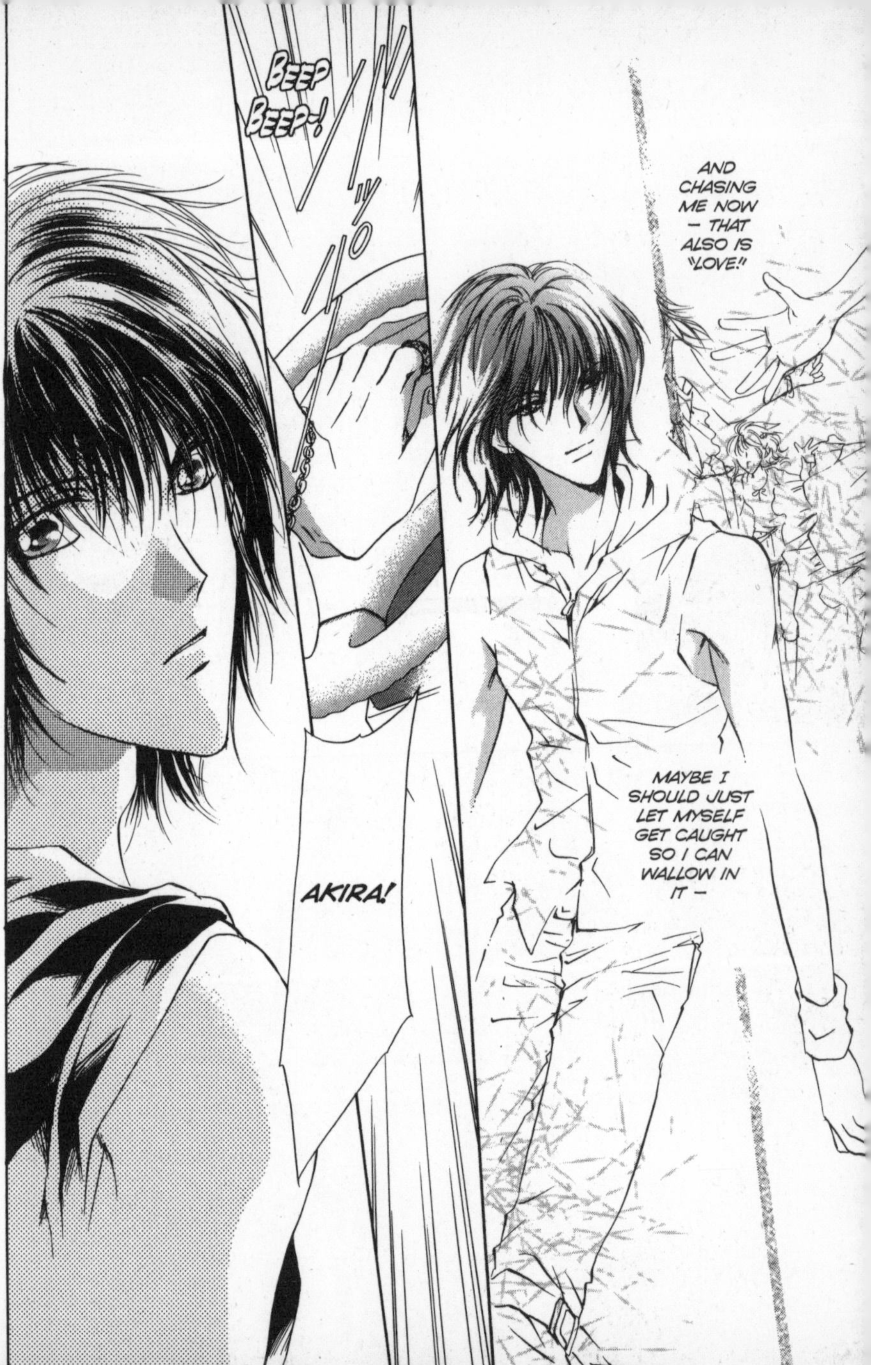
AND CHASING ME NOW — THAT ALSO IS "LOVE."
MAYBE I SHOULD JUST LET MYSELF GET CAUGHT SO I CAN WALLOW IN IT —
BEEP BEEP-!
AKIRA!

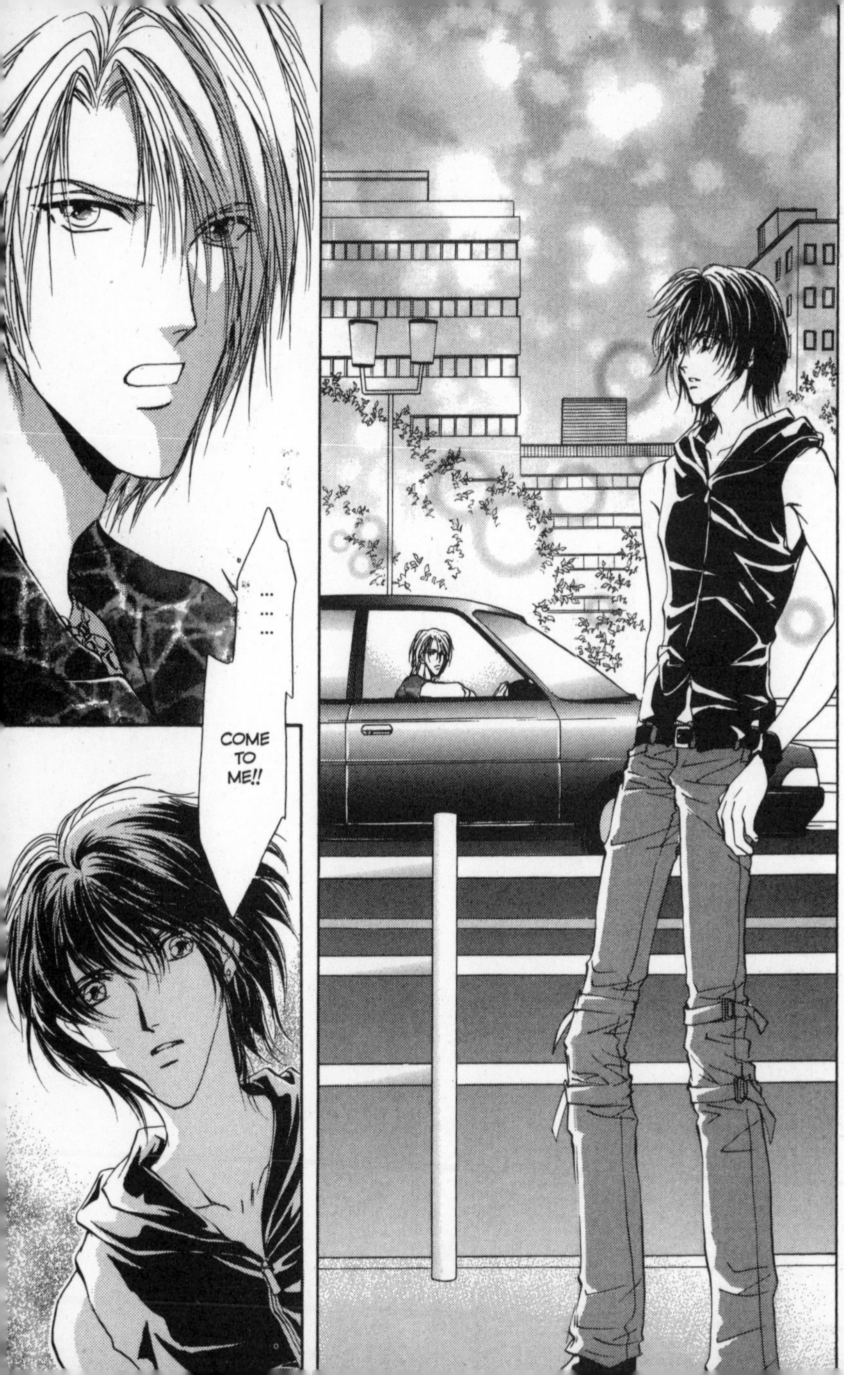
...
...
...
COME TO ME!!

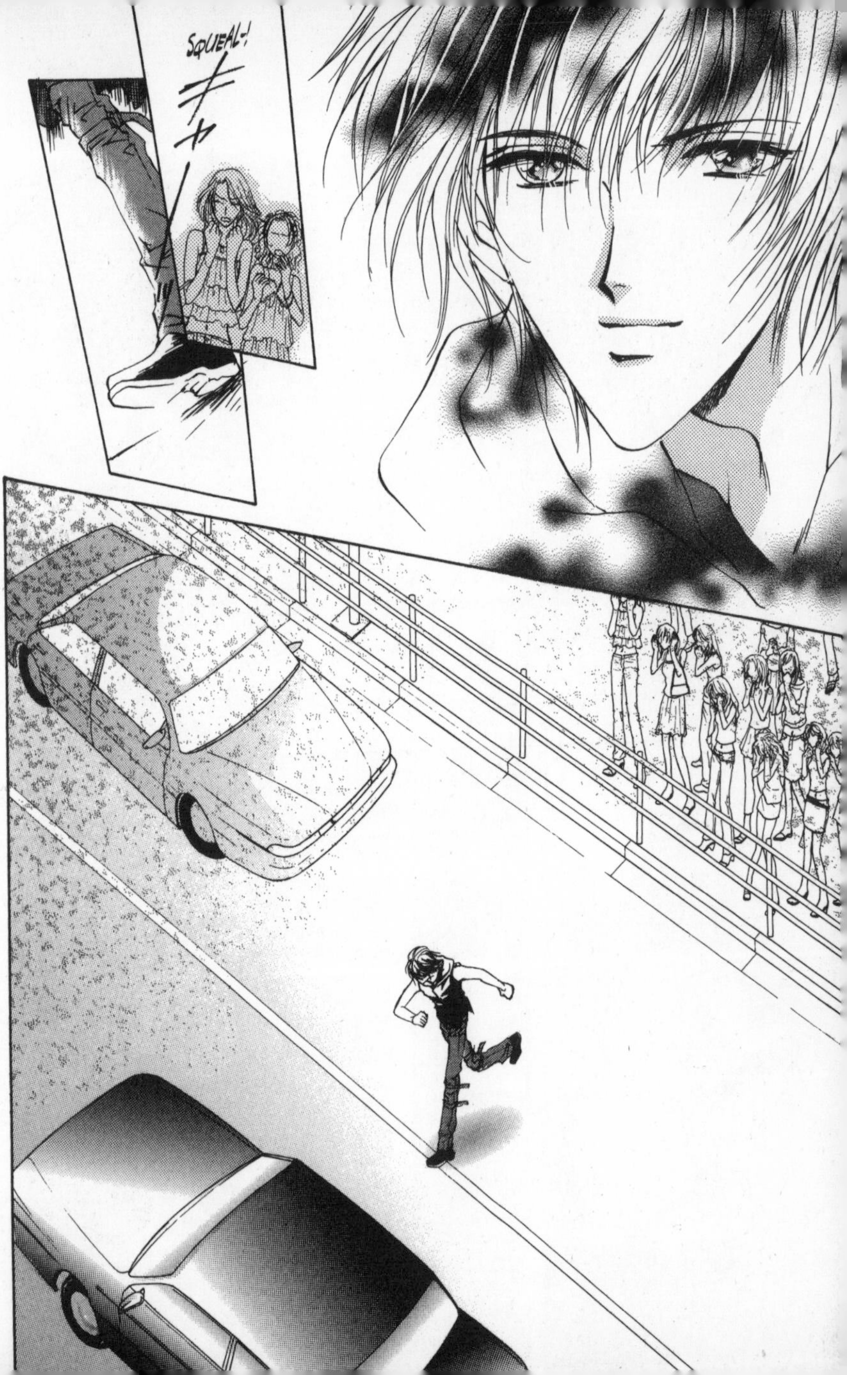
SQUEAL-!

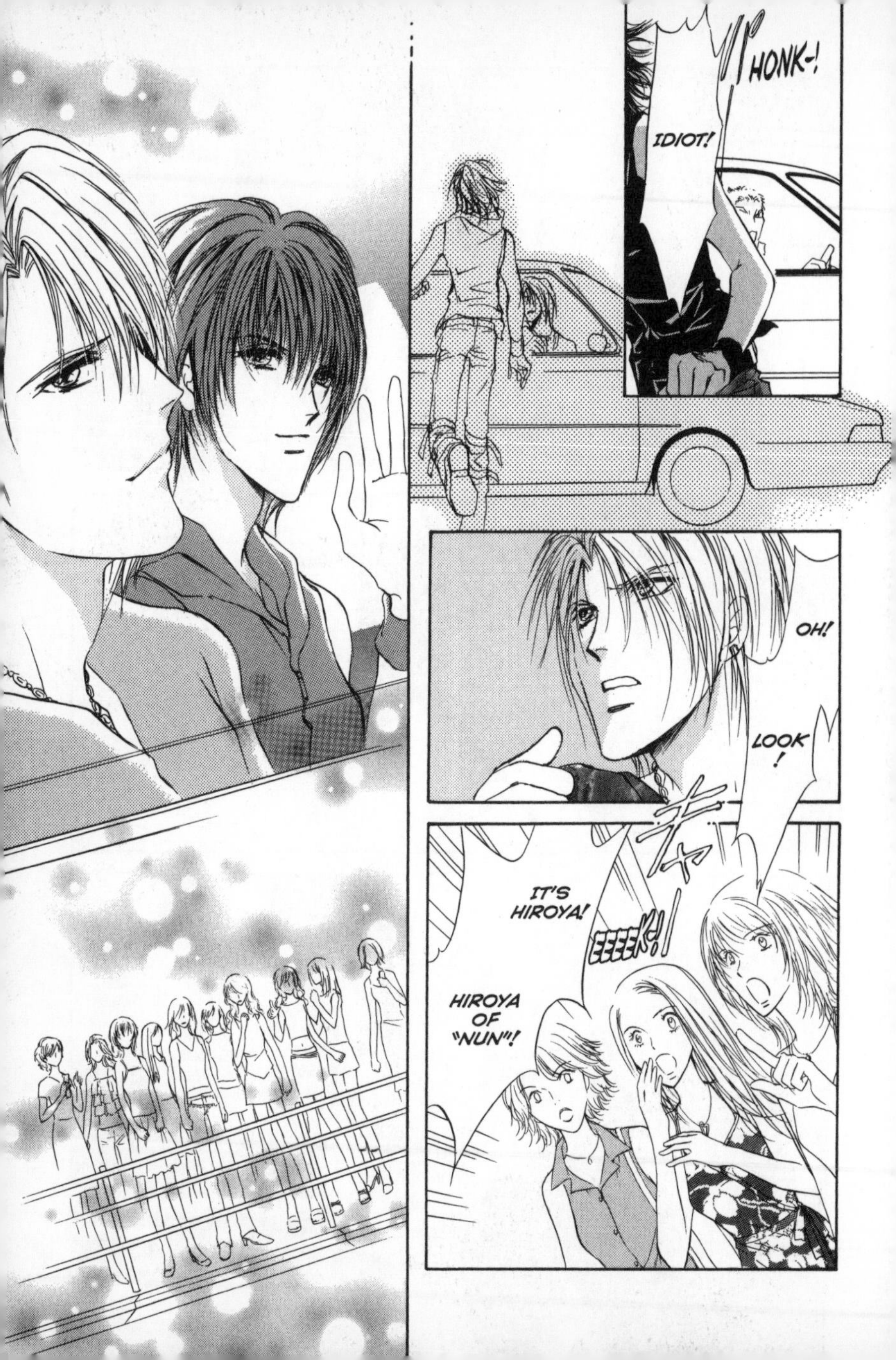
HONK-!
IDIOT!
OH!
LOOK!
キャ
IT'S HIROYA!
EEEEEK!!
HIROYA OF "NUN"!

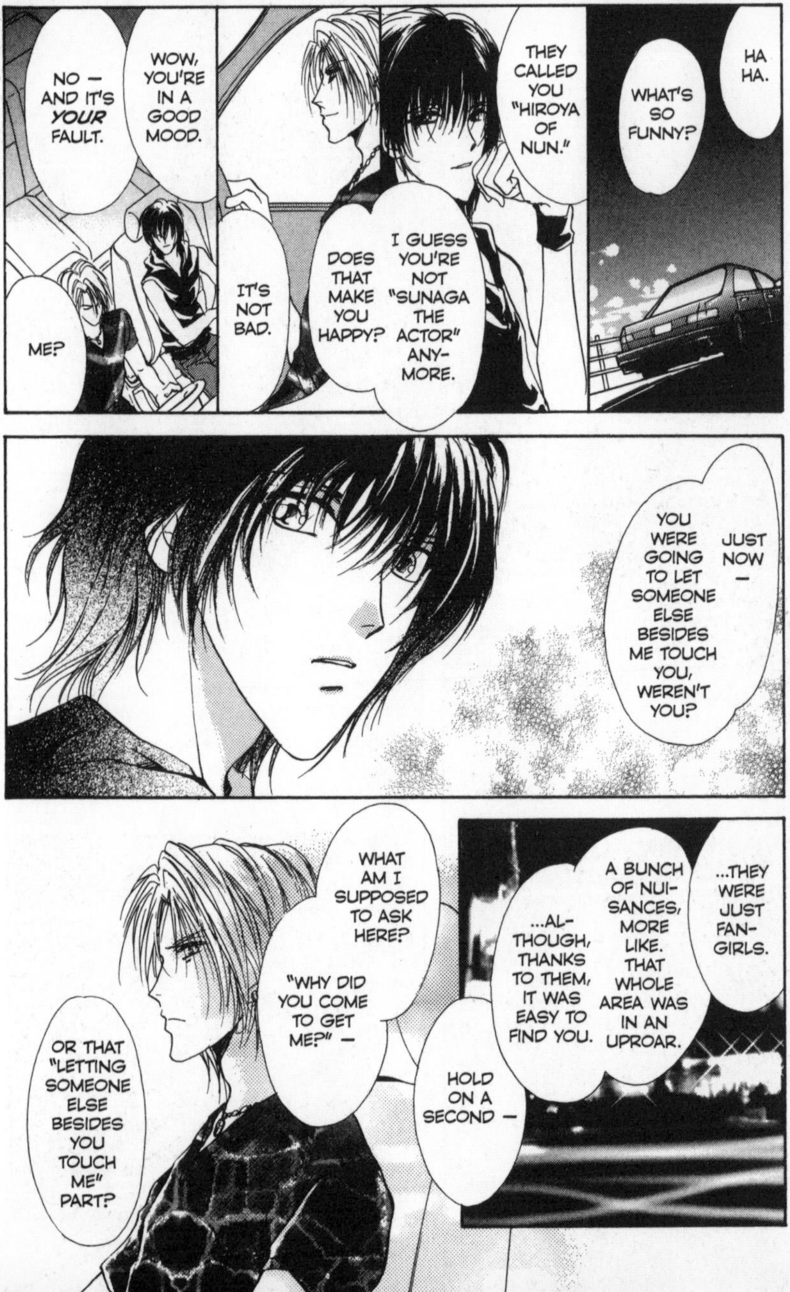
HA HA.
WHAT'S SO FUNNY?
THEY CALLED YOU "HIROYA OF NUN."
I GUESS YOU'RE NOT "SUNAGA THE ACTOR" ANYMORE.
DOES THAT MAKE YOU HAPPY?
IT'S NOT BAD.
WOW, YOU'RE IN A GOOD MOOD.
NO — AND IT'S ***YOUR*** FAULT.
ME?
JUST NOW —
YOU WERE GOING TO LET SOMEONE ELSE BESIDES ME TOUCH YOU, WEREN'T YOU?
...THEY WERE JUST FAN-GIRLS.
A BUNCH OF NUI-SANCES, MORE LIKE. THAT WHOLE AREA WAS IN AN UPROAR.
...AL-THOUGH, THANKS TO THEM, IT WAS EASY TO FIND YOU.
HOLD ON A SECOND —
WHAT AM I SUPPOSED TO ASK HERE?
"WHY DID YOU COME TO GET ME?" —
OR THAT "LETTING SOMEONE ELSE BESIDES YOU TOUCH ME" PART?

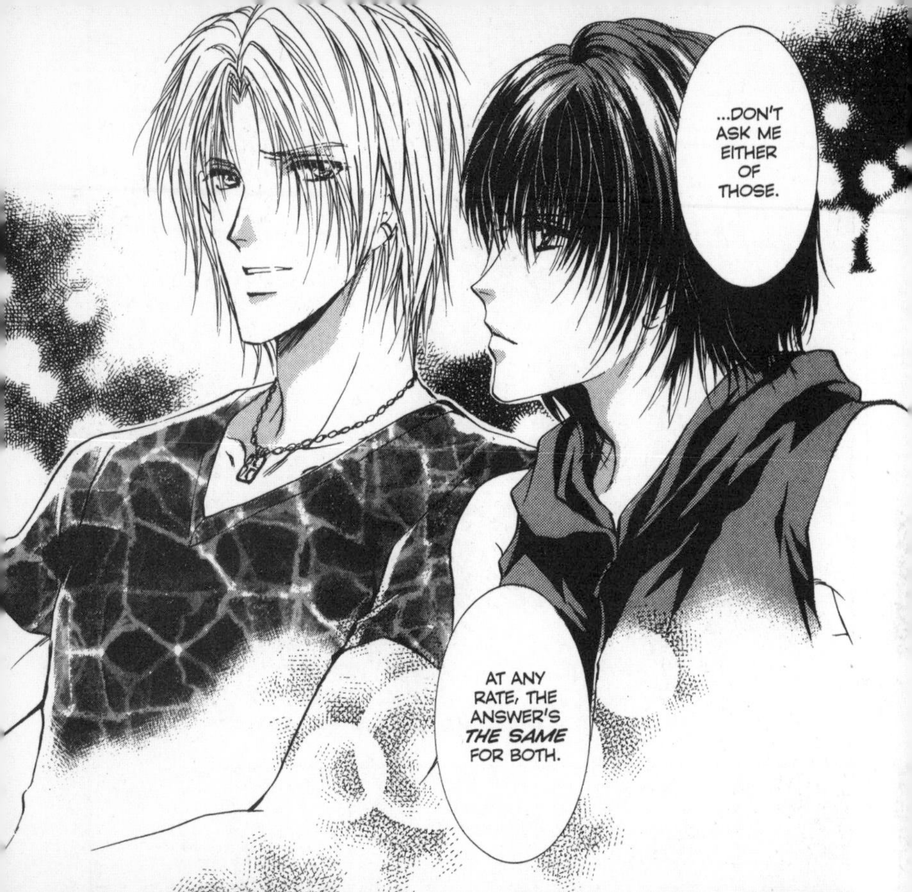
...DON'T ASK ME EITHER OF THOSE.
AT ANY RATE, THE ANSWER'S *THE SAME* FOR BOTH.

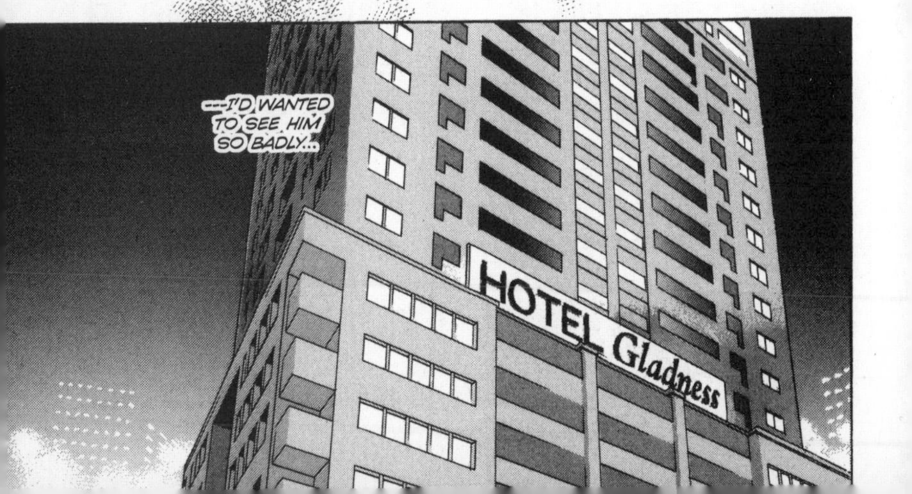
---I'D WANTED TO SEE HIM SO BADLY...
HOTEL Gladness

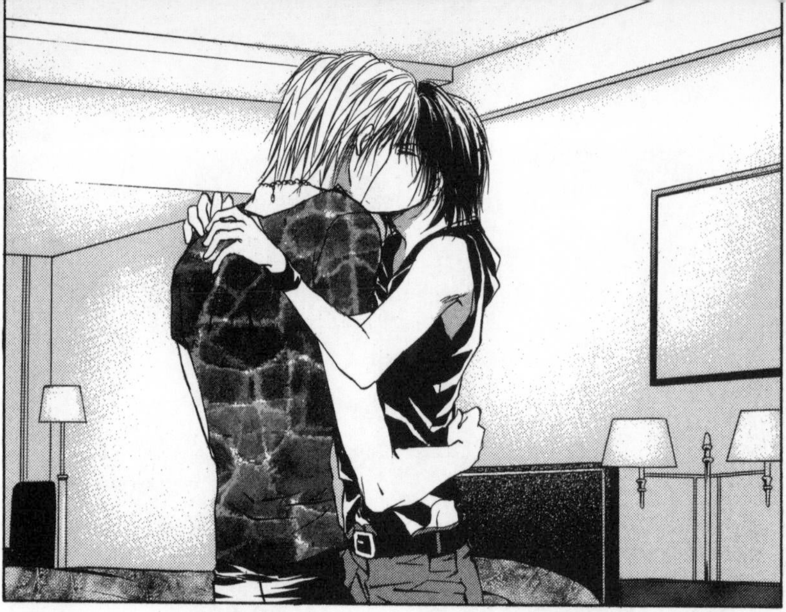

FIRST I SAY, "I LOVE YOU," AND THEN, "I HATE YOU!" WHICHEVER WAY MY THOUGHTS WAVER, THE FACT REMAINS THAT YOU'RE **CONSTANTLY** *ON MY MIND.*

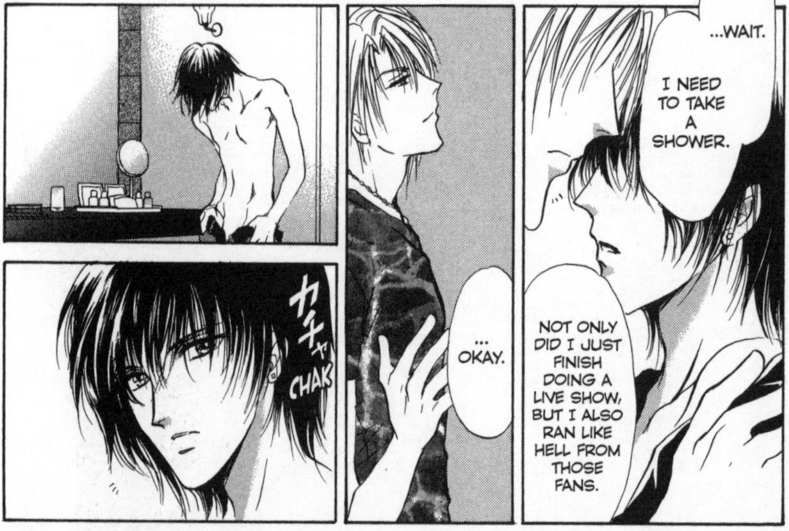
...WAIT.
I NEED TO TAKE A SHOWER.
NOT ONLY DID I JUST FINISH DOING A LIVE SHOW, BUT I ALSO RAN LIKE HELL FROM THOSE FANS.
... OKAY.
カチャ
CHAK

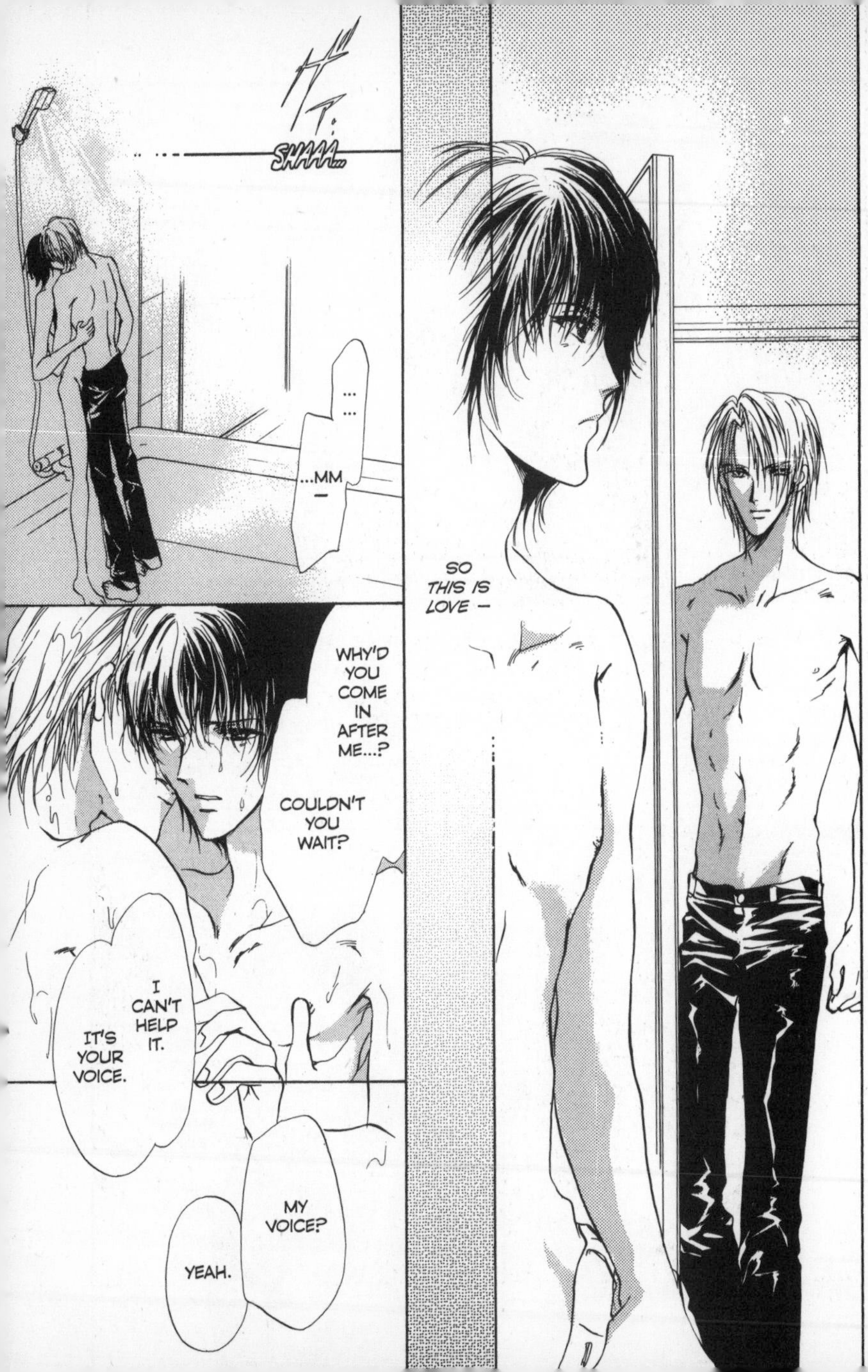
SO THIS IS LOVE —
SHAAA...
...
...
...MM —
WHY'D YOU COME IN AFTER ME...?
COULDN'T YOU WAIT?
I CAN'T HELP IT.
IT'S YOUR VOICE.
MY VOICE?
YEAH.

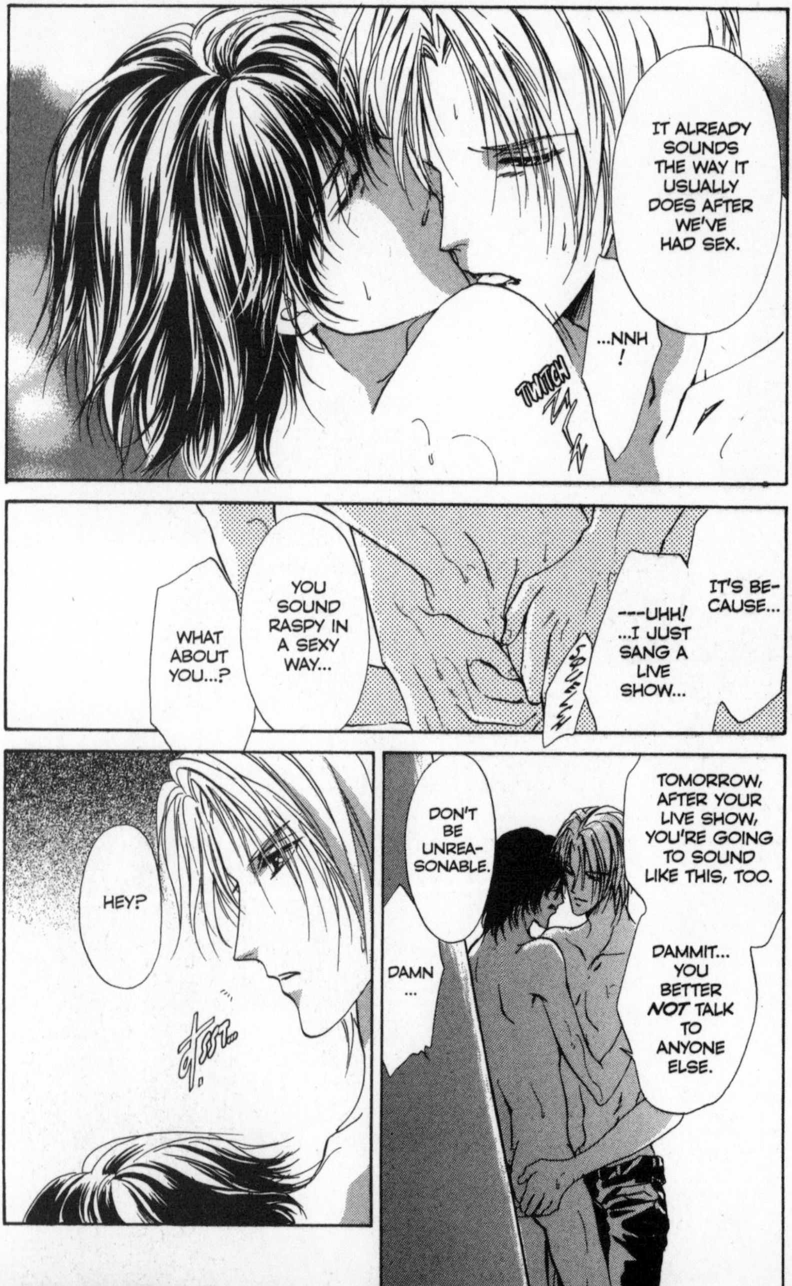
IT ALREADY SOUNDS THE WAY IT USUALLY DOES AFTER WE'VE HAD SEX.
...NNH!
TWITCH
IT'S BE-CAUSE...
---UHH! ...I JUST SANG A LIVE SHOW...
YOU SOUND RASPY IN A SEXY WAY...
WHAT ABOUT YOU...?
TOMORROW, AFTER YOUR LIVE SHOW, YOU'RE GOING TO SOUND LIKE THIS, TOO.
DON'T BE UNREA-SONABLE.
DAMMIT... YOU BETTER *NOT* TALK TO ANYONE ELSE.
DAMN ...
HEY?

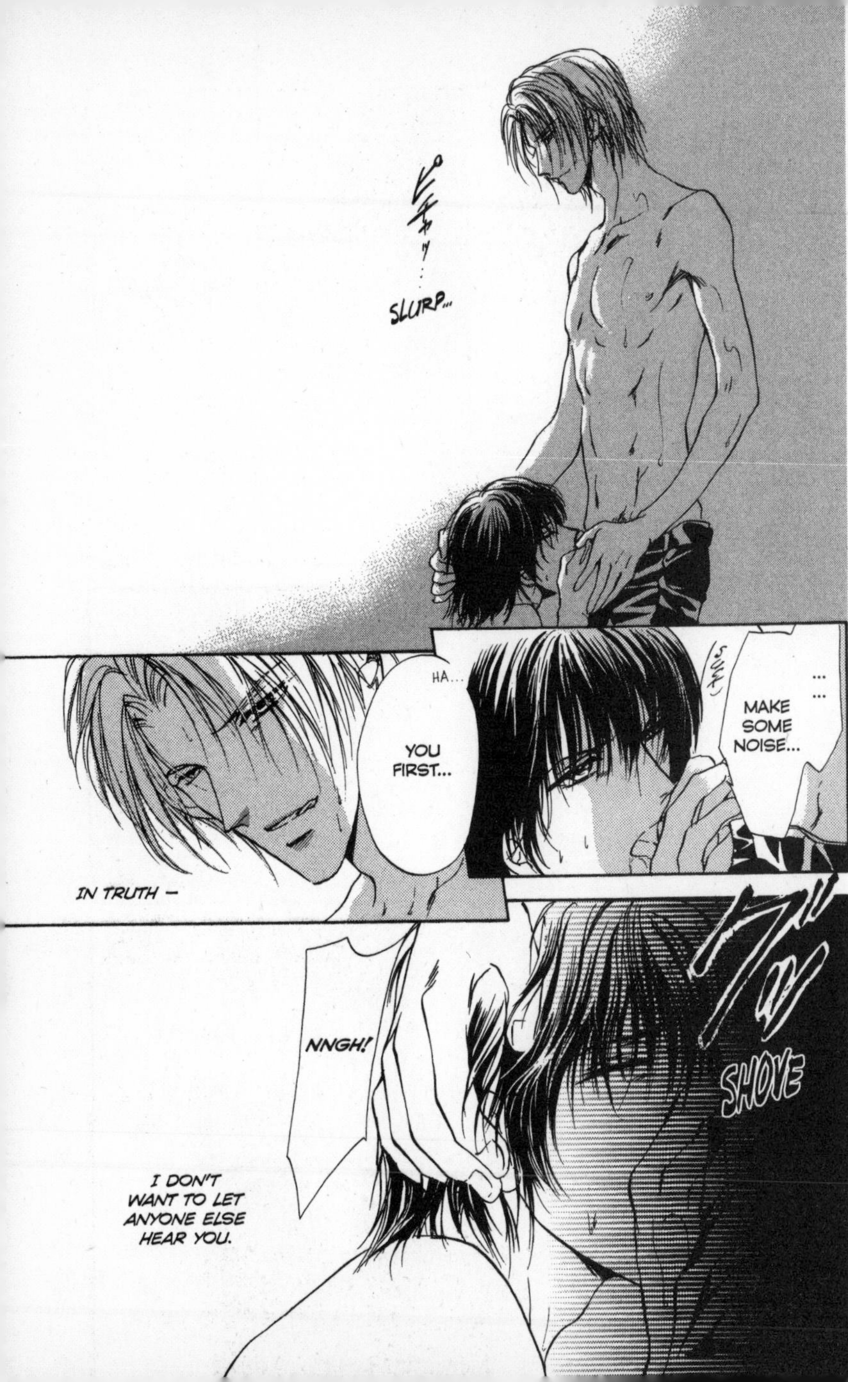
ピチャッ
SLURP...
... ...
(SUCK)
MAKE SOME NOISE...
HA...
YOU FIRST...
IN TRUTH —
SHOVE
NNGH!
I DON'T WANT TO LET ANYONE ELSE HEAR YOU.

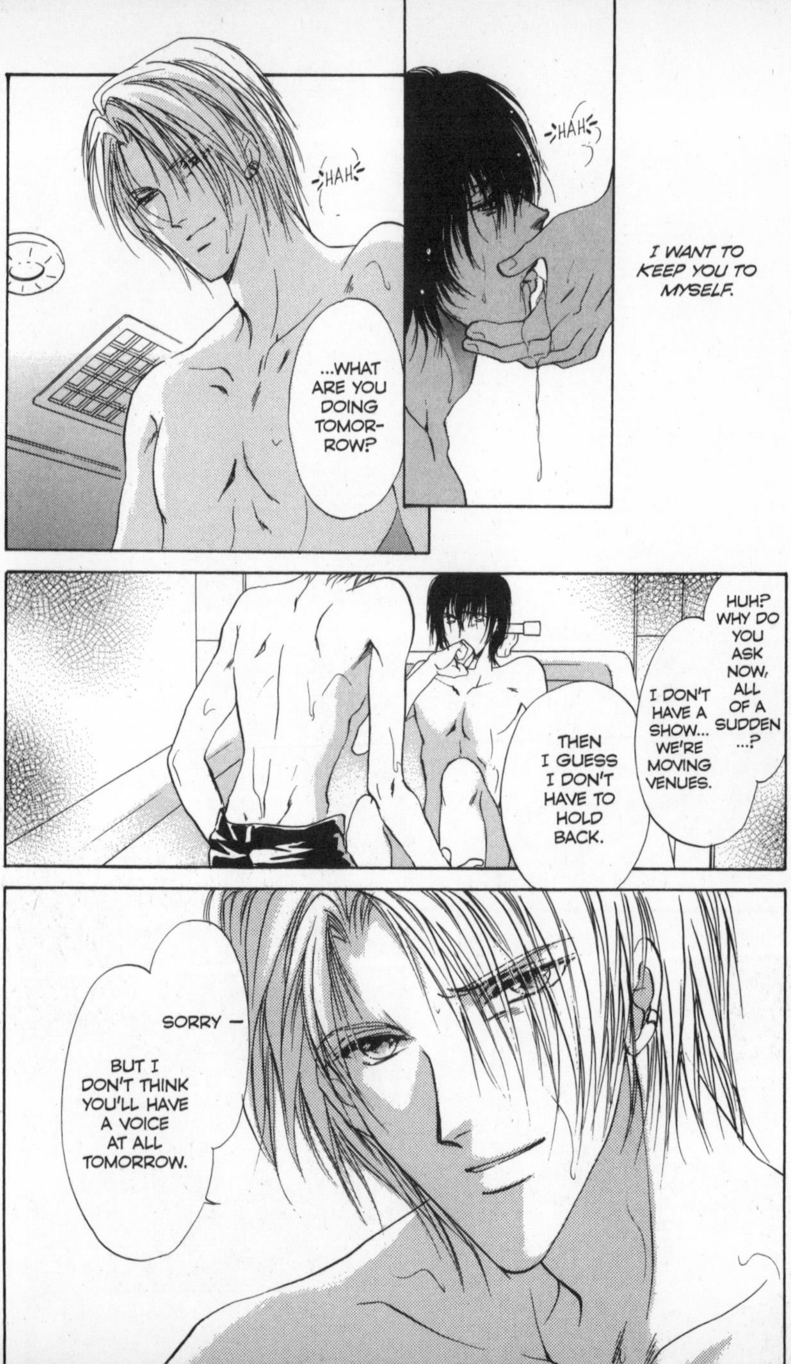
I WANT TO KEEP YOU TO MYSELF.
HAH
HAH
...WHAT ARE YOU DOING TOMORROW?
HUH? WHY DO YOU ASK NOW, ALL OF A SUDDEN ...?
I DON'T HAVE A SHOW... WE'RE MOVING VENUES.
THEN I GUESS I DON'T HAVE TO HOLD BACK.
SORRY —
BUT I DON'T THINK YOU'LL HAVE A VOICE AT ALL TOMORROW.

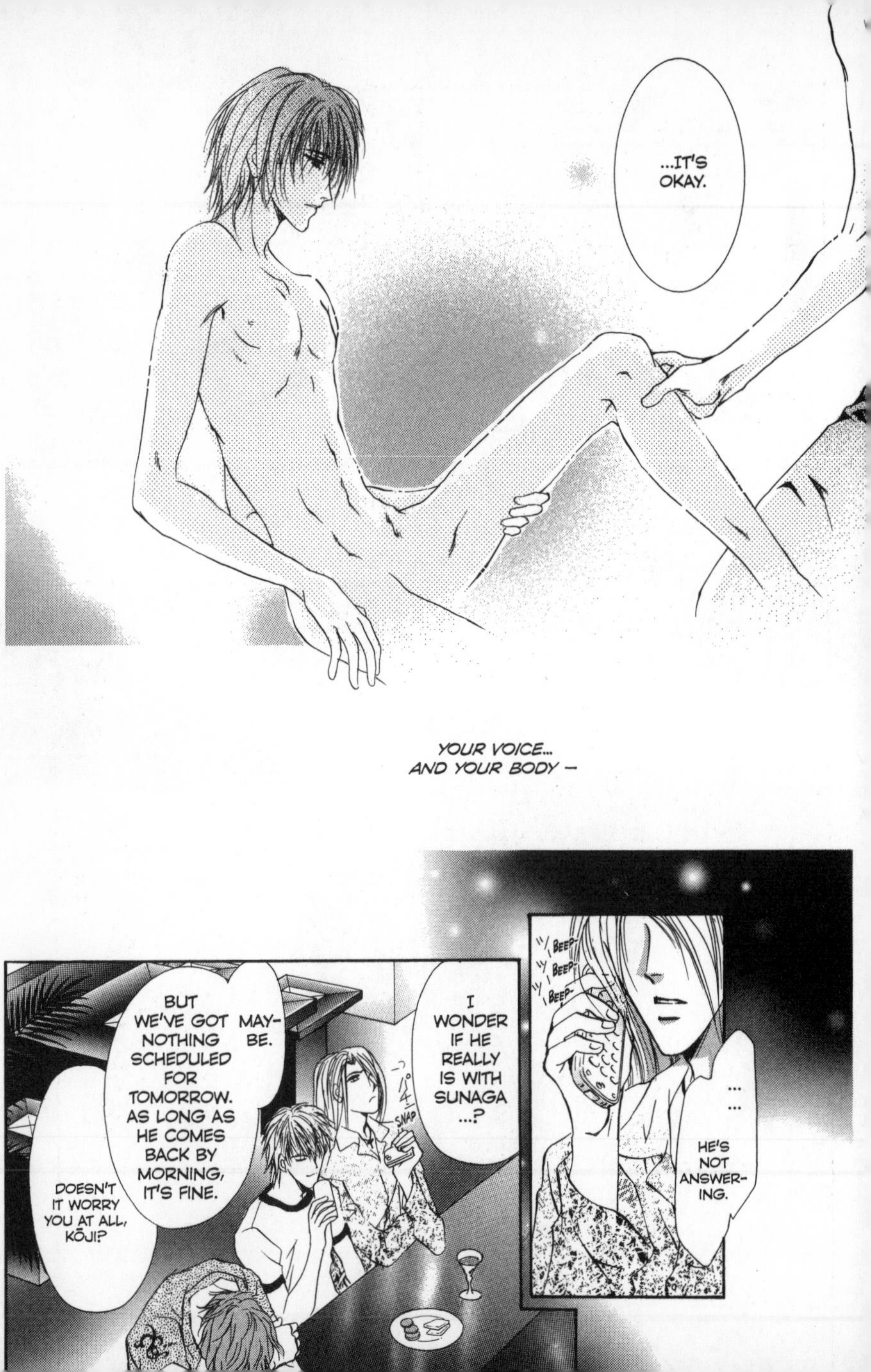
...IT'S OKAY.
YOUR VOICE... AND YOUR BODY —
BEEP BEEP BEEP
... ...
HE'S NOT ANSWERING.
I WONDER IF HE REALLY IS WITH SUNAGA ...?
SNAP
MAY-BE.
BUT WE'VE GOT NOTHING SCHEDULED FOR TOMORROW. AS LONG AS HE COMES BACK BY MORNING, IT'S FINE.
DOESN'T IT WORRY YOU AT ALL, KŌJI?

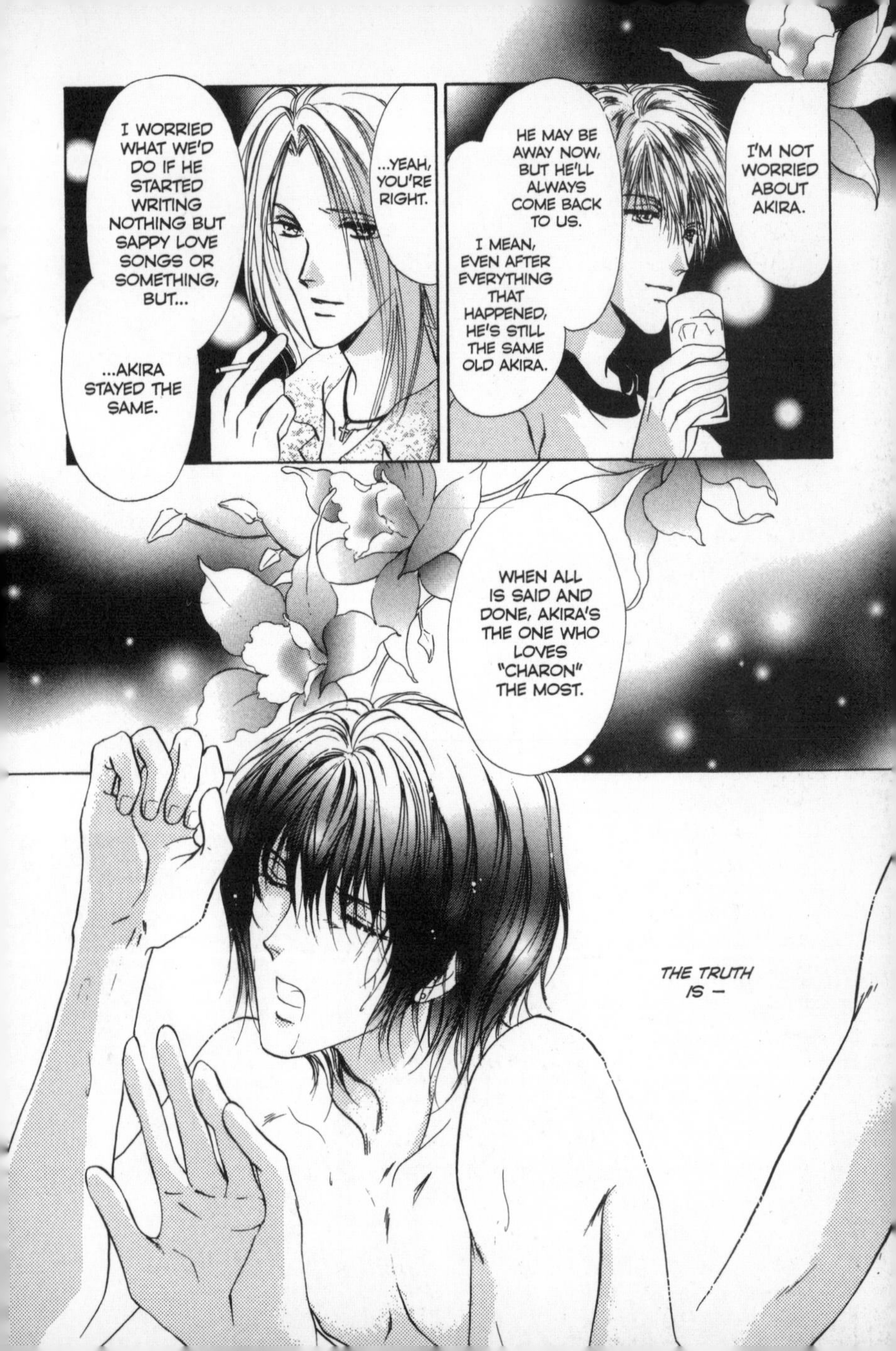
I'M NOT WORRIED ABOUT AKIRA.
HE MAY BE AWAY NOW, BUT HE'LL ALWAYS COME BACK TO US.
I MEAN, EVEN AFTER EVERYTHING THAT HAPPENED, HE'S STILL THE SAME OLD AKIRA.
...YEAH, YOU'RE RIGHT.
I WORRIED WHAT WE'D DO IF HE STARTED WRITING NOTHING BUT SAPPY LOVE SONGS OR SOMETHING, BUT...
...AKIRA STAYED THE SAME.
WHEN ALL IS SAID AND DONE, AKIRA'S THE ONE WHO LOVES "CHARON" THE MOST.
THE TRUTH IS —

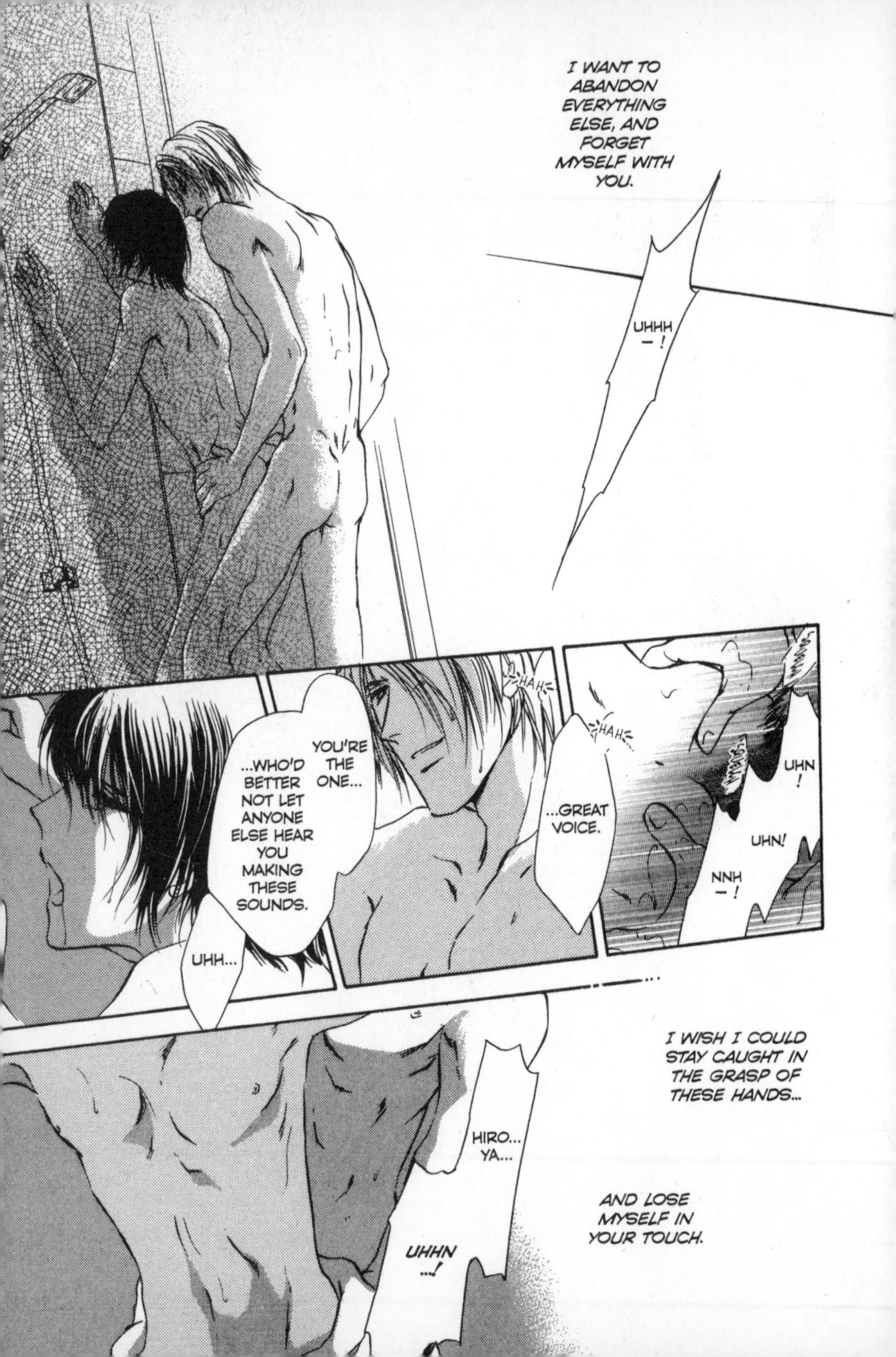
I WANT TO ABANDON EVERYTHING ELSE, AND FORGET MYSELF WITH YOU.
UHHH—!
UHN!
UHN!
NNH—!
HAH
HAH
...GREAT VOICE.
YOU'RE THE ONE...
...WHO'D BETTER NOT LET ANYONE ELSE HEAR YOU MAKING THESE SOUNDS.
UHH...
——...
I WISH I COULD STAY CAUGHT IN THE GRASP OF THESE HANDS...
HIRO... YA...
AND LOSE MYSELF IN YOUR TOUCH.
UHHN...!

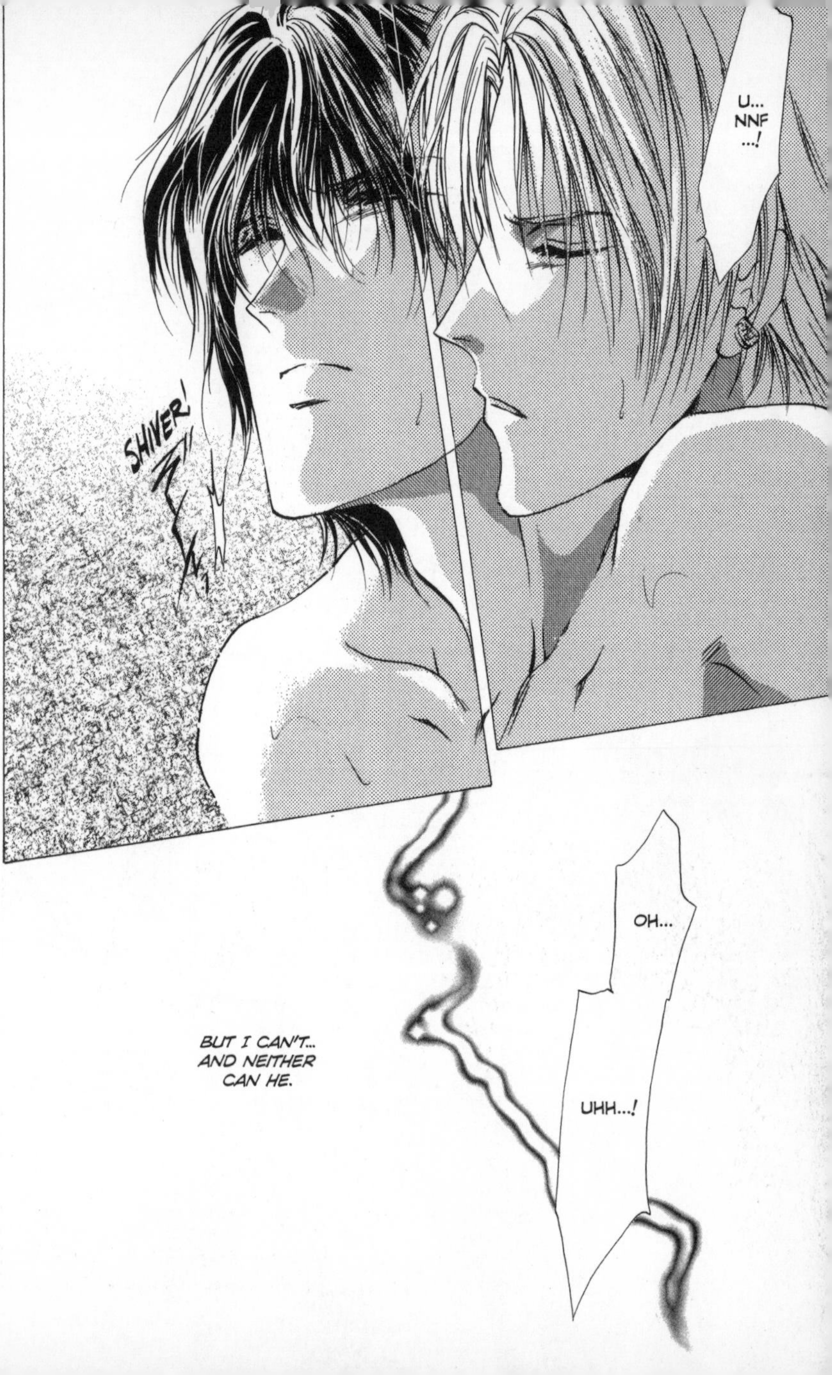
U... NNF ...!
SHIVER!
OH...
UHH...!
BUT I CAN'T... AND NEITHER CAN HE.

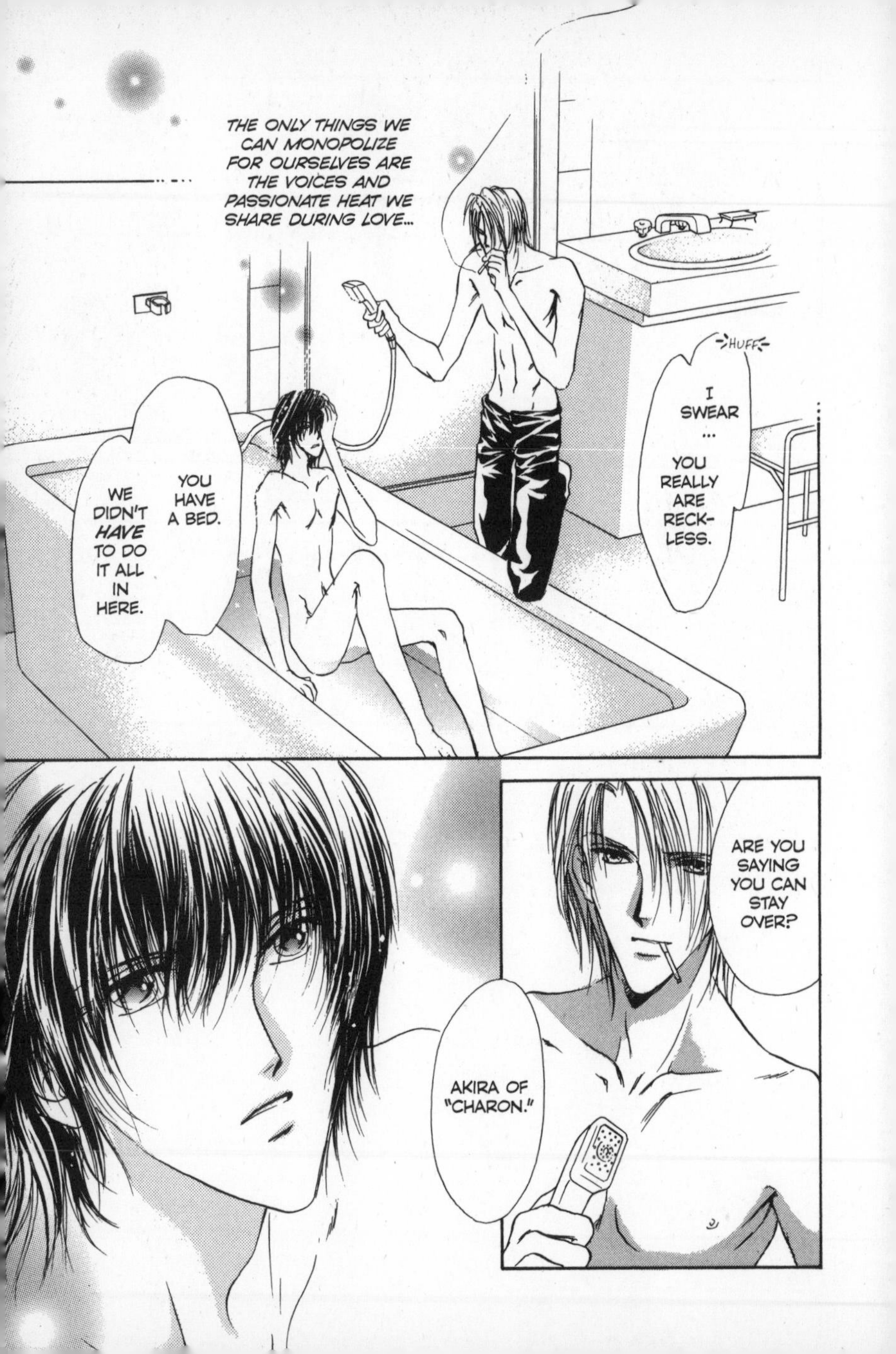
THE ONLY THINGS WE CAN MONOPOLIZE FOR OURSELVES ARE THE VOICES AND PASSIONATE HEAT WE SHARE DURING LOVE...
HUFF
I SWEAR... YOU REALLY ARE RECKLESS.
YOU HAVE A BED. WE DIDN'T HAVE TO DO IT ALL IN HERE.
ARE YOU SAYING YOU CAN STAY OVER?
AKIRA OF "CHARON."

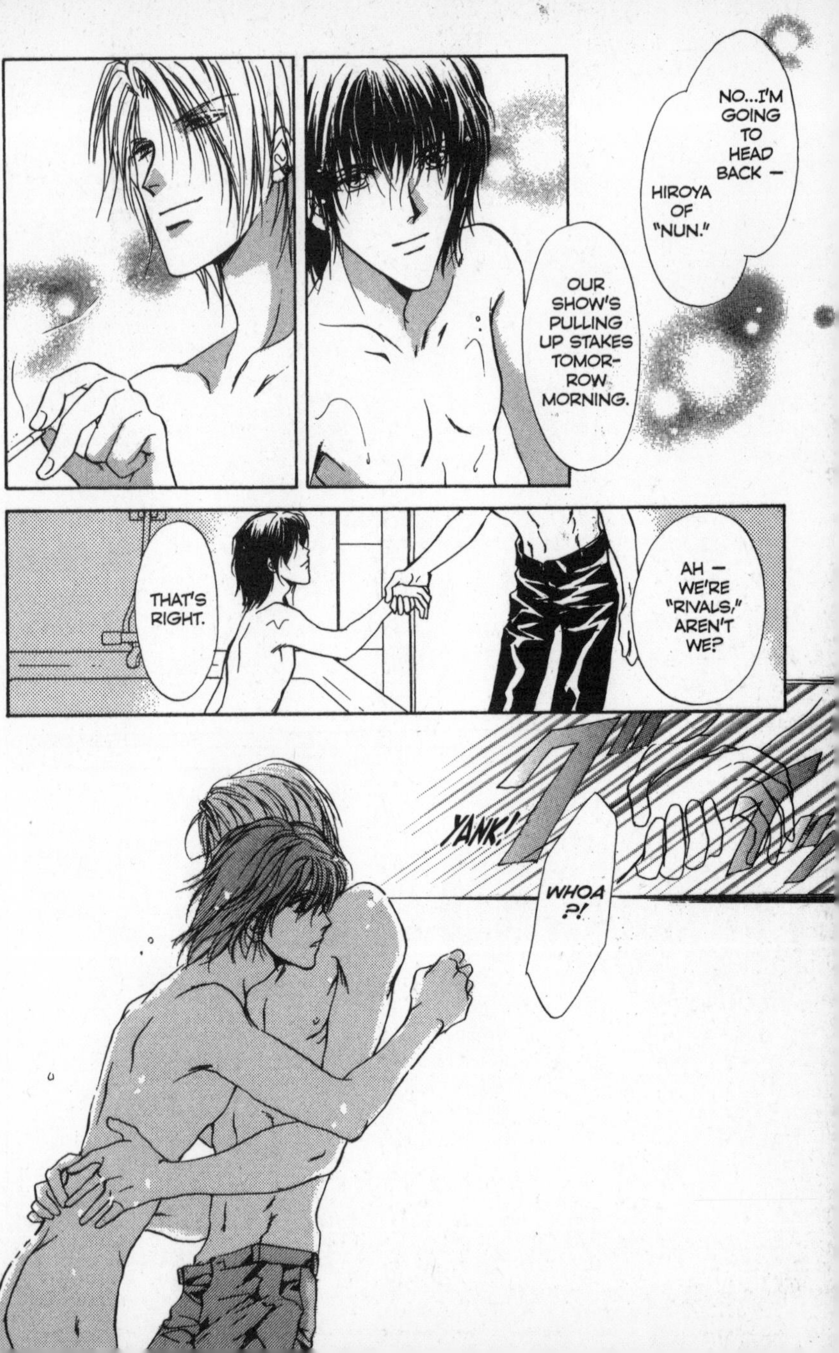
NO...I'M GOING TO HEAD BACK — HIROYA OF "NUN."
OUR SHOW'S PULLING UP STAKES TOMOR-ROW MORNING.
AH — WE'RE "RIVALS," AREN'T WE?
THAT'S RIGHT.
YANK!
WHOA ?!

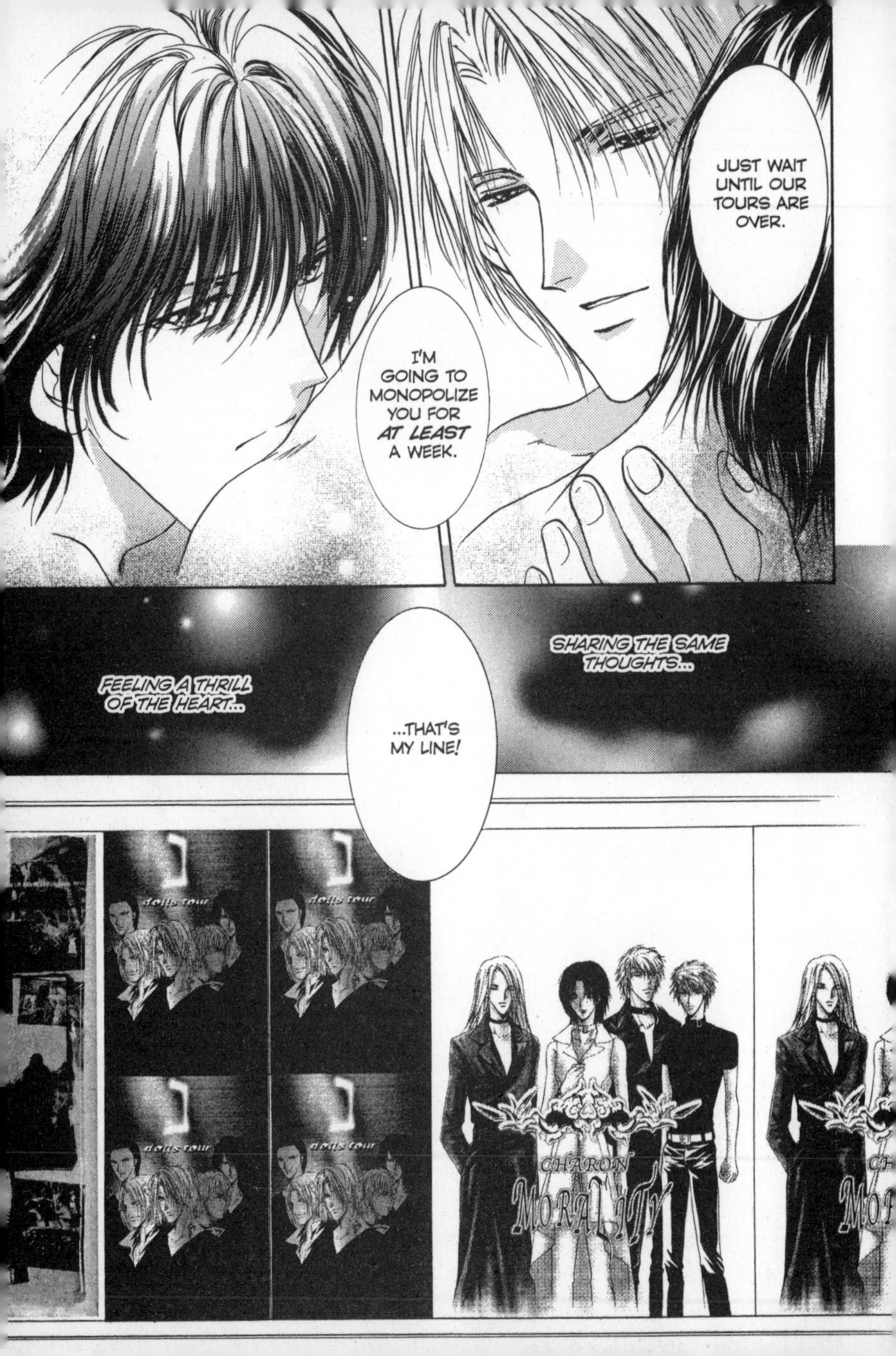
JUST WAIT UNTIL OUR TOURS ARE OVER.
I'M GOING TO MONOPOLIZE YOU FOR *AT LEAST* A WEEK.
SHARING THE SAME THOUGHTS...
...THAT'S MY LINE!
FEELING A THRILL OF THE HEART...
CHARON MORALITY
dolls tour
dolls tour
dolls tour
dolls tour

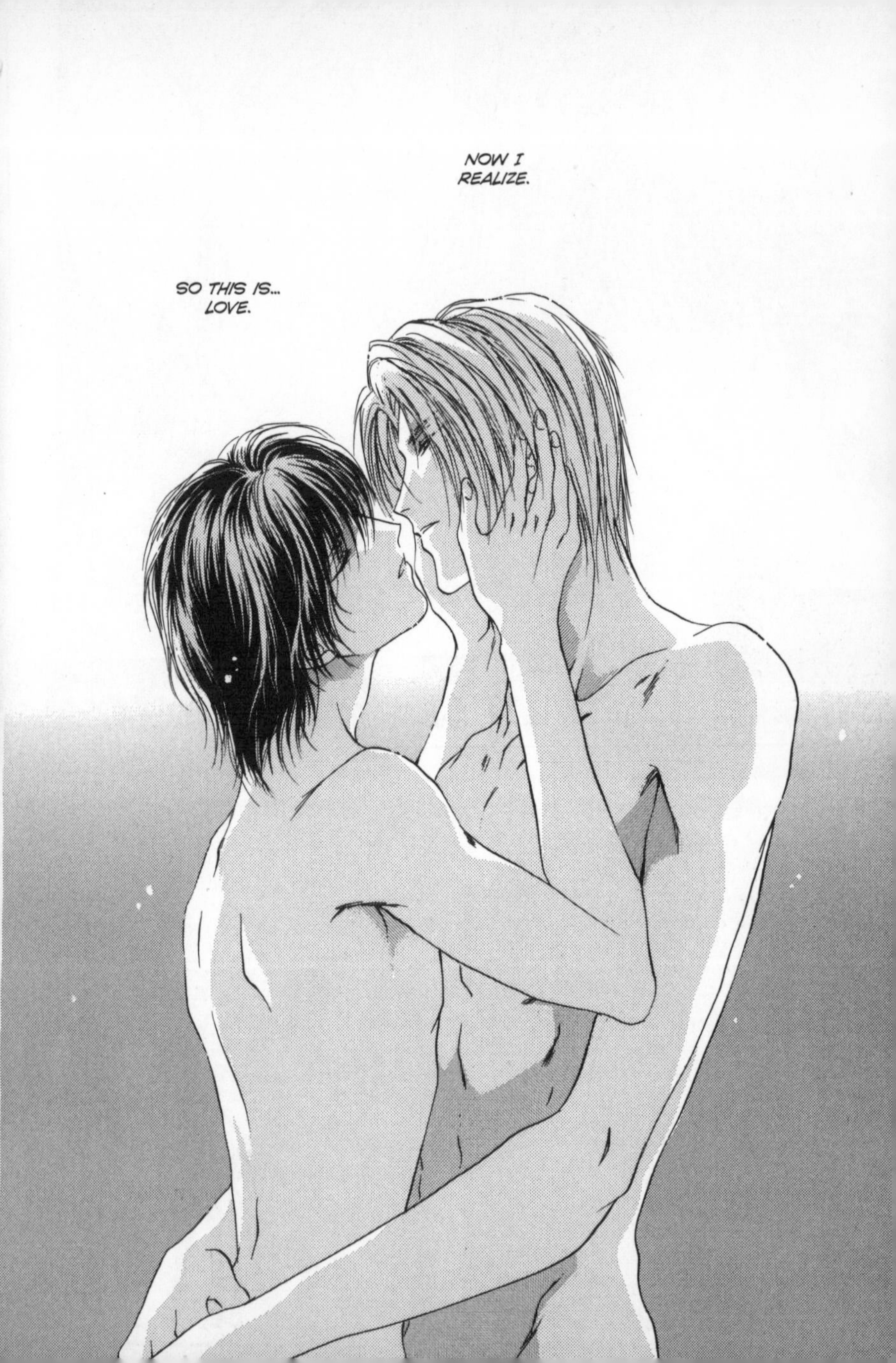
NOW I REALIZE.
SO THIS IS... LOVE.

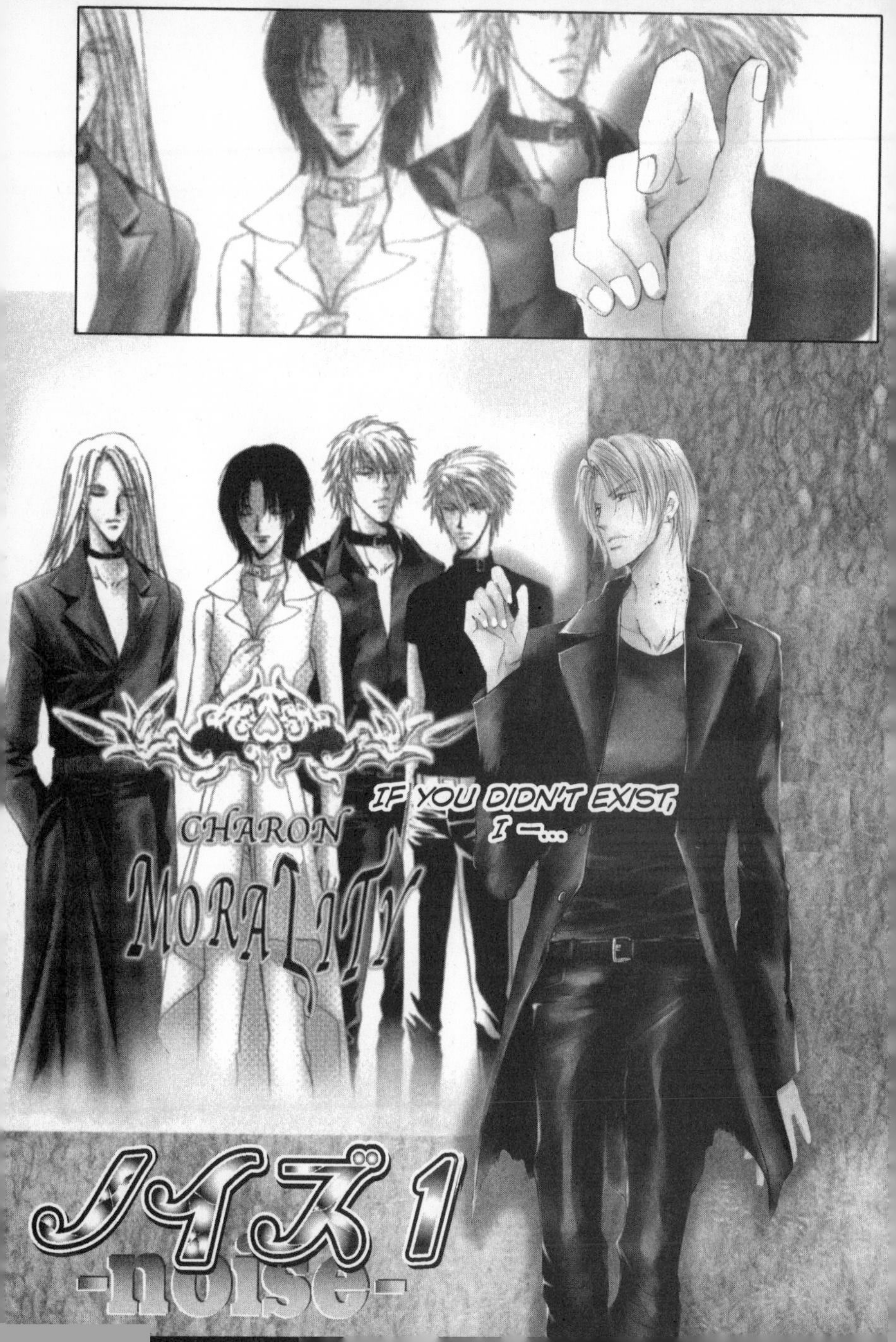
IF YOU DIDN'T EXIST, I —...
CHARON
MORALITY
ノイズ1
-noise-

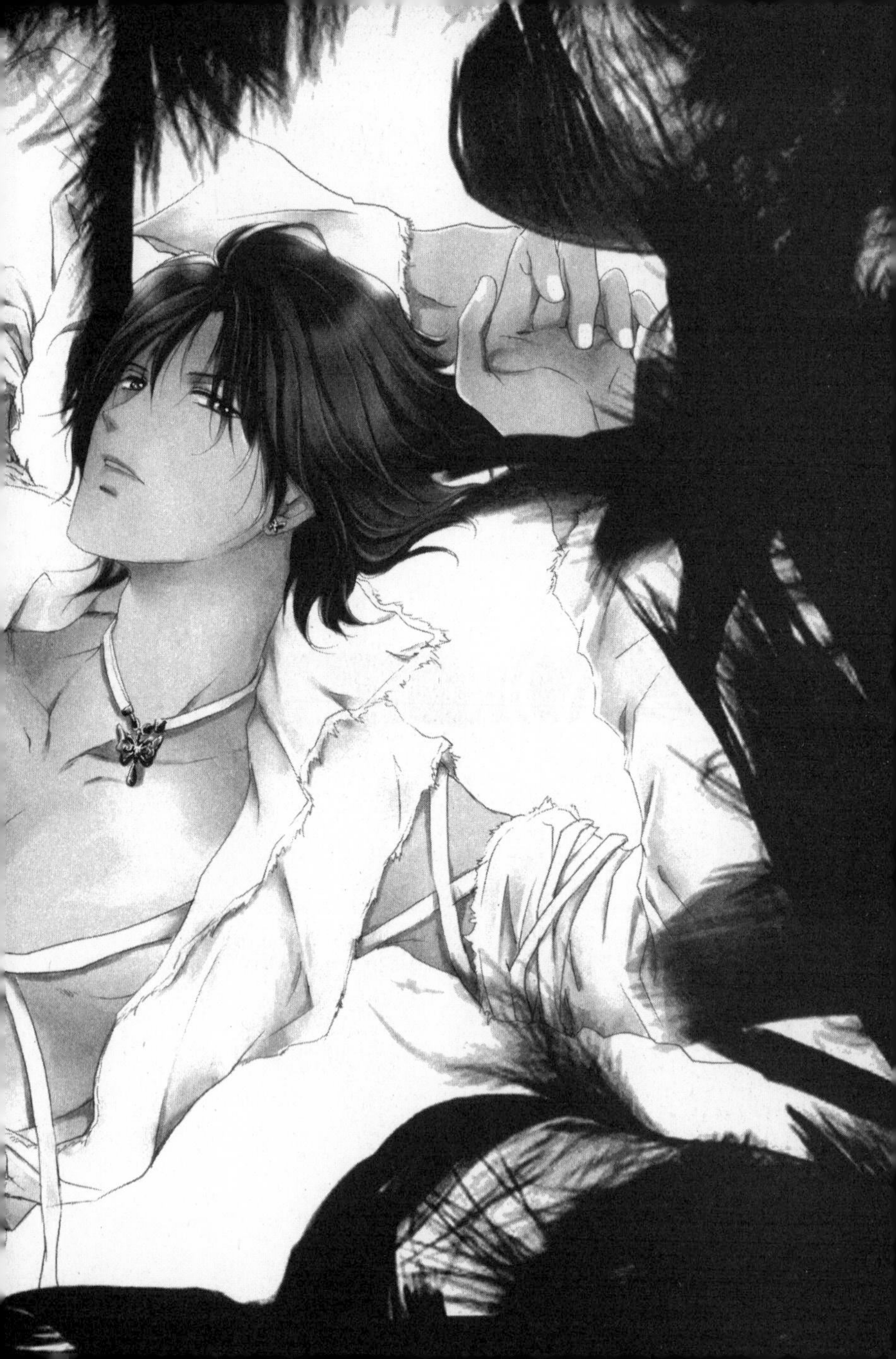

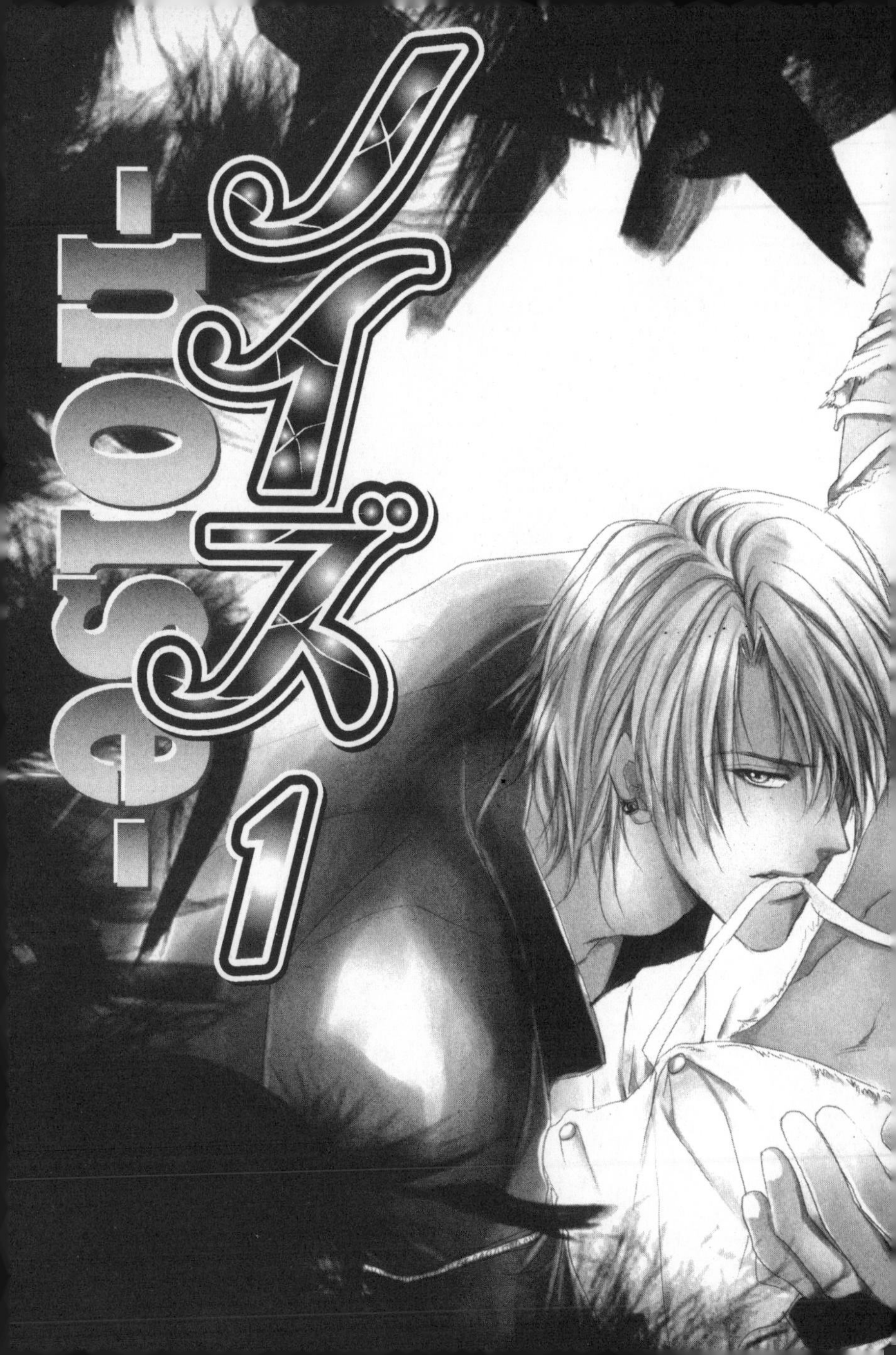
ノイズ 1
-noise-

Noise

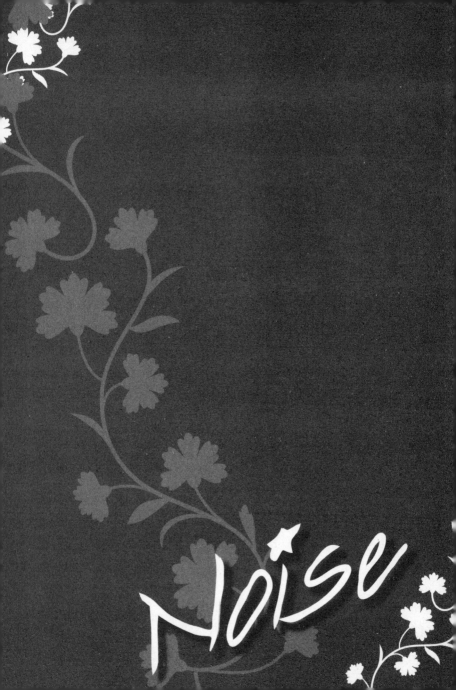

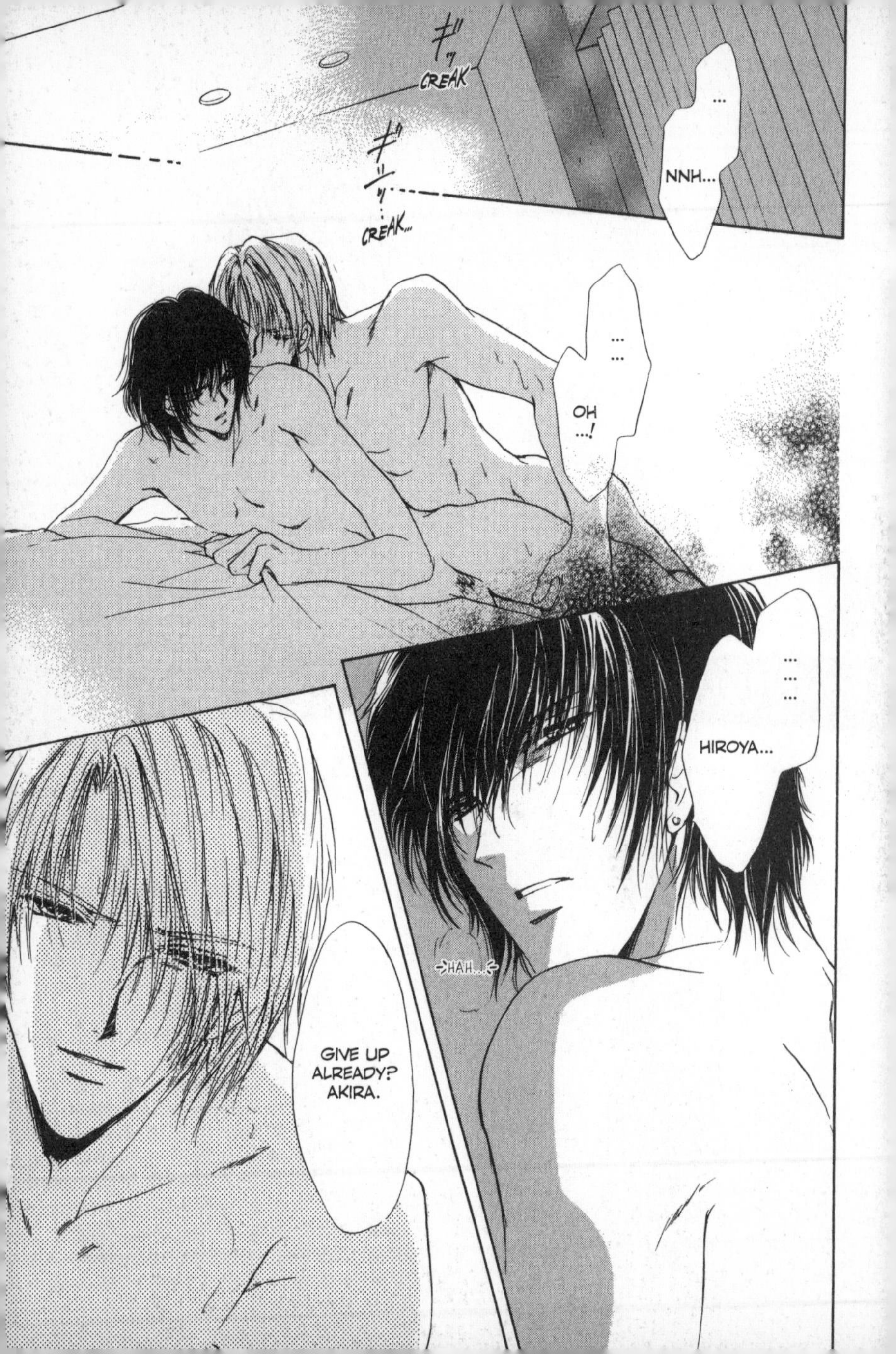

... NNH...
CREAK
CREAK...
... ... OH ...!
... ... HIROYA...
HAH...
GIVE UP ALREADY? AKIRA.

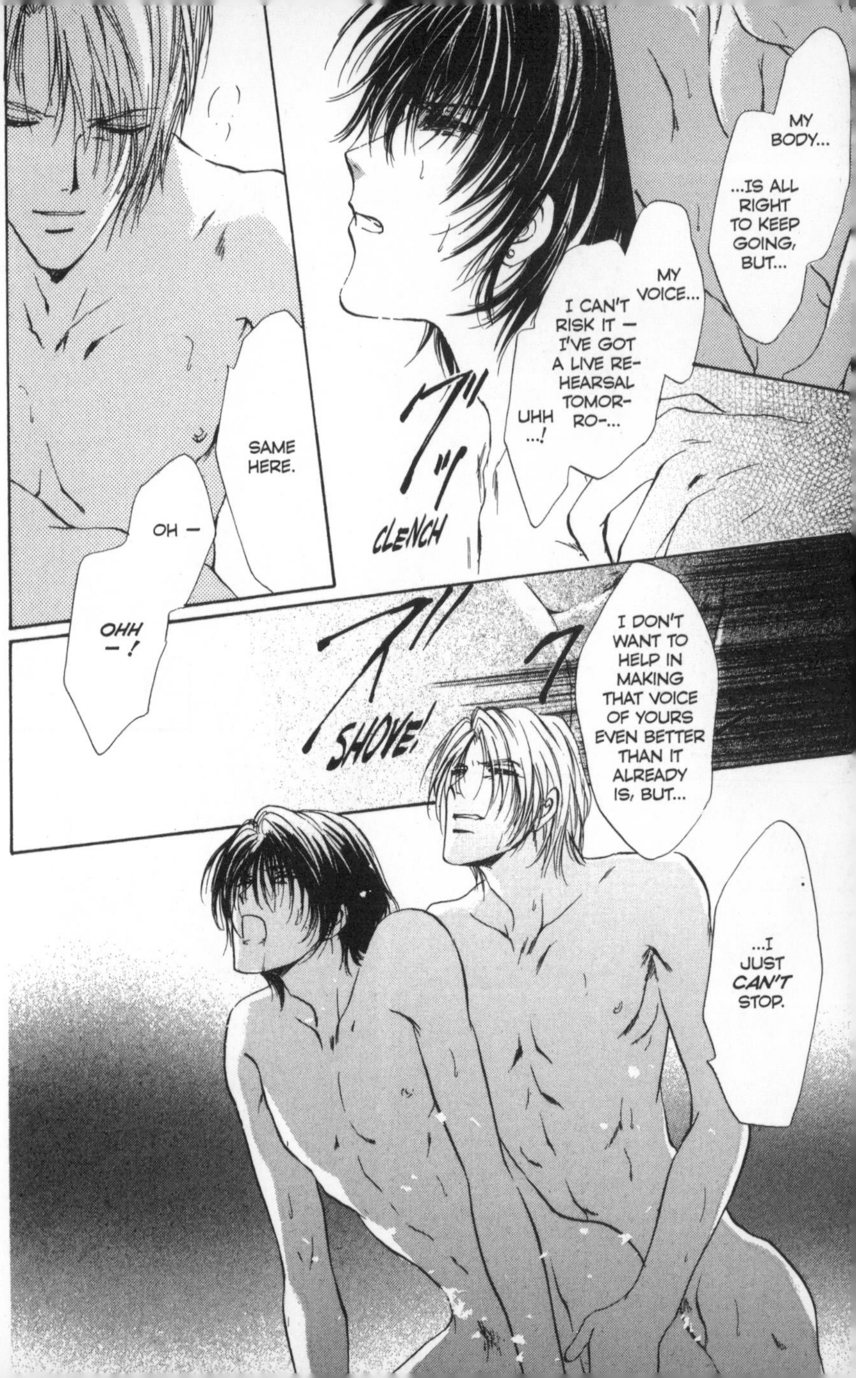
MY BODY...
...IS ALL RIGHT TO KEEP GOING, BUT...
MY VOICE...
I CAN'T RISK IT — I'VE GOT A LIVE REHEARSAL TOMORRO-...
UHH ...!
CLENCH
SAME HERE.
OH —
OHH —!
SHOVE!
I DON'T WANT TO HELP IN MAKING THAT VOICE OF YOURS EVEN BETTER THAN IT ALREADY IS, BUT...
...I JUST *CAN'T* STOP.

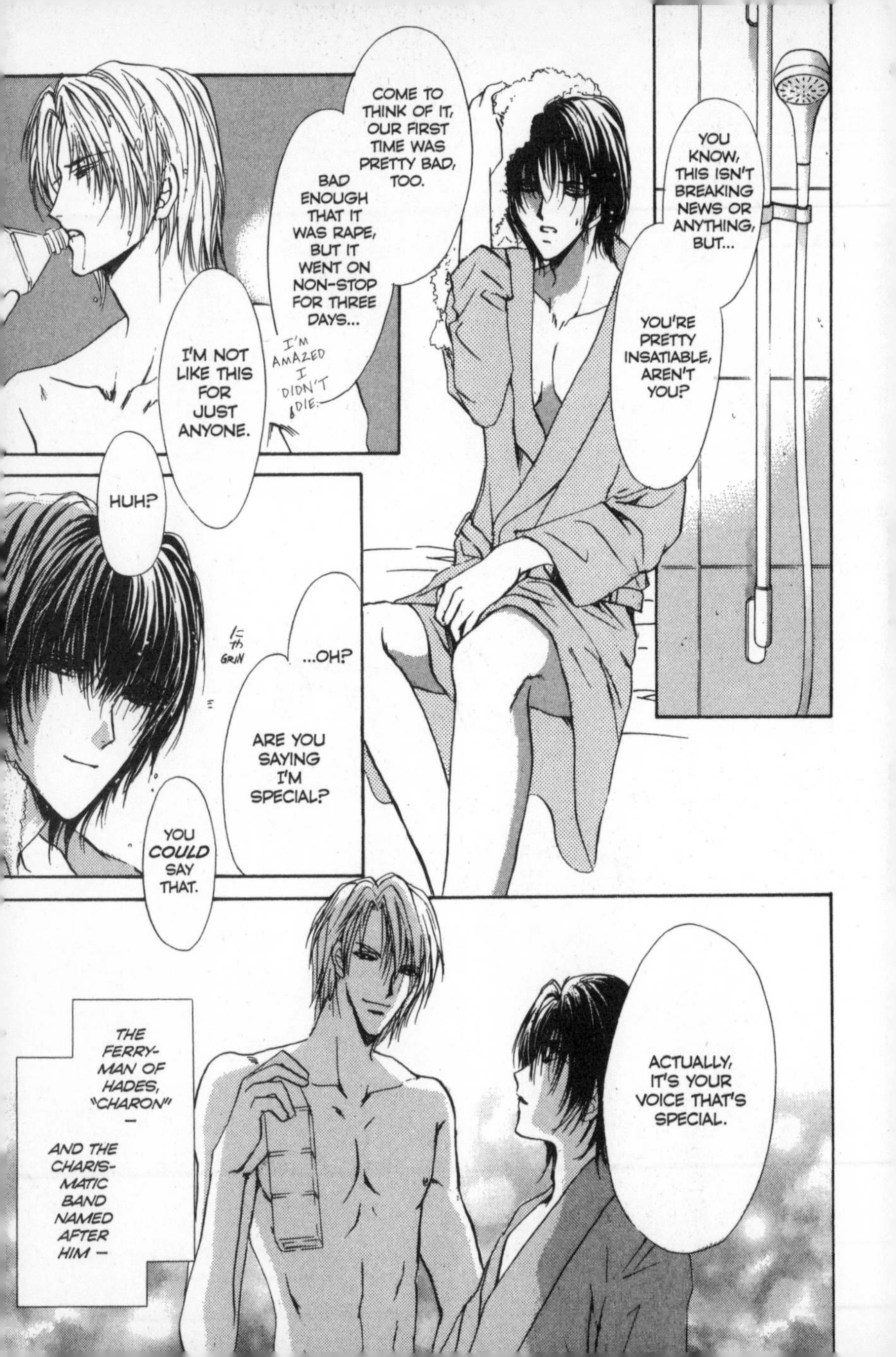
YOU KNOW, THIS ISN'T BREAKING NEWS OR ANYTHING, BUT...
YOU'RE PRETTY INSATIABLE, AREN'T YOU?
COME TO THINK OF IT, OUR FIRST TIME WAS PRETTY BAD, TOO.
BAD ENOUGH THAT IT WAS RAPE, BUT IT WENT ON NON-STOP FOR THREE DAYS...
I'M AMAZED I DIDN'T DIE.
I'M NOT LIKE THIS FOR JUST ANYONE.
HUH?
...OH?
GRIN
ARE YOU SAYING I'M SPECIAL?
YOU COULD SAY THAT.
ACTUALLY, IT'S YOUR VOICE THAT'S SPECIAL.
THE FERRY-MAN OF HADES, "CHARON" —
AND THE CHARIS-MATIC BAND NAMED AFTER HIM —

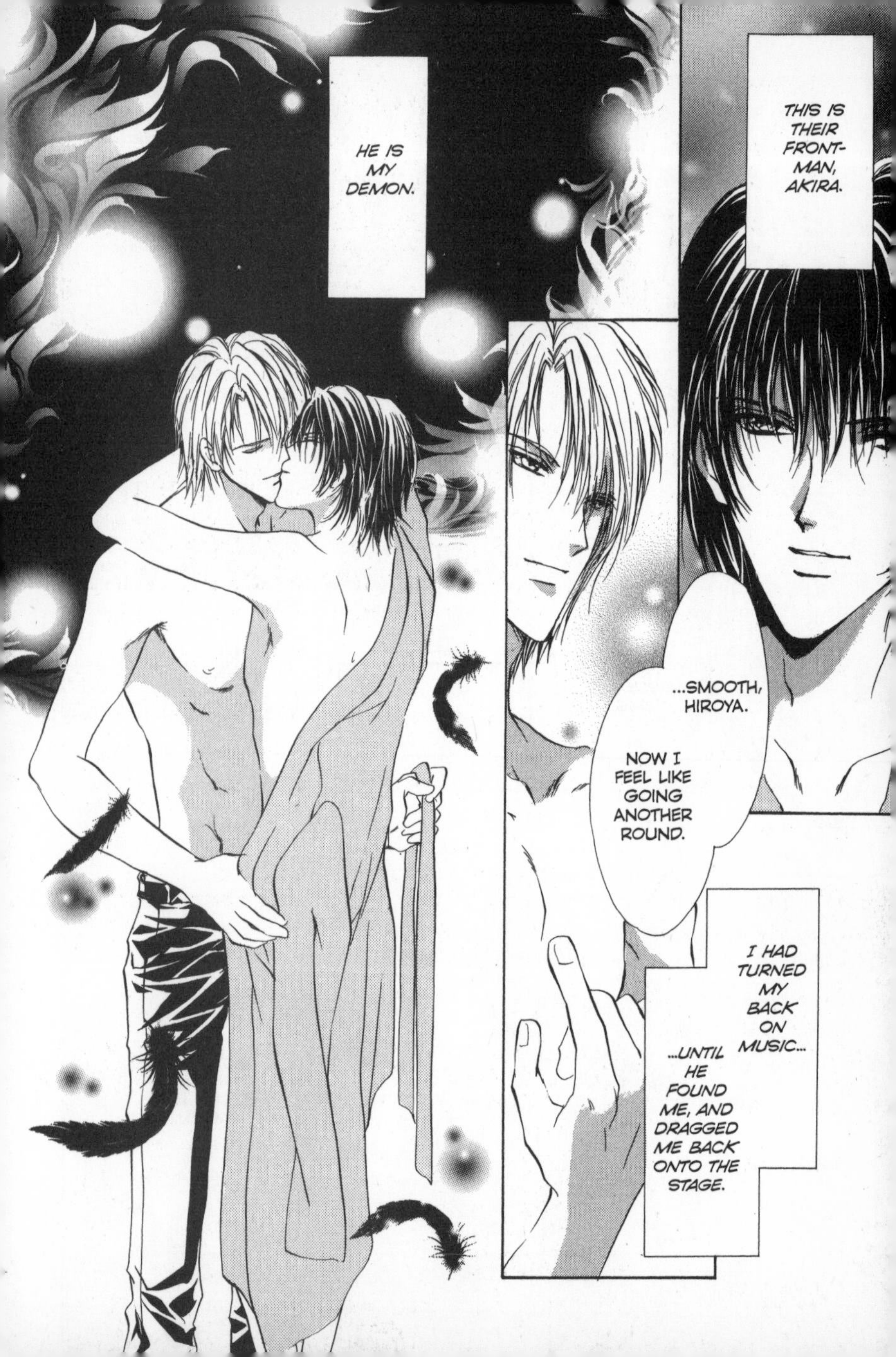
THIS IS THEIR FRONT-MAN, AKIRA.
...SMOOTH, HIROYA.
NOW I FEEL LIKE GOING ANOTHER ROUND.
I HAD TURNED MY BACK ON MUSIC...
...UNTIL HE FOUND ME, AND DRAGGED ME BACK ONTO THE STAGE.
HE IS MY DEMON.

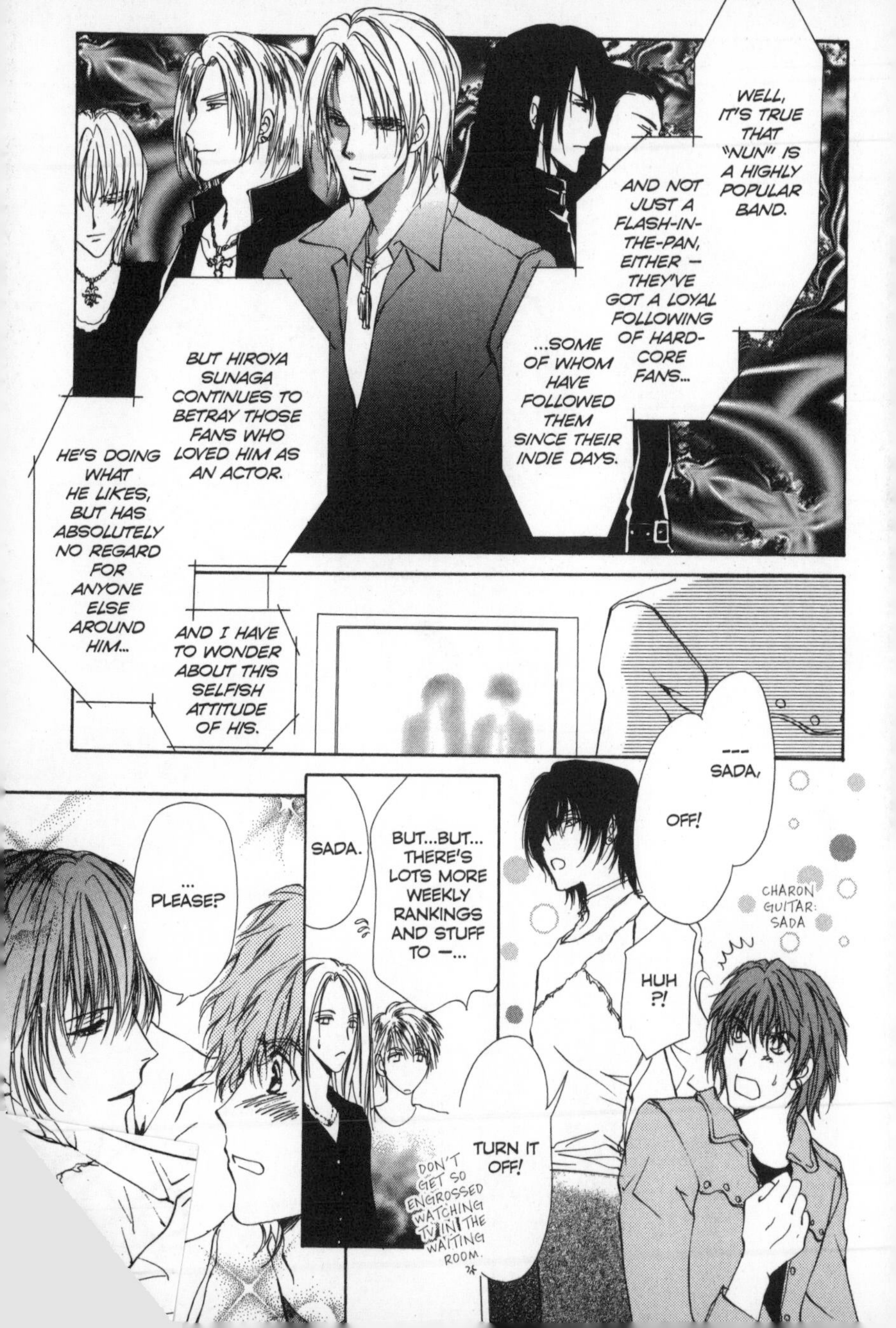
WELL, IT'S TRUE THAT "NUN" IS A HIGHLY POPULAR BAND.
AND NOT JUST A FLASH-IN-THE-PAN, EITHER — THEY'VE GOT A LOYAL FOLLOWING OF HARD-CORE FANS...
...SOME OF WHOM HAVE FOLLOWED THEM SINCE THEIR INDIE DAYS.
BUT HIROYA SUNAGA CONTINUES TO BETRAY THOSE FANS WHO LOVED HIM AS AN ACTOR.
HE'S DOING WHAT HE LIKES, BUT HAS ABSOLUTELY NO REGARD FOR ANYONE ELSE AROUND HIM...
AND I HAVE TO WONDER ABOUT THIS SELFISH ATTITUDE OF HIS.
---SADA,
OFF!
CHARON GUITAR: SADA
HUH ?!
TURN IT OFF!
DON'T GET SO ENGROSSED WATCHING TV IN THE WAITING ROOM.
SADA.
BUT...BUT... THERE'S LOTS MORE WEEKLY RANKINGS AND STUFF TO —...
... PLEASE?

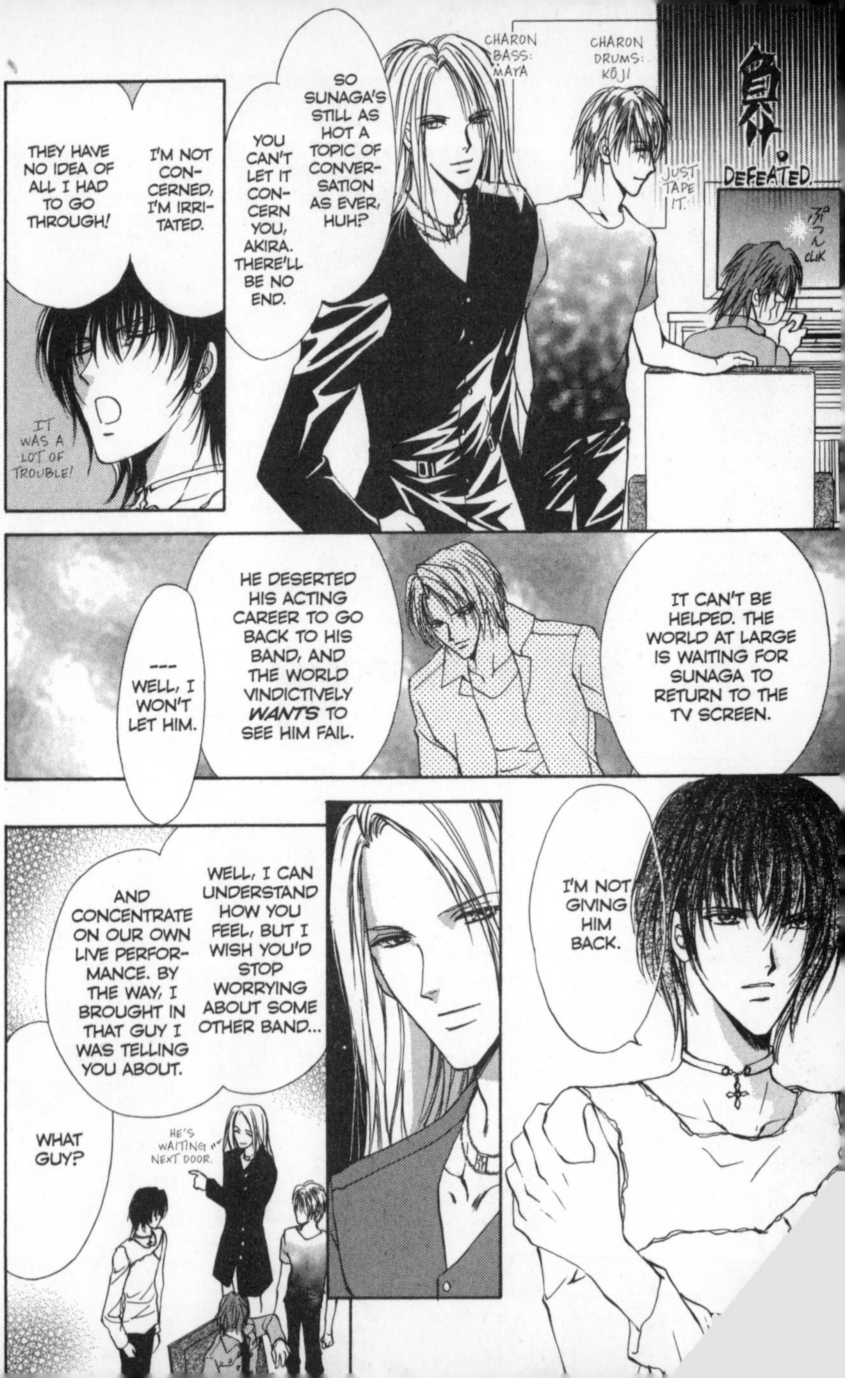
CHARON DRUMS: KŌJI
CHARON BASS: MAYA
DEFEATED.
JUST TAPE IT.
ぷつん
CLIK
SO SUNAGA'S STILL AS HOT A TOPIC OF CONVERSATION AS EVER, HUH?
YOU CAN'T LET IT CONCERN YOU, AKIRA. THERE'LL BE NO END.
I'M NOT CONCERNED, I'M IRRITATED.
THEY HAVE NO IDEA OF ALL I HAD TO GO THROUGH!
IT WAS A LOT OF TROUBLE!
IT CAN'T BE HELPED. THE WORLD AT LARGE IS WAITING FOR SUNAGA TO RETURN TO THE TV SCREEN.
HE DESERTED HIS ACTING CAREER TO GO BACK TO HIS BAND, AND THE WORLD VINDICTIVELY *WANTS* TO SEE HIM FAIL.
--- WELL, I WON'T LET HIM.
I'M NOT GIVING HIM BACK.
WELL, I CAN UNDERSTAND HOW YOU FEEL, BUT I WISH YOU'D STOP WORRYING ABOUT SOME OTHER BAND...
AND CONCENTRATE ON OUR OWN LIVE PERFORMANCE. BY THE WAY, I BROUGHT IN THAT GUY I WAS TELLING YOU ABOUT.
WHAT GUY?
HE'S WAITING NEXT DOOR.

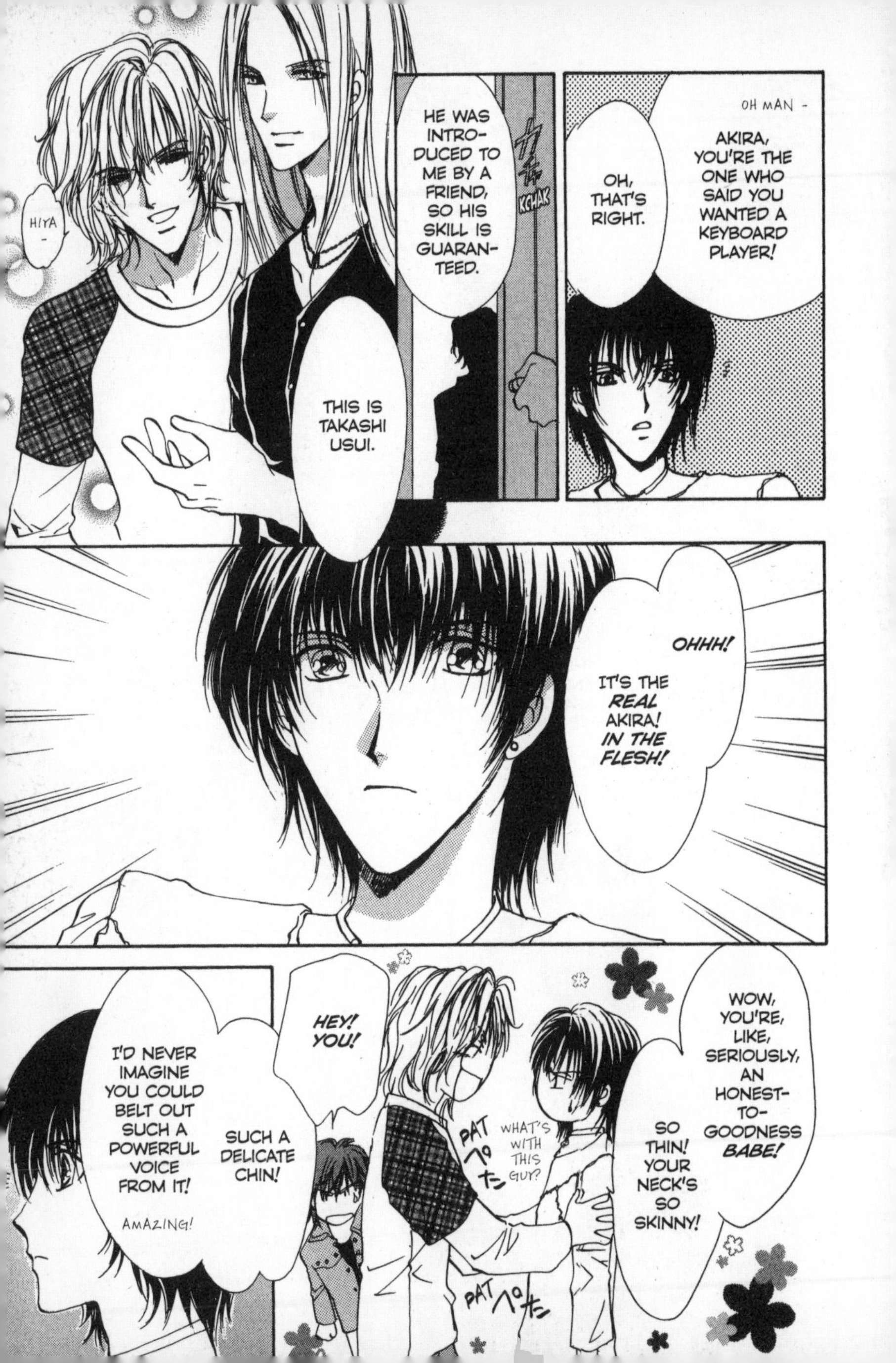

OH MAN -
AKIRA, YOU'RE THE ONE WHO SAID YOU WANTED A KEYBOARD PLAYER!
OH, THAT'S RIGHT.
HE WAS INTRODUCED TO ME BY A FRIEND, SO HIS SKILL IS GUARANTEED.
KCHAK
THIS IS TAKASHI USUI.
HIYA -
OHHH!
IT'S THE *REAL* AKIRA! *IN THE FLESH!*
WOW, YOU'RE, LIKE, SERIOUSLY, AN HONEST-TO-GOODNESS *BABE!*
SO THIN! YOUR NECK'S SO SKINNY!
WHAT'S WITH THIS GUY?
PAT
PAT
HEY! YOU!
SUCH A DELICATE CHIN!
I'D NEVER IMAGINE YOU COULD BELT OUT SUCH A POWERFUL VOICE FROM IT!
AMAZING!

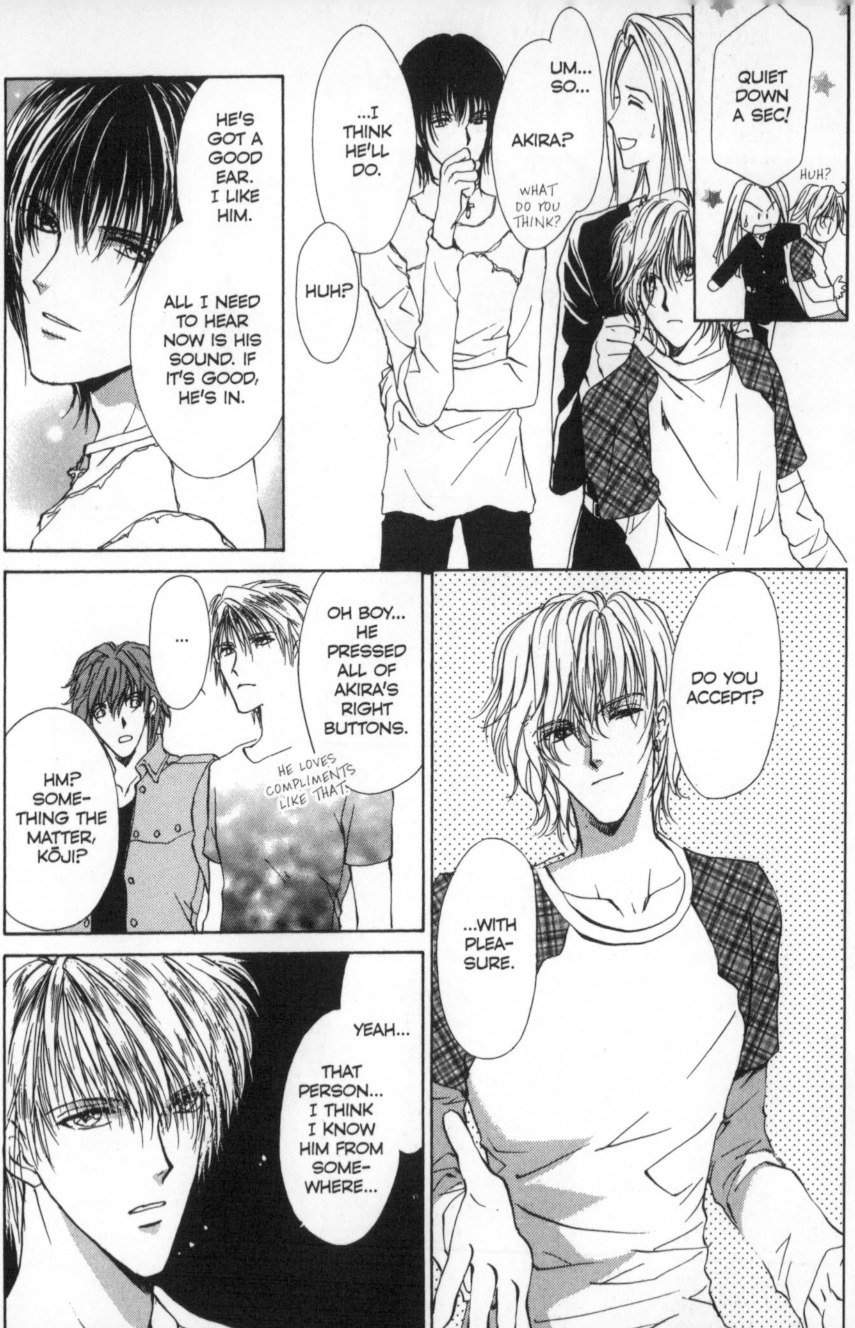
QUIET DOWN A SEC!
HUH?
UM... SO...
AKIRA?
WHAT DO YOU THINK?
...I THINK HE'LL DO.
HUH?
HE'S GOT A GOOD EAR. I LIKE HIM.
ALL I NEED TO HEAR NOW IS HIS SOUND. IF IT'S GOOD, HE'S IN.
DO YOU ACCEPT?
...WITH PLEA-SURE.
OH BOY... HE PRESSED ALL OF AKIRA'S RIGHT BUTTONS.
HE LOVES COMPLIMENTS LIKE THAT.
...
HM? SOME-THING THE MATTER, KŌJI?
YEAH...
THAT PERSON... I THINK I KNOW HIM FROM SOME-WHERE...

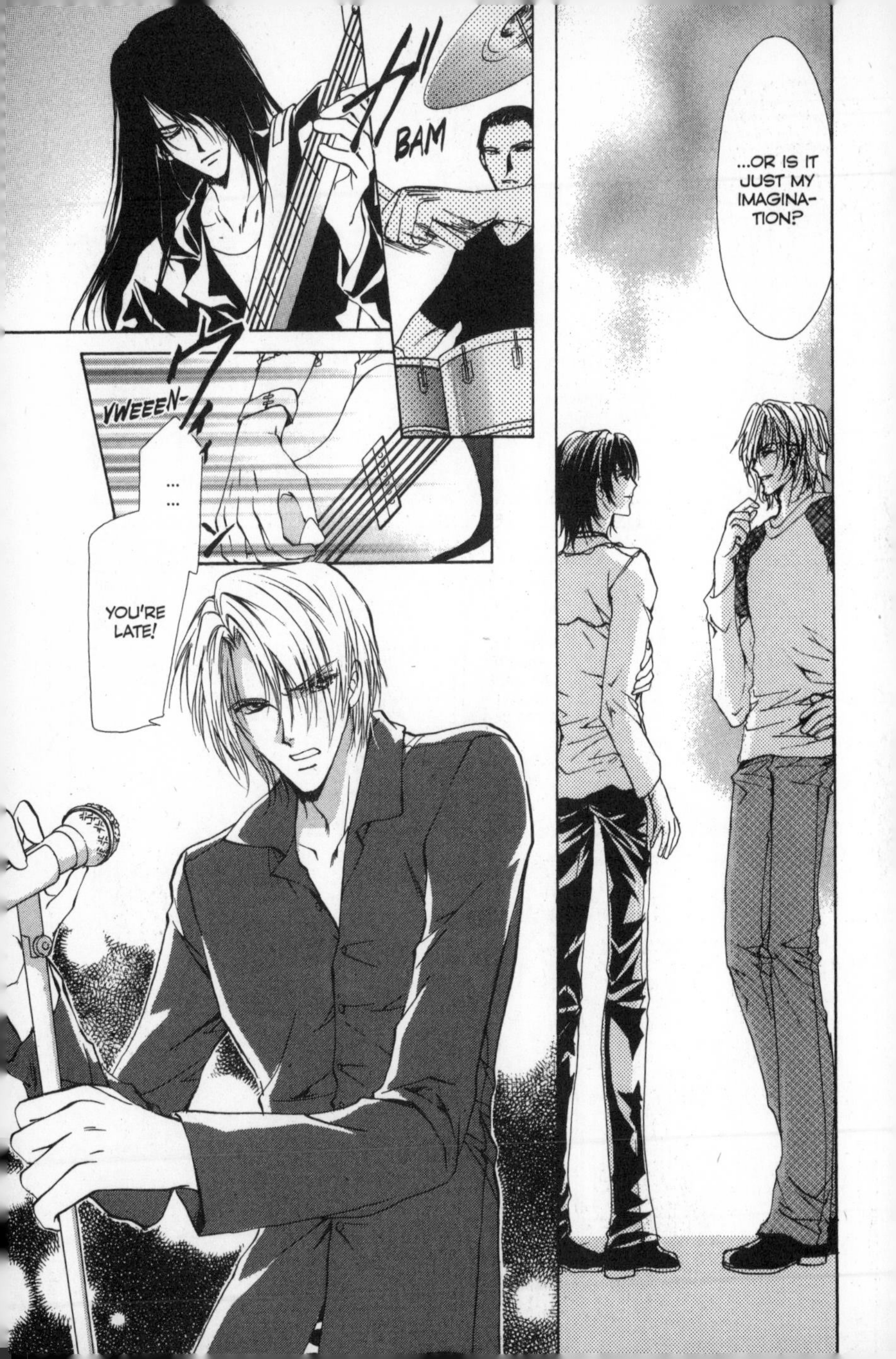
...OR IS IT JUST MY IMAGINATION?
BAM
VWEEEN-
...
...
YOU'RE LATE!

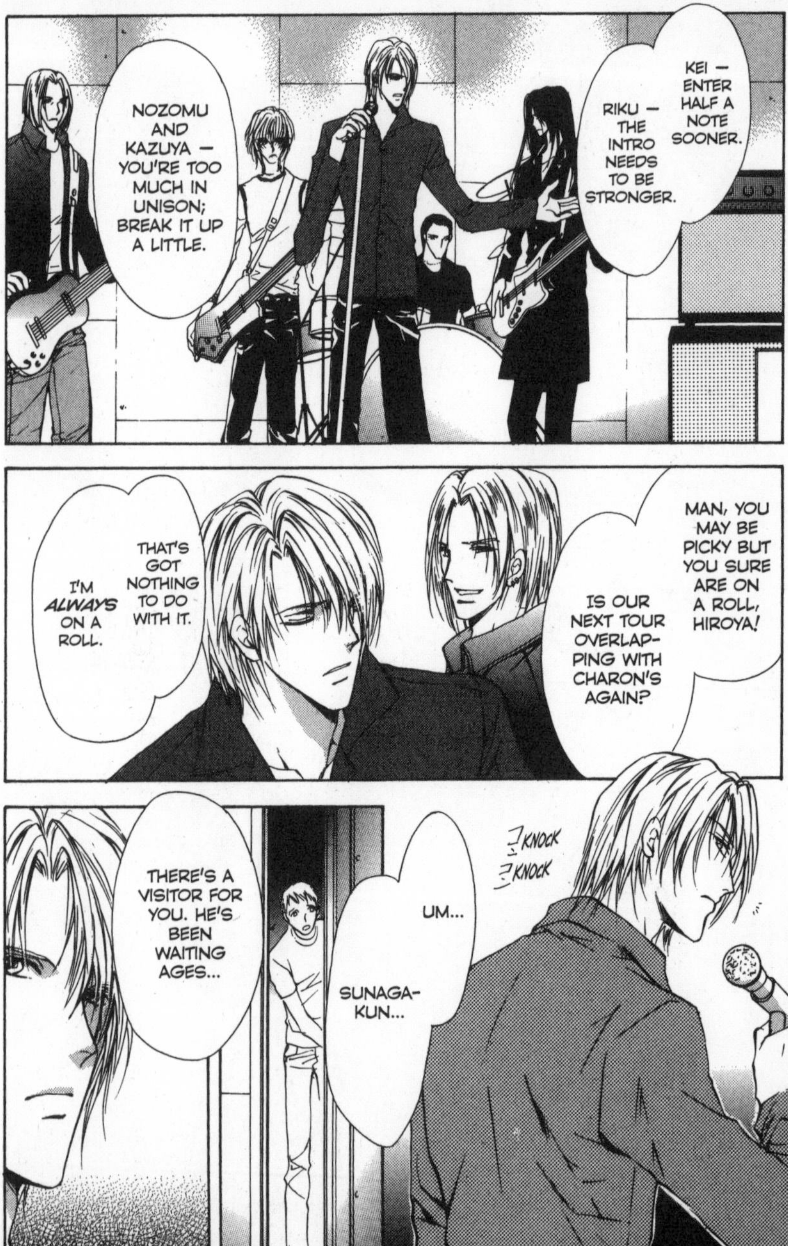
KEI — ENTER HALF A NOTE SOONER.
RIKU — THE INTRO NEEDS TO BE STRONGER.
NOZOMU AND KAZUYA — YOU'RE TOO MUCH IN UNISON; BREAK IT UP A LITTLE.
MAN, YOU MAY BE PICKY BUT YOU SURE ARE ON A ROLL, HIROYA!
IS OUR NEXT TOUR OVERLAP-PING WITH CHARON'S AGAIN?
THAT'S GOT NOTHING TO DO WITH IT.
I'M *ALWAYS* ON A ROLL.
KNOCK KNOCK
UM...
SUNAGA-KUN...
THERE'S A VISITOR FOR YOU. HE'S BEEN WAITING AGES...

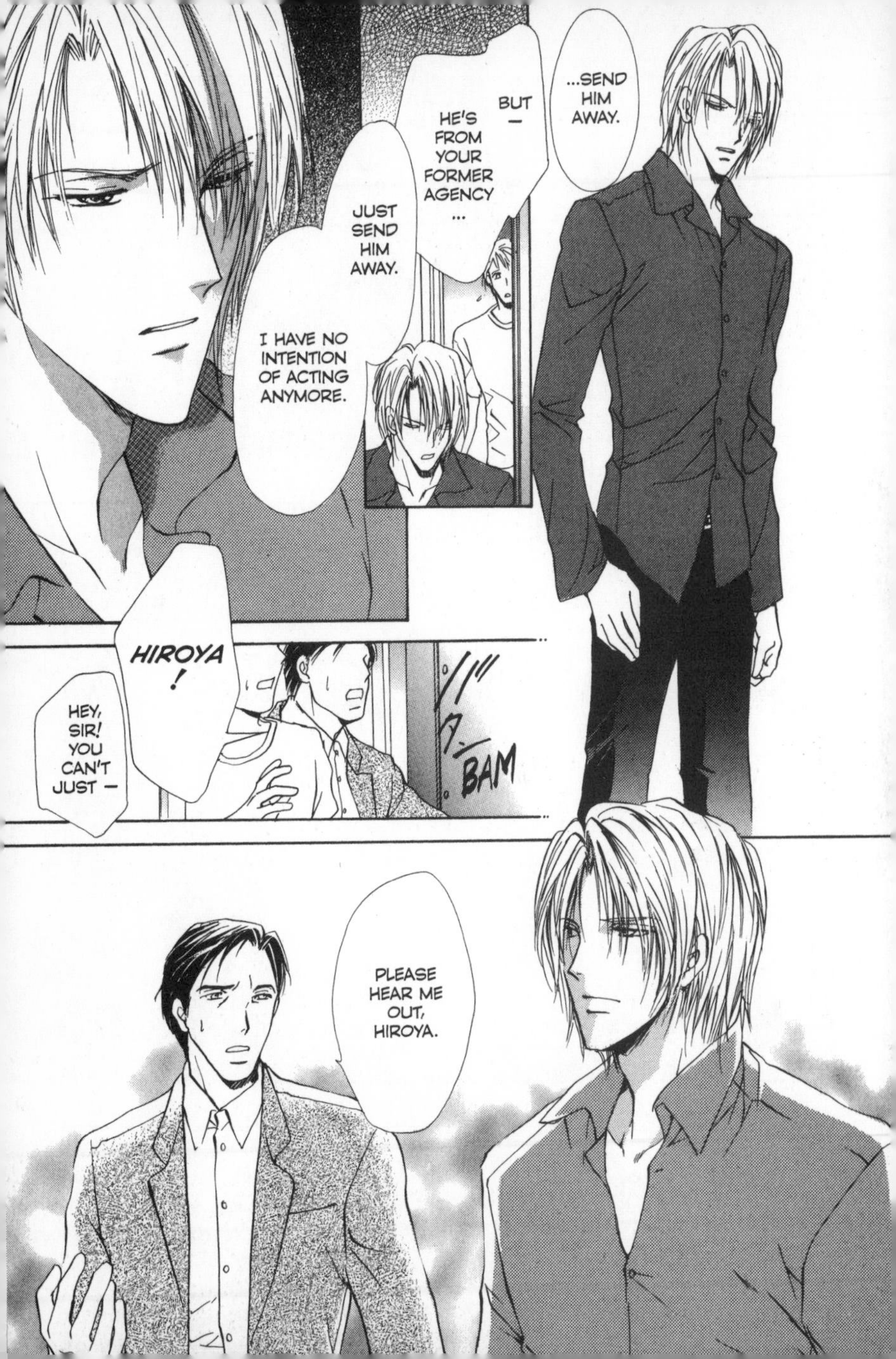

...SEND HIM AWAY.
BUT —
HE'S FROM YOUR FORMER AGENCY ...
JUST SEND HIM AWAY.
I HAVE NO INTENTION OF ACTING ANYMORE.
BAM
HIROYA!
HEY, SIR! YOU CAN'T JUST —
PLEASE HEAR ME OUT, HIROYA.

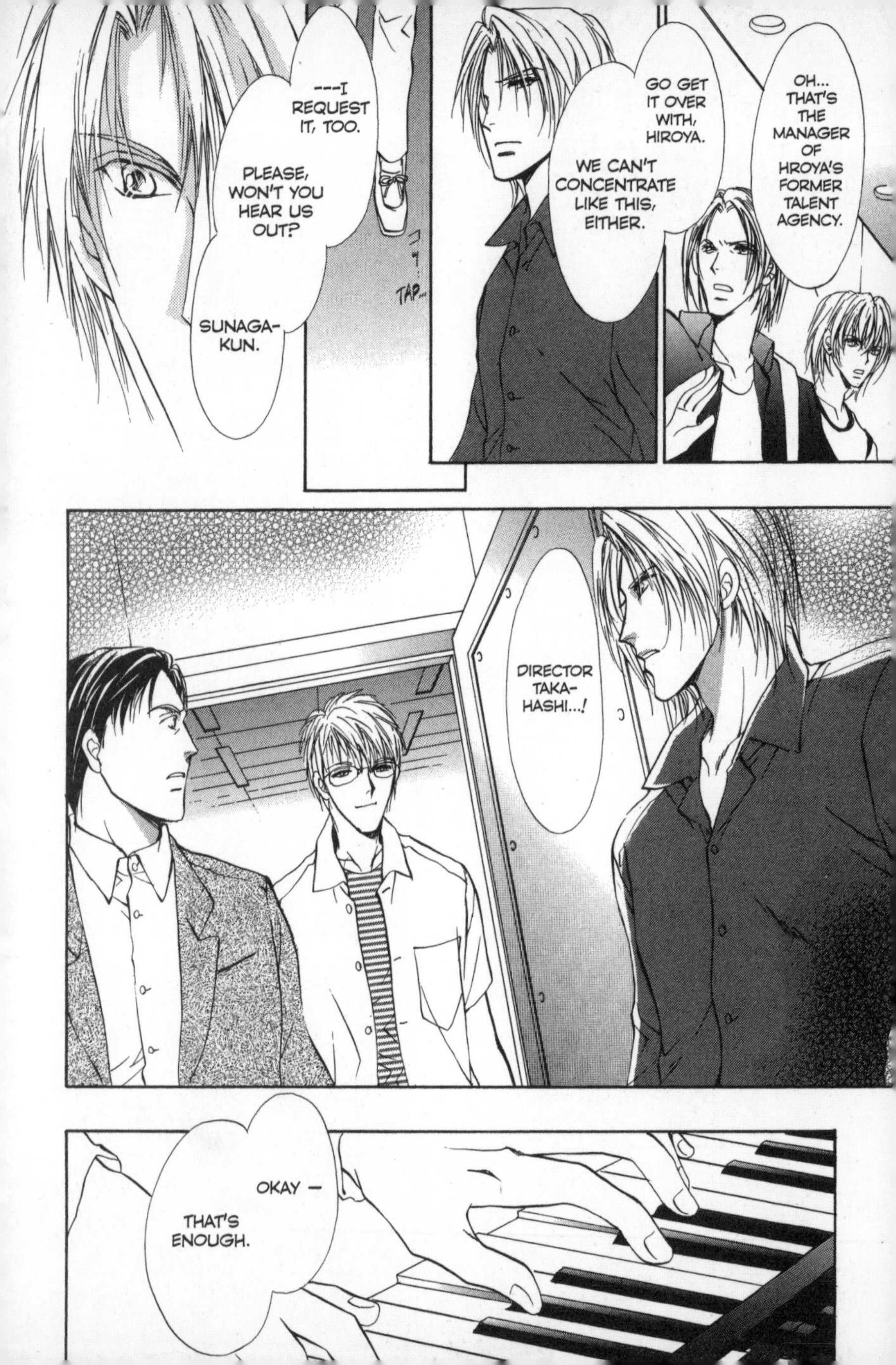
OH... THAT'S THE MANAGER OF HROYA'S FORMER TALENT AGENCY.
GO GET IT OVER WITH, HIROYA.
WE CAN'T CONCENTRATE LIKE THIS, EITHER.
TAP...
---I REQUEST IT, TOO.
PLEASE, WON'T YOU HEAR US OUT?
SUNAGA-KUN.
DIRECTOR TAKA-HASHI...!
OKAY — THAT'S ENOUGH.

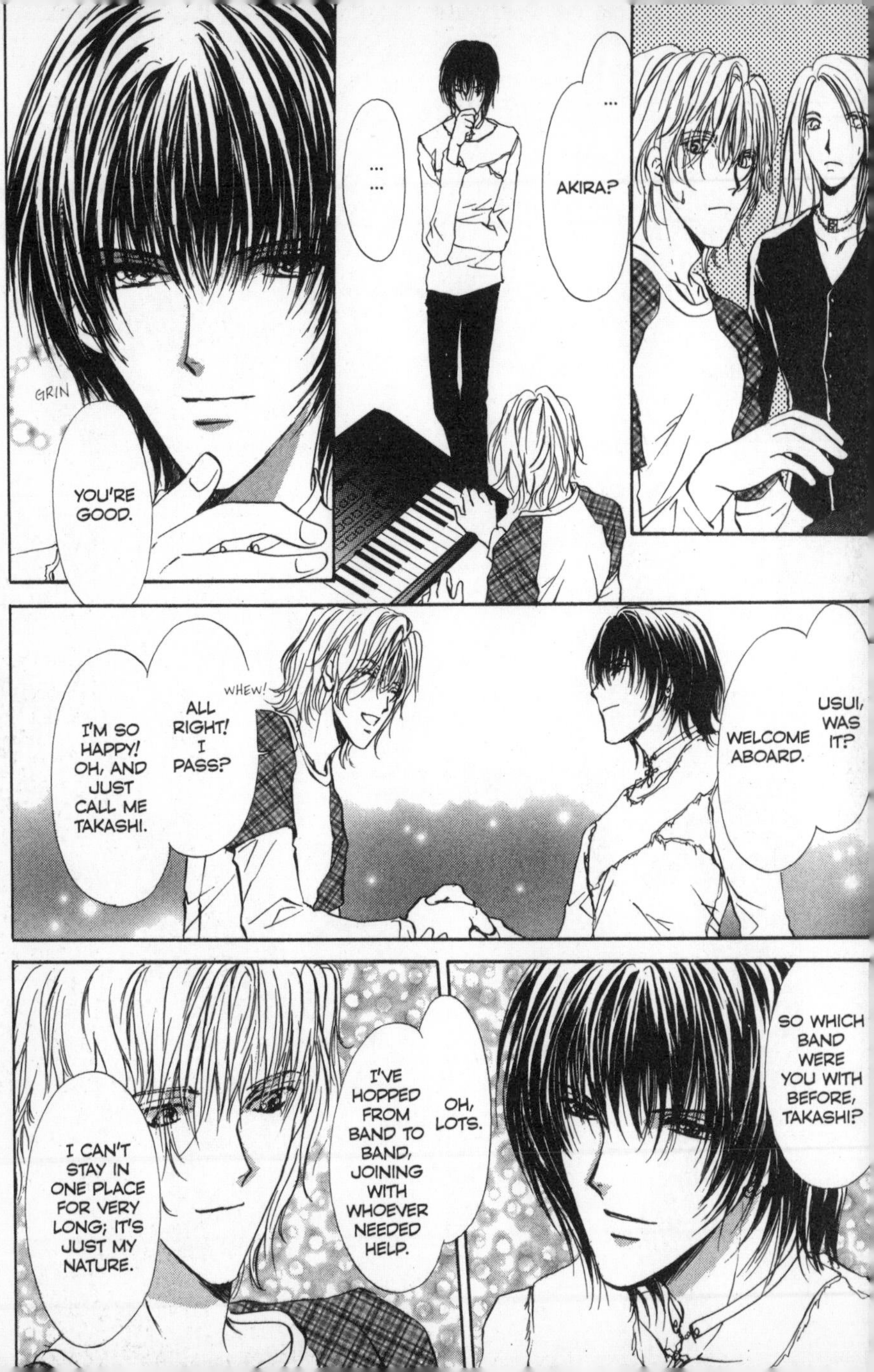
... AKIRA?
... ...
GRIN
YOU'RE GOOD.
USUI, WAS IT?
WELCOME ABOARD.
WHEW!
ALL RIGHT! I PASS?
I'M SO HAPPY! OH, AND JUST CALL ME TAKASHI.
SO WHICH BAND WERE YOU WITH BEFORE, TAKASHI?
OH, LOTS.
I'VE HOPPED FROM BAND TO BAND, JOINING WITH WHOEVER NEEDED HELP.
I CAN'T STAY IN ONE PLACE FOR VERY LONG; IT'S JUST MY NATURE.

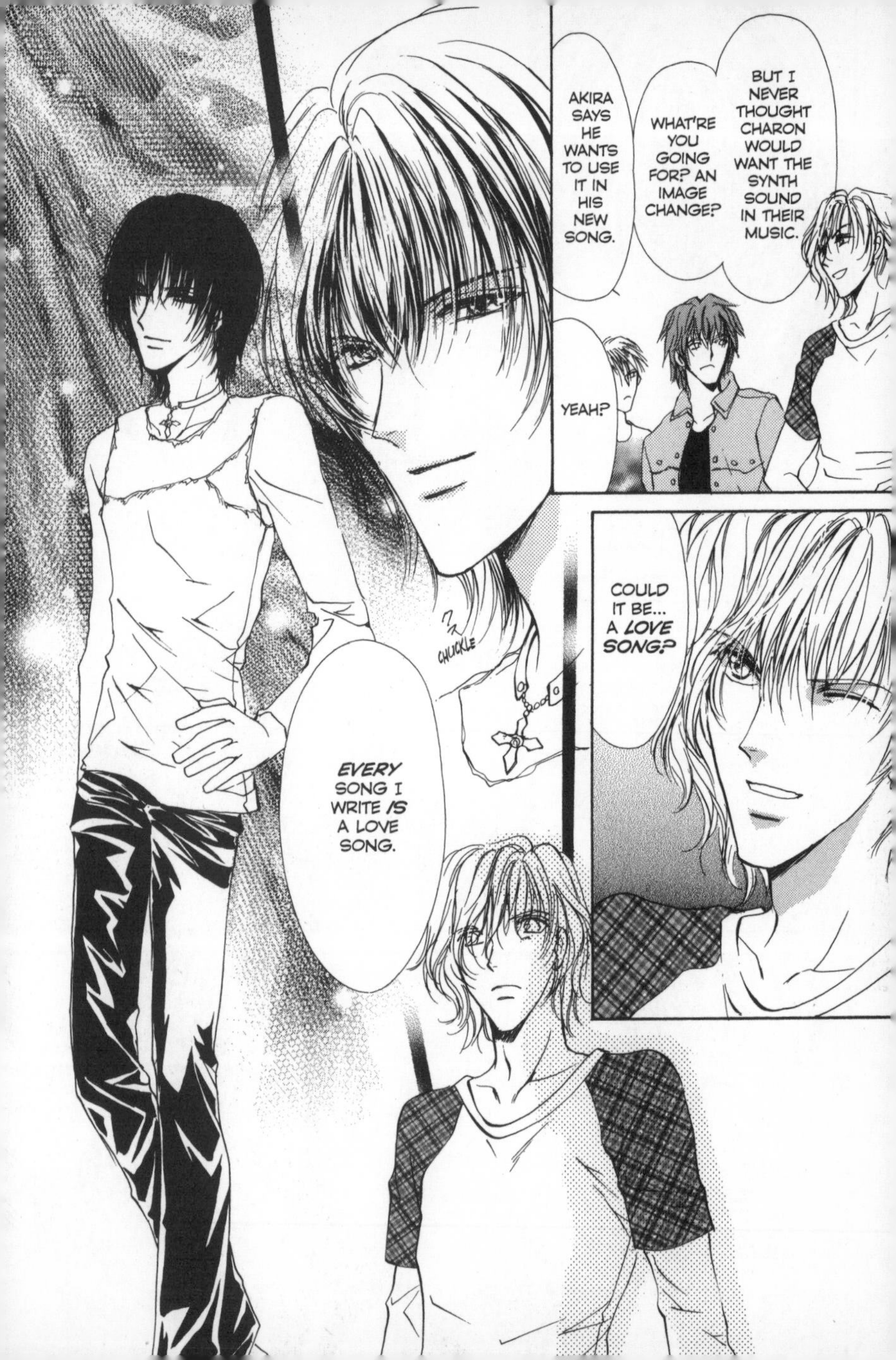
BUT I NEVER THOUGHT CHARON WOULD WANT THE SYNTH SOUND IN THEIR MUSIC.
WHAT'RE YOU GOING FOR? AN IMAGE CHANGE?
AKIRA SAYS HE WANTS TO USE IT IN HIS NEW SONG.
YEAH?
COULD IT BE... A *LOVE SONG?*
CHUCKLE
EVERY SONG I WRITE *IS* A LOVE SONG.

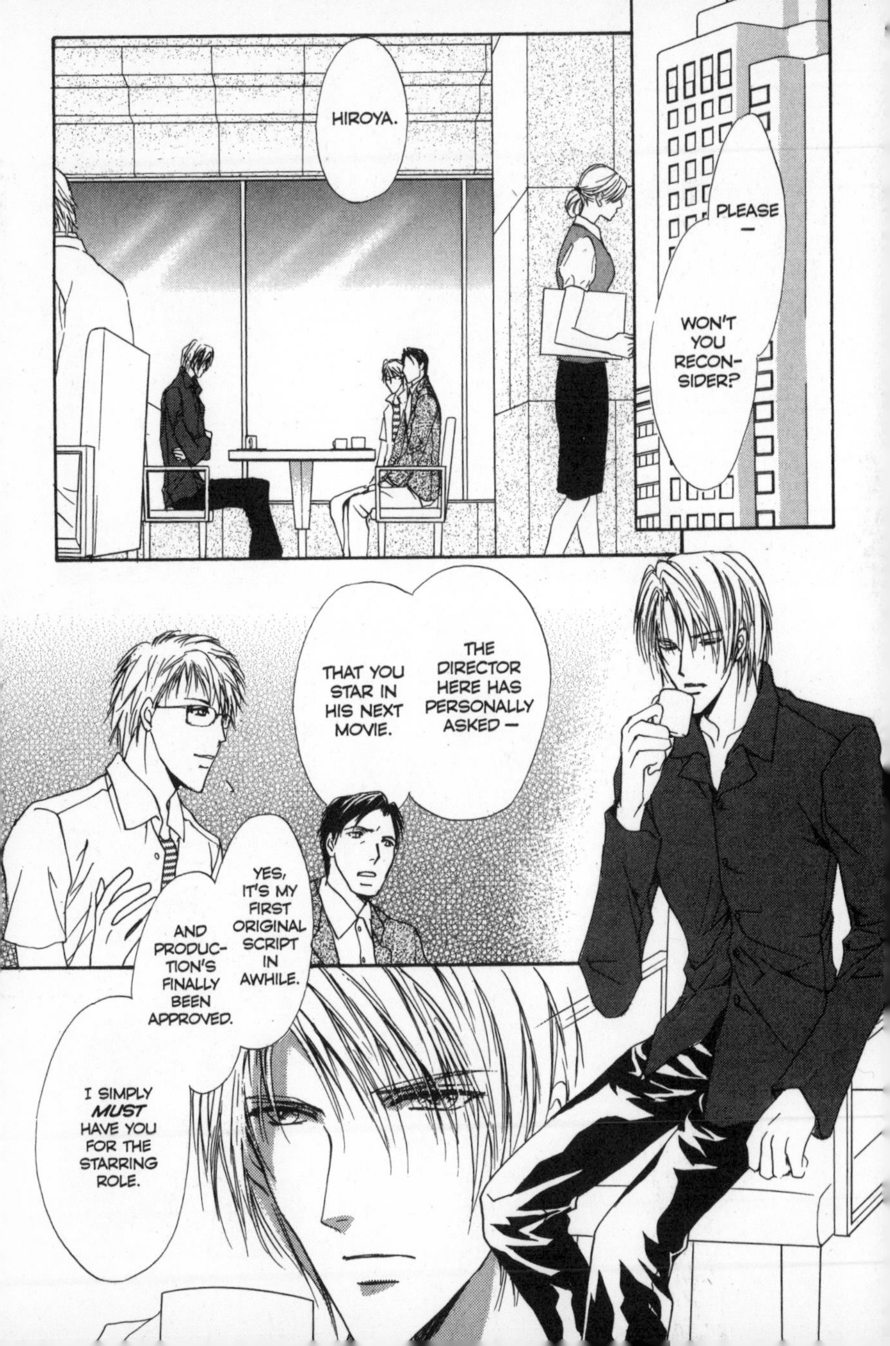
PLEASE —
WON'T YOU RECONSIDER?
HIROYA.
THE DIRECTOR HERE HAS PERSONALLY ASKED —
THAT YOU STAR IN HIS NEXT MOVIE.
YES, IT'S MY FIRST ORIGINAL SCRIPT IN AWHILE.
AND PRODUCTION'S FINALLY BEEN APPROVED.
I SIMPLY *MUST* HAVE YOU FOR THE STARRING ROLE.

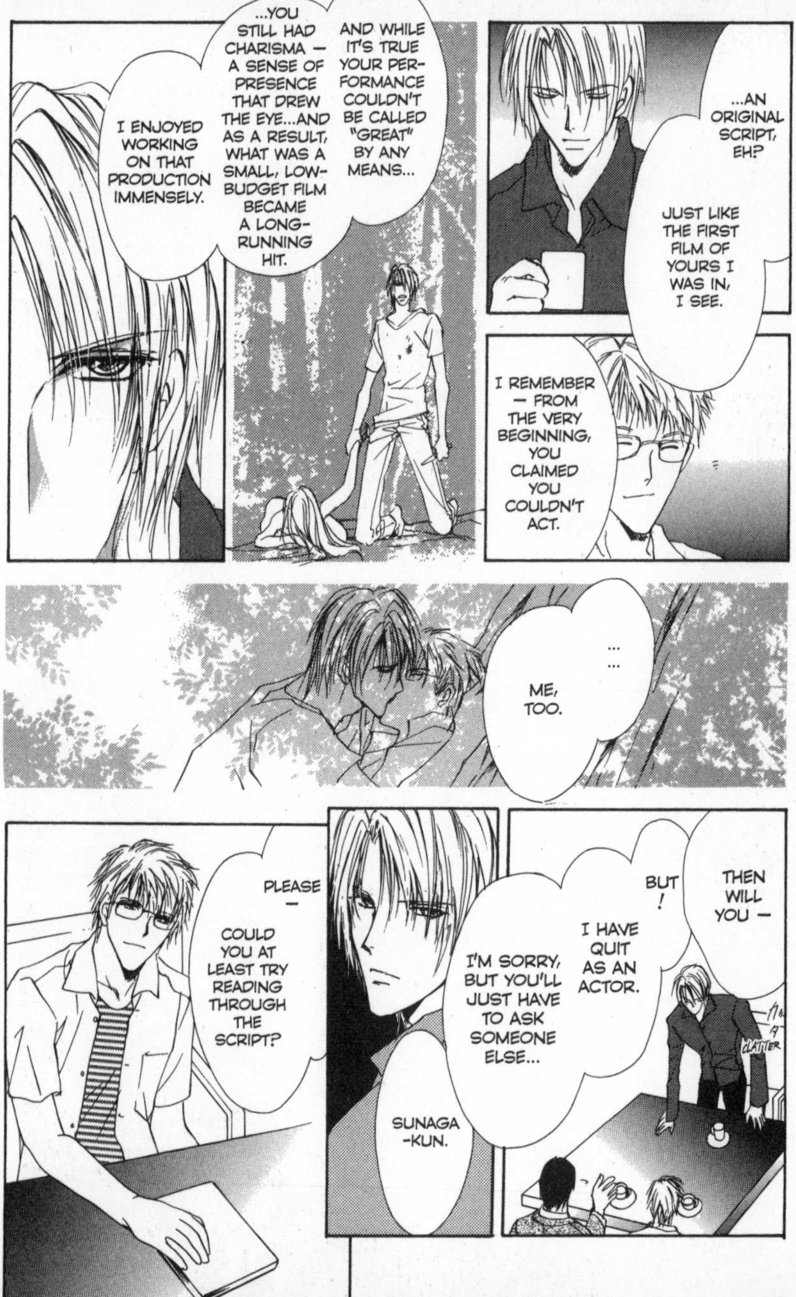
...AN ORIGINAL SCRIPT, EH?
JUST LIKE THE FIRST FILM OF YOURS I WAS IN, I SEE.
I REMEMBER — FROM THE VERY BEGINNING, YOU CLAIMED YOU COULDN'T ACT.
AND WHILE IT'S TRUE YOUR PERFORMANCE COULDN'T BE CALLED "GREAT" BY ANY MEANS...
...YOU STILL HAD CHARISMA — A SENSE OF PRESENCE THAT DREW THE EYE...AND AS A RESULT, WHAT WAS A SMALL, LOW-BUDGET FILM BECAME A LONG-RUNNING HIT.
I ENJOYED WORKING ON THAT PRODUCTION IMMENSELY.
......
ME, TOO.
THEN WILL YOU —
BUT!
I HAVE QUIT AS AN ACTOR.
CLATTER
I'M SORRY, BUT YOU'LL JUST HAVE TO ASK SOMEONE ELSE...
SUNAGA-KUN.
PLEASE —
COULD YOU AT LEAST TRY READING THROUGH THE SCRIPT?

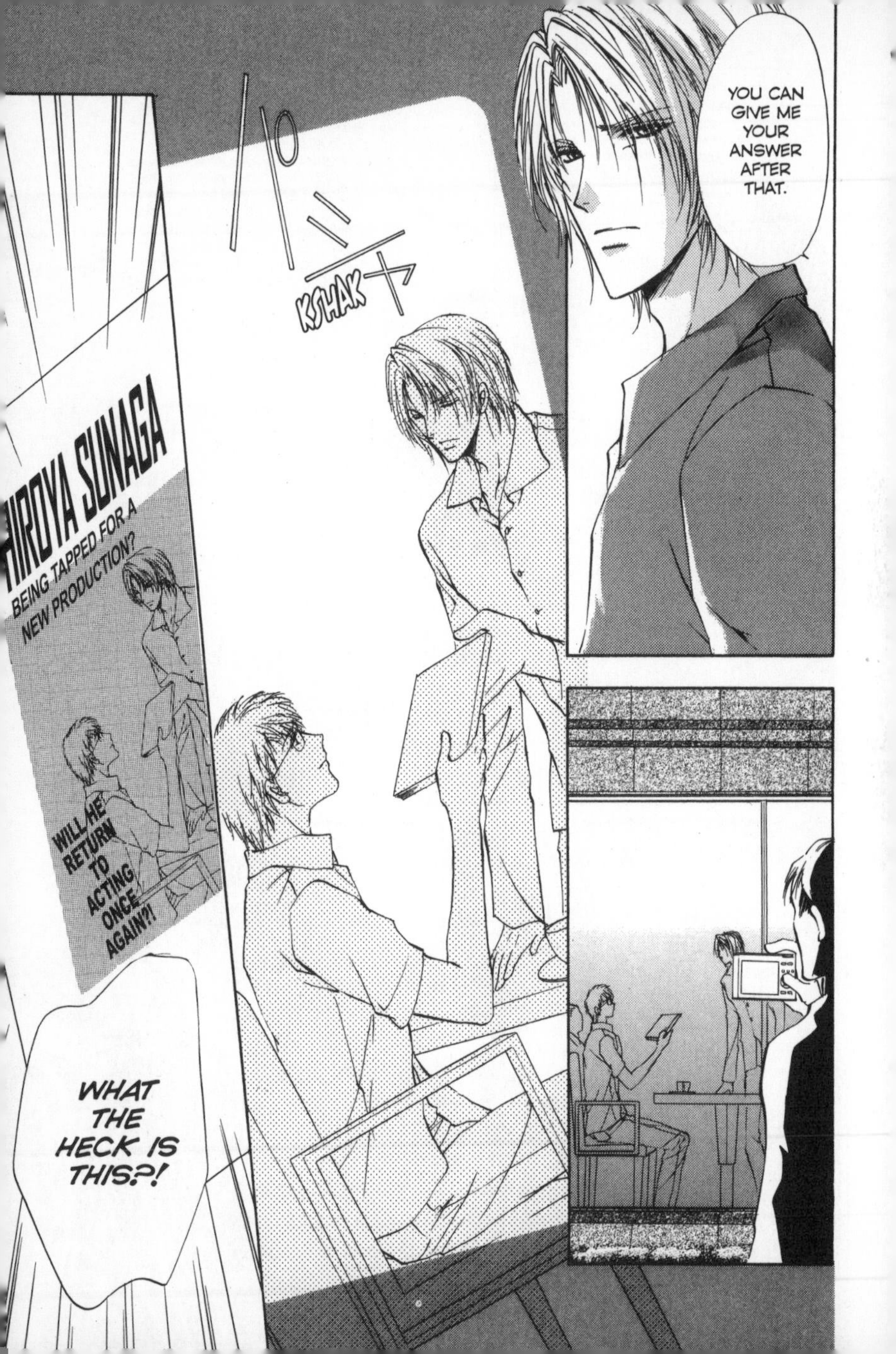
YOU CAN GIVE ME YOUR ANSWER AFTER THAT.
KSHAK
HIROYA SUNAGA
BEING TAPPED FOR A NEW PRODUCTION?
WILL HE RETURN TO ACTING ONCE AGAIN?!
WHAT THE HECK IS THIS?!

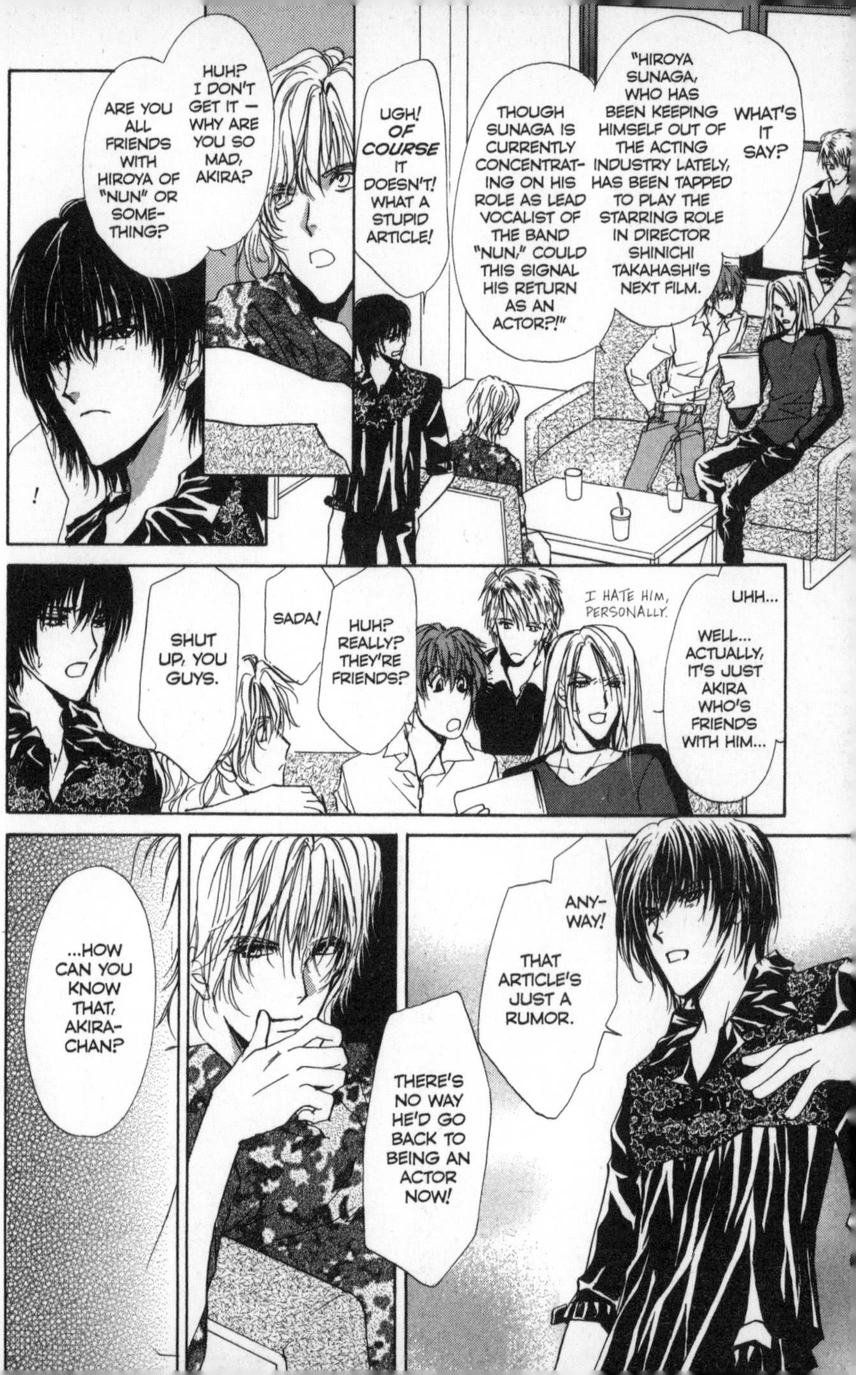
WHAT'S IT SAY?
"HIROYA SUNAGA, WHO HAS BEEN KEEPING HIMSELF OUT OF THE ACTING INDUSTRY LATELY, HAS BEEN TAPPED TO PLAY THE STARRING ROLE IN DIRECTOR SHINICHI TAKAHASHI'S NEXT FILM.
THOUGH SUNAGA IS CURRENTLY CONCENTRAT-ING ON HIS ROLE AS LEAD VOCALIST OF THE BAND "NUN," COULD THIS SIGNAL HIS RETURN AS AN ACTOR?!"
UGH! *OF COURSE* IT DOESN'T! WHAT A STUPID ARTICLE!
HUH? I DON'T GET IT — WHY ARE YOU SO MAD, AKIRA?
ARE YOU ALL FRIENDS WITH HIROYA OF "NUN" OR SOME-THING?
!
UHH...
WELL... ACTUALLY, IT'S JUST AKIRA WHO'S FRIENDS WITH HIM...
I HATE HIM, PERSONALLY.
HUH? REALLY? THEY'RE FRIENDS?
SADA!
SHUT UP, YOU GUYS.
ANY-WAY!
THAT ARTICLE'S JUST A RUMOR.
THERE'S NO WAY HE'D GO BACK TO BEING AN ACTOR NOW!
...HOW CAN YOU KNOW THAT, AKIRA-CHAN?

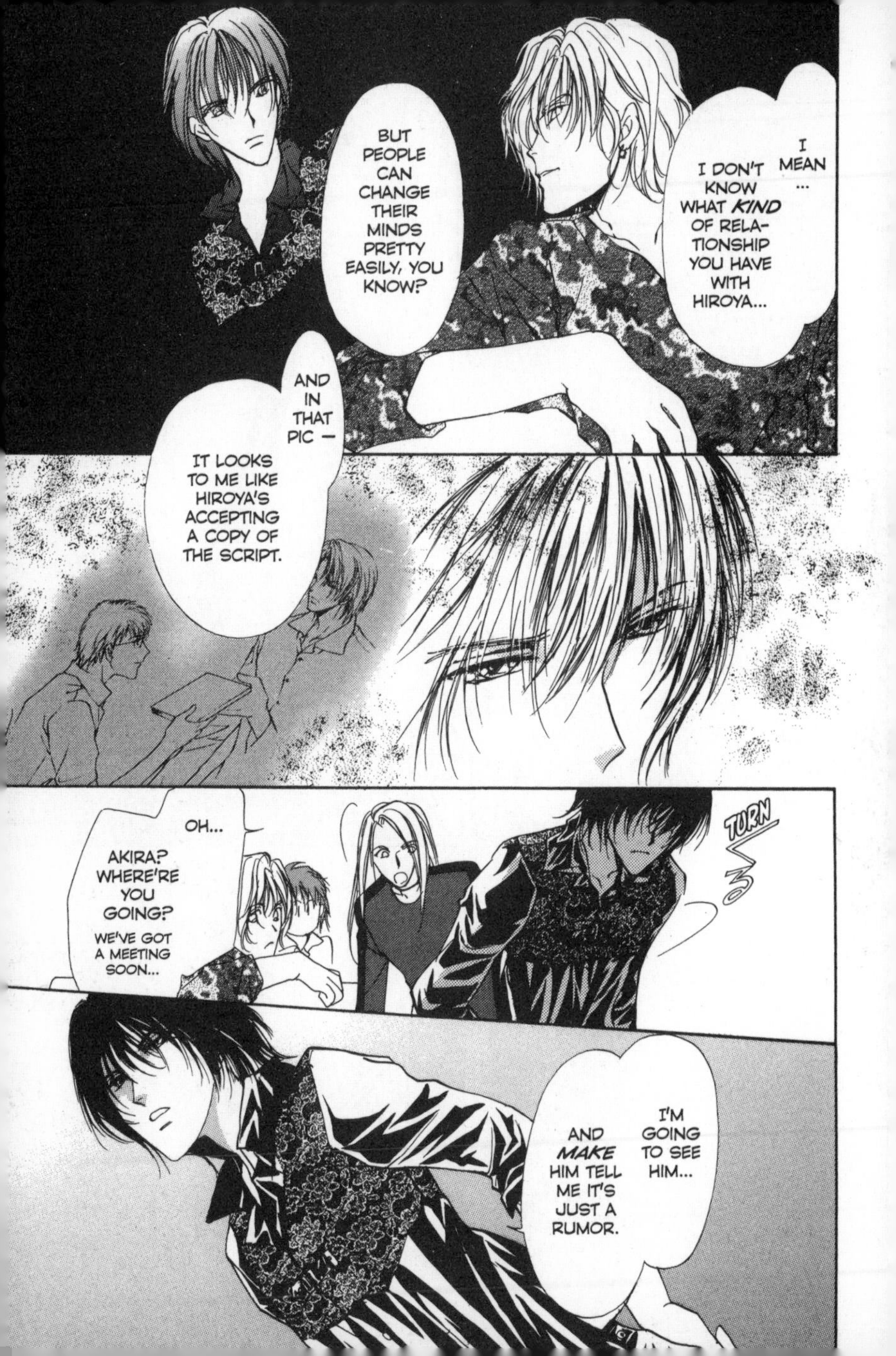
I MEAN... I DON'T KNOW WHAT KIND OF RELATIONSHIP YOU HAVE WITH HIROYA...
BUT PEOPLE CAN CHANGE THEIR MINDS PRETTY EASILY, YOU KNOW?
AND IN THAT PIC —
IT LOOKS TO ME LIKE HIROYA'S ACCEPTING A COPY OF THE SCRIPT.
TURN
OH...
AKIRA? WHERE'RE YOU GOING? WE'VE GOT A MEETING SOON...
I'M GOING TO SEE HIM...
AND MAKE HIM TELL ME IT'S JUST A RUMOR.

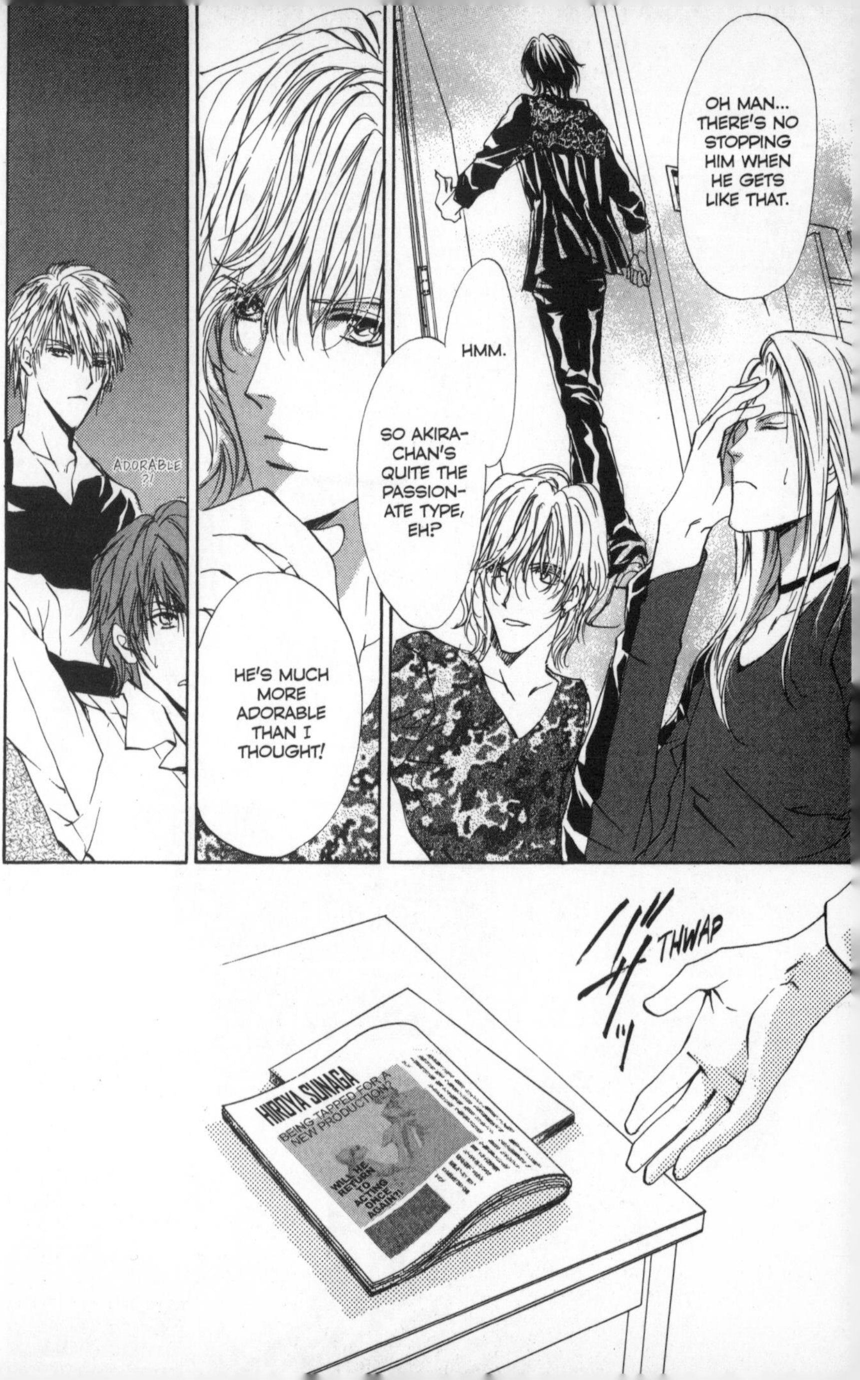
OH MAN... THERE'S NO STOPPING HIM WHEN HE GETS LIKE THAT.
HMM.
SO AKIRA-CHAN'S QUITE THE PASSION-ATE TYPE, EH?
HE'S MUCH MORE ADORABLE THAN I THOUGHT!
ADORABLE ?!
THWAP
HIROYA SUNAGA
BEING TAPPED FOR A NEW PRODUCTION?!
WILL HE RETURN TO ACTING ONCE AGAIN?!

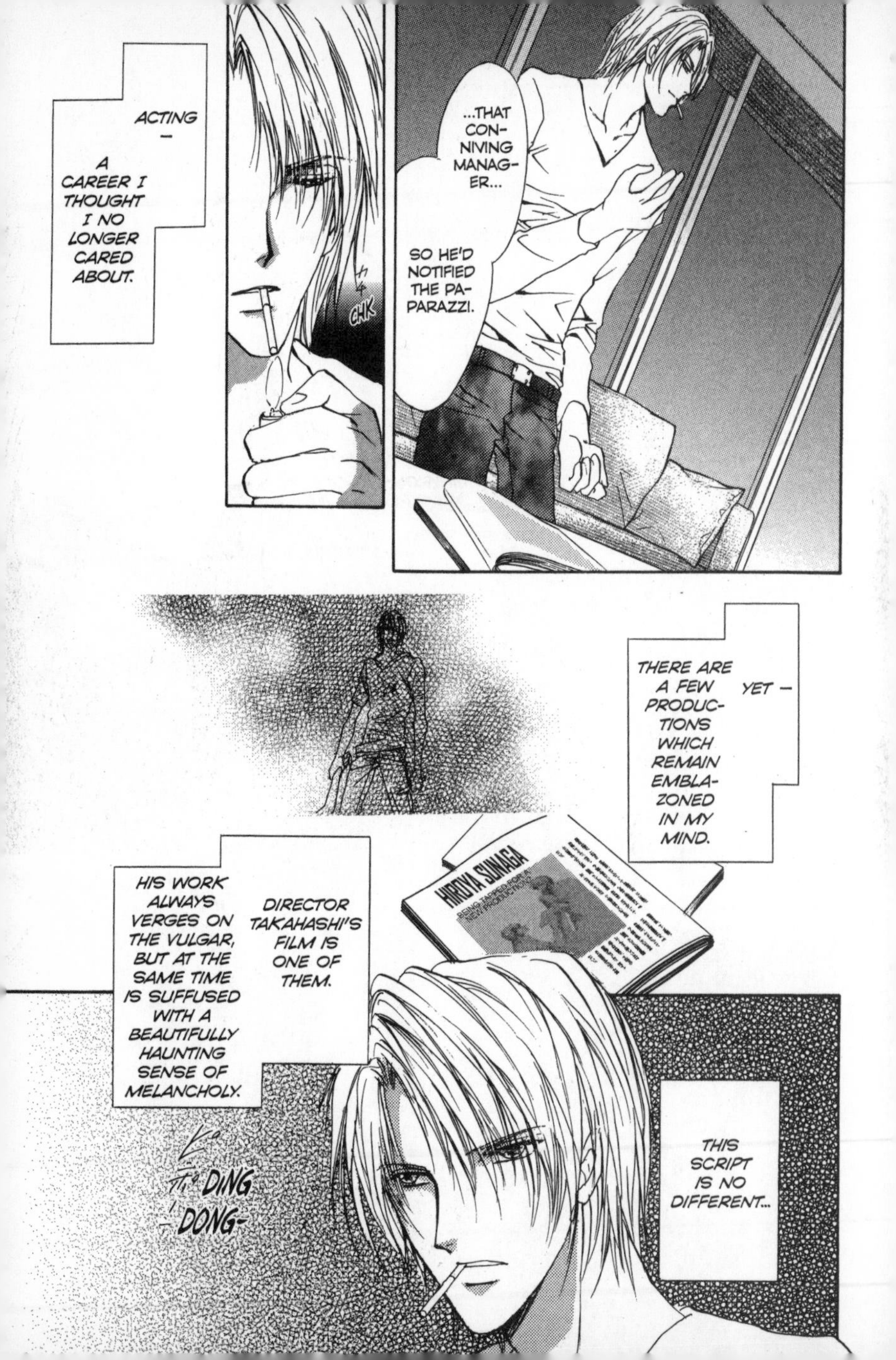
...THAT CONNIVING MANAGER...
SO HE'D NOTIFIED THE PAPARAZZI.
CHK
ACTING — A CAREER I THOUGHT I NO LONGER CARED ABOUT.
YET —
THERE ARE A FEW PRODUCTIONS WHICH REMAIN EMBLAZONED IN MY MIND.
DIRECTOR TAKAHASHI'S FILM IS ONE OF THEM.
HIS WORK ALWAYS VERGES ON THE VULGAR, BUT AT THE SAME TIME IS SUFFUSED WITH A BEAUTIFULLY HAUNTING SENSE OF MELANCHOLY.
HIROYA SUNAGA
BEING TAPPED FOR A NEW PRODUCTION?
THIS SCRIPT IS NO DIFFERENT...
DING DONG-

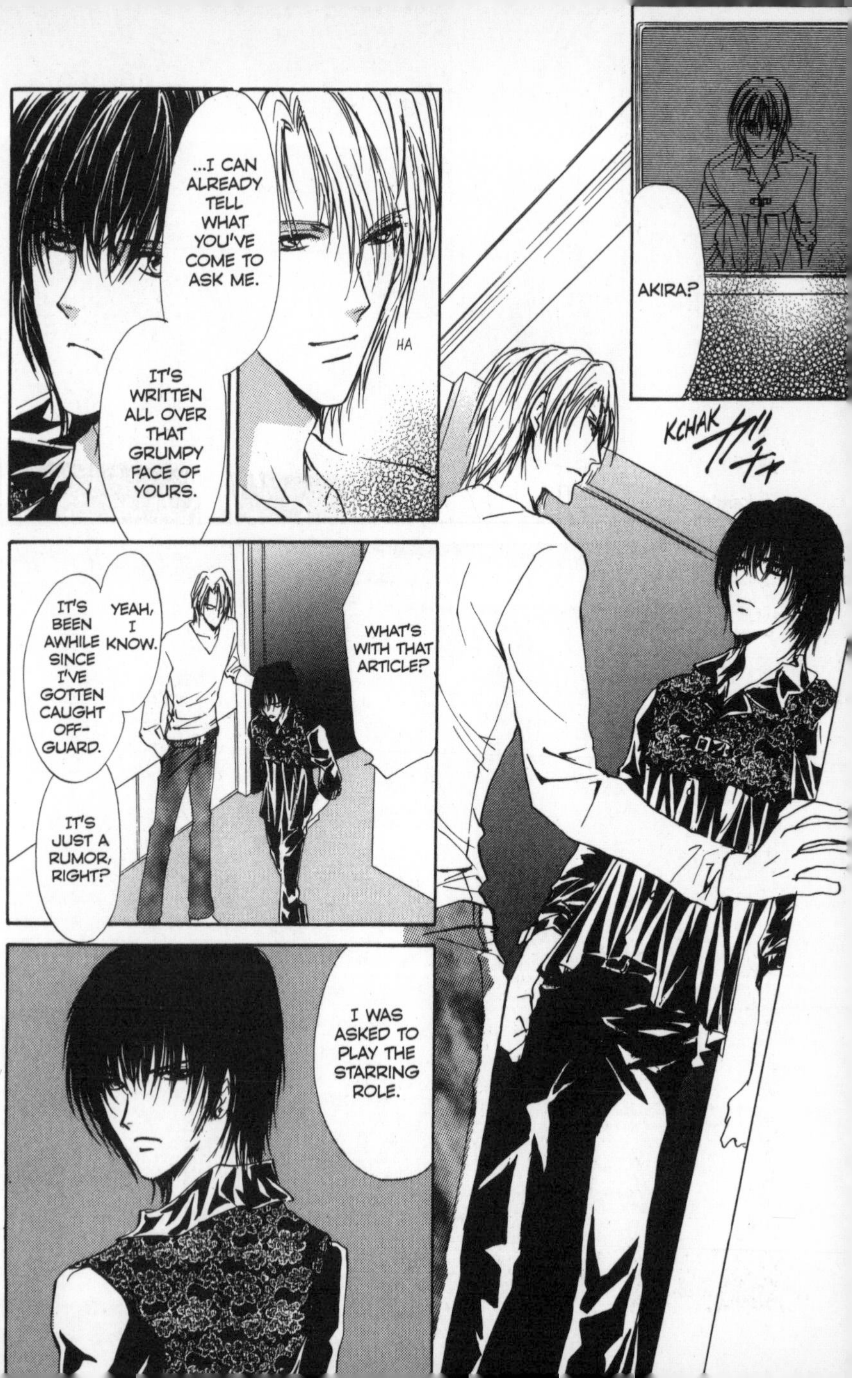
AKIRA?
KCHAK
...I CAN ALREADY TELL WHAT YOU'VE COME TO ASK ME.
HA
IT'S WRITTEN ALL OVER THAT GRUMPY FACE OF YOURS.
WHAT'S WITH THAT ARTICLE?
YEAH, I KNOW.
IT'S BEEN AWHILE SINCE I'VE GOTTEN CAUGHT OFF-GUARD.
IT'S JUST A RUMOR, RIGHT?
I WAS ASKED TO PLAY THE STARRING ROLE.

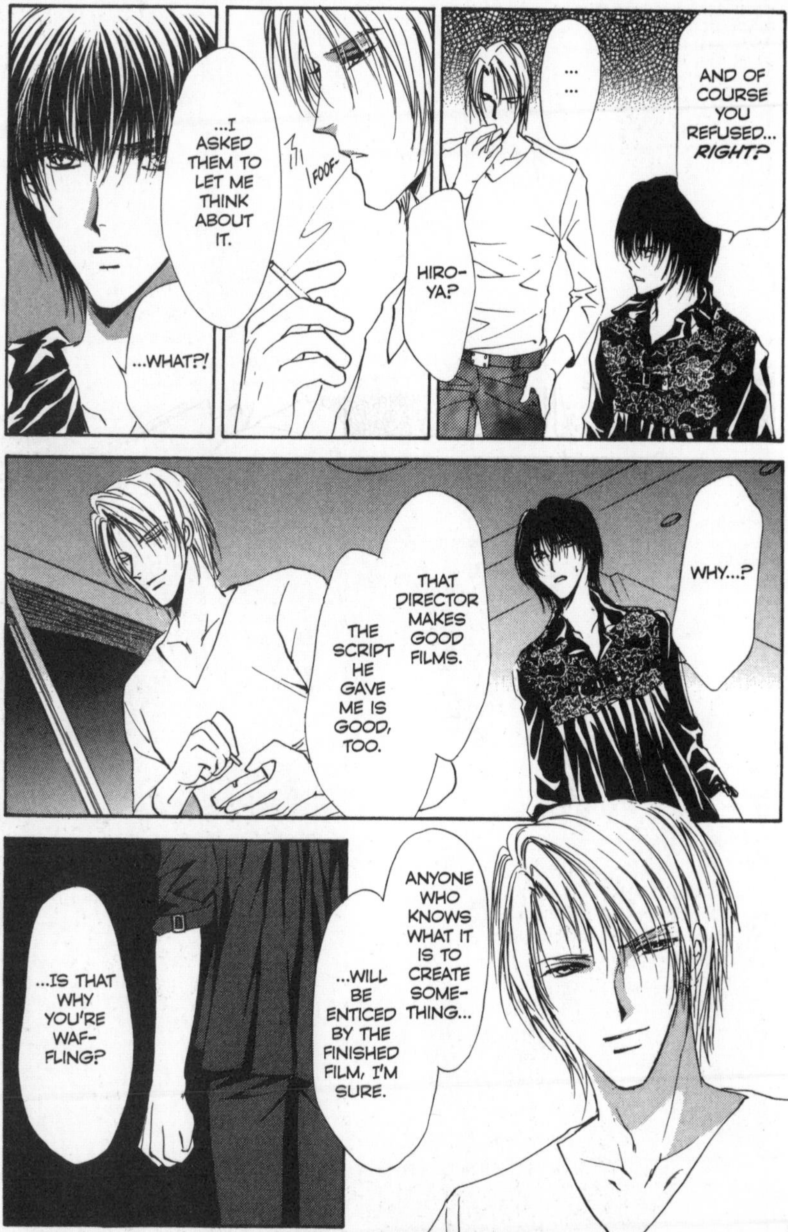
AND OF COURSE YOU REFUSED... RIGHT?
...
...
HIRO-YA?
FOOF
...I ASKED THEM TO LET ME THINK ABOUT IT.
...WHAT?!
WHY...?
THAT DIRECTOR MAKES GOOD FILMS.
THE SCRIPT HE GAVE ME IS GOOD, TOO.
ANYONE WHO KNOWS WHAT IT IS TO CREATE SOME-THING...
...WILL BE ENTICED BY THE FINISHED FILM, I'M SURE.
...IS THAT WHY YOU'RE WAF-FLING?

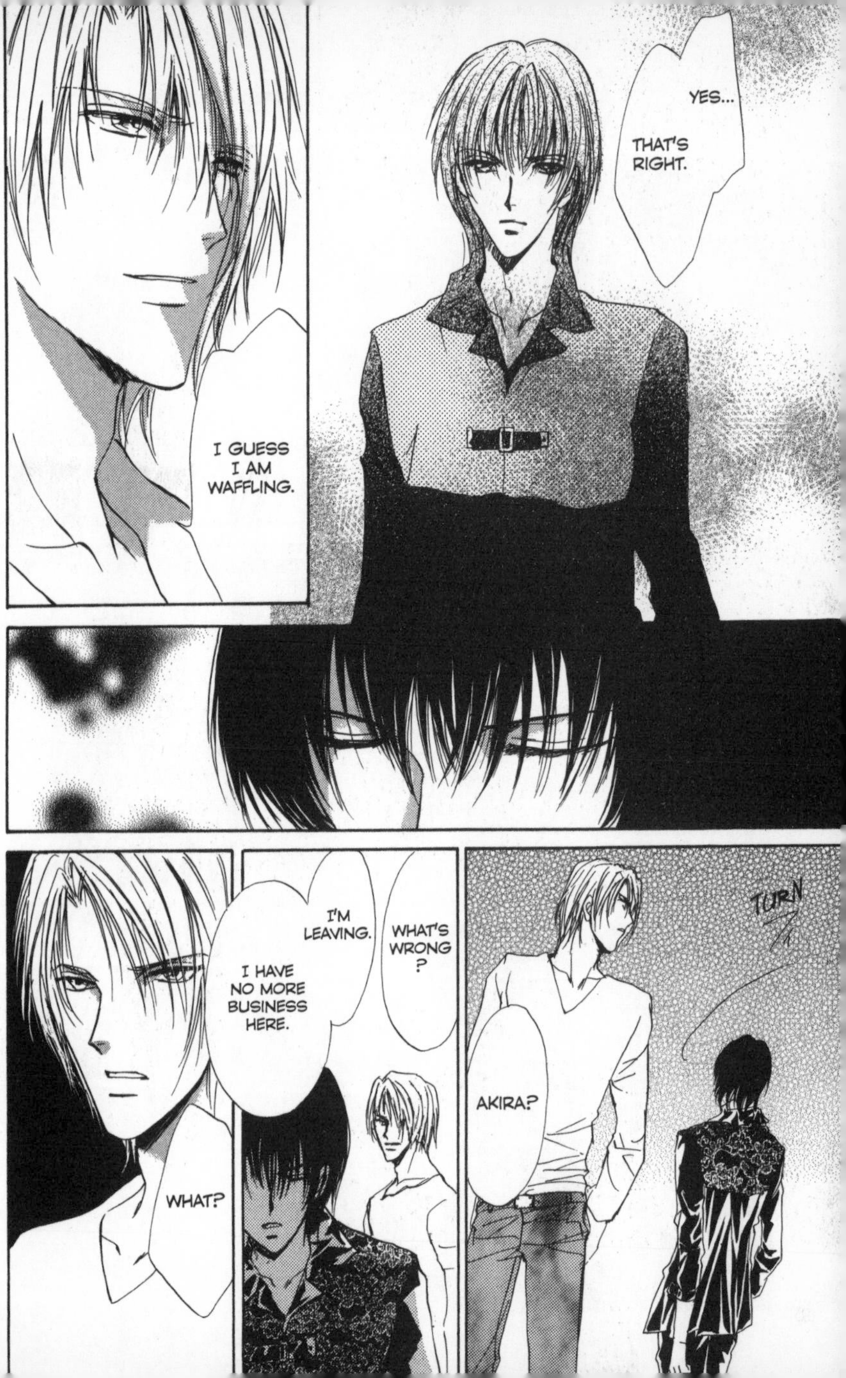
YES...
THAT'S RIGHT.
I GUESS I AM WAFFLING.
TURN
AKIRA?
WHAT'S WRONG?
I'M LEAVING.
I HAVE NO MORE BUSINESS HERE.
WHAT?

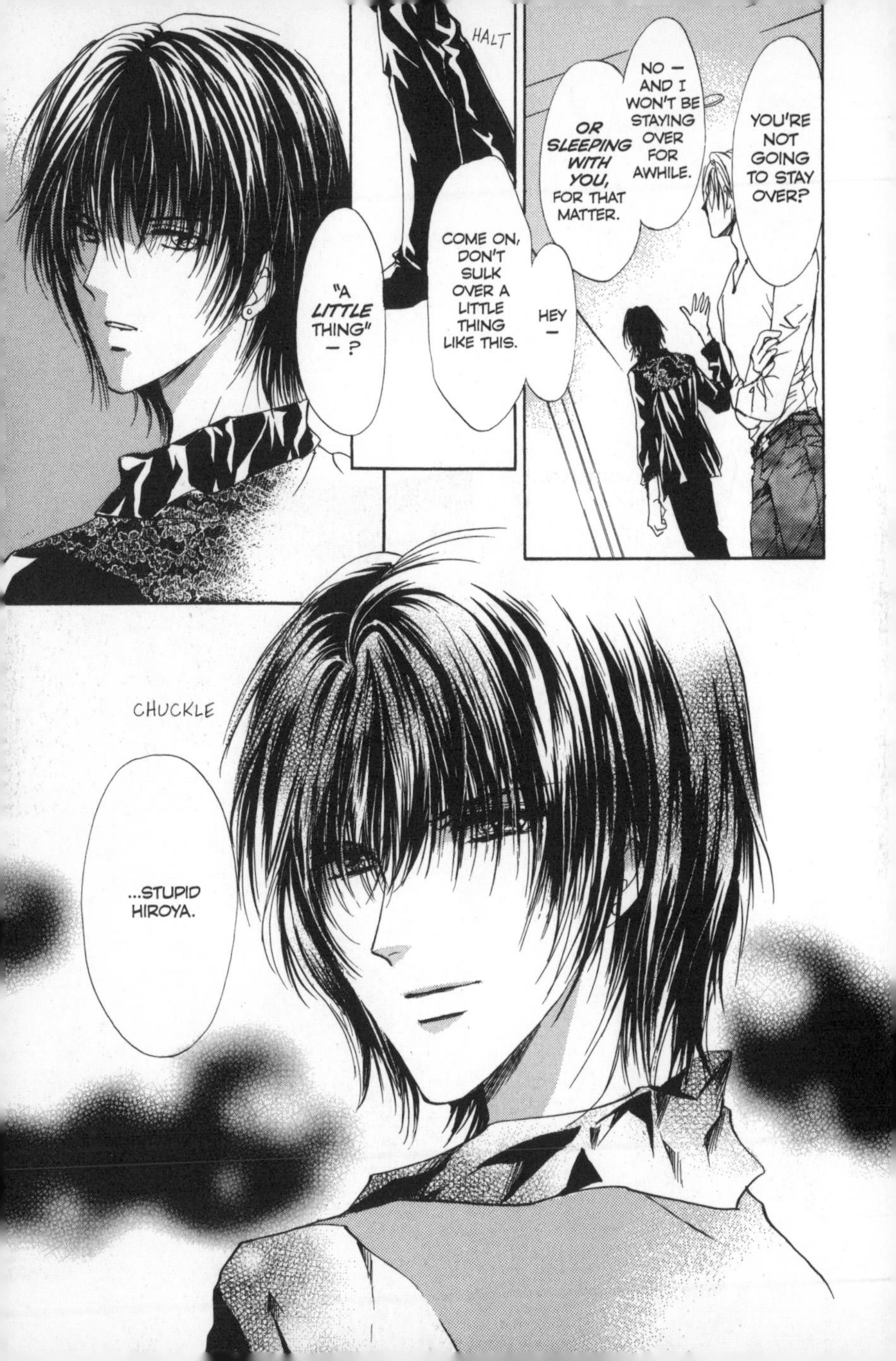
YOU'RE NOT GOING TO STAY OVER?
NO — AND I WON'T BE STAYING OVER FOR AWHILE.
OR SLEEPING WITH YOU, FOR THAT MATTER.
HEY —
COME ON, DON'T SULK OVER A LITTLE THING LIKE THIS.
HALT
"A *LITTLE* THING" — ?
CHUCKLE
...STUPID HIROYA.

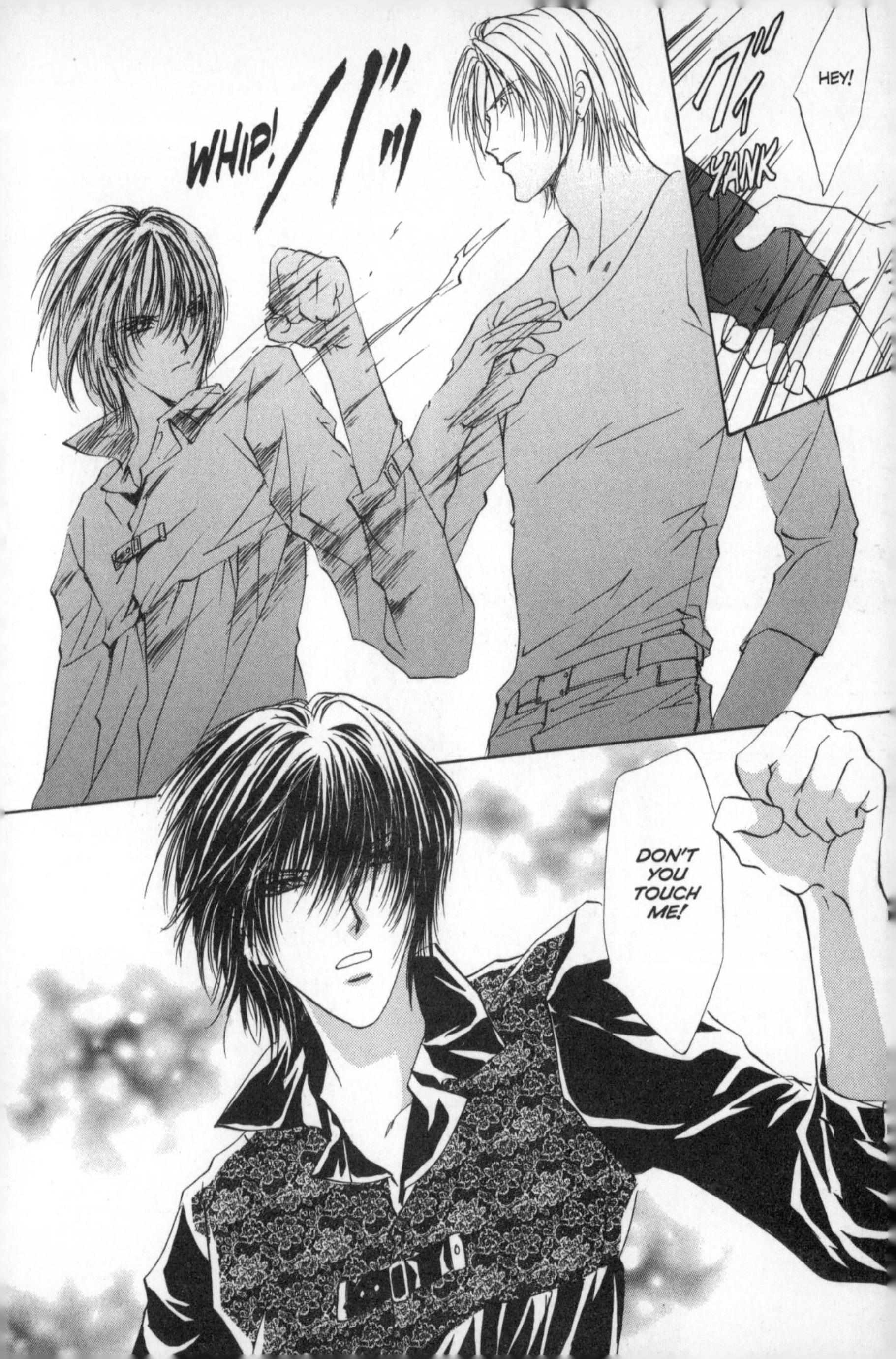
HEY!
YANK
WHIP!
DON'T YOU TOUCH ME!

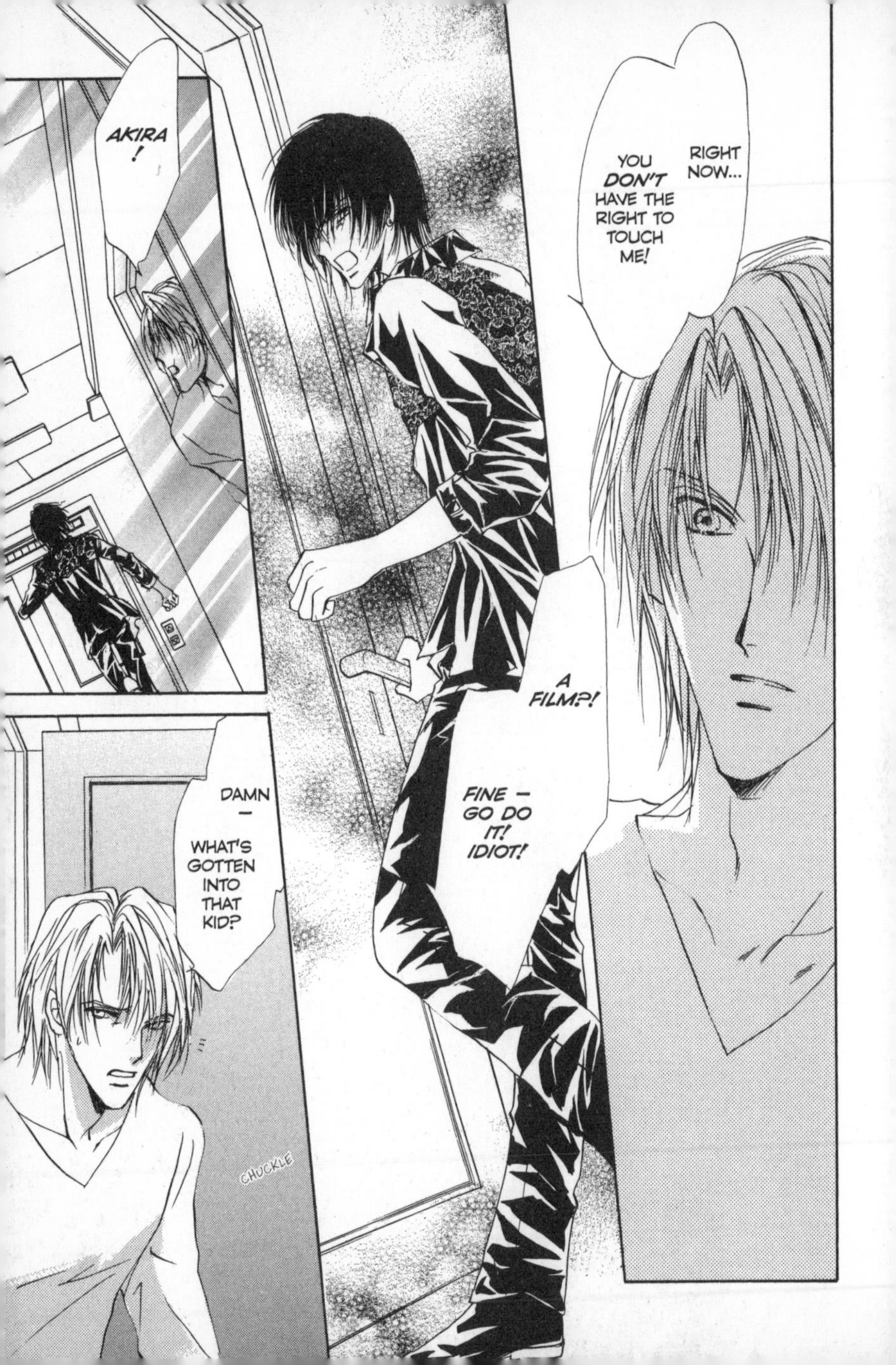
RIGHT NOW...
YOU *DON'T* HAVE THE RIGHT TO TOUCH ME!
A FILM?!
FINE — GO DO IT! IDIOT!
AKIRA!
DAMN —
WHAT'S GOTTEN INTO THAT KID?
CHUCKLE

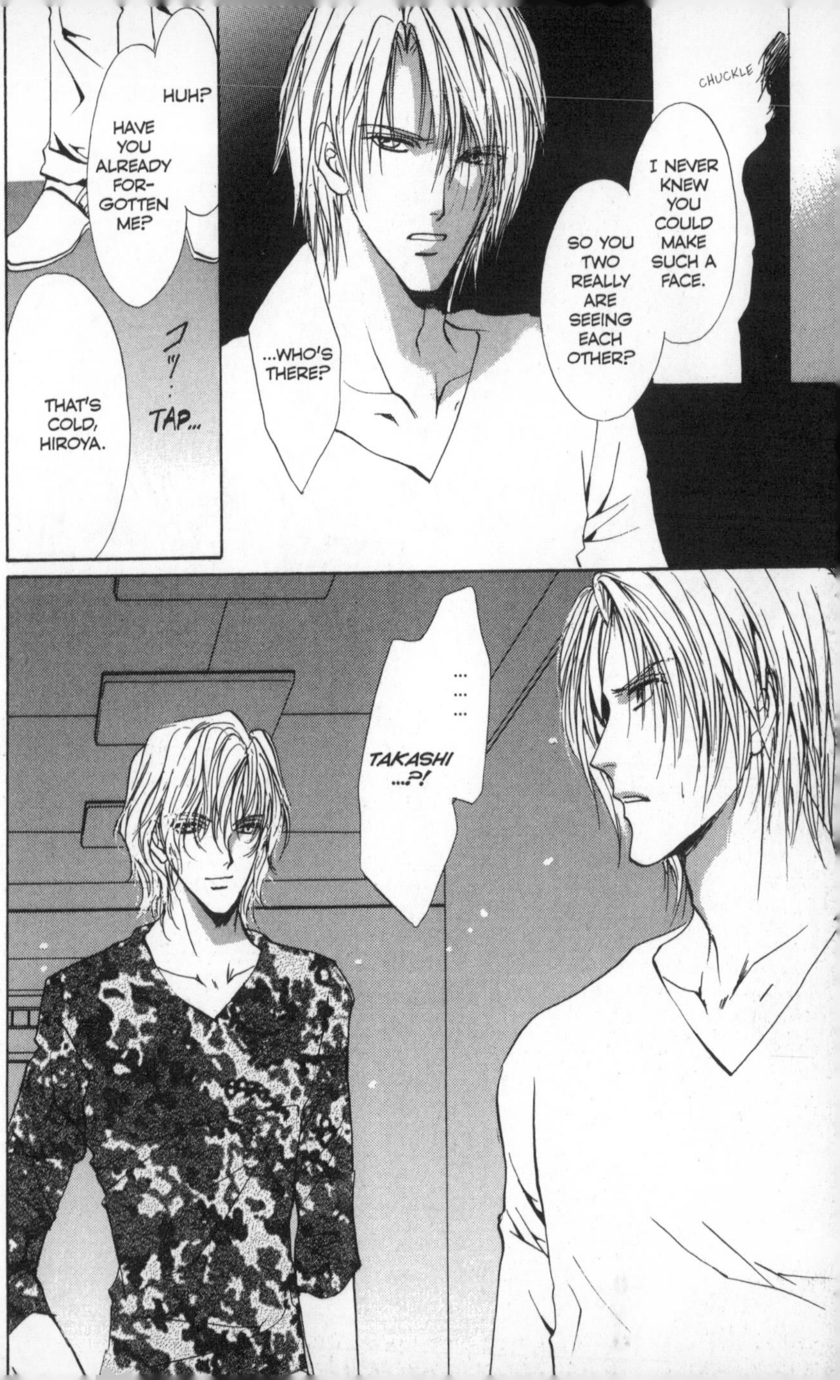
CHUCKLE
I NEVER KNEW YOU COULD MAKE SUCH A FACE.
SO YOU TWO REALLY ARE SEEING EACH OTHER?
...WHO'S THERE?
HUH? HAVE YOU ALREADY FOR-GOTTEN ME?
TAP...
THAT'S COLD, HIROYA.
... ...
TAKASHI ...?!

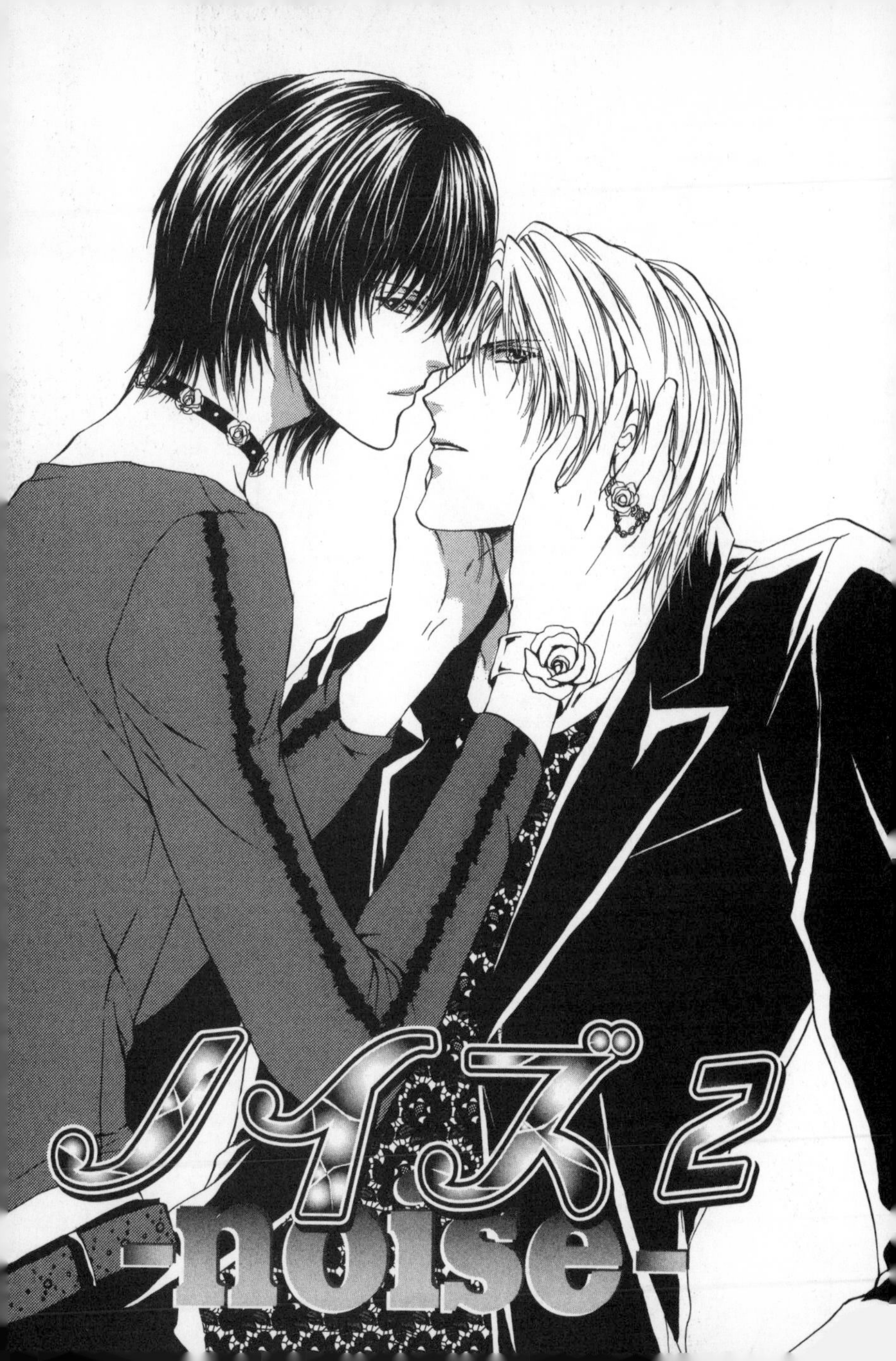
ノイズ 2
-noise-

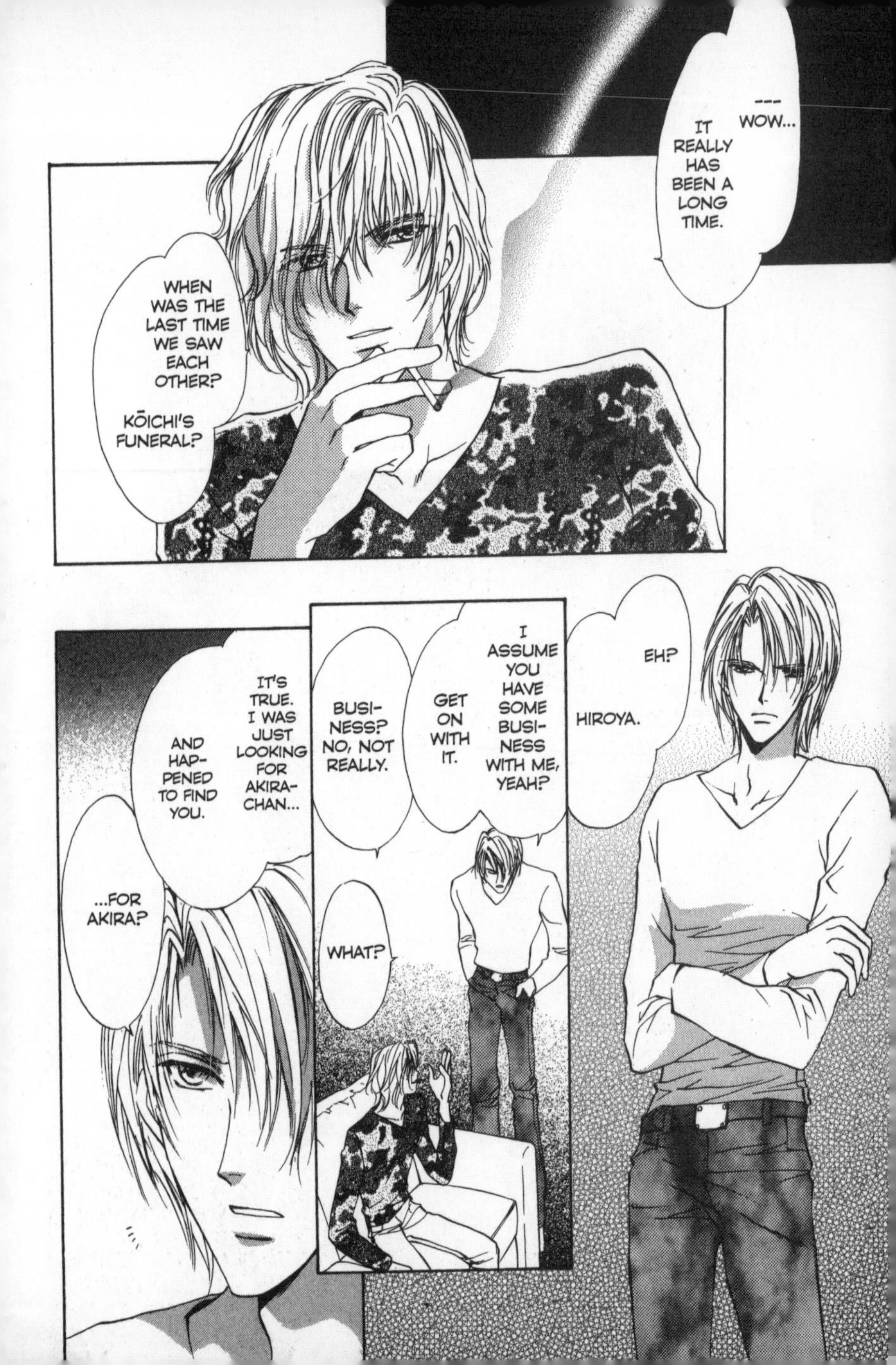
--- WOW... IT REALLY HAS BEEN A LONG TIME.
WHEN WAS THE LAST TIME WE SAW EACH OTHER?
KŌICHI'S FUNERAL?
EH?
HIROYA.
I ASSUME YOU HAVE SOME BUSI-NESS WITH ME, YEAH?
GET ON WITH IT.
BUSI-NESS? NO, NOT REALLY.
WHAT?
IT'S TRUE. I WAS JUST LOOKING FOR AKIRA-CHAN...
AND HAP-PENED TO FIND YOU.
...FOR AKIRA?

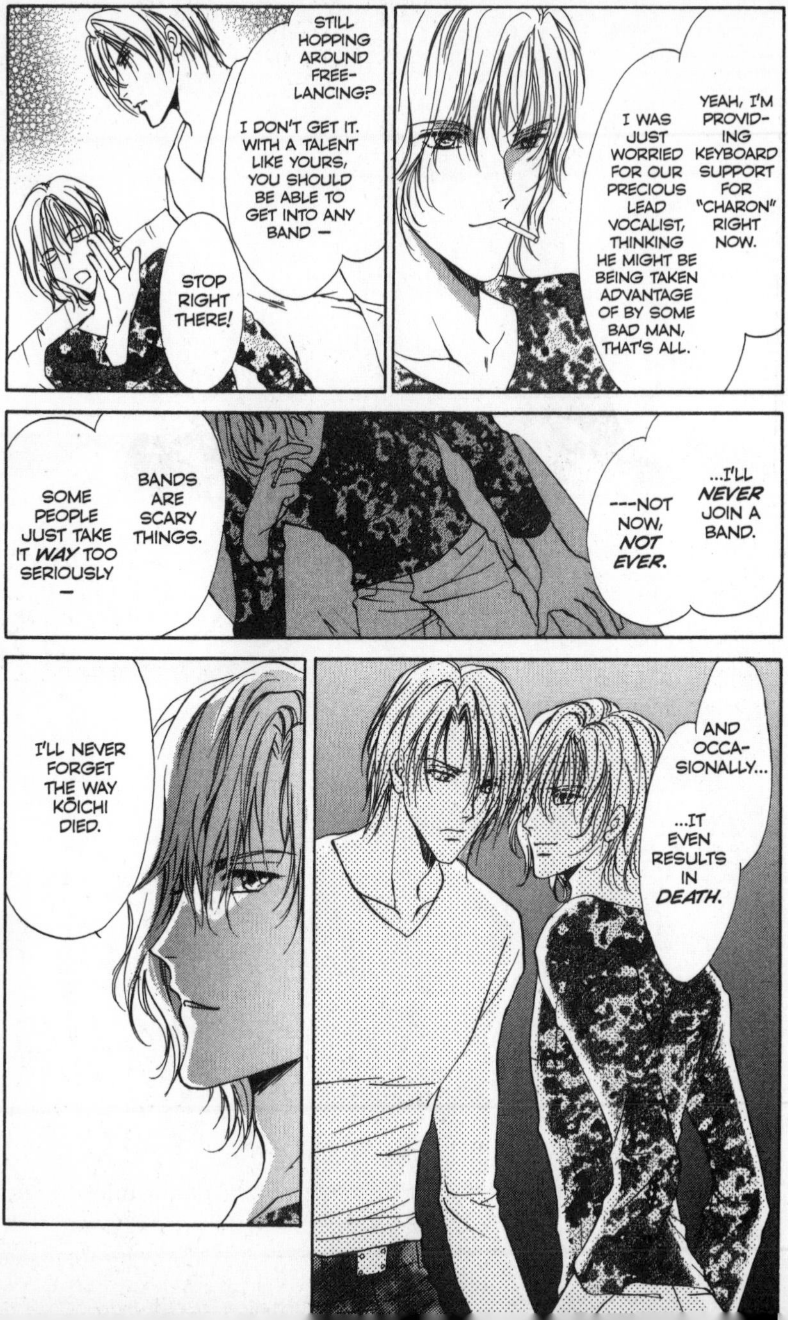
STILL HOPPING AROUND FREE-LANCING?
I DON'T GET IT. WITH A TALENT LIKE YOURS, YOU SHOULD BE ABLE TO GET INTO ANY BAND —
STOP RIGHT THERE!
I WAS JUST WORRIED FOR OUR PRECIOUS LEAD VOCALIST, THINKING HE MIGHT BE BEING TAKEN ADVANTAGE OF BY SOME BAD MAN, THAT'S ALL.
YEAH, I'M PROVIDING KEYBOARD SUPPORT FOR "CHARON" RIGHT NOW.
BANDS ARE SCARY THINGS.
SOME PEOPLE JUST TAKE IT *WAY* TOO SERIOUSLY —
...I'LL *NEVER* JOIN A BAND.
---NOT NOW, *NOT EVER*.
I'LL NEVER FORGET THE WAY KŌICHI DIED.
AND OCCA-SIONALLY...
...IT EVEN RESULTS IN *DEATH*.

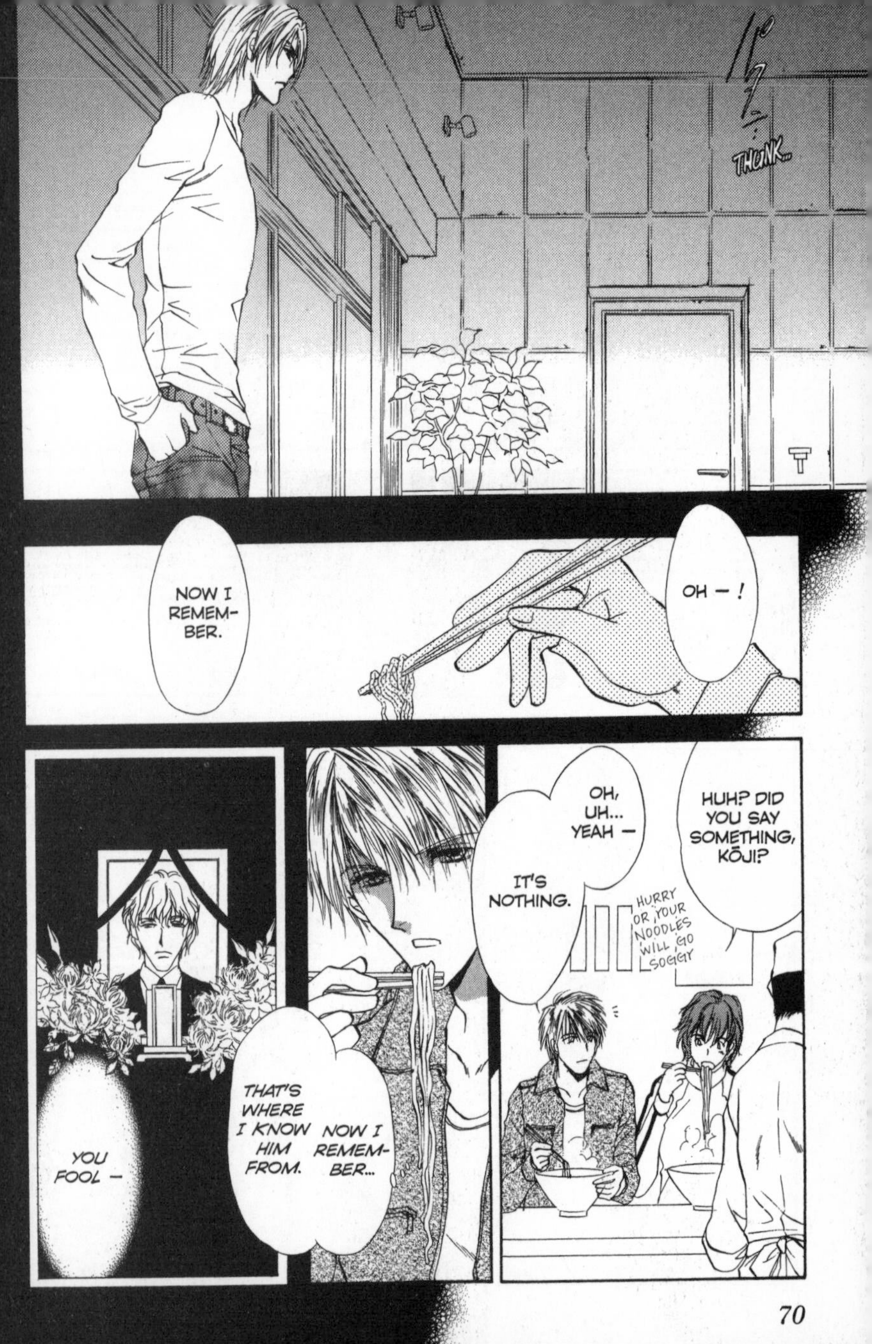
THUNK...
OH — !
NOW I REMEMBER.
HUH? DID YOU SAY SOMETHING, KŌJI?
HURRY OR YOUR NOODLES WILL GO SOGGY
OH, UH... YEAH —
IT'S NOTHING.
NOW I REMEMBER...
THAT'S WHERE I KNOW HIM FROM.
YOU FOOL —

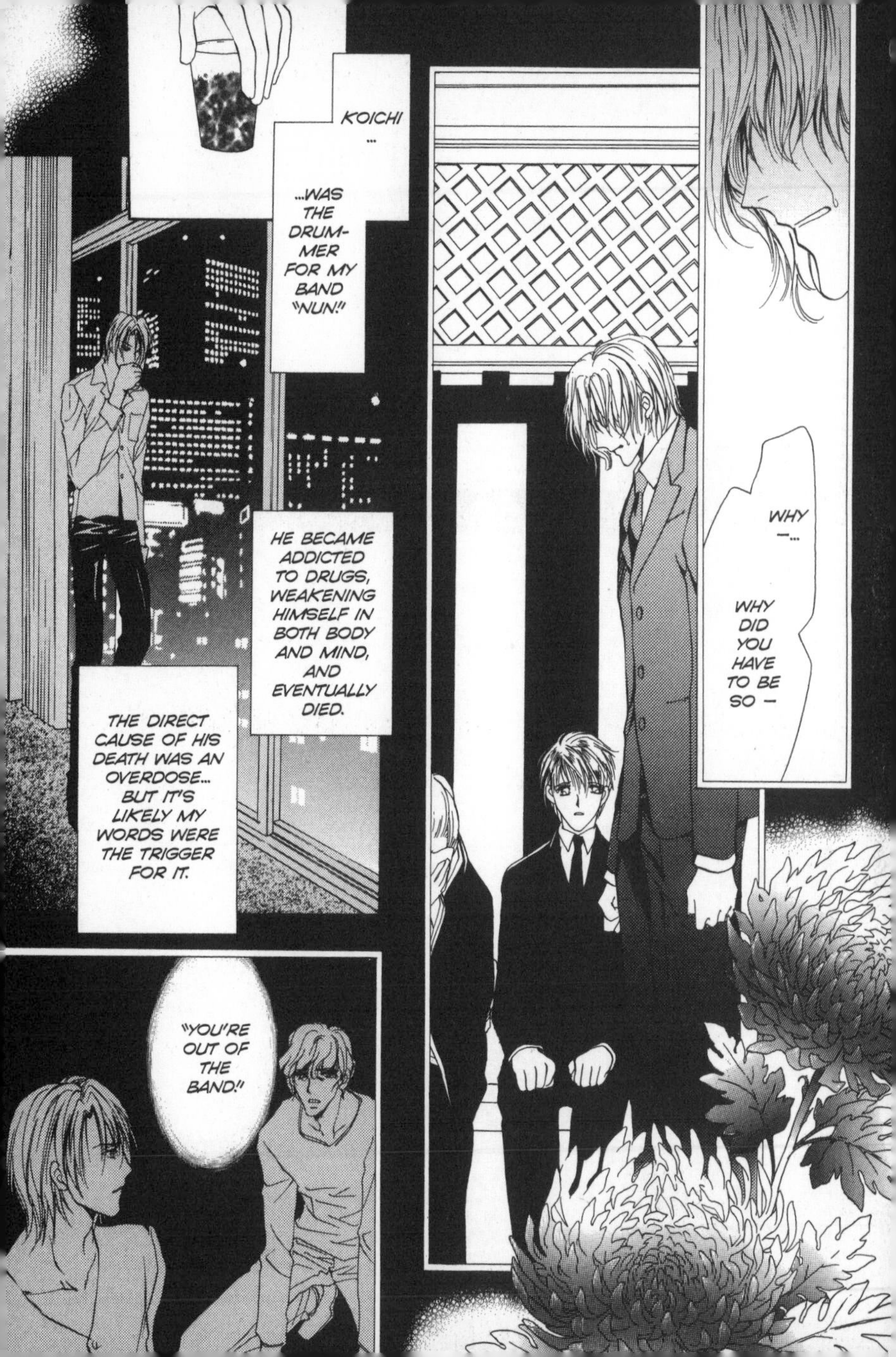

WHY —...
WHY DID YOU HAVE TO BE SO —
KOICHI ...
...WAS THE DRUMMER FOR MY BAND "NUN!"
HE BECAME ADDICTED TO DRUGS, WEAKENING HIMSELF IN BOTH BODY AND MIND, AND EVENTUALLY DIED.
THE DIRECT CAUSE OF HIS DEATH WAS AN OVERDOSE... BUT IT'S LIKELY MY WORDS WERE THE TRIGGER FOR IT.
"YOU'RE OUT OF THE BAND!"

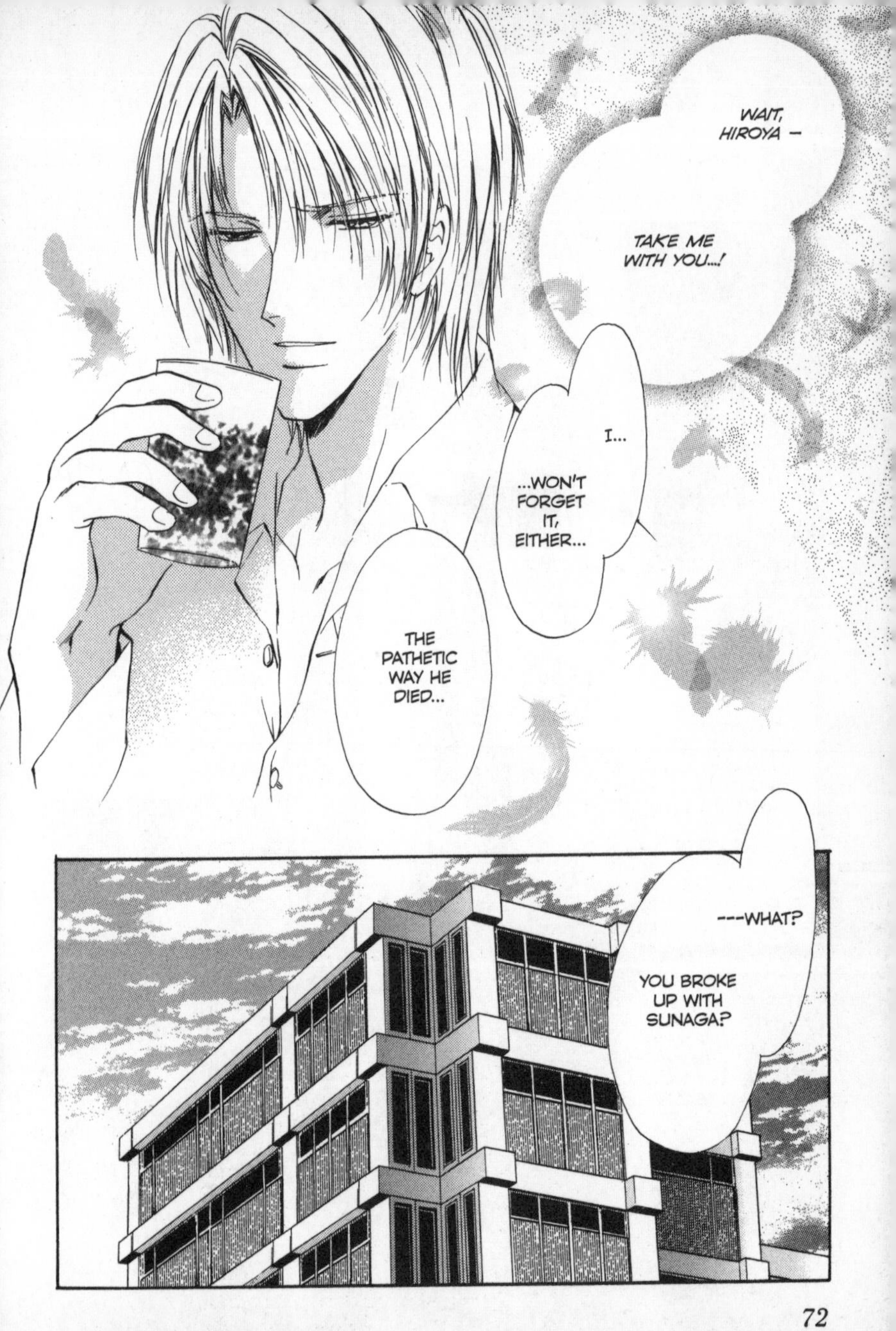
WAIT, HIROYA –
TAKE ME WITH YOU...!
I...
...WON'T FORGET IT, EITHER...
THE PATHETIC WAY HE DIED...
---WHAT?
YOU BROKE UP WITH SUNAGA?

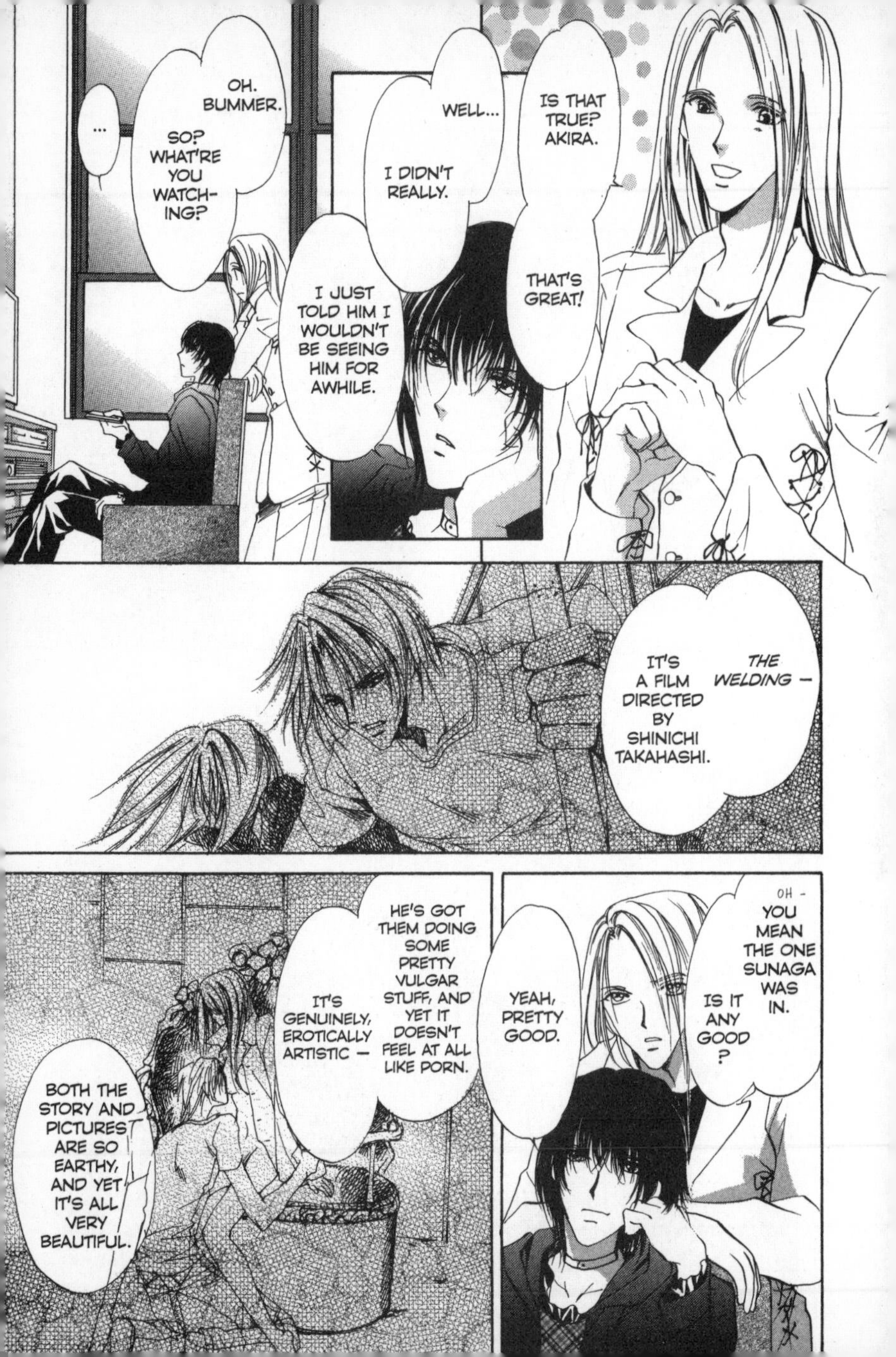
IS THAT TRUE? AKIRA.
THAT'S GREAT!
WELL...
I DIDN'T REALLY.
I JUST TOLD HIM I WOULDN'T BE SEEING HIM FOR AWHILE.
OH. BUMMER.
SO? WHAT'RE YOU WATCHING?
...
THE WELDING —
IT'S A FILM DIRECTED BY SHINICHI TAKAHASHI.
OH — YOU MEAN THE ONE SUNAGA WAS IN.
IS IT ANY GOOD?
YEAH, PRETTY GOOD.
HE'S GOT THEM DOING SOME PRETTY VULGAR STUFF, AND YET IT DOESN'T FEEL AT ALL LIKE PORN.
IT'S GENUINELY, EROTICALLY ARTISTIC —
BOTH THE STORY AND PICTURES ARE SO EARTHY, AND YET IT'S ALL VERY BEAUTIFUL.

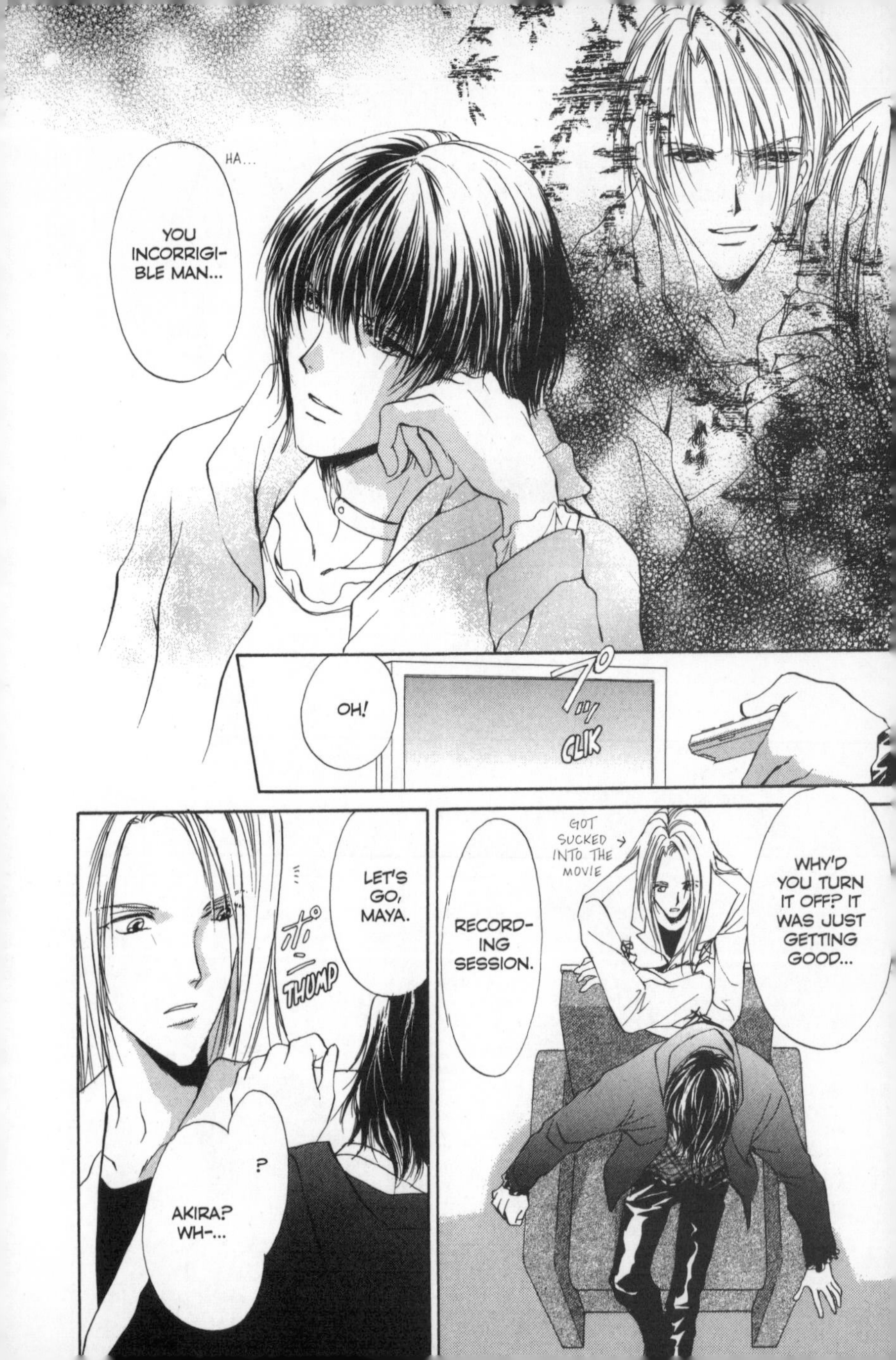
HA...
YOU INCORRIGIBLE MAN...
OH!
CLIK
WHY'D YOU TURN IT OFF? IT WAS JUST GETTING GOOD...
GOT SUCKED INTO THE MOVIE
RECORDING SESSION.
LET'S GO, MAYA.
THUMP
?
AKIRA? WH-...

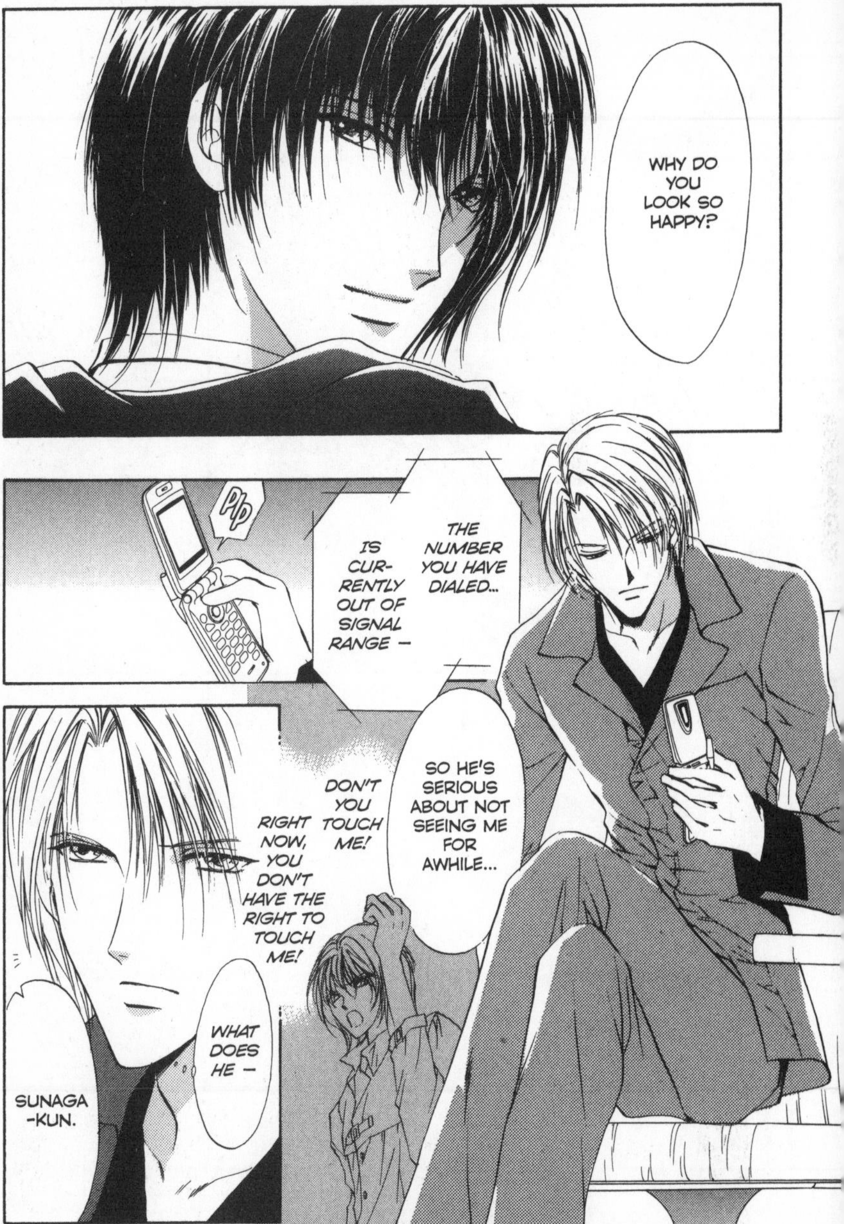
WHY DO YOU LOOK SO HAPPY?
PIP
THE NUMBER YOU HAVE DIALED...
IS CURRENTLY OUT OF SIGNAL RANGE —
SO HE'S SERIOUS ABOUT NOT SEEING ME FOR AWHILE...
DON'T YOU TOUCH ME!
RIGHT NOW, YOU DON'T HAVE THE RIGHT TO TOUCH ME!
WHAT DOES HE —
SUNAGA-KUN.

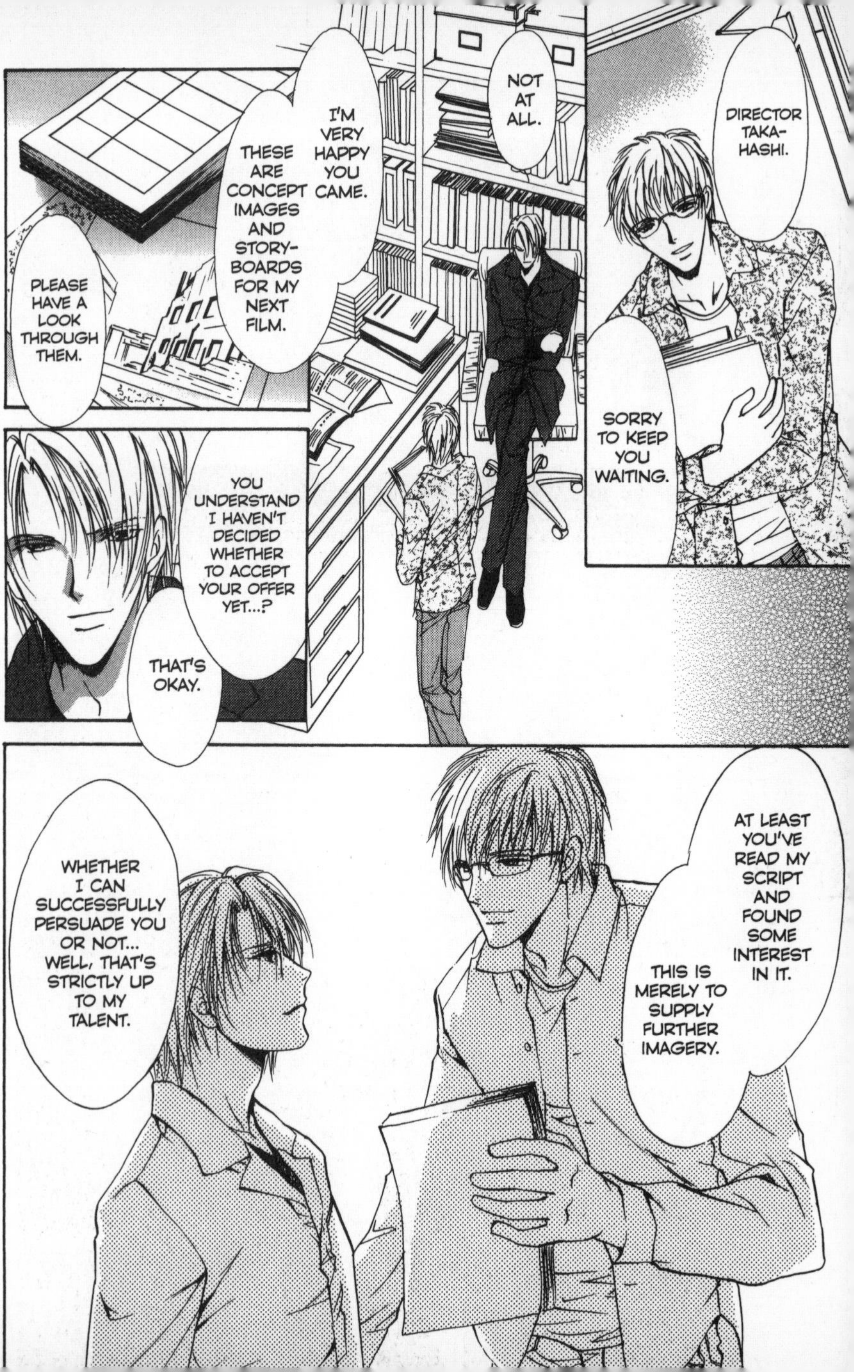
DIRECTOR TAKA-HASHI.
SORRY TO KEEP YOU WAITING.
NOT AT ALL.
I'M VERY HAPPY YOU CAME.
THESE ARE CONCEPT IMAGES AND STORY-BOARDS FOR MY NEXT FILM.
PLEASE HAVE A LOOK THROUGH THEM.
YOU UNDERSTAND I HAVEN'T DECIDED WHETHER TO ACCEPT YOUR OFFER YET...?
THAT'S OKAY.
AT LEAST YOU'VE READ MY SCRIPT AND FOUND SOME INTEREST IN IT.
THIS IS MERELY TO SUPPLY FURTHER IMAGERY.
WHETHER I CAN SUCCESSFULLY PERSUADE YOU OR NOT... WELL, THAT'S STRICTLY UP TO MY TALENT.

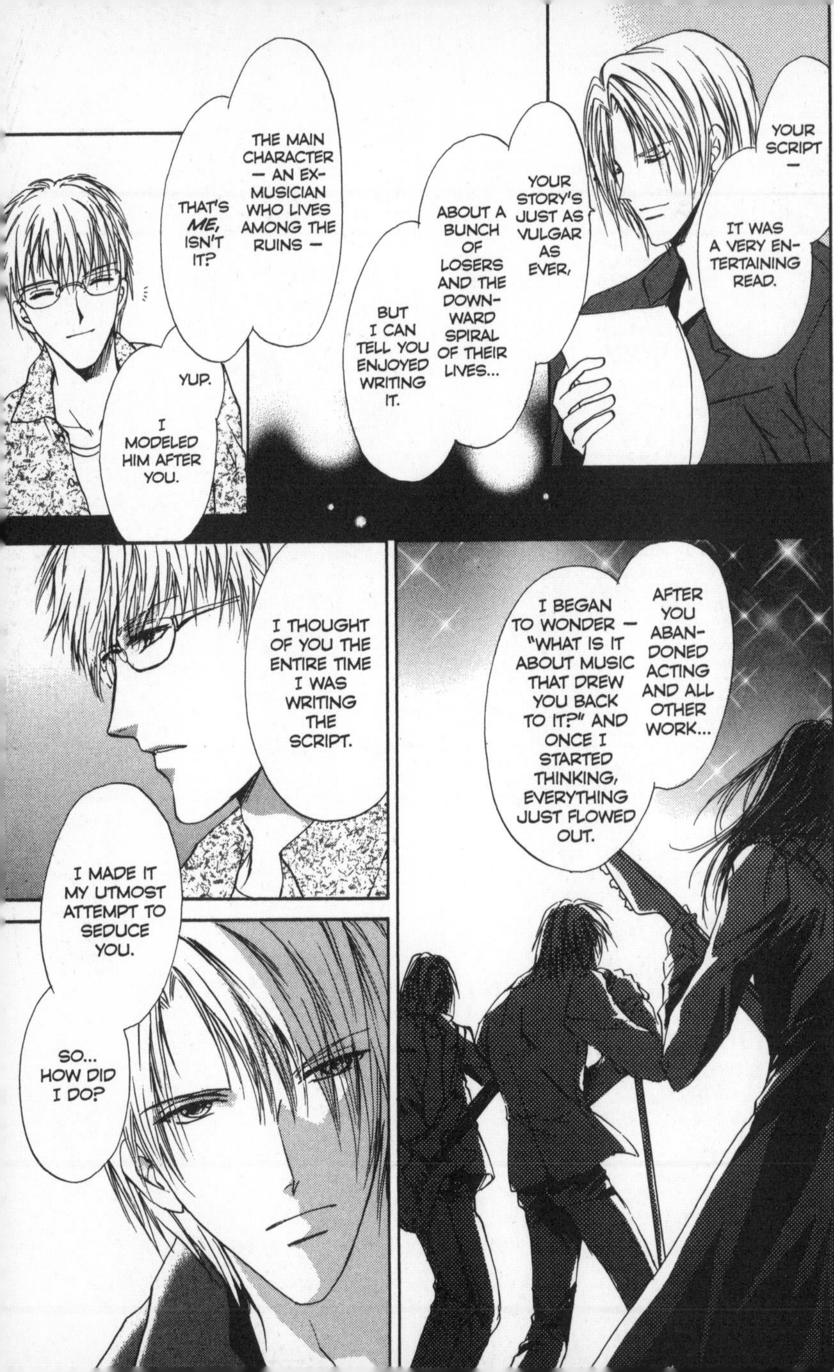
YOUR SCRIPT —
IT WAS A VERY ENTERTAINING READ.
YOUR STORY'S JUST AS VULGAR AS EVER,
ABOUT A BUNCH OF LOSERS AND THE DOWNWARD SPIRAL OF THEIR LIVES...
BUT I CAN TELL YOU ENJOYED WRITING IT.
THE MAIN CHARACTER — AN EX-MUSICIAN WHO LIVES AMONG THE RUINS —
THAT'S *ME,* ISN'T IT?
YUP.
I MODELED HIM AFTER YOU.
AFTER YOU ABANDONED ACTING AND ALL OTHER WORK...
I BEGAN TO WONDER — "WHAT IS IT ABOUT MUSIC THAT DREW YOU BACK TO IT?" AND ONCE I STARTED THINKING, EVERYTHING JUST FLOWED OUT.
I THOUGHT OF YOU THE ENTIRE TIME I WAS WRITING THE SCRIPT.
I MADE IT MY UTMOST ATTEMPT TO SEDUCE YOU.
SO... HOW DID I DO?

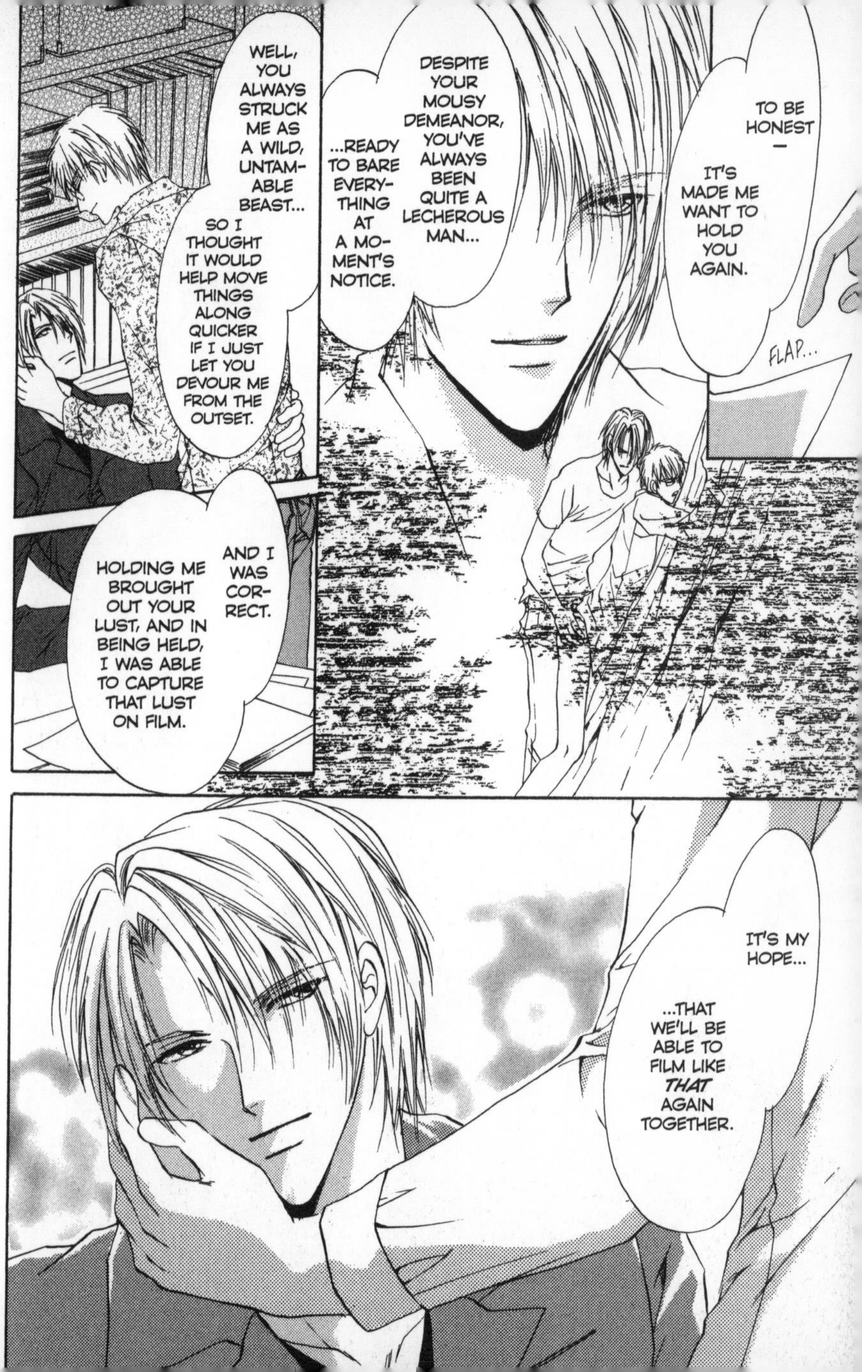
TO BE HONEST—
IT'S MADE ME WANT TO HOLD YOU AGAIN.
FLAP...
DESPITE YOUR MOUSY DEMEANOR, YOU'VE ALWAYS BEEN QUITE A LECHEROUS MAN...
...READY TO BARE EVERYTHING AT A MOMENT'S NOTICE.
WELL, YOU ALWAYS STRUCK ME AS A WILD, UNTAMABLE BEAST...
SO I THOUGHT IT WOULD HELP MOVE THINGS ALONG QUICKER IF I JUST LET YOU DEVOUR ME FROM THE OUTSET.
AND I WAS CORRECT.
HOLDING ME BROUGHT OUT YOUR LUST, AND IN BEING HELD, I WAS ABLE TO CAPTURE THAT LUST ON FILM.
IT'S MY HOPE...
...THAT WE'LL BE ABLE TO FILM LIKE *THAT* AGAIN TOGETHER.

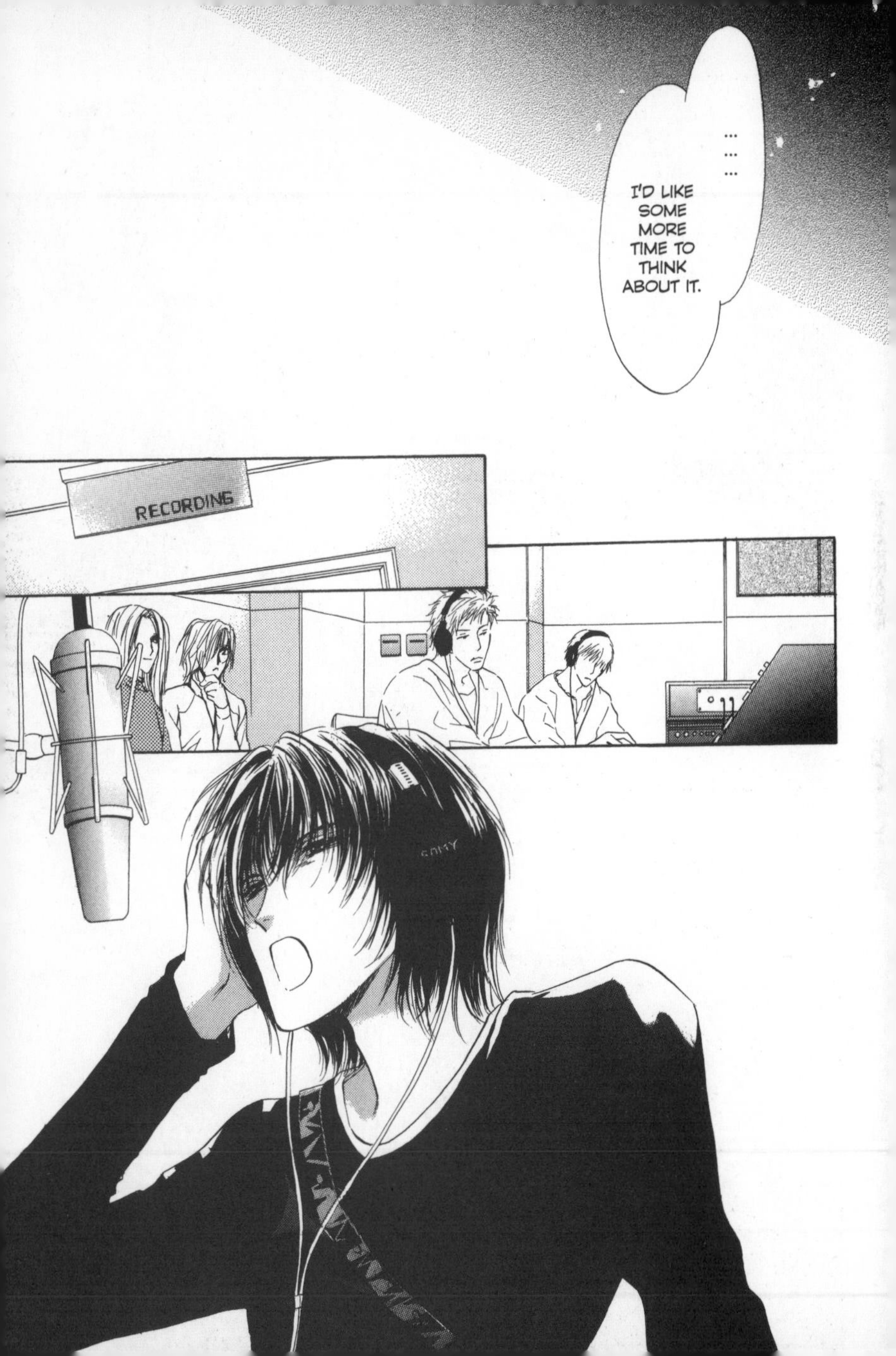

... ... I'D LIKE SOME MORE TIME TO THINK ABOUT IT.
RECORDING

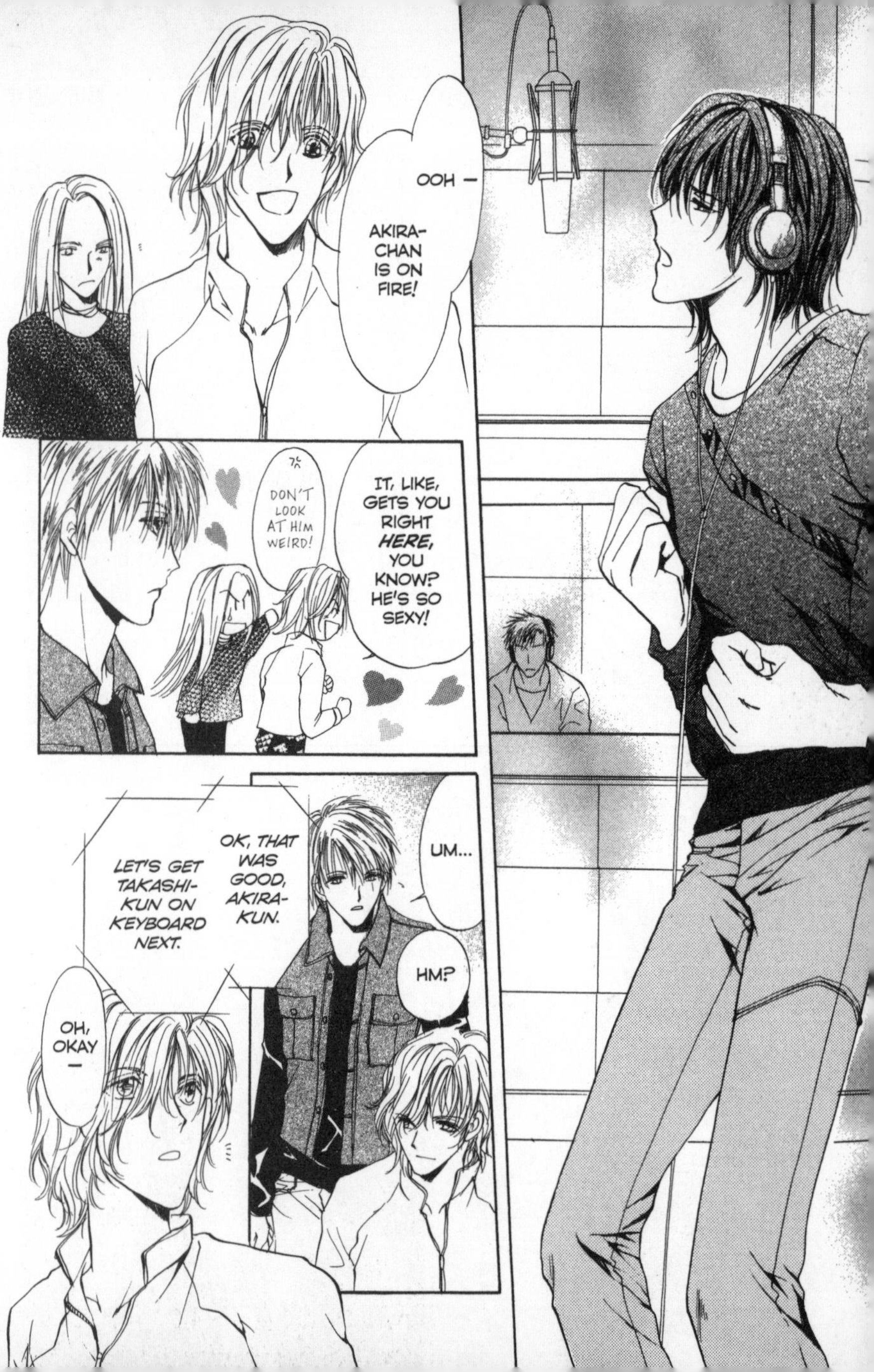
OOH —
AKIRA-CHAN IS ON FIRE!
IT, LIKE, GETS YOU RIGHT *HERE,* YOU KNOW? HE'S SO SEXY!
DON'T LOOK AT HIM WEIRD!
UM...
OK, THAT WAS GOOD, AKIRA-KUN.
LET'S GET TAKASHI-KUN ON KEYBOARD NEXT.
HM?
OH, OKAY —

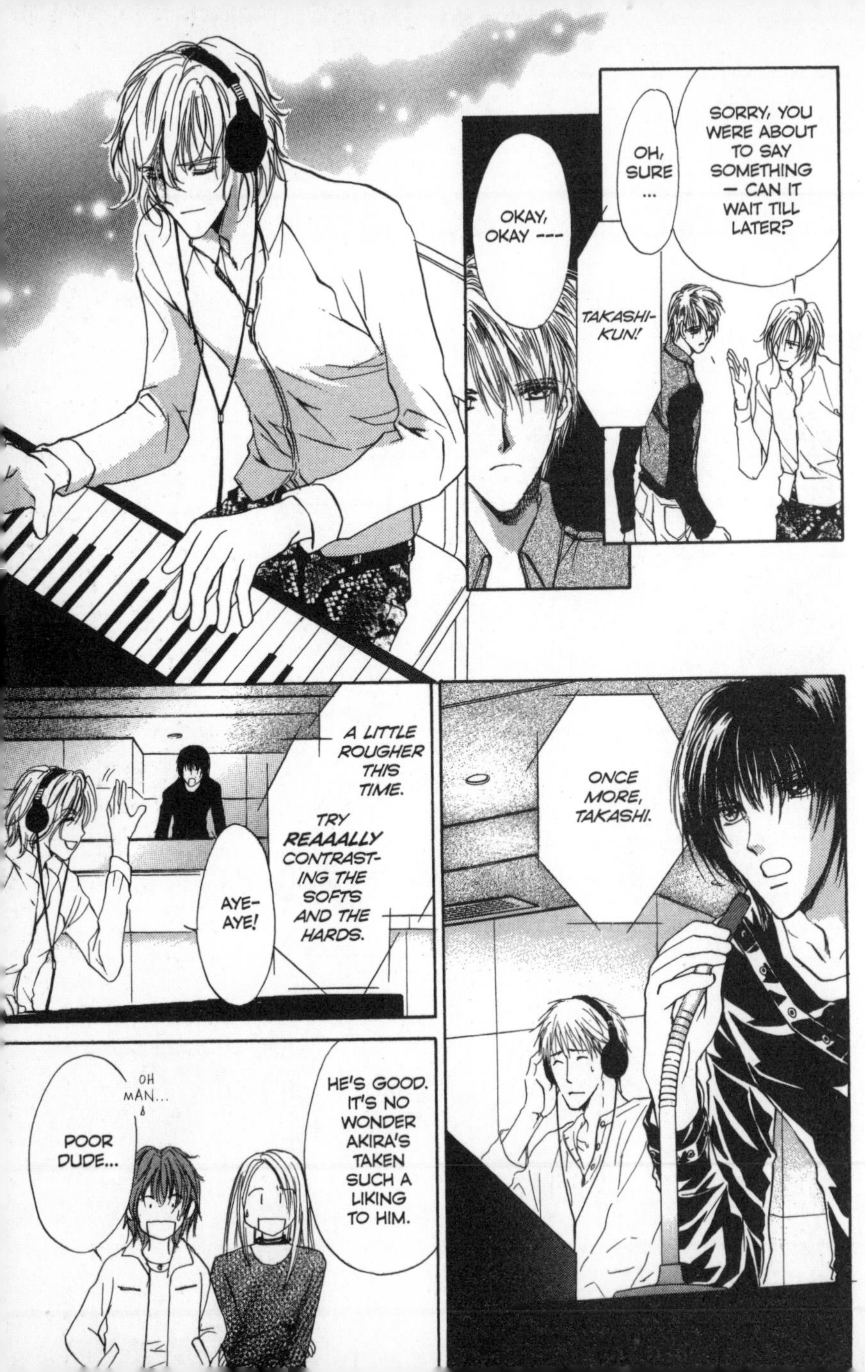

SORRY, YOU WERE ABOUT TO SAY SOMETHING — CAN IT WAIT TILL LATER?
OH, SURE ...
TAKASHI-KUN!
OKAY, OKAY ---
ONCE MORE, TAKASHI.
A LITTLE ROUGHER THIS TIME.
TRY REAAALLY CONTRASTING THE SOFTS AND THE HARDS.
AYE-AYE!
HE'S GOOD. IT'S NO WONDER AKIRA'S TAKEN SUCH A LIKING TO HIM.
OH MAN...
POOR DUDE...

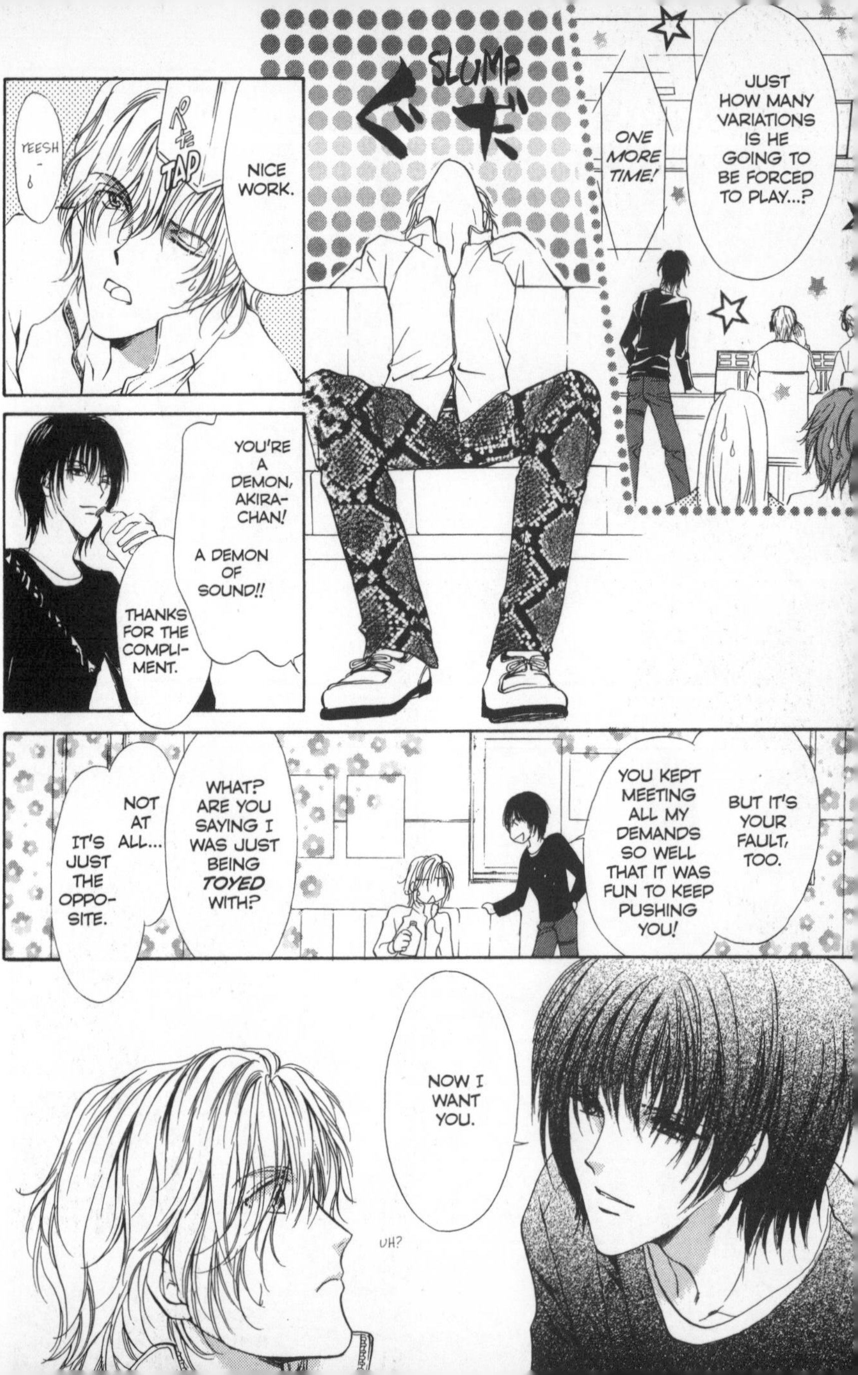
JUST HOW MANY VARIATIONS IS HE GOING TO BE FORCED TO PLAY...?
ONE MORE TIME!
SLUMP
ぐだ
NICE WORK.
ぺた
TAP
YEESH
YOU'RE A DEMON, AKIRA-CHAN!
A DEMON OF SOUND!!
THANKS FOR THE COMPLI-MENT.
BUT IT'S YOUR FAULT, TOO.
YOU KEPT MEETING ALL MY DEMANDS SO WELL THAT IT WAS FUN TO KEEP PUSHING YOU!
WHAT? ARE YOU SAYING I WAS JUST BEING *TOYED* WITH?
NOT AT ALL...
IT'S JUST THE OPPO-SITE.
NOW I WANT YOU.
UH?

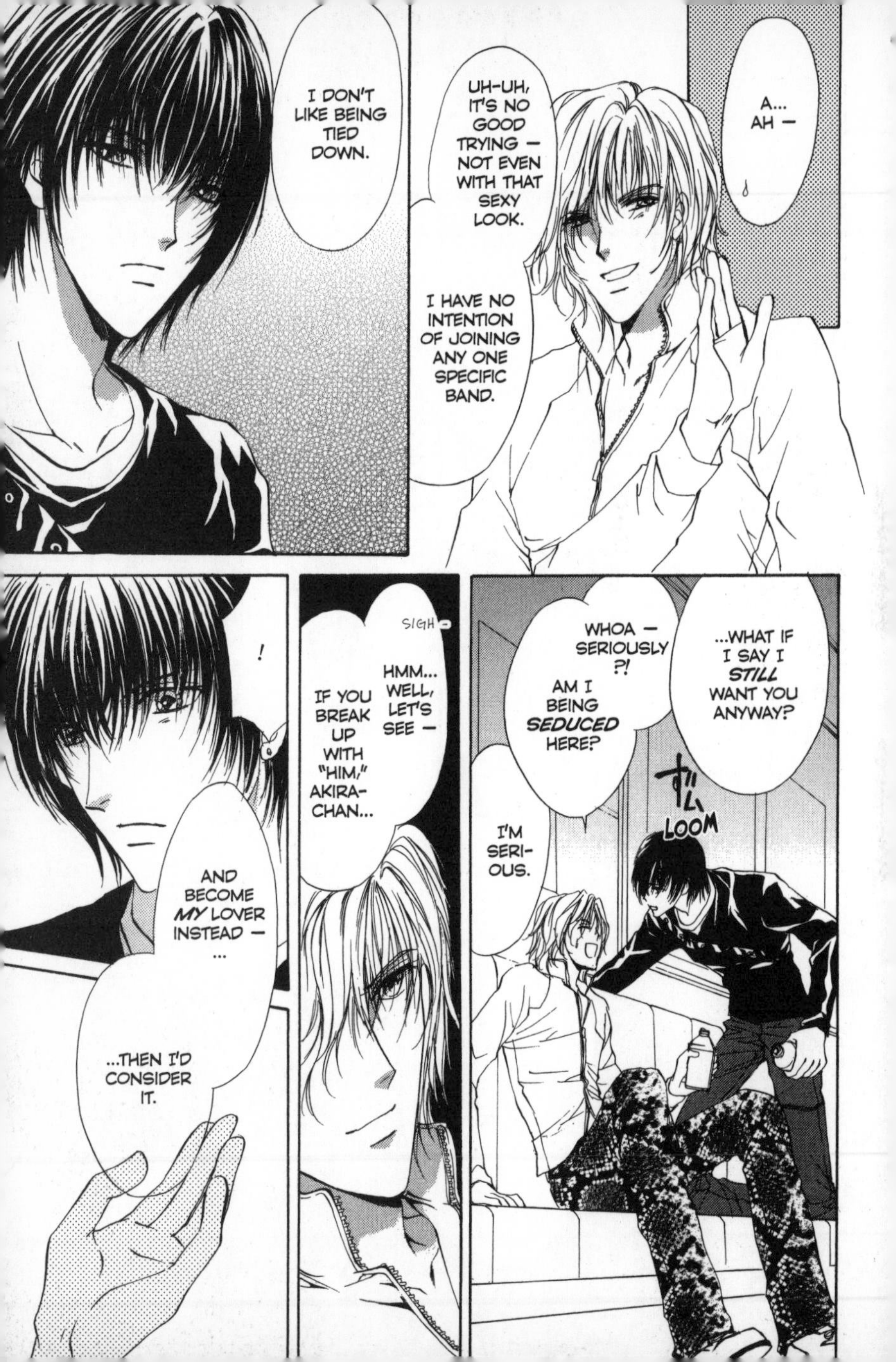
A... AH —
UH-UH, IT'S NO GOOD TRYING — NOT EVEN WITH THAT SEXY LOOK.
I HAVE NO INTENTION OF JOINING ANY ONE SPECIFIC BAND.
I DON'T LIKE BEING TIED DOWN.
...WHAT IF I SAY I *STILL* WANT YOU ANYWAY?
WHOA — SERIOUSLY ?!
AM I BEING *SEDUCED* HERE?
I'M SERI- OUS.
LOOM
SIGH
HMM... WELL, LET'S SEE —
IF YOU BREAK UP WITH "HIM," AKIRA-CHAN...
!
AND BECOME *MY* LOVER INSTEAD — ...
...THEN I'D CONSIDER IT.

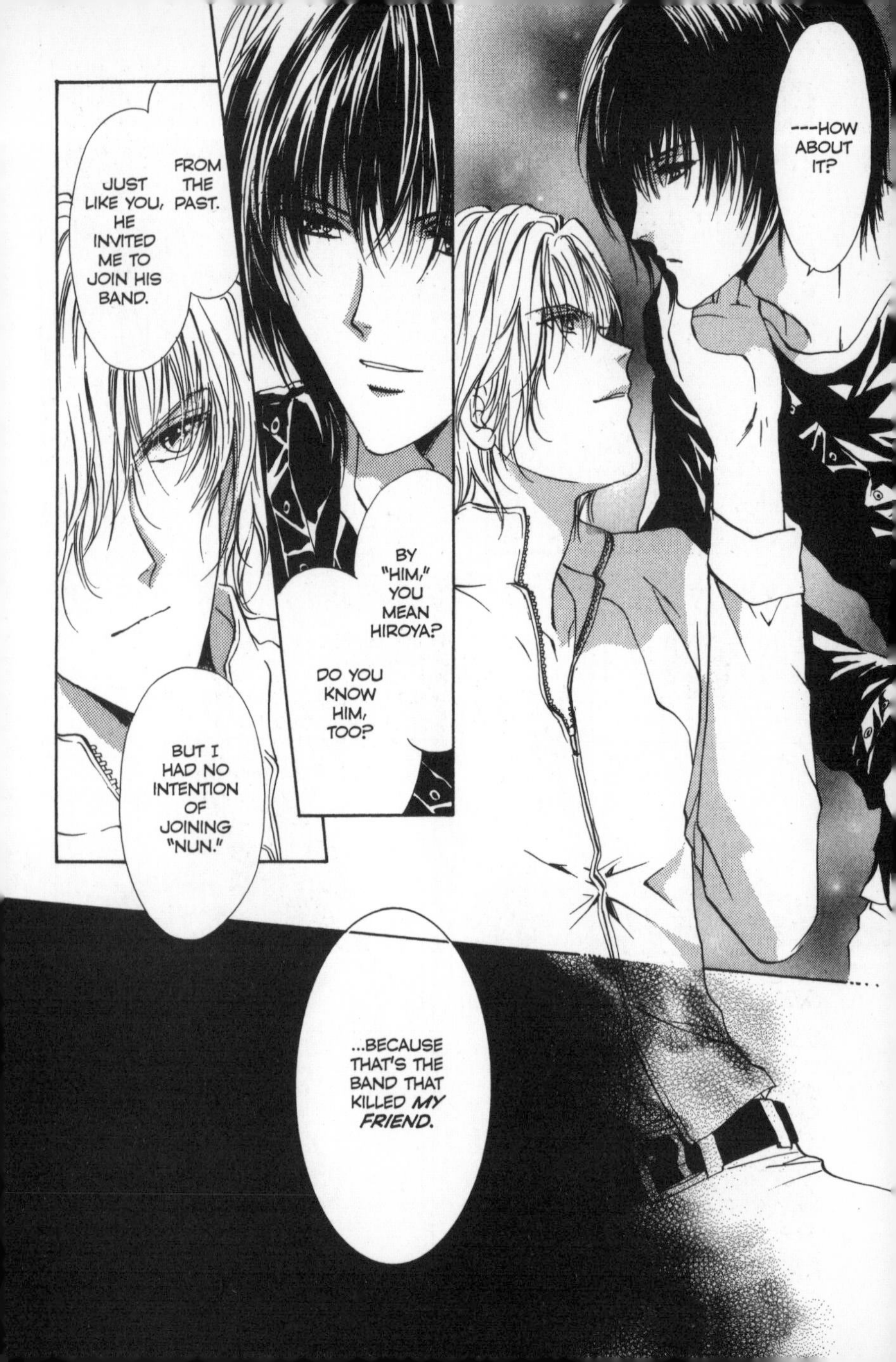
---HOW ABOUT IT?
FROM THE PAST. JUST LIKE YOU, HE INVITED ME TO JOIN HIS BAND.
BY "HIM," YOU MEAN HIROYA?
DO YOU KNOW HIM, TOO?
BUT I HAD NO INTENTION OF JOINING "NUN."
...BECAUSE THAT'S THE BAND THAT KILLED *MY FRIEND*.

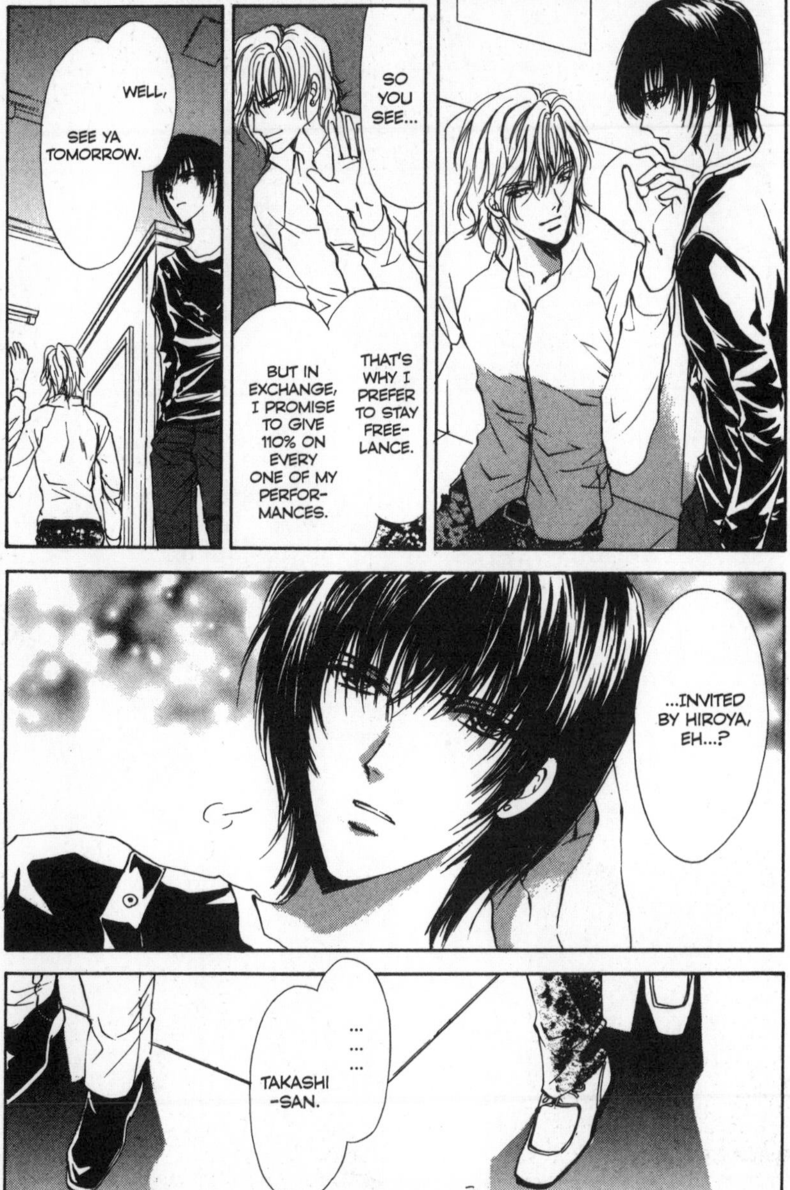
SO YOU SEE...
THAT'S WHY I PREFER TO STAY FREE-LANCE.
BUT IN EXCHANGE, I PROMISE TO GIVE 110% ON EVERY ONE OF MY PERFORMANCES.
WELL,
SEE YA TOMORROW.
...INVITED BY HIROYA, EH...?
... ... TAKASHI-SAN.

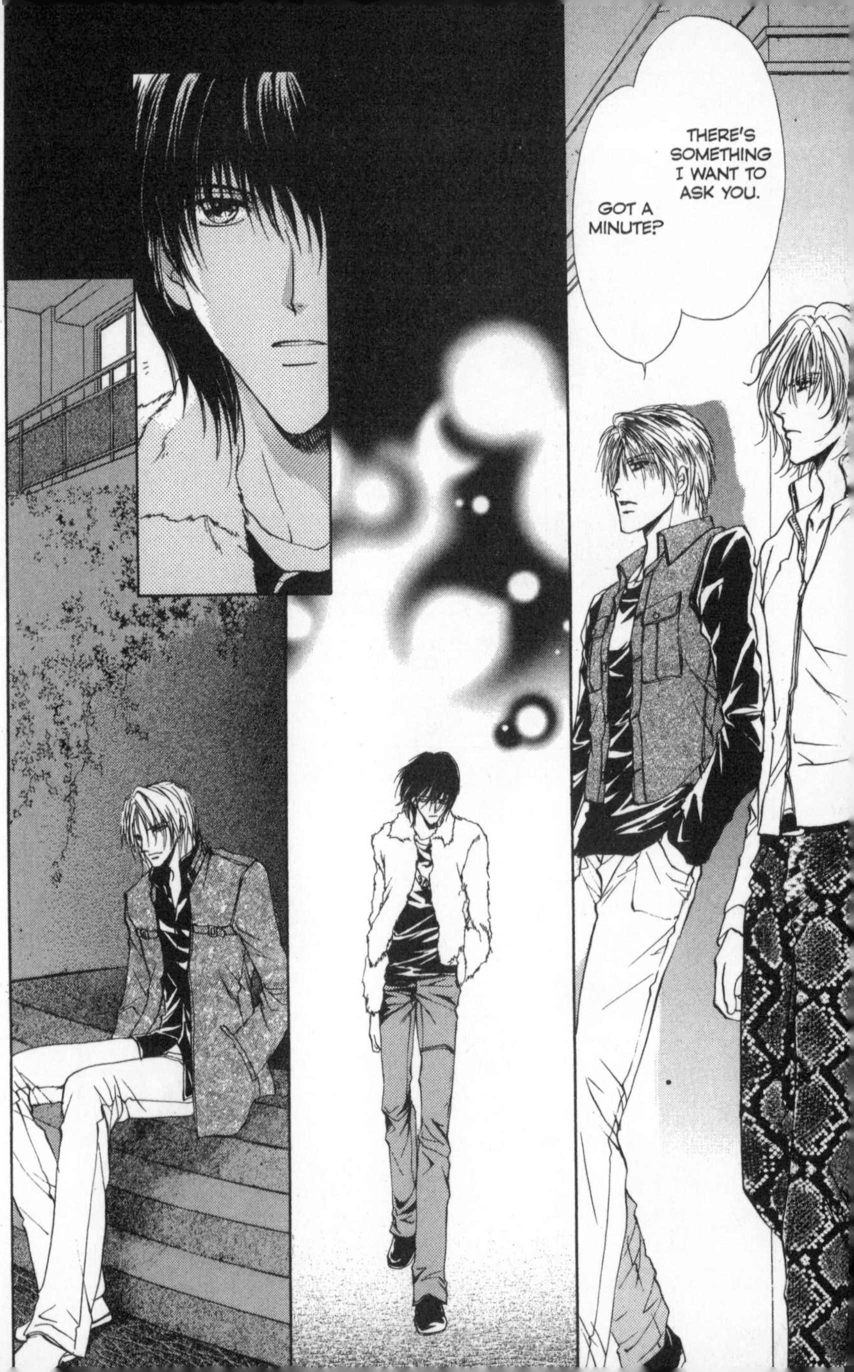
THERE'S SOMETHING I WANT TO ASK YOU.
GOT A MINUTE?

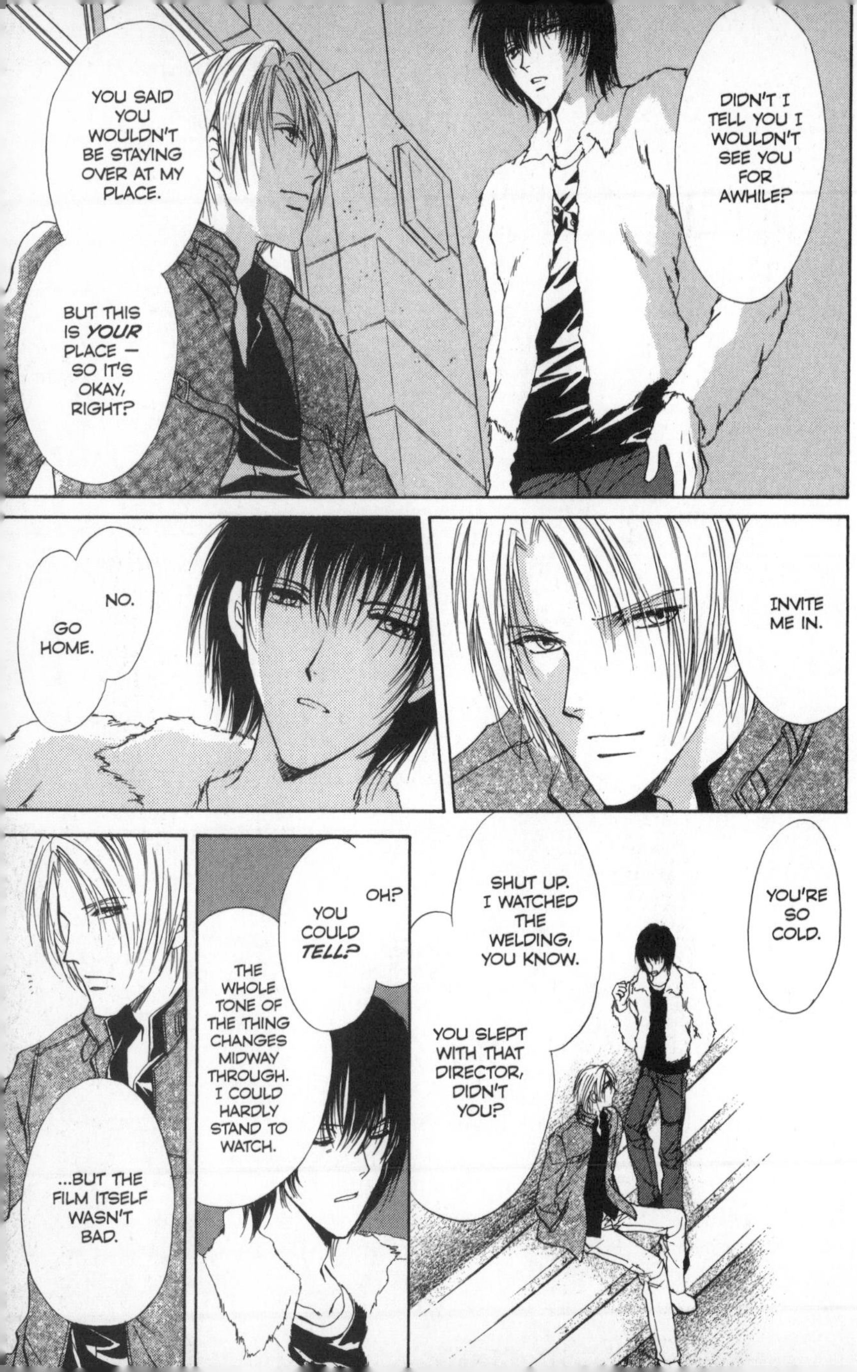
DIDN'T I TELL YOU I WOULDN'T SEE YOU FOR AWHILE?
YOU SAID YOU WOULDN'T BE STAYING OVER AT MY PLACE.
BUT THIS IS *YOUR* PLACE — SO IT'S OKAY, RIGHT?
INVITE ME IN.
NO. GO HOME.
YOU'RE SO COLD.
SHUT UP. I WATCHED THE WELDING, YOU KNOW.
YOU SLEPT WITH THAT DIRECTOR, DIDN'T YOU?
OH? YOU COULD *TELL?*
THE WHOLE TONE OF THE THING CHANGES MIDWAY THROUGH. I COULD HARDLY STAND TO WATCH.
...BUT THE FILM ITSELF WASN'T BAD.

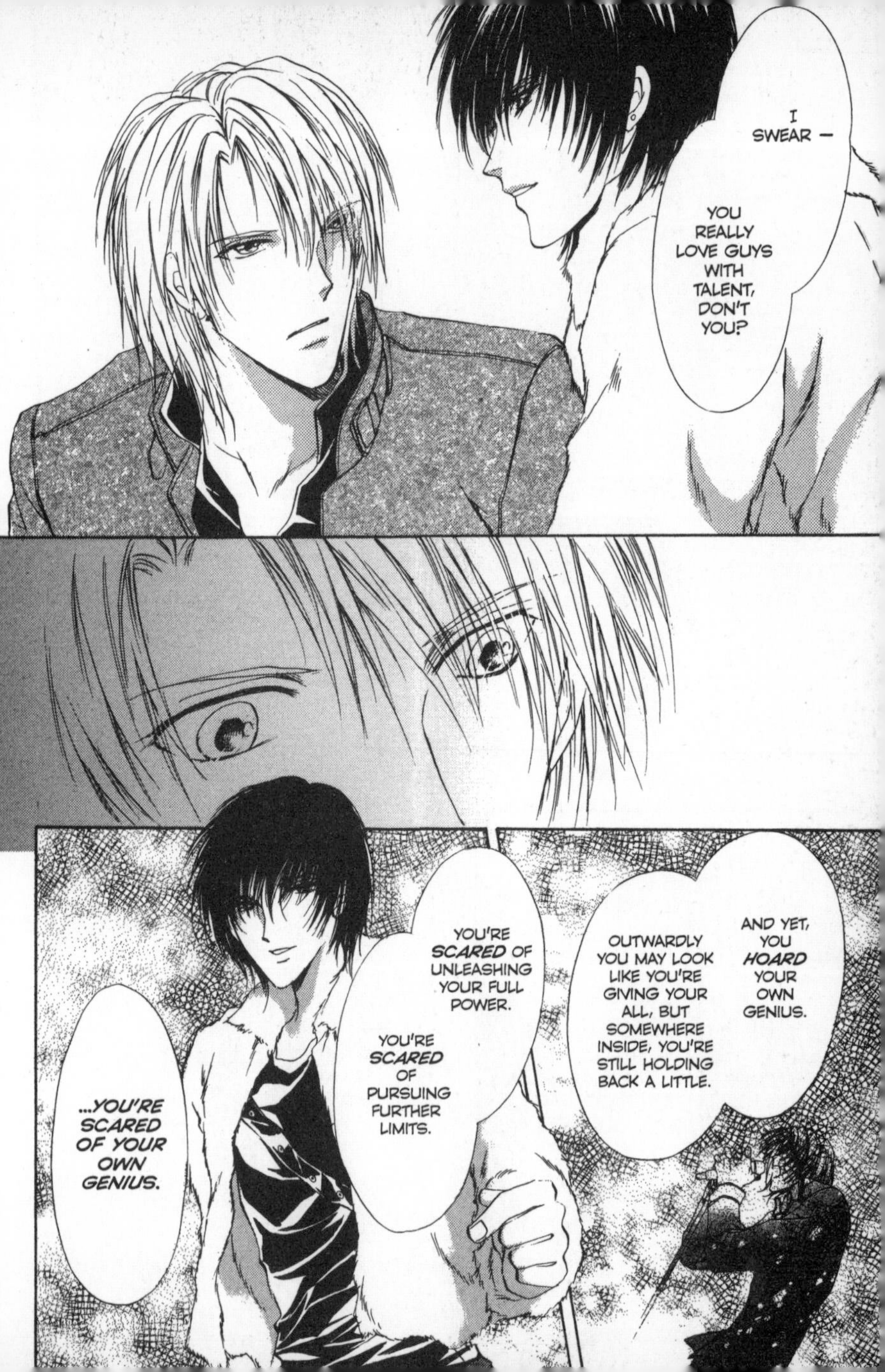
I SWEAR —
YOU REALLY LOVE GUYS WITH TALENT, DON'T YOU?
AND YET, YOU **HOARD** YOUR OWN GENIUS.
OUTWARDLY YOU MAY LOOK LIKE YOU'RE GIVING YOUR ALL, BUT SOMEWHERE INSIDE, YOU'RE STILL HOLDING BACK A LITTLE.
YOU'RE **SCARED** OF UNLEASHING YOUR FULL POWER.
YOU'RE **SCARED** OF PURSUING FURTHER LIMITS.
...YOU'RE SCARED OF YOUR OWN GENIUS.

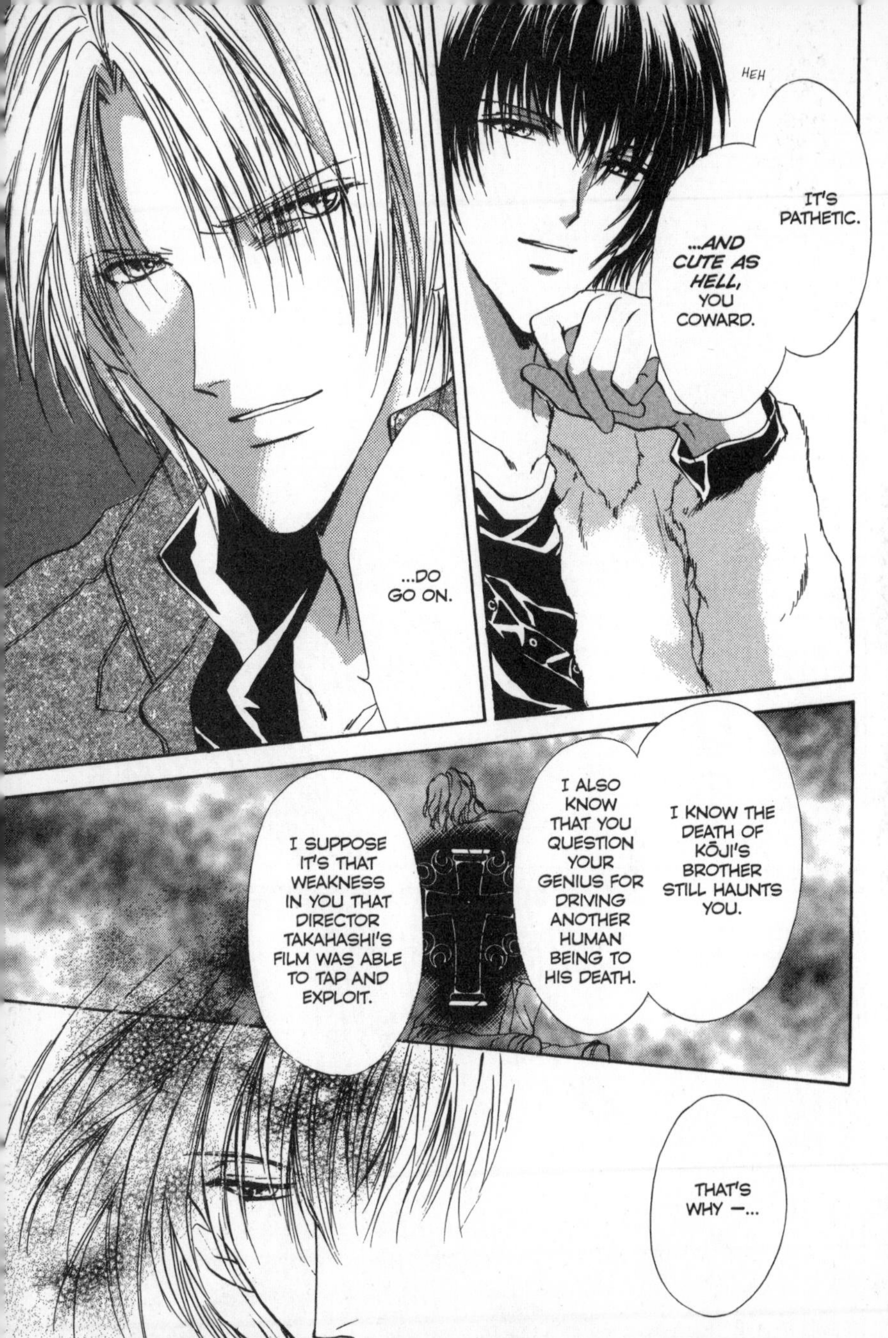
HEH
IT'S PATHETIC.
...AND CUTE AS HELL, YOU COWARD.
...DO GO ON.
I KNOW THE DEATH OF KŌJI'S BROTHER STILL HAUNTS YOU.
I ALSO KNOW THAT YOU QUESTION YOUR GENIUS FOR DRIVING ANOTHER HUMAN BEING TO HIS DEATH.
I SUPPOSE IT'S THAT WEAKNESS IN YOU THAT DIRECTOR TAKAHASHI'S FILM WAS ABLE TO TAP AND EXPLOIT.
THAT'S WHY —...

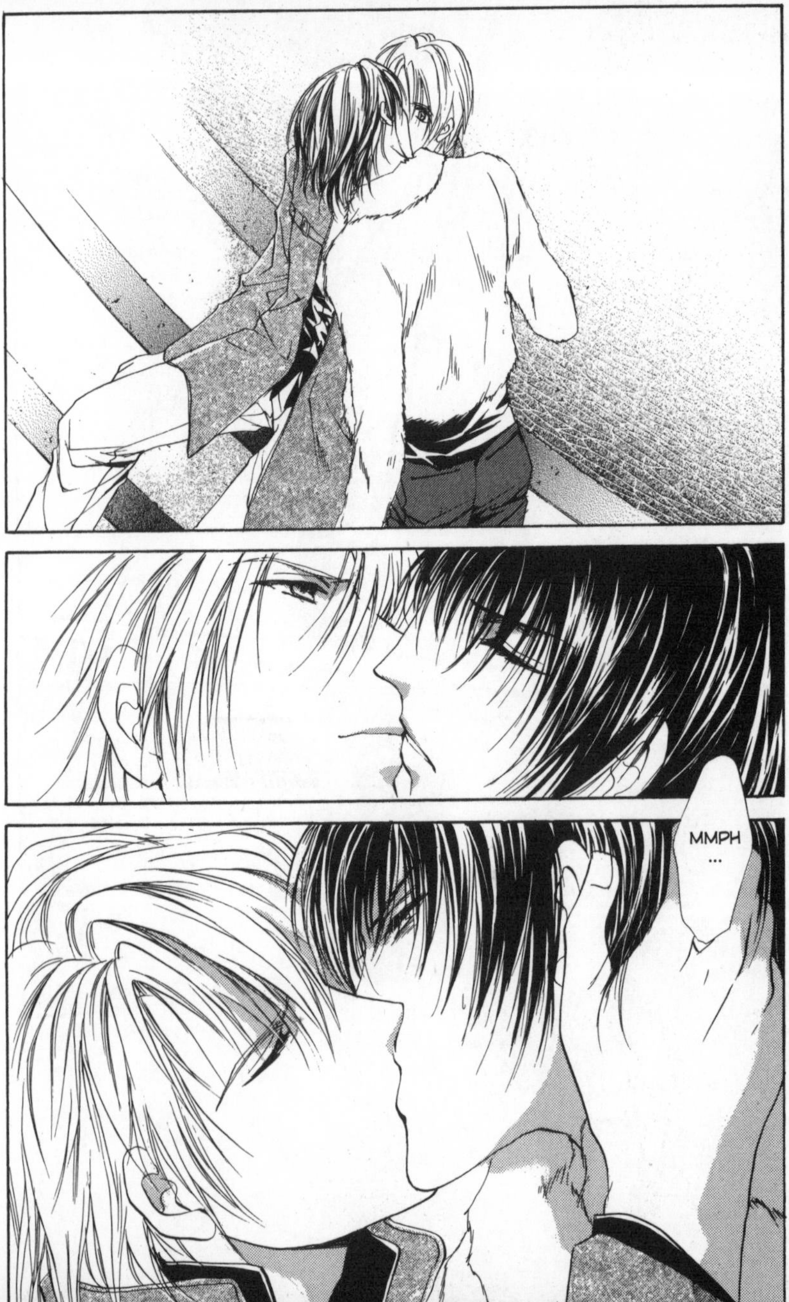
MMPH
...

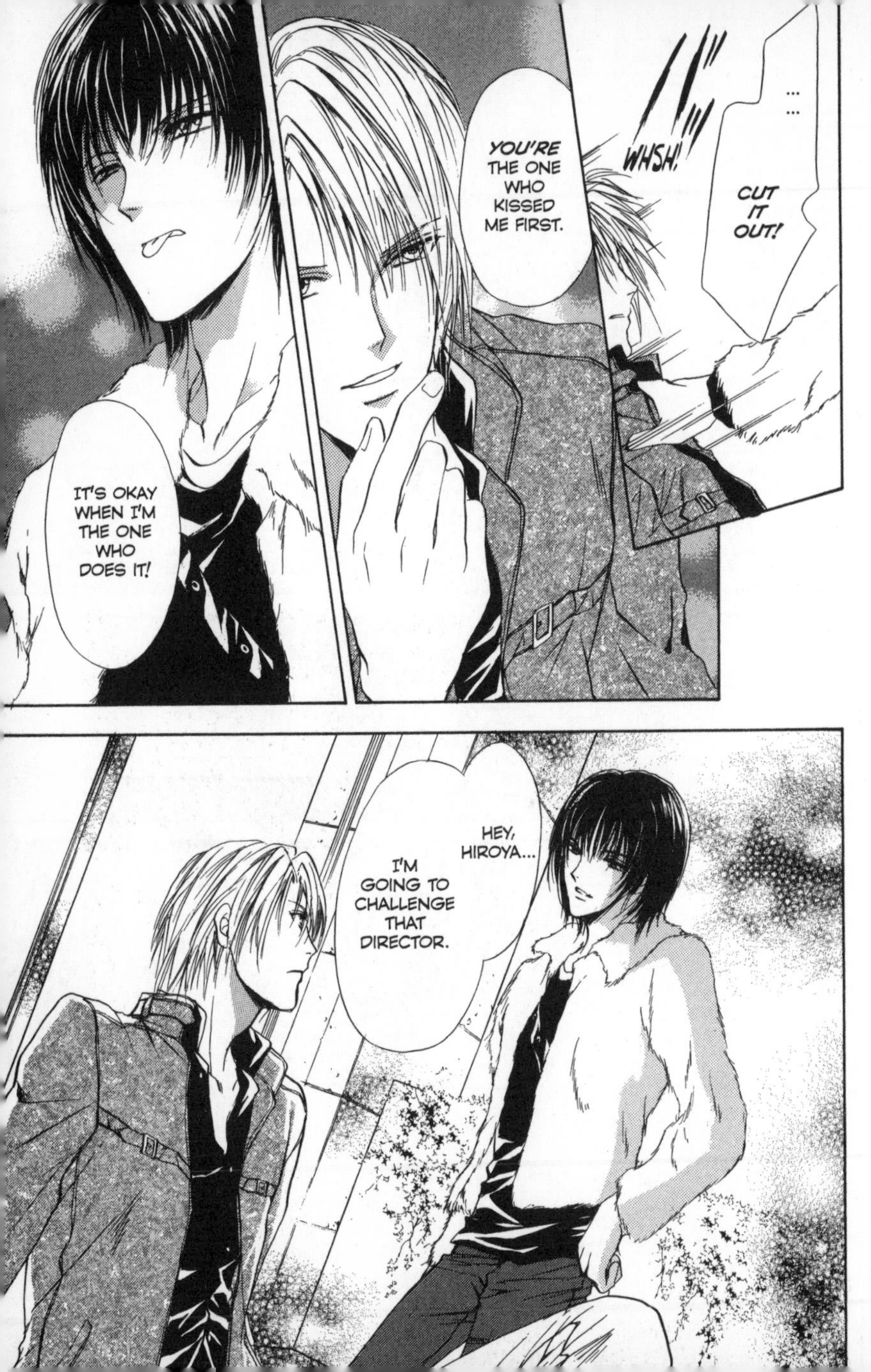
... ... CUT IT OUT!
WHSH!
YOU'RE THE ONE WHO KISSED ME FIRST.
IT'S OKAY WHEN I'M THE ONE WHO DOES IT!
HEY, HIROYA...
I'M GOING TO CHALLENGE THAT DIRECTOR.

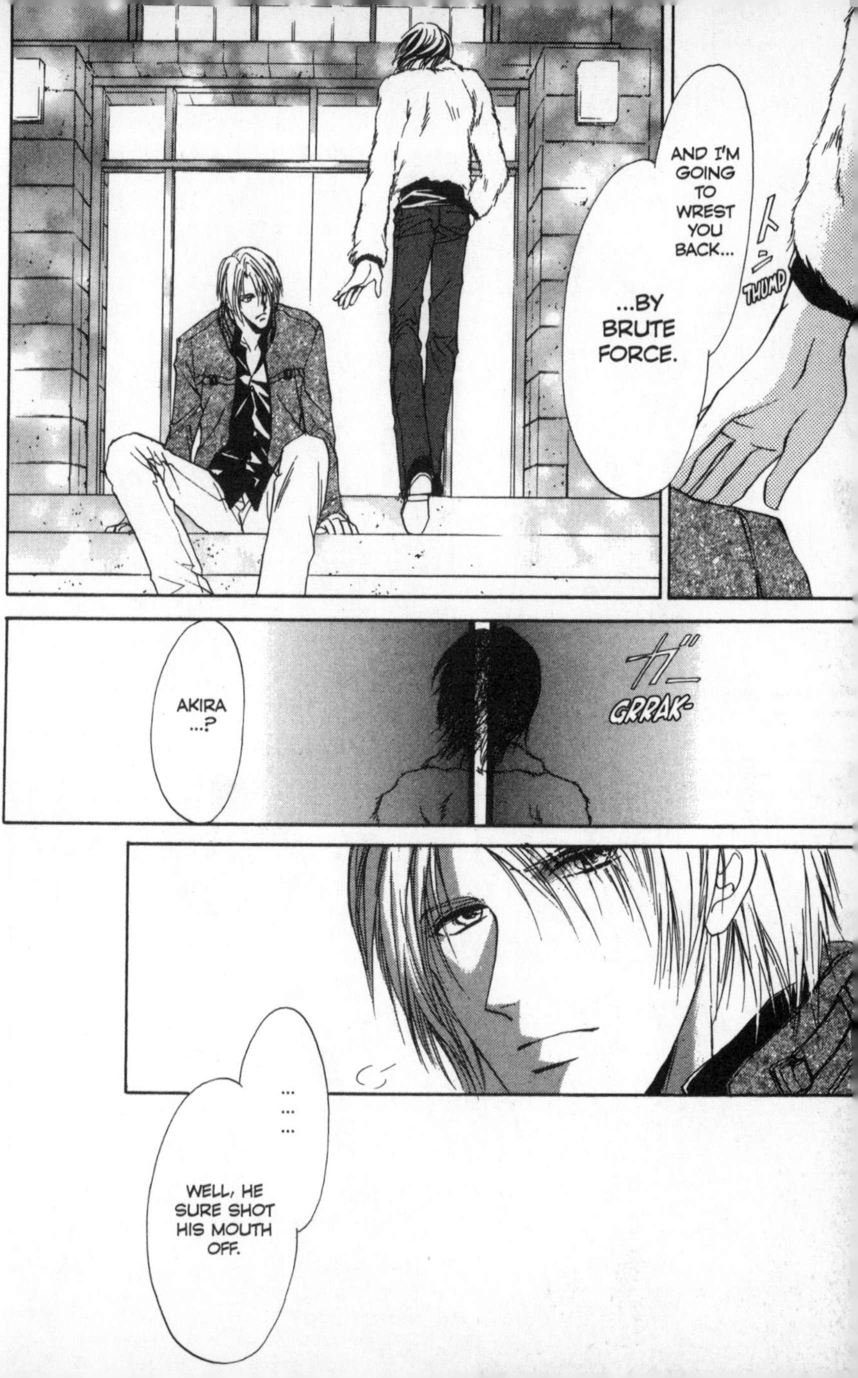
AND I'M GOING TO WREST YOU BACK...
...BY BRUTE FORCE.
トン
THUMP
ガー
GRRAK-
AKIRA ...?
... ...
WELL, HE SURE SHOT HIS MOUTH OFF.

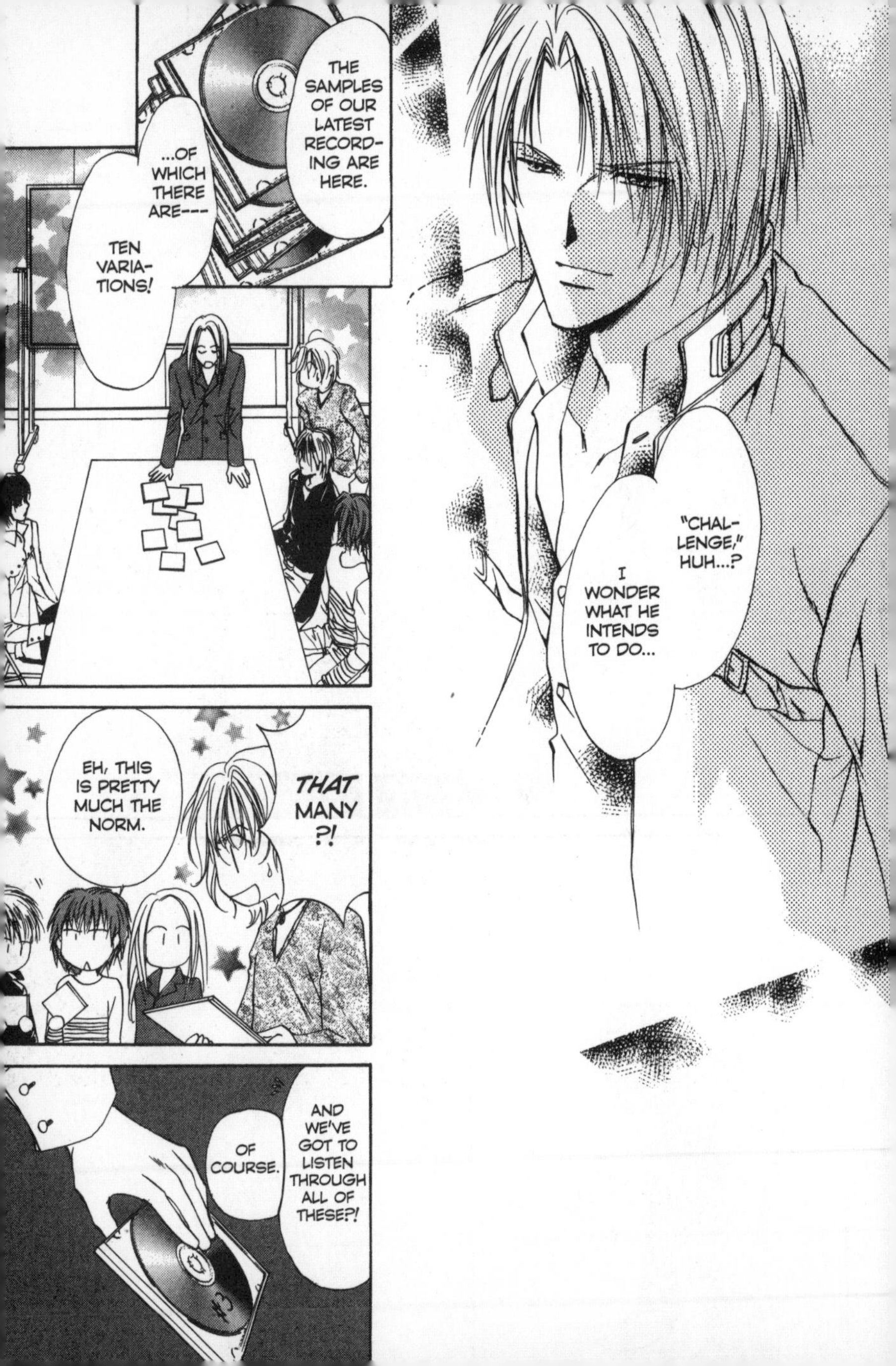
"CHAL-LENGE," HUH...?
I WONDER WHAT HE INTENDS TO DO...
THE SAMPLES OF OUR LATEST RECORD-ING ARE HERE.
...OF WHICH THERE ARE---
TEN VARIA-TIONS!
THAT MANY?!
EH, THIS IS PRETTY MUCH THE NORM.
AND WE'VE GOT TO LISTEN THROUGH ALL OF THESE?!
OF COURSE.

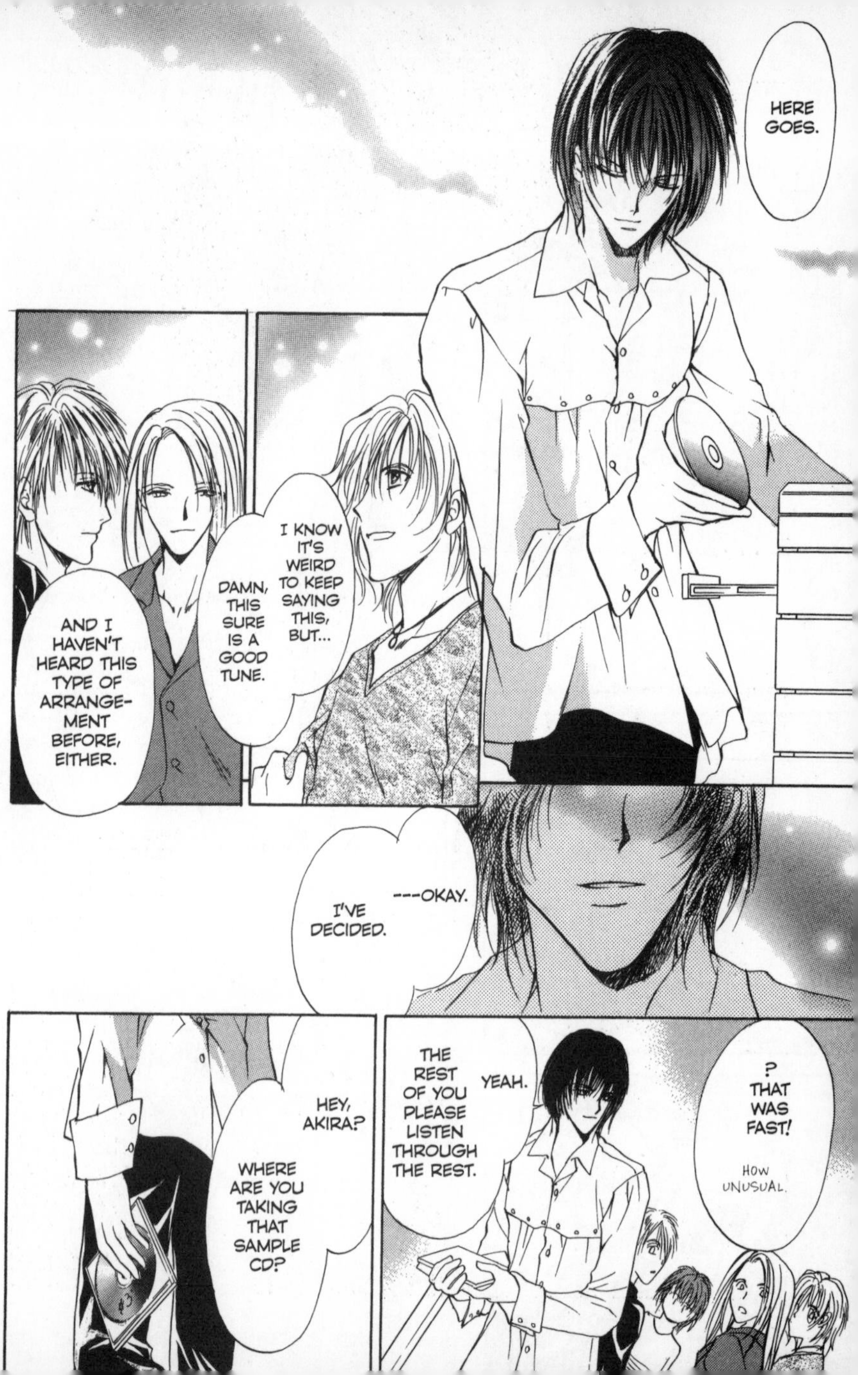
HERE GOES.
I KNOW IT'S WEIRD TO KEEP SAYING THIS, BUT...
DAMN, THIS SURE IS A GOOD TUNE.
AND I HAVEN'T HEARD THIS TYPE OF ARRANGE-MENT BEFORE, EITHER.
---OKAY.
I'VE DECIDED.
? THAT WAS FAST!
HOW UNUSUAL.
YEAH.
THE REST OF YOU PLEASE LISTEN THROUGH THE REST.
HEY, AKIRA?
WHERE ARE YOU TAKING THAT SAMPLE CD?

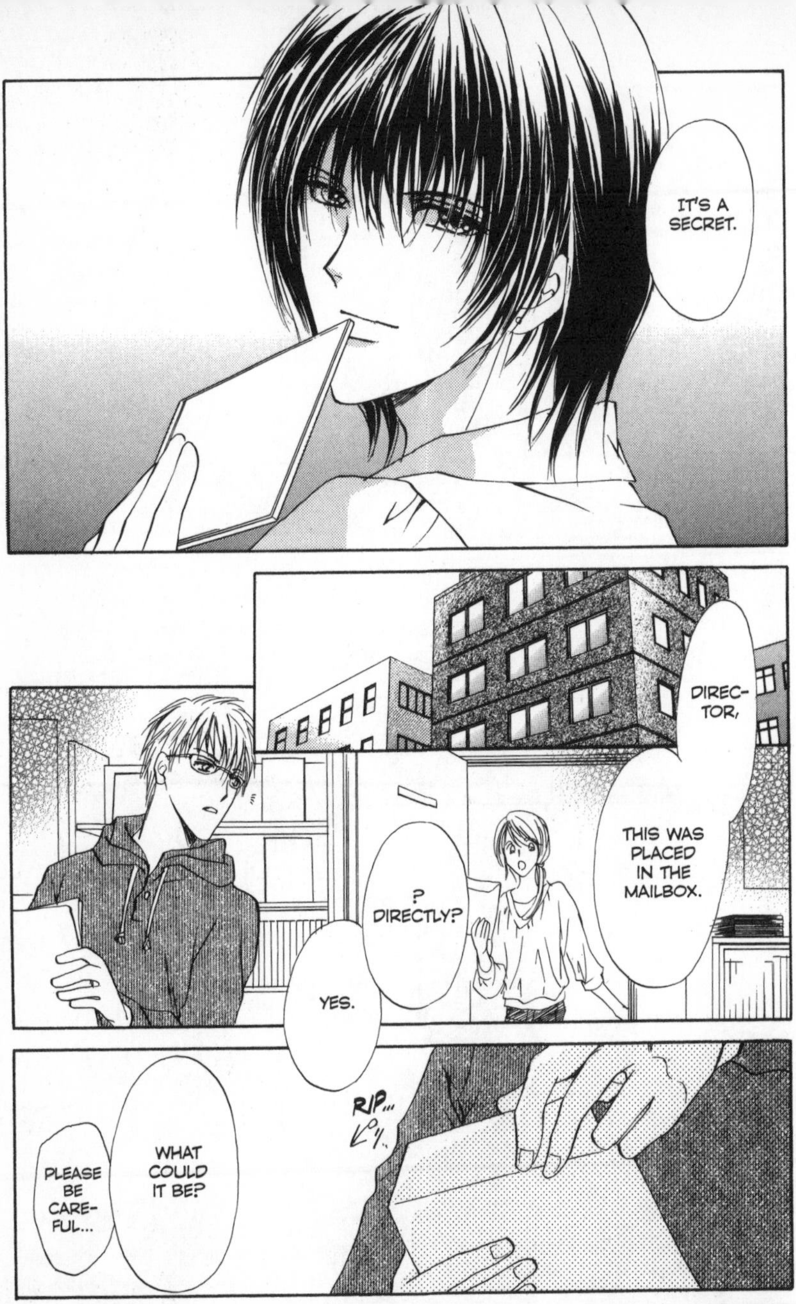
IT'S A SECRET.
DIRECTOR,
THIS WAS PLACED IN THE MAILBOX.
? DIRECTLY?
YES.
RIP...
WHAT COULD IT BE?
PLEASE BE CARE-FUL...

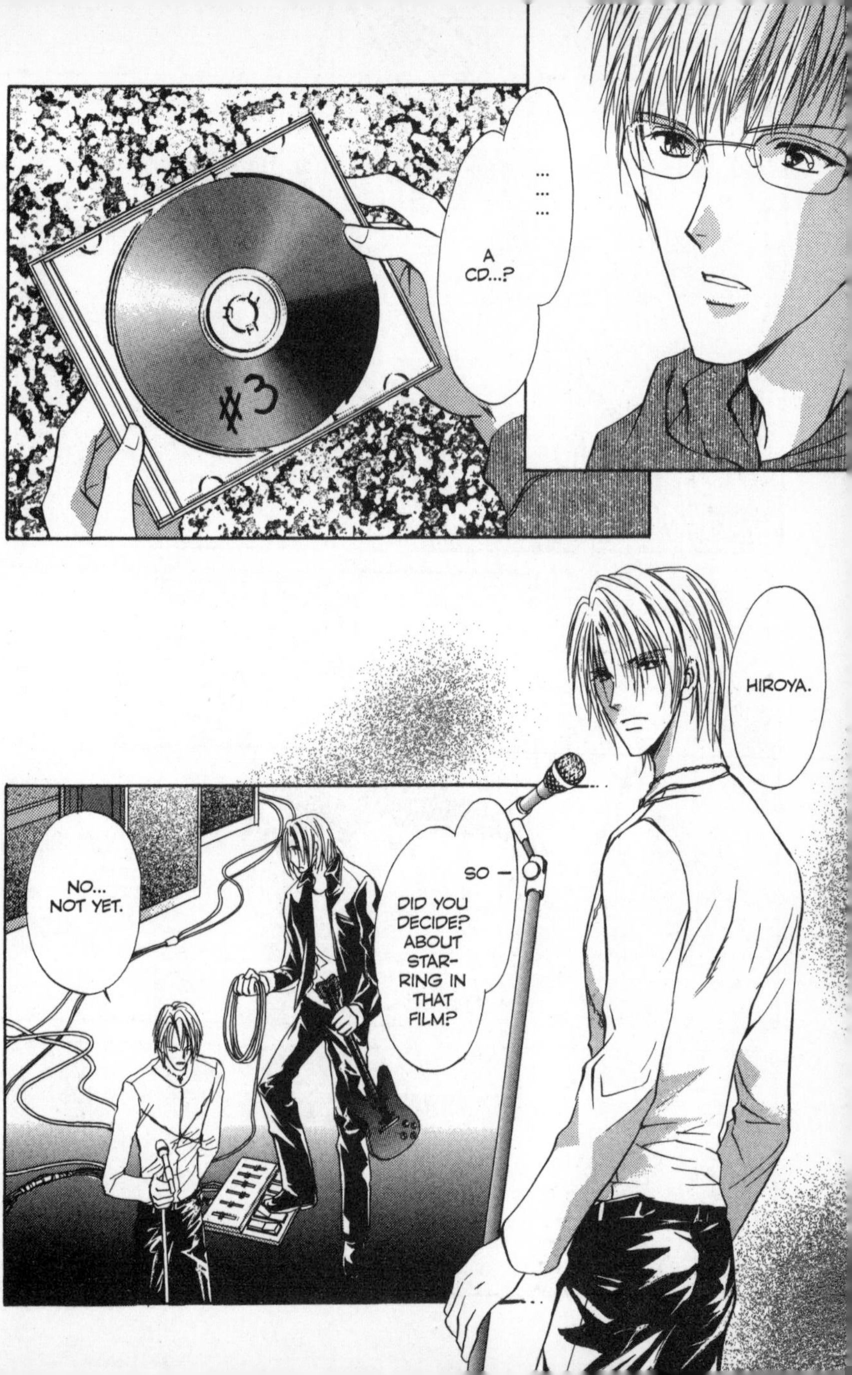
... ... A CD...?
HIROYA.
SO — DID YOU DECIDE? ABOUT STAR-RING IN THAT FILM?
NO... NOT YET.

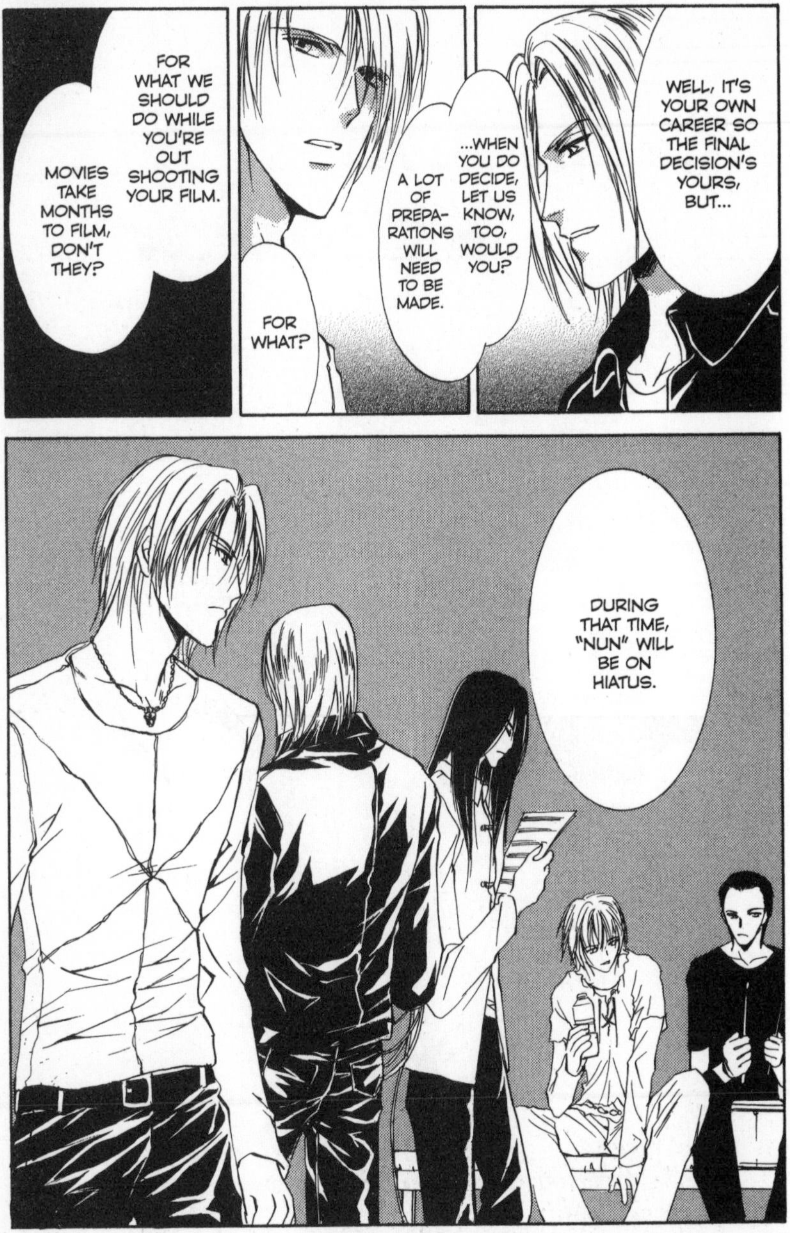
WELL, IT'S YOUR OWN CAREER SO THE FINAL DECISION'S YOURS, BUT...
...WHEN YOU DO DECIDE, LET US KNOW, TOO, WOULD YOU?
A LOT OF PREPARATIONS WILL NEED TO BE MADE.
FOR WHAT?
FOR WHAT WE SHOULD DO WHILE YOU'RE OUT SHOOTING YOUR FILM.
MOVIES TAKE MONTHS TO FILM, DON'T THEY?
DURING THAT TIME, "NUN" WILL BE ON HIATUS.

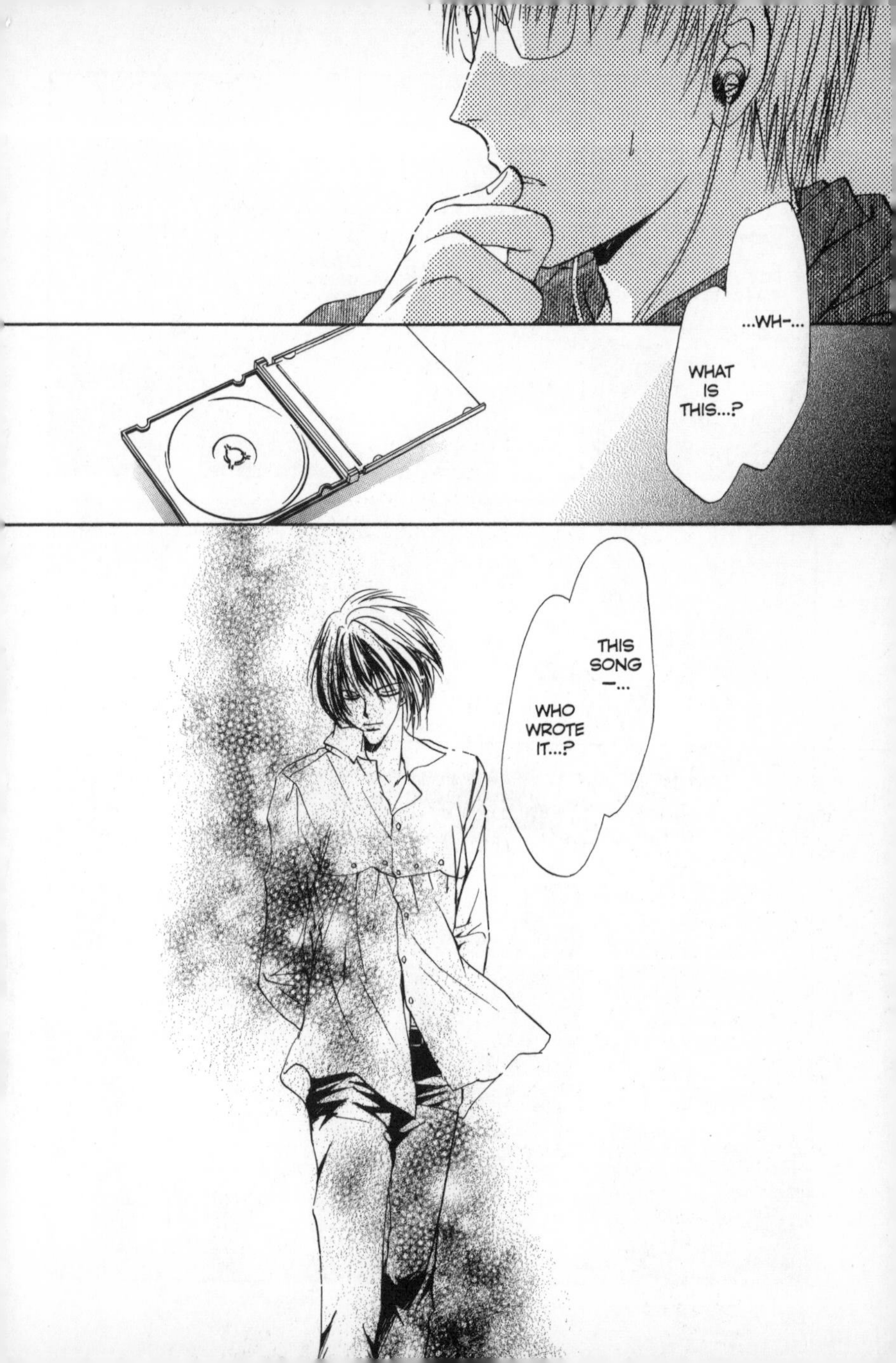
...WH-... WHAT IS THIS...?
THIS SONG —... WHO WROTE IT...?

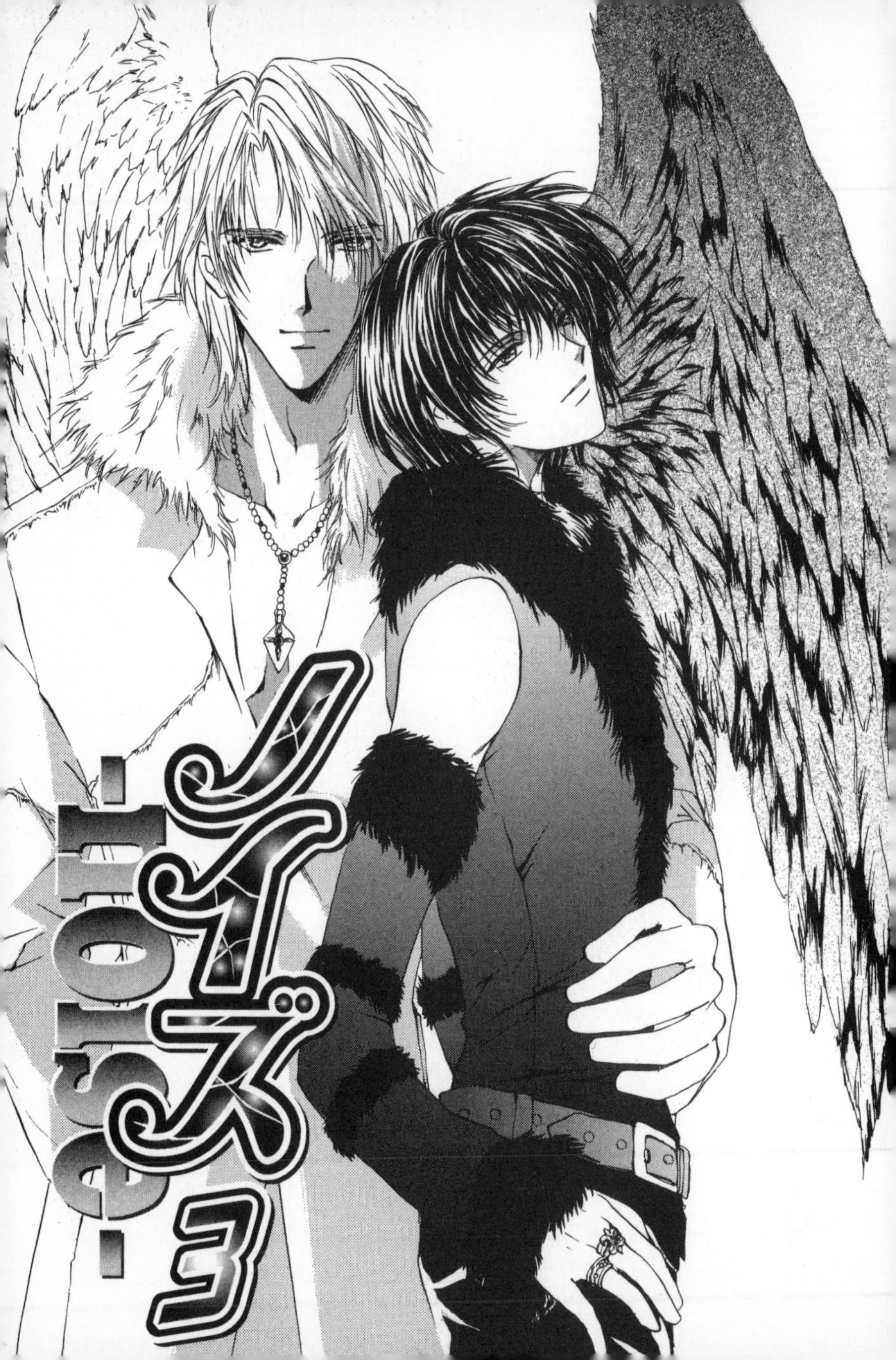
noise-
ノイズ
3

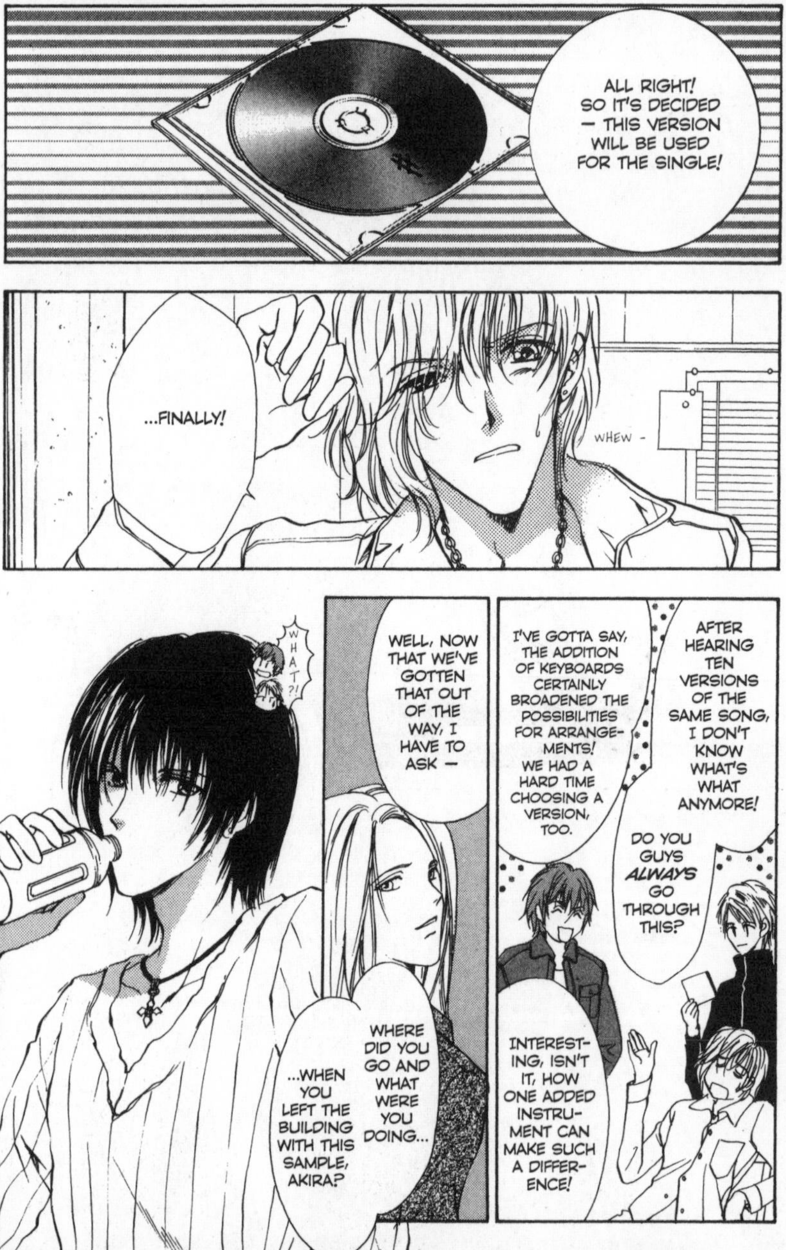
ALL RIGHT! SO IT'S DECIDED — THIS VERSION WILL BE USED FOR THE SINGLE!
...FINALLY!
WHEW -
AFTER HEARING TEN VERSIONS OF THE SAME SONG, I DON'T KNOW WHAT'S WHAT ANYMORE!
I'VE GOTTA SAY, THE ADDITION OF KEYBOARDS CERTAINLY BROADENED THE POSSIBILITIES FOR ARRANGE-MENTS! WE HAD A HARD TIME CHOOSING A VERSION, TOO.
DO YOU GUYS *ALWAYS* GO THROUGH THIS?
INTERESTING, ISN'T IT, HOW ONE ADDED INSTRU-MENT CAN MAKE SUCH A DIFFERENCE!
WELL, NOW THAT WE'VE GOTTEN THAT OUT OF THE WAY, I HAVE TO ASK —
WHERE DID YOU GO AND WHAT WERE YOU DOING...
...WHEN YOU LEFT THE BUILDING WITH THIS SAMPLE, AKIRA?
WHAT?!

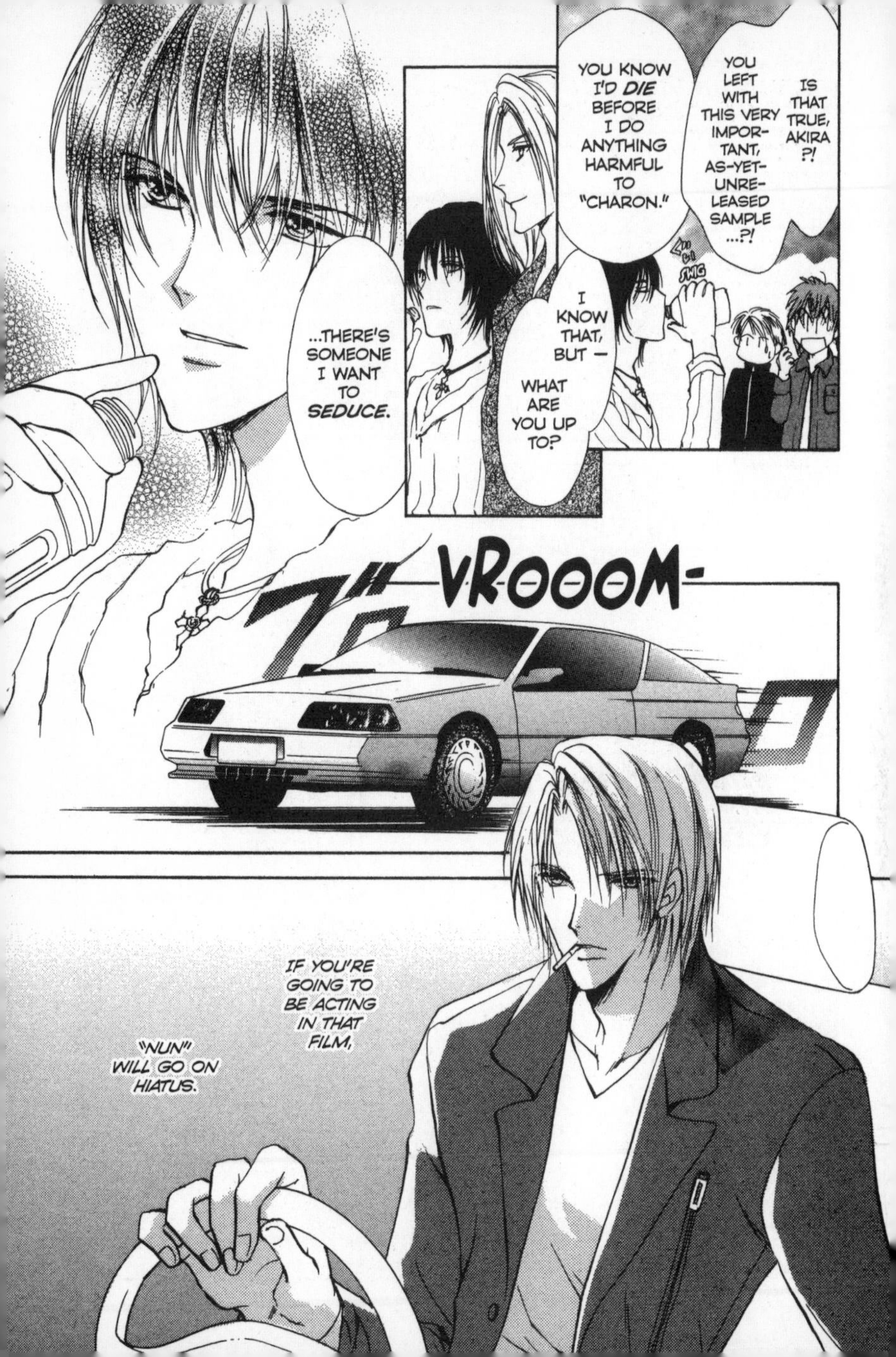

IS THAT TRUE, AKIRA?!
YOU LEFT WITH THIS VERY IMPORTANT, AS-YET-UNRELEASED SAMPLE ...?!
YOU KNOW I'D *DIE* BEFORE I DO ANYTHING HARMFUL TO "CHARON."
SWIG
I KNOW THAT, BUT —
WHAT ARE YOU UP TO?
...THERE'S SOMEONE I WANT TO *SEDUCE.*
VROOOM
IF YOU'RE GOING TO BE ACTING IN THAT FILM,
"NUN" WILL GO ON HIATUS.

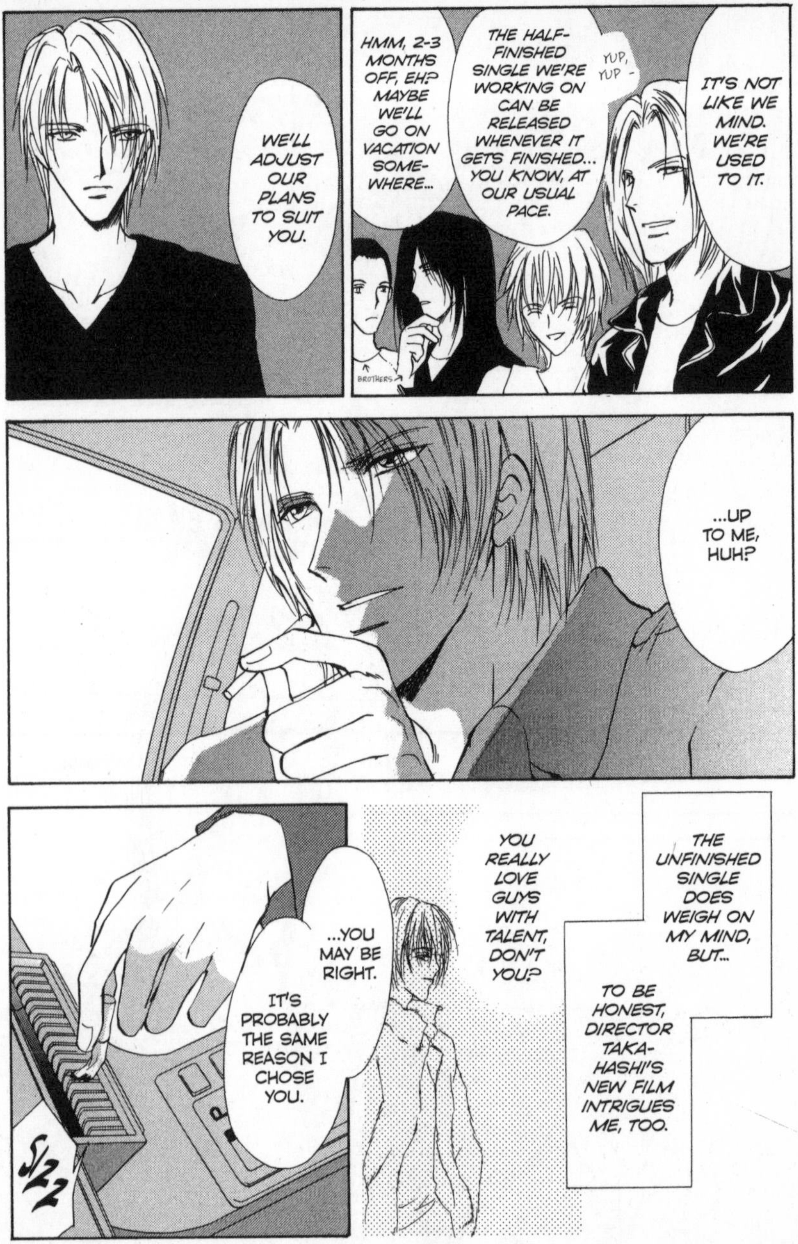
IT'S NOT LIKE WE MIND. WE'RE USED TO IT.
YUP, YUP -
THE HALF-FINISHED SINGLE WE'RE WORKING ON CAN BE RELEASED WHENEVER IT GETS FINISHED... YOU KNOW, AT OUR USUAL PACE.
HMM, 2-3 MONTHS OFF, EH? MAYBE WE'LL GO ON VACATION SOMEWHERE...
BROTHERS
WE'LL ADJUST OUR PLANS TO SUIT YOU.
...UP TO ME, HUH?
THE UNFINISHED SINGLE DOES WEIGH ON MY MIND, BUT...
TO BE HONEST, DIRECTOR TAKAHASHI'S NEW FILM INTRIGUES ME, TOO.
YOU REALLY LOVE GUYS WITH TALENT, DON'T YOU?
...YOU MAY BE RIGHT.
IT'S PROBABLY THE SAME REASON I CHOSE YOU.

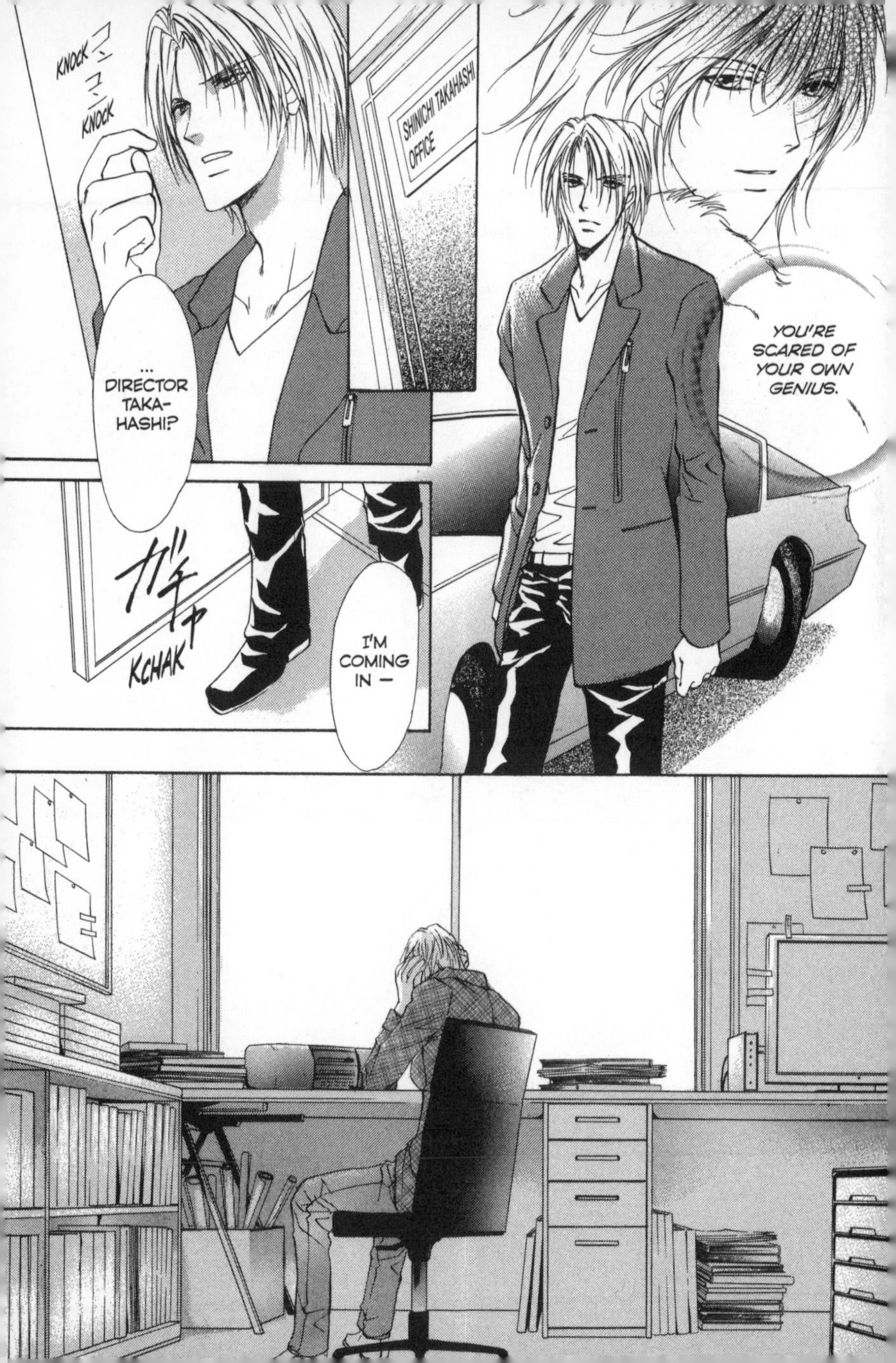
YOU'RE SCARED OF YOUR OWN GENIUS.
コン コン
KNOCK KNOCK
SHINICHI TAKAHASHI OFFICE
... DIRECTOR TAKA-HASHI?
ガチャ
KCHAK
I'M COMING IN —

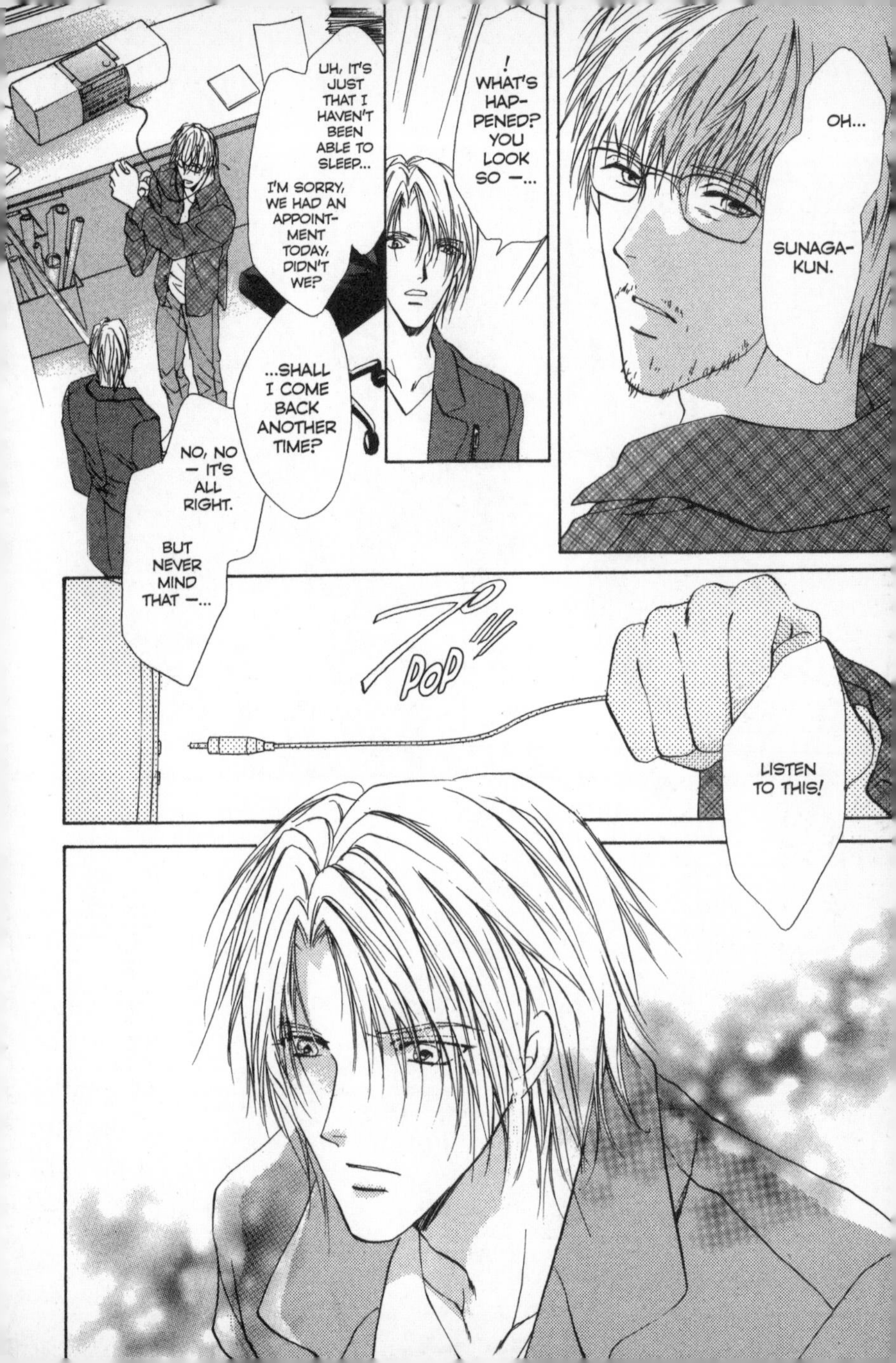
OH...
SUNAGA-KUN.
! WHAT'S HAP-PENED? YOU LOOK SO —...
UH, IT'S JUST THAT I HAVEN'T BEEN ABLE TO SLEEP...
I'M SORRY, WE HAD AN APPOINT-MENT TODAY, DIDN'T WE?
...SHALL I COME BACK ANOTHER TIME?
NO, NO — IT'S ALL RIGHT.
BUT NEVER MIND THAT —...
POP
LISTEN TO THIS!

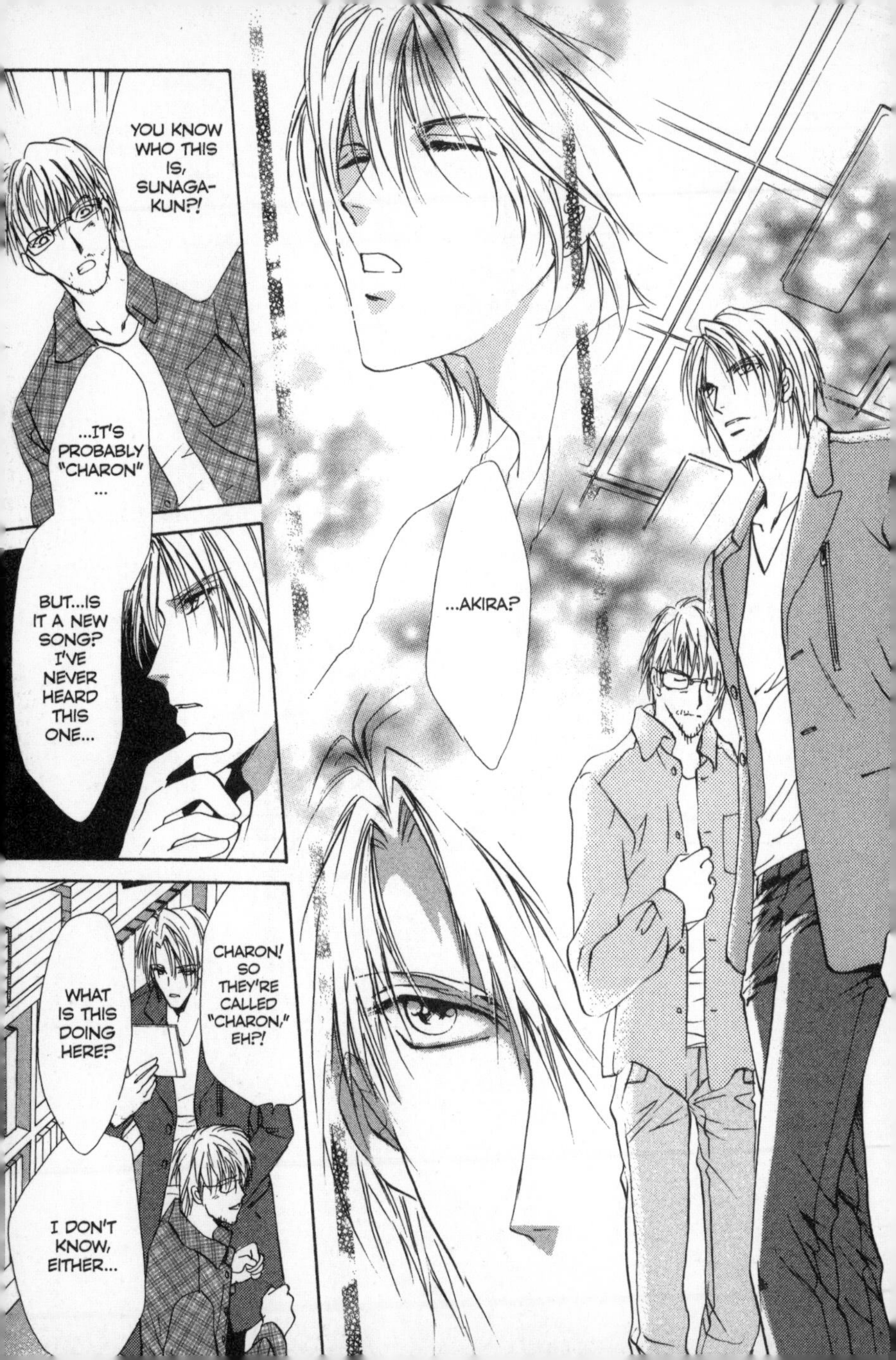
...AKIRA?
YOU KNOW WHO THIS IS, SUNAGA-KUN?!
...IT'S PROBABLY "CHARON"...
BUT...IS IT A NEW SONG? I'VE NEVER HEARD THIS ONE...
CHARON! SO THEY'RE CALLED "CHARON," EH?!
WHAT IS THIS DOING HERE?
I DON'T KNOW, EITHER...

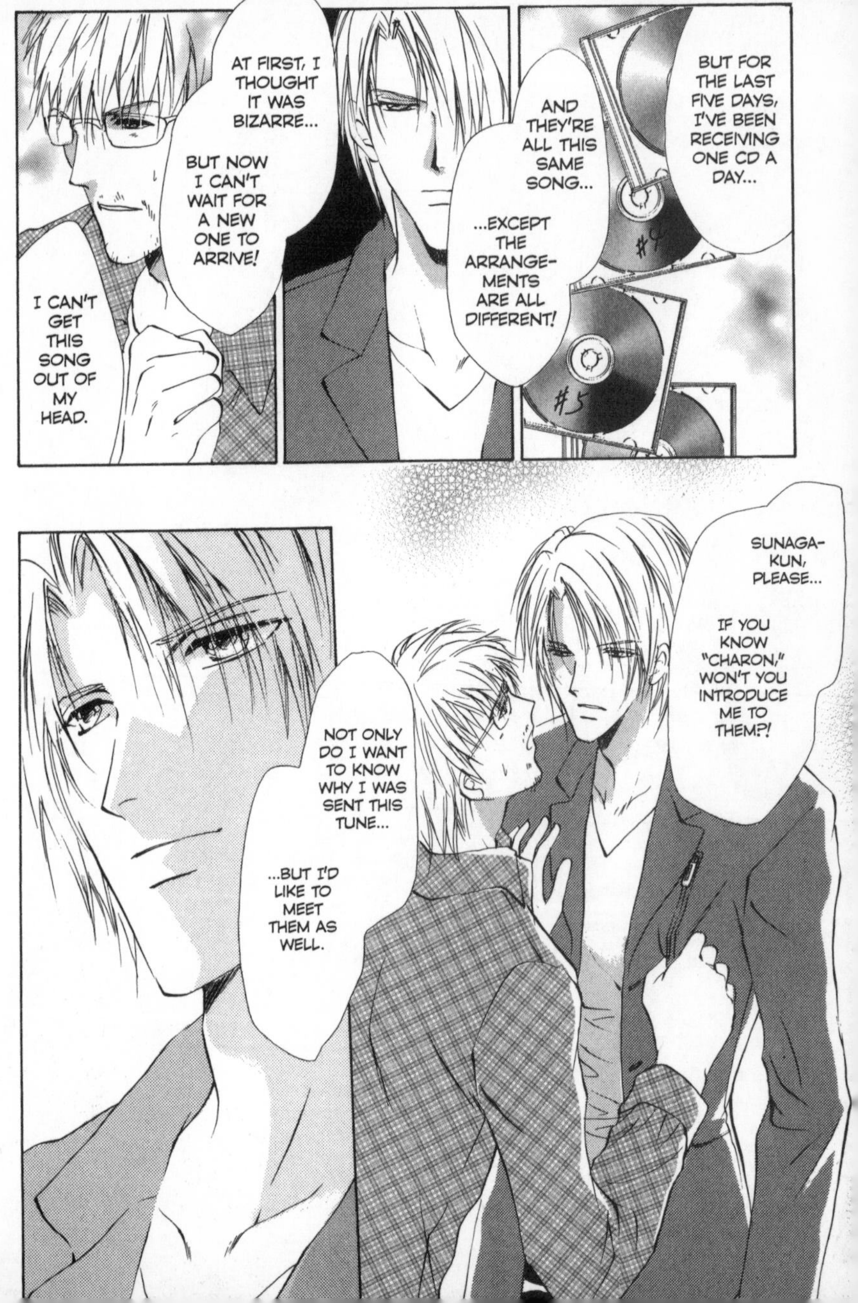
BUT FOR THE LAST FIVE DAYS, I'VE BEEN RECEIVING ONE CD A DAY...
AND THEY'RE ALL THIS SAME SONG...
...EXCEPT THE ARRANGEMENTS ARE ALL DIFFERENT!
AT FIRST, I THOUGHT IT WAS BIZARRE...
BUT NOW I CAN'T WAIT FOR A NEW ONE TO ARRIVE!
I CAN'T GET THIS SONG OUT OF MY HEAD.
SUNAGA-KUN, PLEASE...
IF YOU KNOW "CHARON," WON'T YOU INTRODUCE ME TO THEM?!
NOT ONLY DO I WANT TO KNOW WHY I WAS SENT THIS TUNE...
...BUT I'D LIKE TO MEET THEM AS WELL.

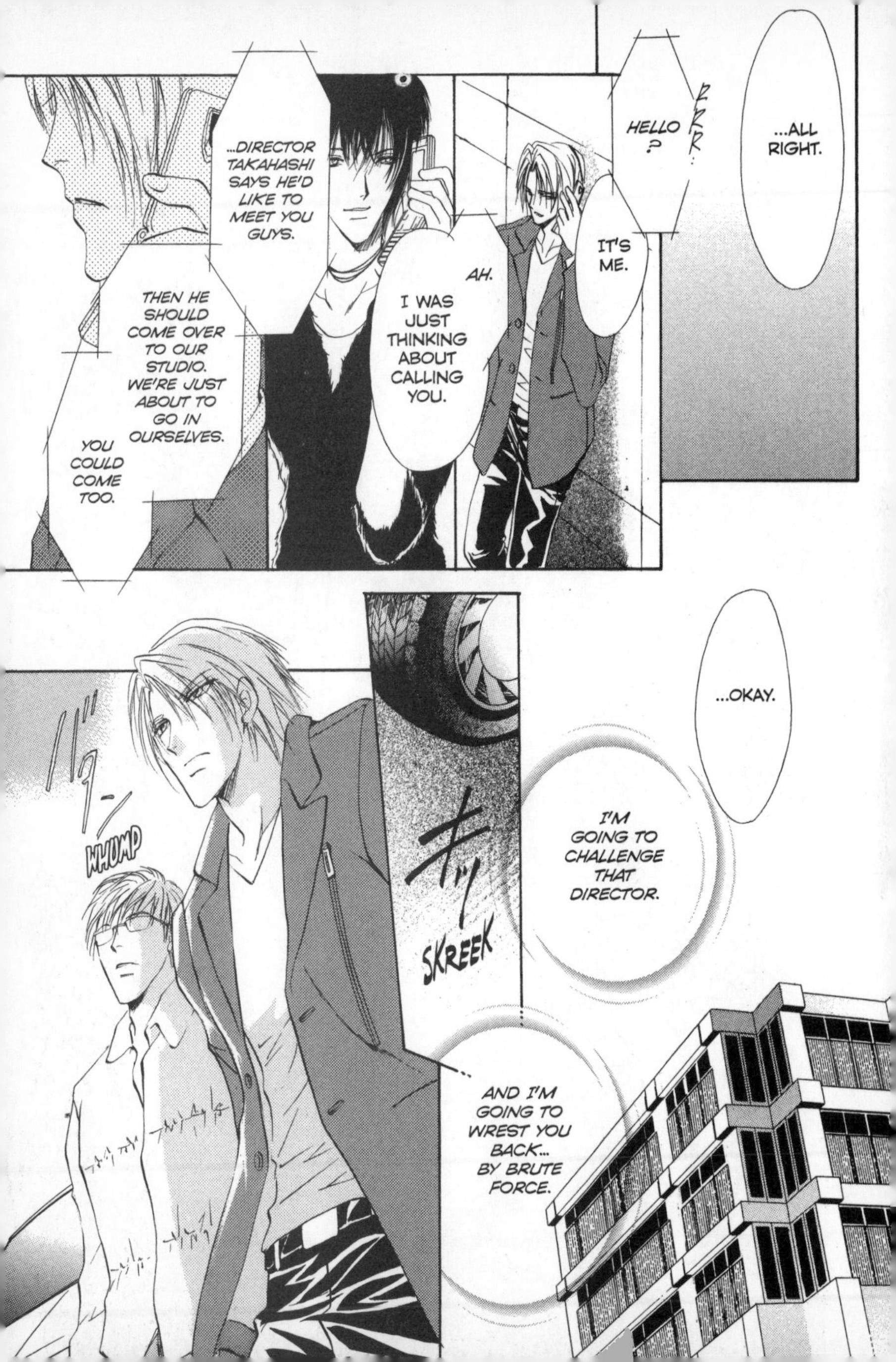
...ALL RIGHT.
RRRR...
HELLO?
IT'S ME.
AH. I WAS JUST THINKING ABOUT CALLING YOU.
...DIRECTOR TAKAHASHI SAYS HE'D LIKE TO MEET YOU GUYS.
THEN HE SHOULD COME OVER TO OUR STUDIO. WE'RE JUST ABOUT TO GO IN OURSELVES.
YOU COULD COME TOO.
...OKAY.
I'M GOING TO CHALLENGE THAT DIRECTOR.
SKREEK
AND I'M GOING TO WREST YOU BACK... BY BRUTE FORCE.
WHUMP

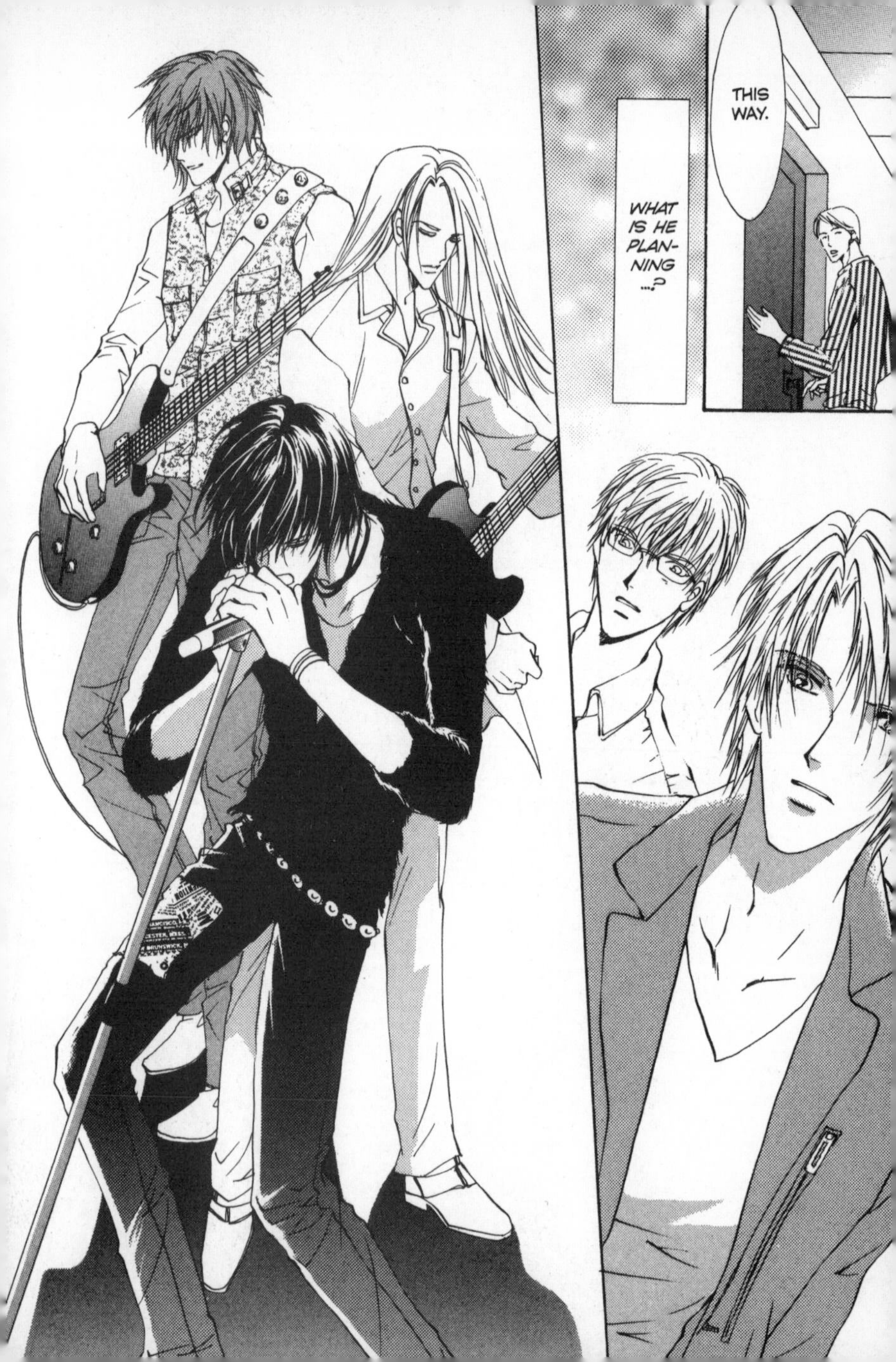
THIS WAY.
WHAT IS HE PLANNING ...?

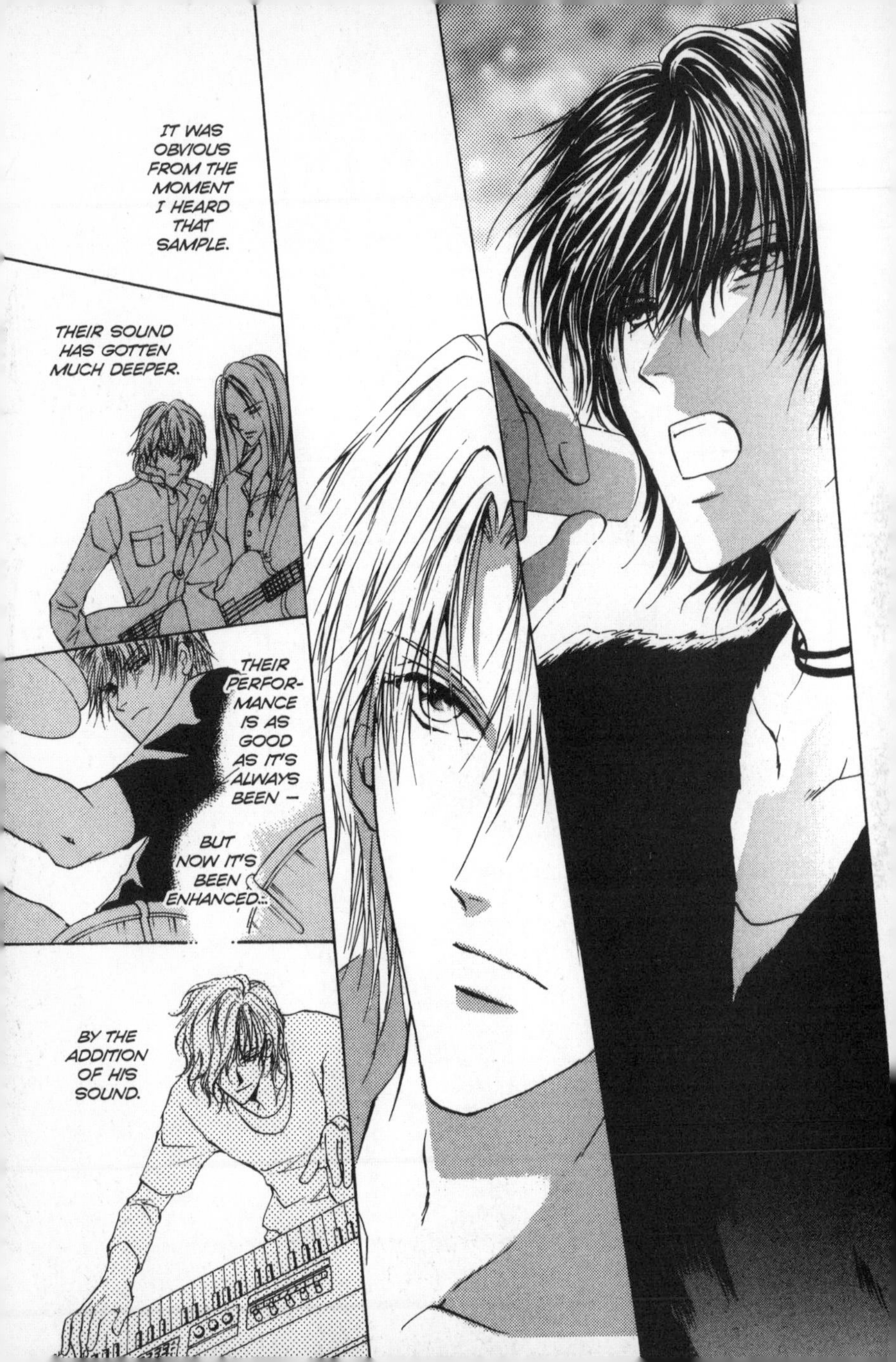
IT WAS OBVIOUS FROM THE MOMENT I HEARD THAT SAMPLE.
THEIR SOUND HAS GOTTEN MUCH DEEPER.
THEIR PERFORMANCE IS AS GOOD AS IT'S ALWAYS BEEN —
BUT NOW IT'S BEEN ENHANCED...
BY THE ADDITION OF HIS SOUND.

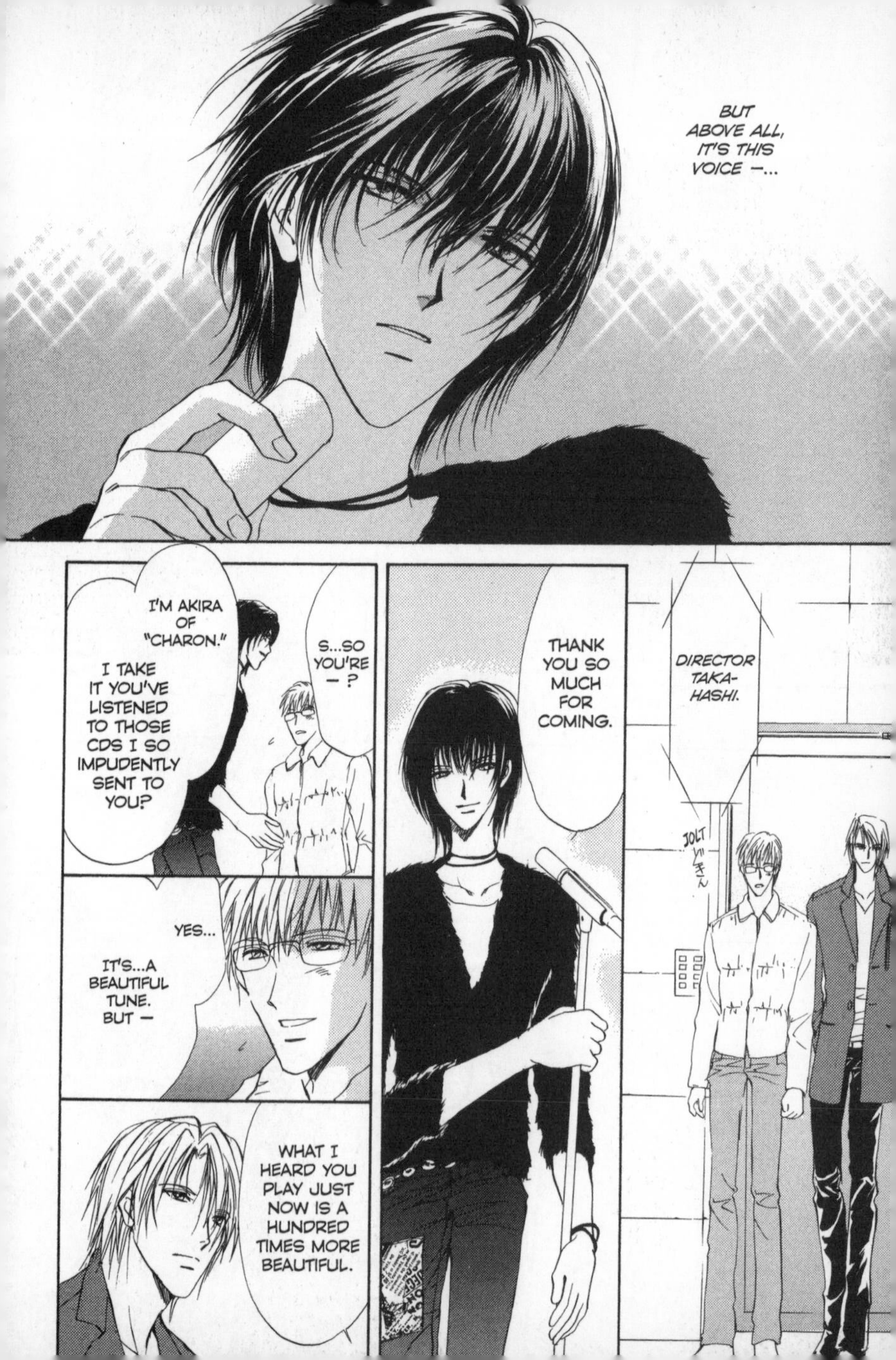
BUT ABOVE ALL, IT'S THIS VOICE —...
DIRECTOR TAKA-HASHI.
JOLT
THANK YOU SO MUCH FOR COMING.
S...SO YOU'RE — ?
I'M AKIRA OF "CHARON."
I TAKE IT YOU'VE LISTENED TO THOSE CDS I SO IMPUDENTLY SENT TO YOU?
YES...
IT'S...A BEAUTIFUL TUNE. BUT —
WHAT I HEARD YOU PLAY JUST NOW IS A HUNDRED TIMES MORE BEAUTIFUL.

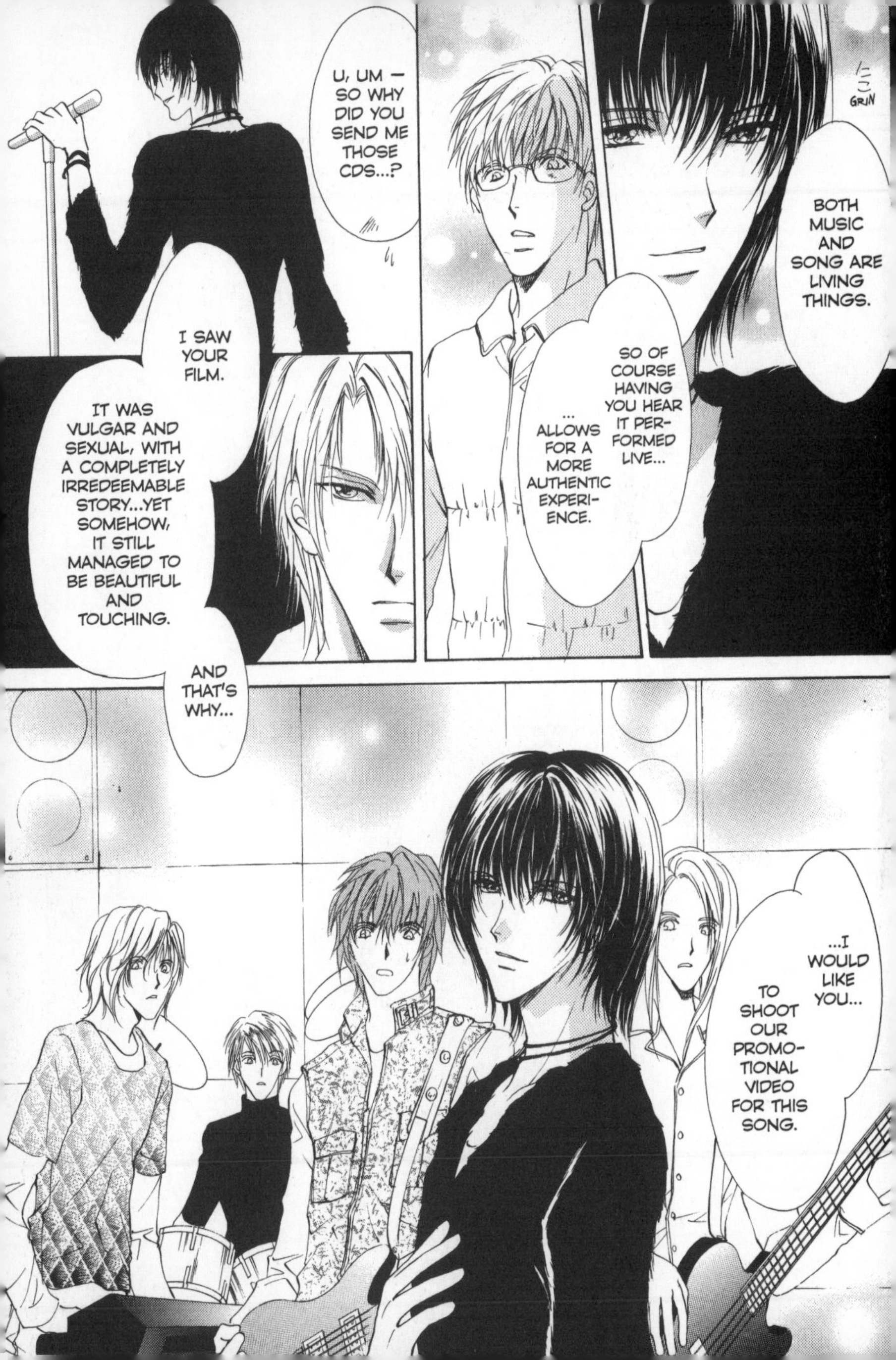
GRIN
BOTH MUSIC AND SONG ARE LIVING THINGS.
SO OF COURSE HAVING YOU HEAR IT PER-FORMED LIVE...
... ALLOWS FOR A MORE AUTHENTIC EXPERI-ENCE.
U, UM — SO WHY DID YOU SEND ME THOSE CDS...?
I SAW YOUR FILM.
IT WAS VULGAR AND SEXUAL, WITH A COMPLETELY IRREDEEMABLE STORY...YET SOMEHOW, IT STILL MANAGED TO BE BEAUTIFUL AND TOUCHING.
AND THAT'S WHY...
...I WOULD LIKE YOU...
TO SHOOT OUR PROMO-TIONAL VIDEO FOR THIS SONG.

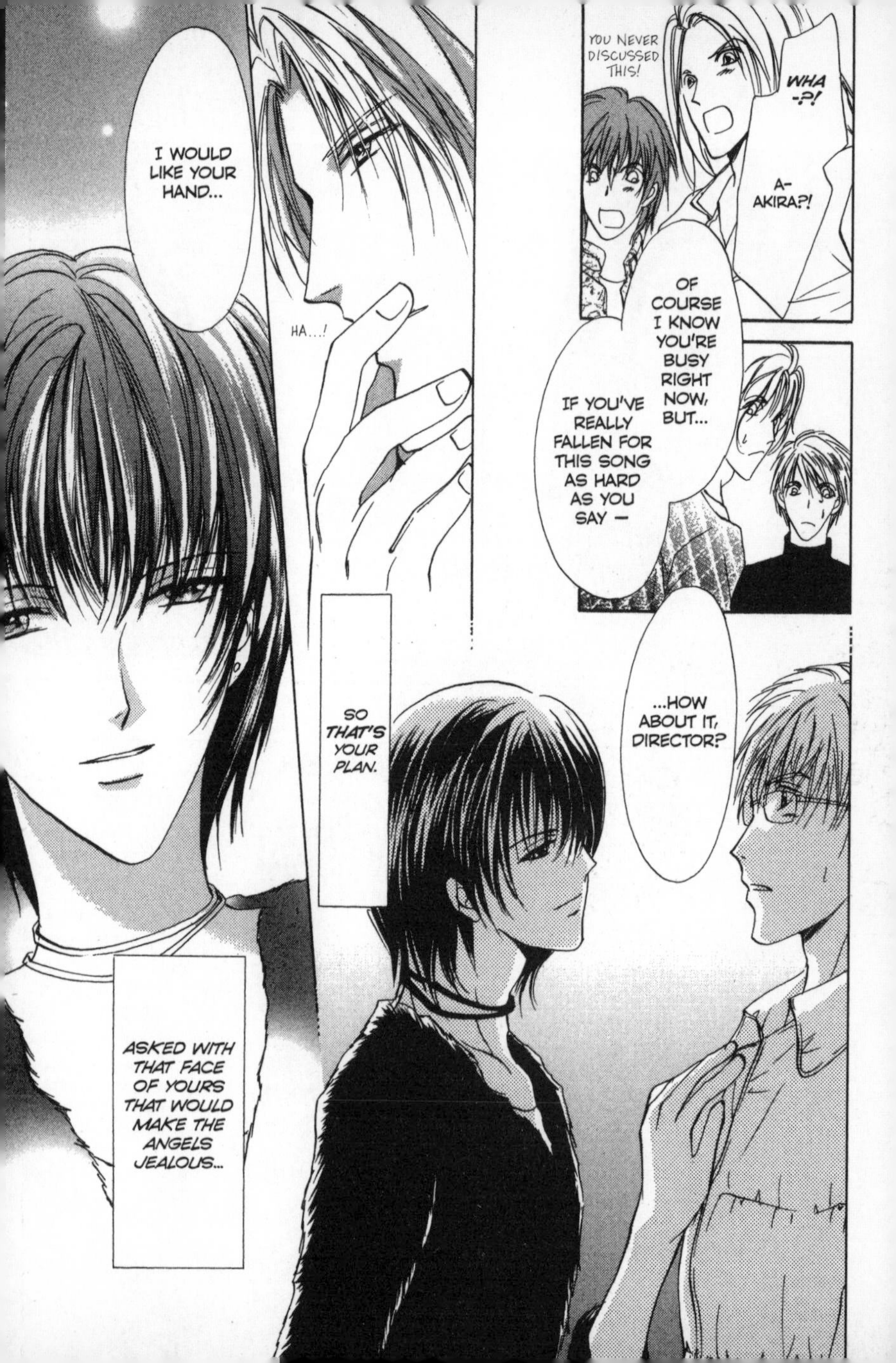
WHA-?!
A-AKIRA?!
YOU NEVER DISCUSSED THIS!
OF COURSE I KNOW YOU'RE BUSY RIGHT NOW, BUT...
IF YOU'VE REALLY FALLEN FOR THIS SONG AS HARD AS YOU SAY —
...HOW ABOUT IT, DIRECTOR?
SO *THAT'S* YOUR PLAN.
HA...!
I WOULD LIKE YOUR HAND...
ASKED WITH THAT FACE OF YOURS THAT WOULD MAKE THE ANGELS JEALOUS...

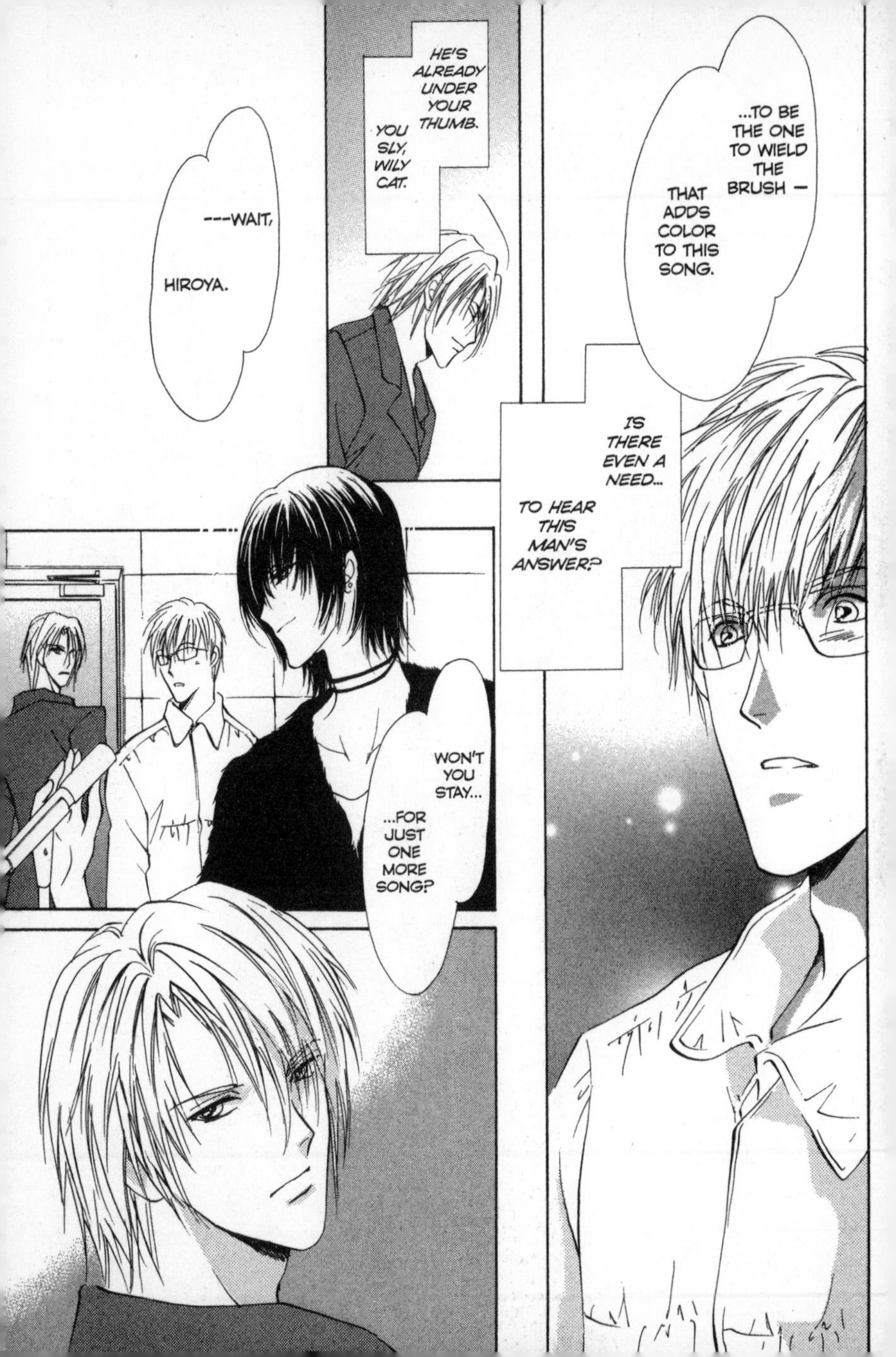
...TO BE THE ONE TO WIELD THE BRUSH —
THAT ADDS COLOR TO THIS SONG.
IS THERE EVEN A NEED...
TO HEAR THIS MAN'S ANSWER?
HE'S ALREADY UNDER YOUR THUMB.
YOU SLY, WILY CAT.
---WAIT,
HIROYA.
WON'T YOU STAY...
...FOR JUST ONE MORE SONG?

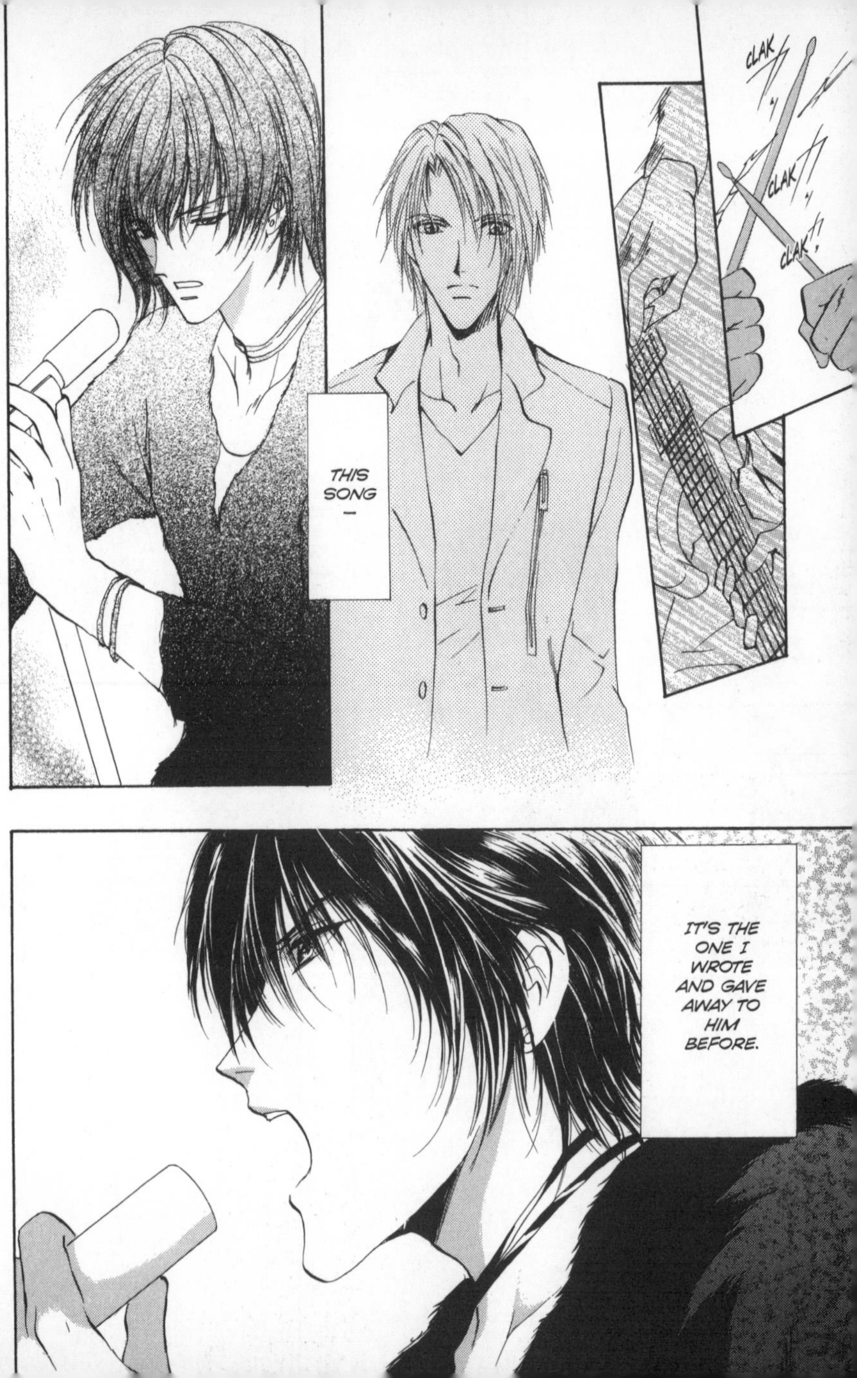
CLAK
CLAK
CLAK!!
THIS SONG —
IT'S THE ONE I WROTE AND GAVE AWAY TO HIM BEFORE.

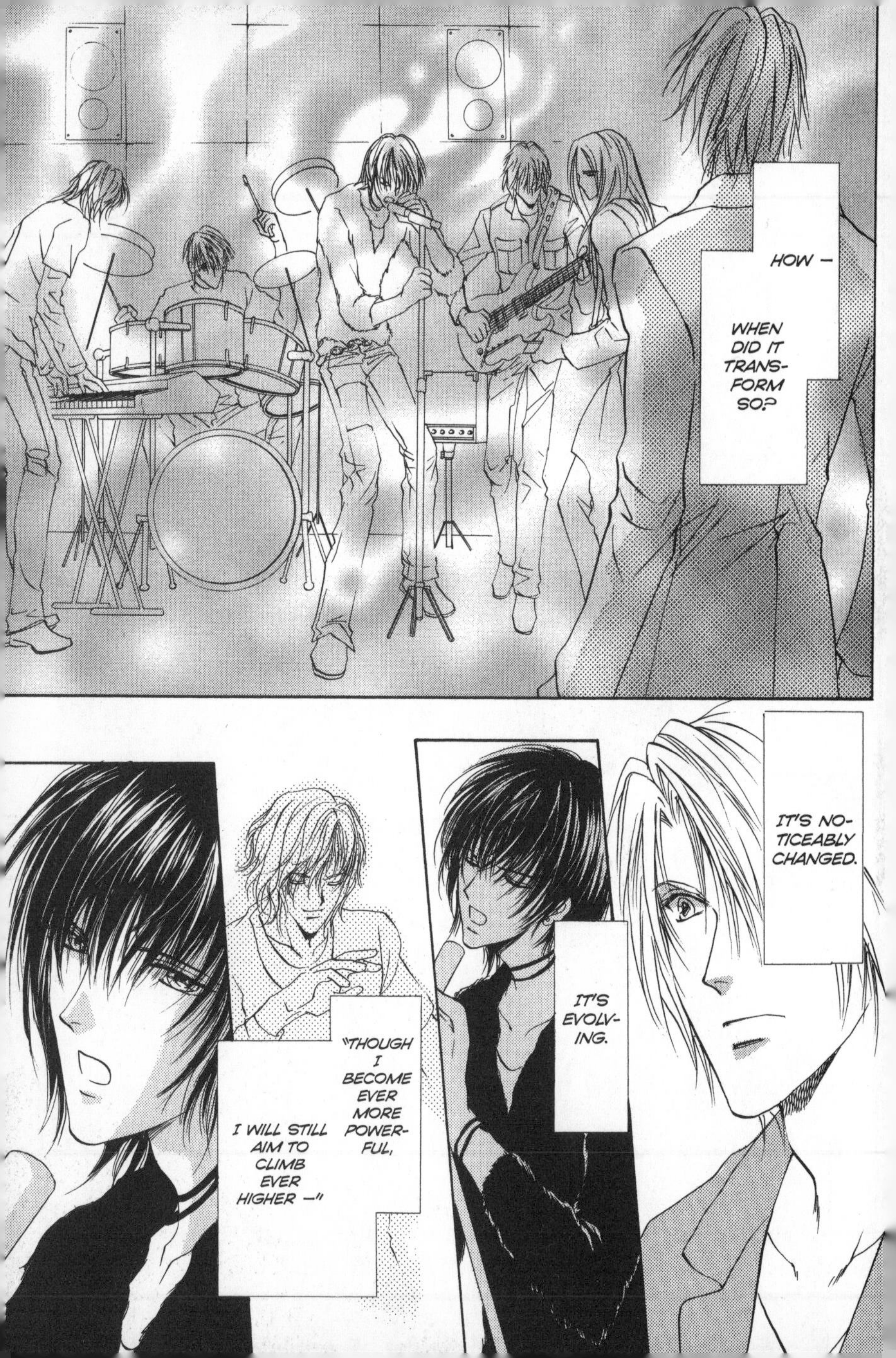
HOW —
WHEN DID IT TRANSFORM SO?
IT'S NOTICEABLY CHANGED.
IT'S EVOLVING.
"THOUGH I BECOME EVER MORE POWERFUL,
I WILL STILL AIM TO CLIMB EVER HIGHER —"

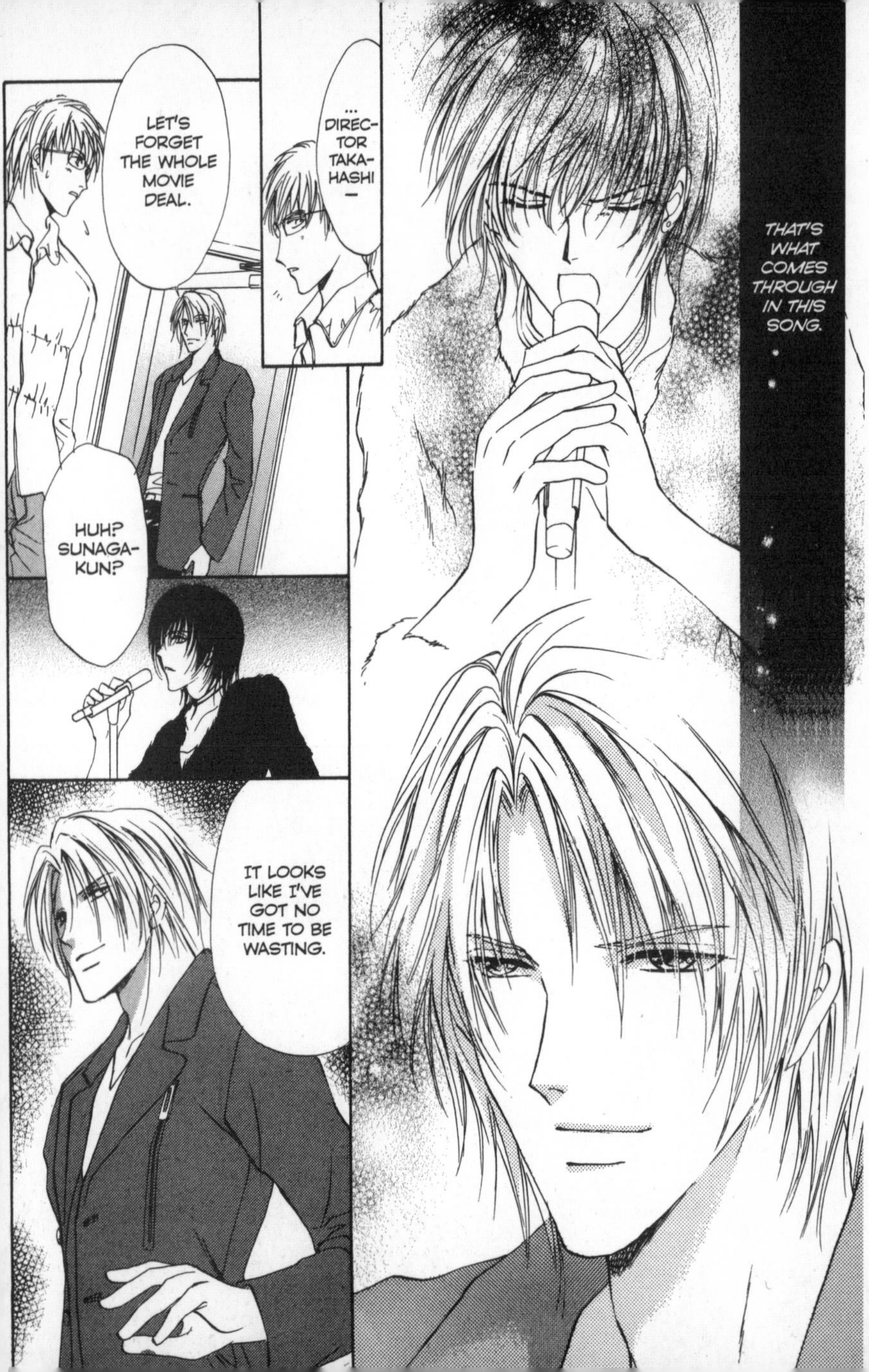
THAT'S WHAT COMES THROUGH IN THIS SONG.
...DIRECTOR TAKAHASHI—
LET'S FORGET THE WHOLE MOVIE DEAL.
HUH? SUNAGA-KUN?
IT LOOKS LIKE I'VE GOT NO TIME TO BE WASTING.

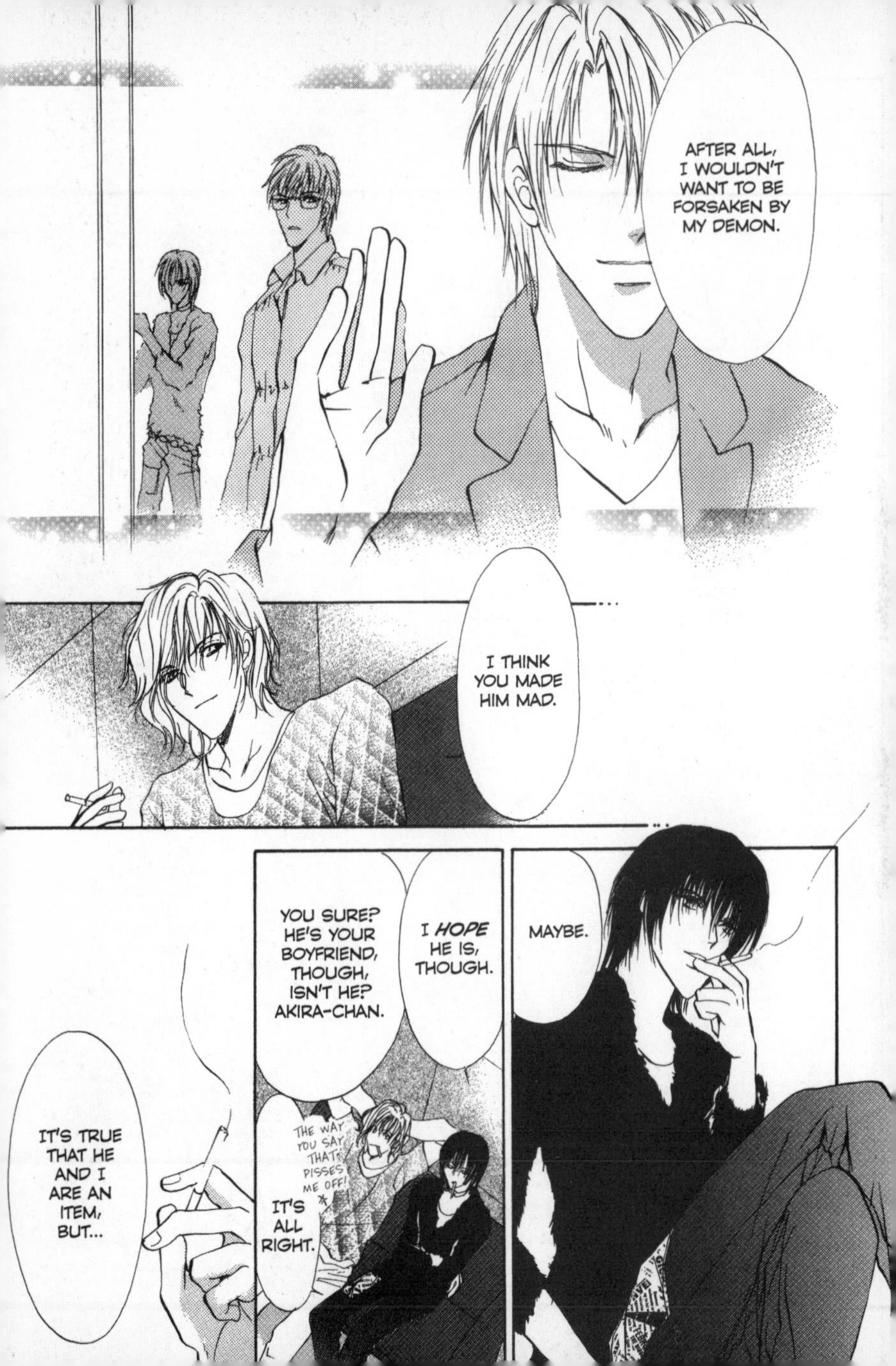
AFTER ALL, I WOULDN'T WANT TO BE FORSAKEN BY MY DEMON.
I THINK YOU MADE HIM MAD.
MAYBE.
I *HOPE* HE IS, THOUGH.
YOU SURE? HE'S YOUR BOYFRIEND, THOUGH, ISN'T HE? AKIRA-CHAN.
THE WAY YOU SAY THAT PISSES ME OFF!
IT'S ALL RIGHT.
IT'S TRUE THAT HE AND I ARE AN ITEM, BUT...

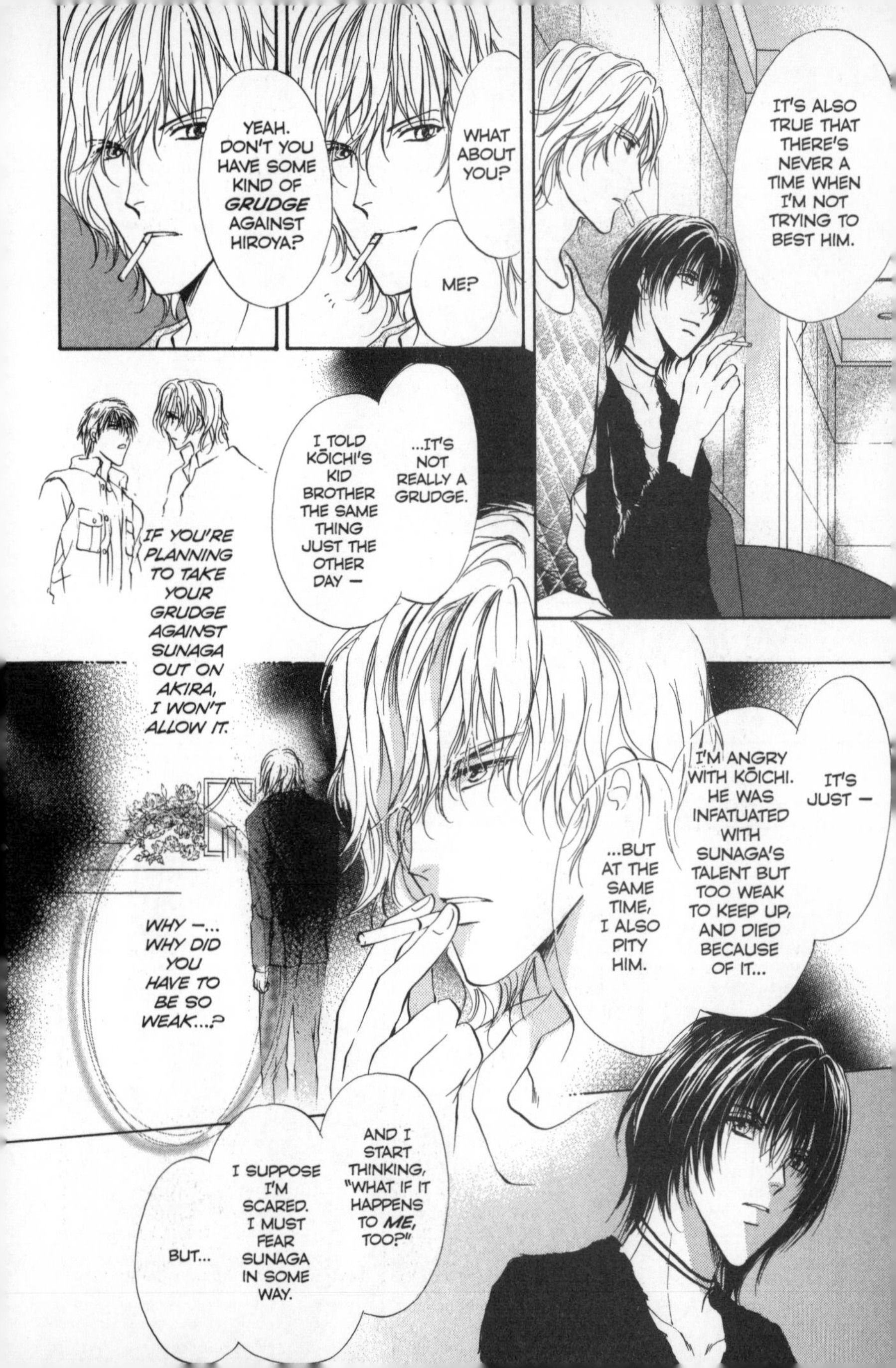
IT'S ALSO TRUE THAT THERE'S NEVER A TIME WHEN I'M NOT TRYING TO BEST HIM.
WHAT ABOUT YOU?
ME?
YEAH. DON'T YOU HAVE SOME KIND OF *GRUDGE* AGAINST HIROYA?
...IT'S NOT REALLY A GRUDGE.
I TOLD KŌICHI'S KID BROTHER THE SAME THING JUST THE OTHER DAY —
IF YOU'RE PLANNING TO TAKE YOUR GRUDGE AGAINST SUNAGA OUT ON AKIRA, I WON'T ALLOW IT.
IT'S JUST —
I'M ANGRY WITH KŌICHI. HE WAS INFATUATED WITH SUNAGA'S TALENT BUT TOO WEAK TO KEEP UP, AND DIED BECAUSE OF IT...
...BUT AT THE SAME TIME, I ALSO PITY HIM.
WHY —... WHY DID YOU HAVE TO BE SO WEAK...?
AND I START THINKING, "WHAT IF IT HAPPENS TO *ME*, TOO?"
I SUPPOSE I'M SCARED. I MUST FEAR SUNAGA IN SOME WAY.
BUT...

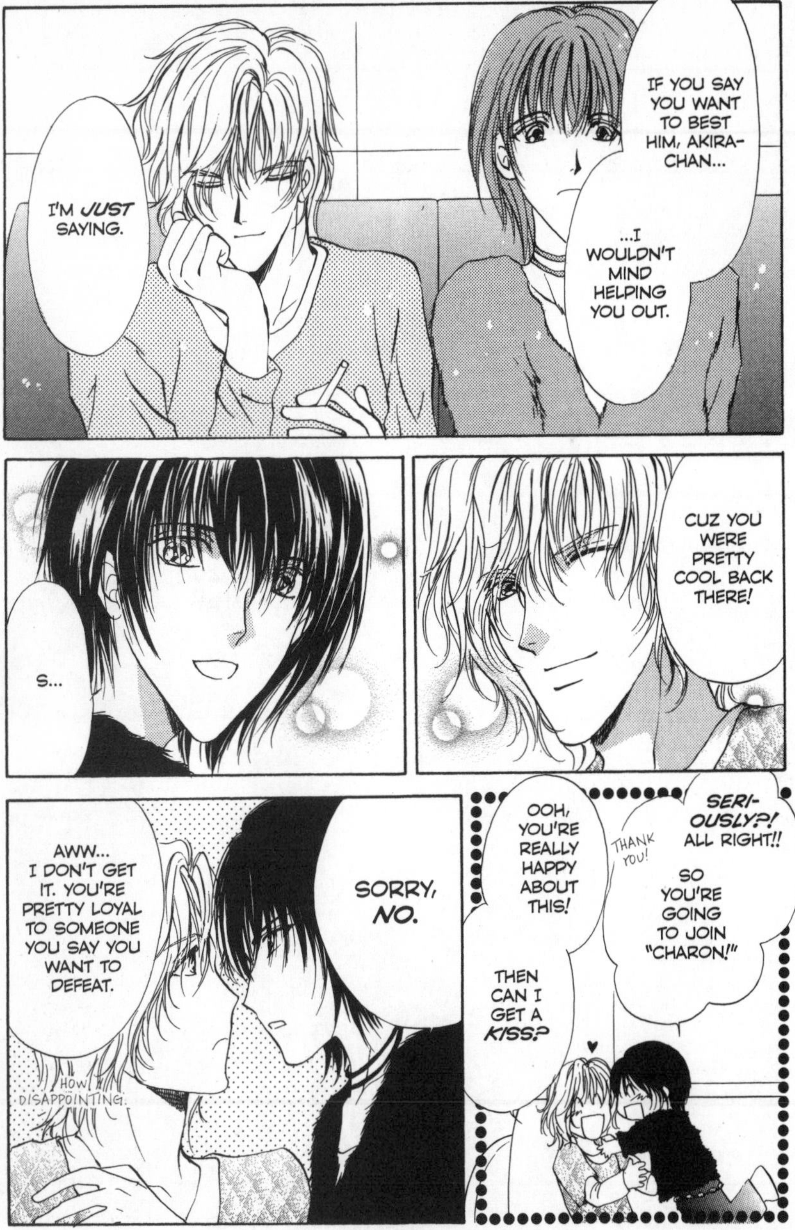
IF YOU SAY YOU WANT TO BEST HIM, AKIRA-CHAN...
...I WOULDN'T MIND HELPING YOU OUT.
I'M *JUST* SAYING.
CUZ YOU WERE PRETTY COOL BACK THERE!
S...
SERI-OUSLY?! ALL RIGHT!!
THANK YOU!
SO YOU'RE GOING TO JOIN "CHARON!"
OOH, YOU'RE REALLY HAPPY ABOUT THIS!
THEN CAN I GET A *KISS?*
SORRY, *NO.*
AWW... I DON'T GET IT. YOU'RE PRETTY LOYAL TO SOMEONE YOU SAY YOU WANT TO DEFEAT.
HOW DISAPPOINTING.

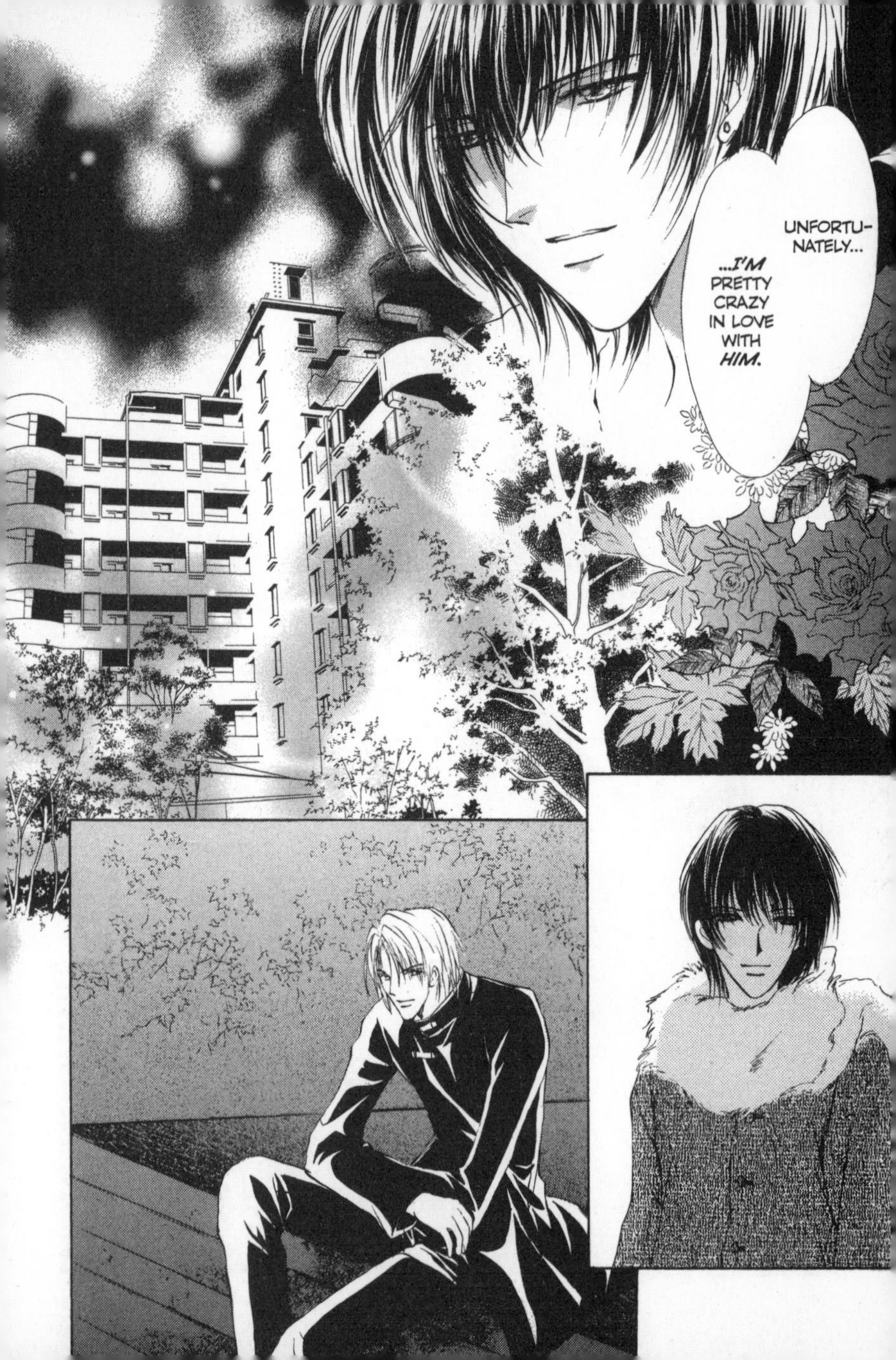
UNFORTU-
NATELY...
...I'M PRETTY CRAZY IN LOVE WITH *HIM*.

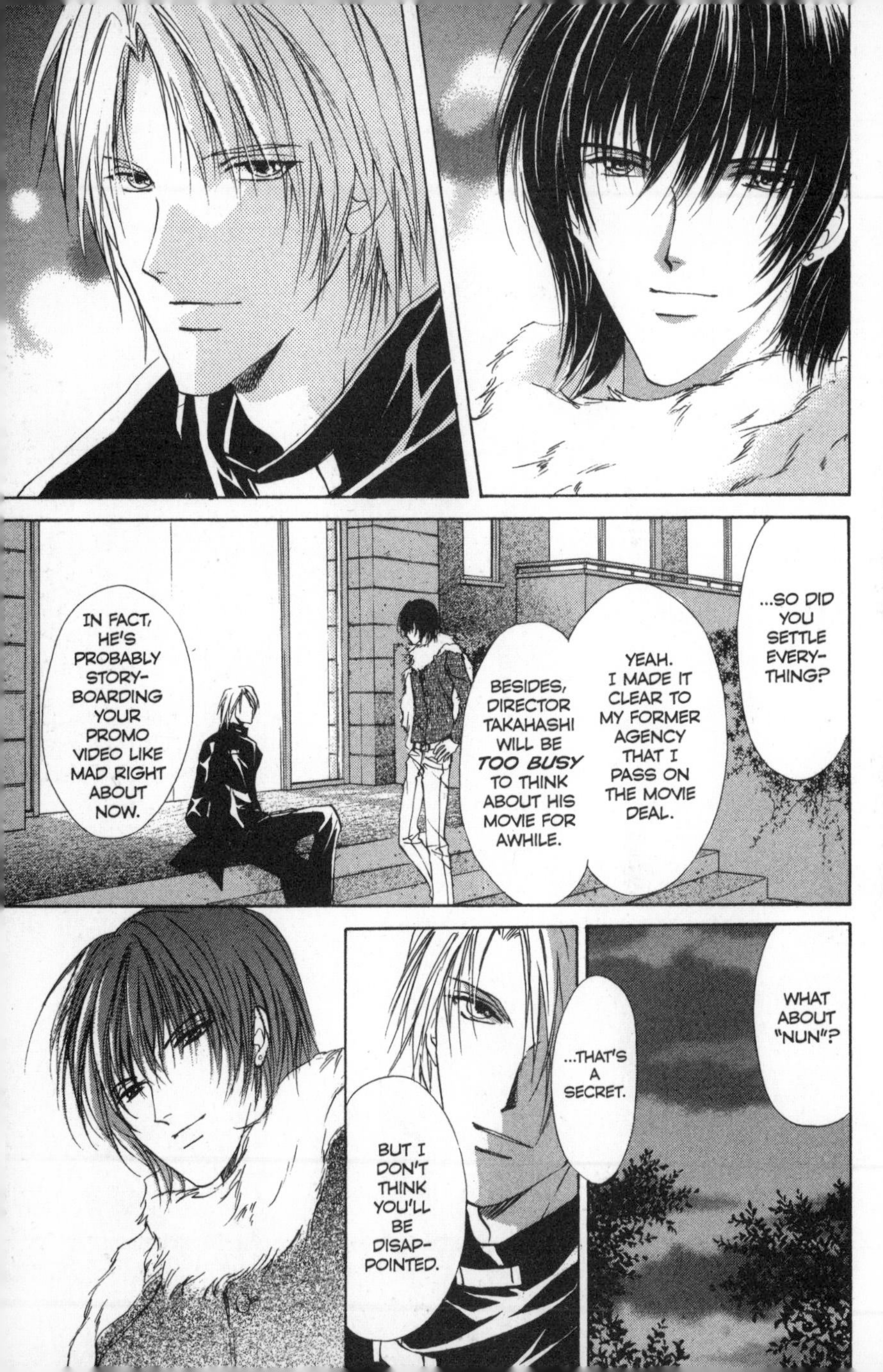
...SO DID YOU SETTLE EVERY-THING?
YEAH. I MADE IT CLEAR TO MY FORMER AGENCY THAT I PASS ON THE MOVIE DEAL.
BESIDES, DIRECTOR TAKAHASHI WILL BE *TOO BUSY* TO THINK ABOUT HIS MOVIE FOR AWHILE.
IN FACT, HE'S PROBABLY STORY-BOARDING YOUR PROMO VIDEO LIKE MAD RIGHT ABOUT NOW.
WHAT ABOUT "NUN"?
...THAT'S A SECRET.
BUT I DON'T THINK YOU'LL BE DISAP-POINTED.

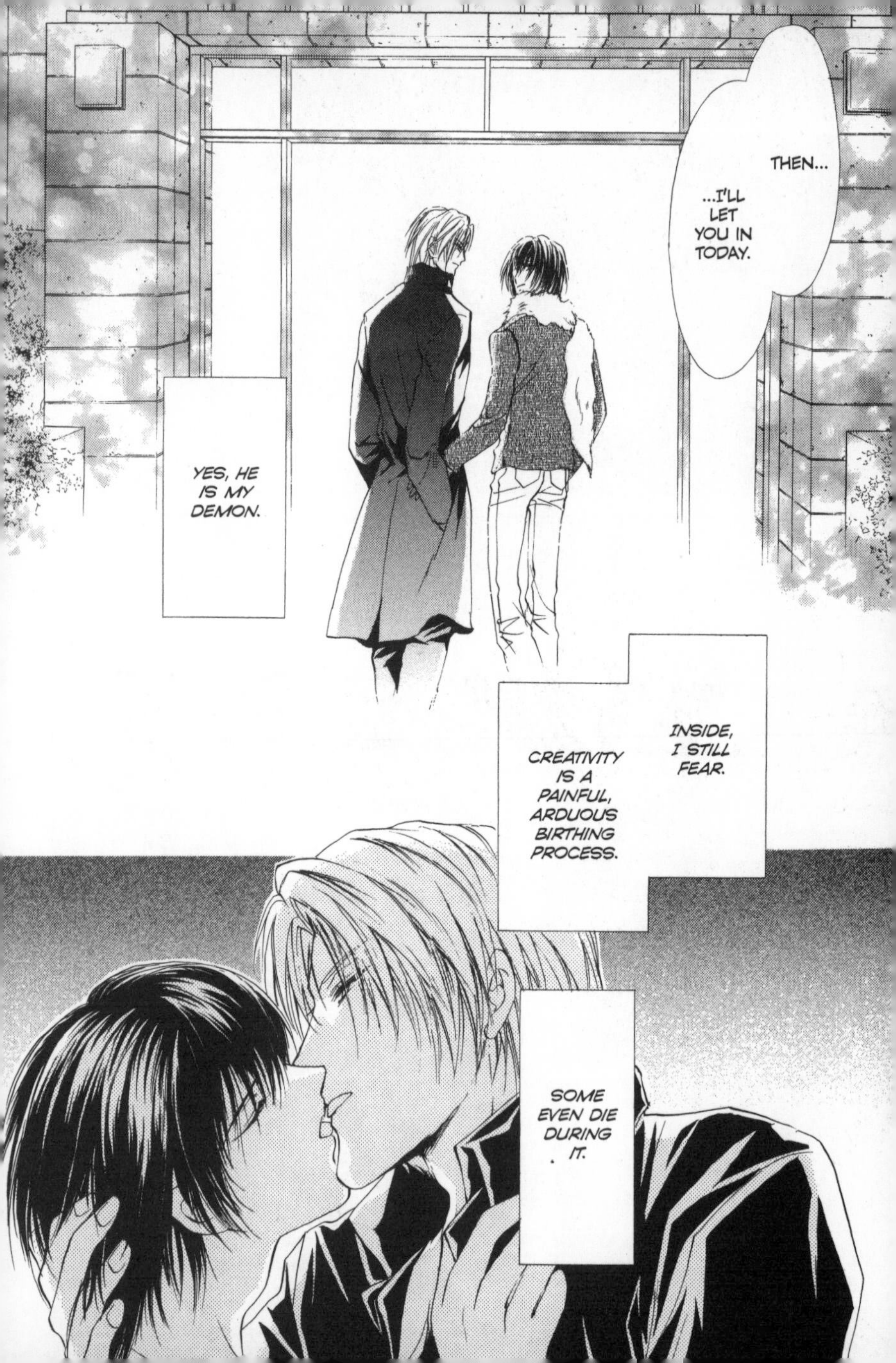
THEN...
...I'LL LET YOU IN TODAY.
YES, HE IS MY DEMON.
INSIDE, I STILL FEAR.
CREATIVITY IS A PAINFUL, ARDUOUS BIRTHING PROCESS.
SOME EVEN DIE DURING IT.

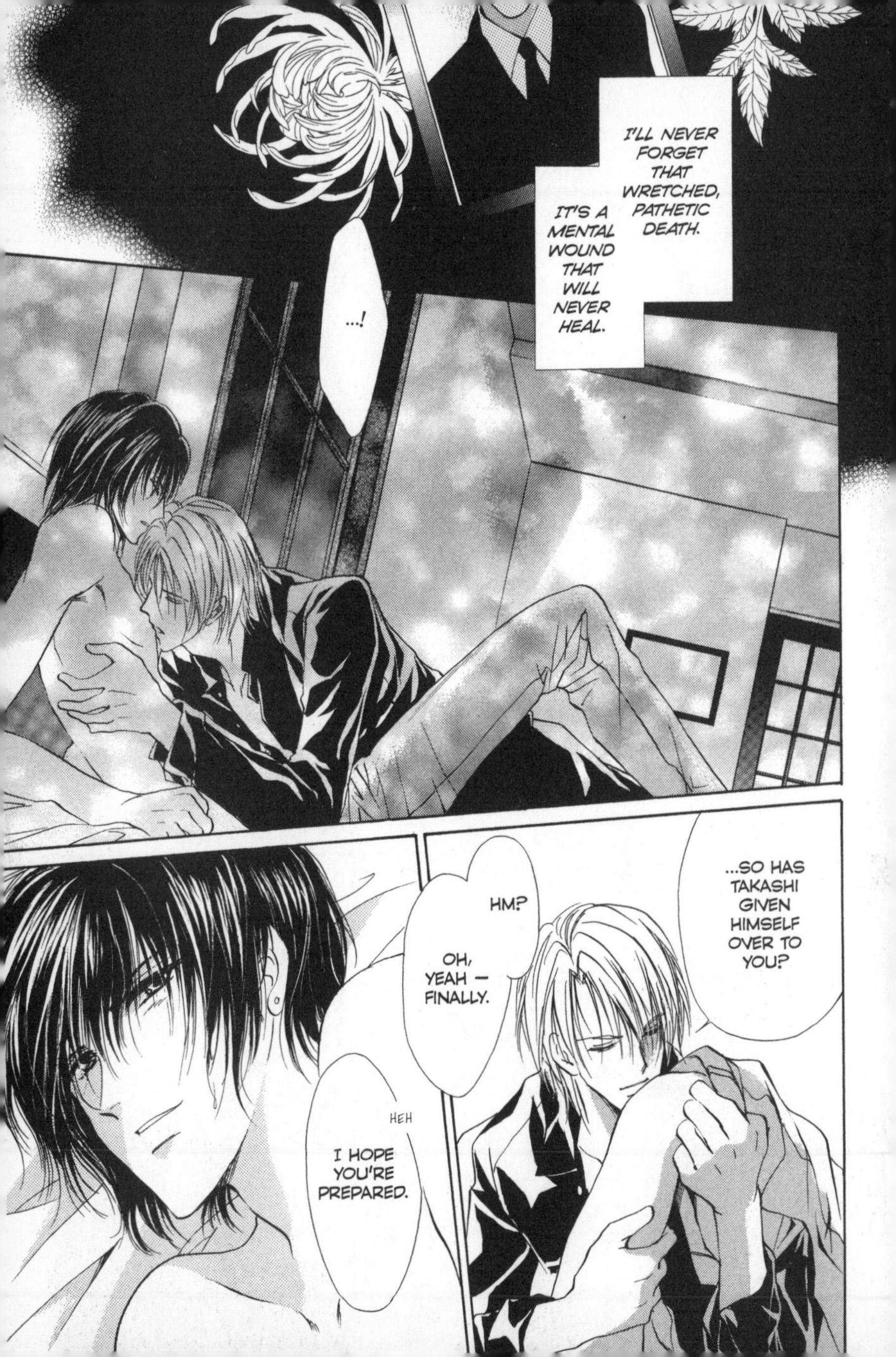
I'LL NEVER FORGET THAT WRETCHED, PATHETIC DEATH.
IT'S A MENTAL WOUND THAT WILL NEVER HEAL.
...!
...SO HAS TAKASHI GIVEN HIMSELF OVER TO YOU?
HM?
OH, YEAH — FINALLY.
HEH
I HOPE YOU'RE PREPARED.

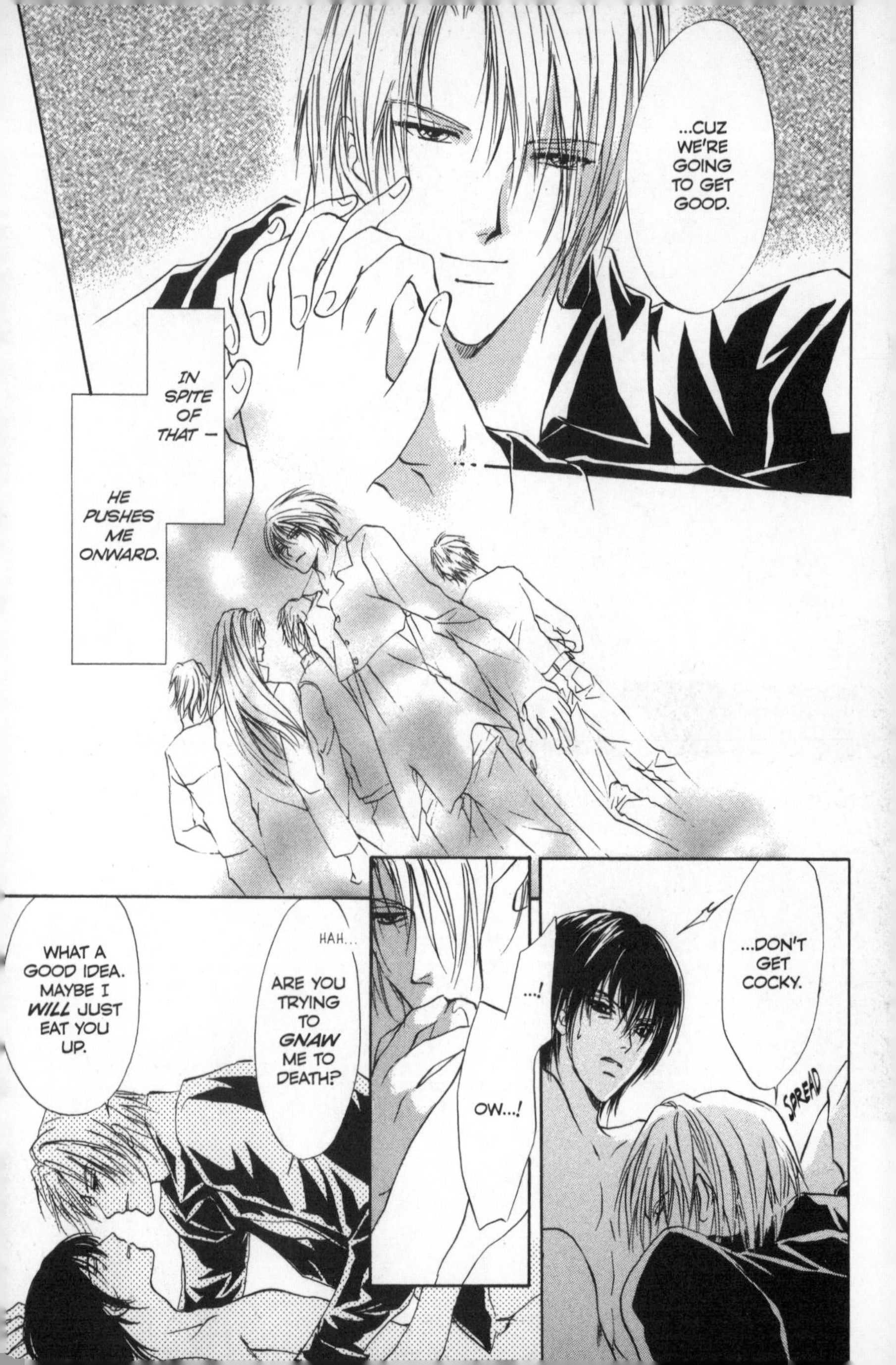

...CUZ WE'RE GOING TO GET GOOD.
IN SPITE OF THAT —
HE PUSHES ME ONWARD.
...DON'T GET COCKY.
SPREAD
...!
HAH...
ARE YOU TRYING TO GNAW ME TO DEATH?
OW...!
WHAT A GOOD IDEA. MAYBE I WILL JUST EAT YOU UP.

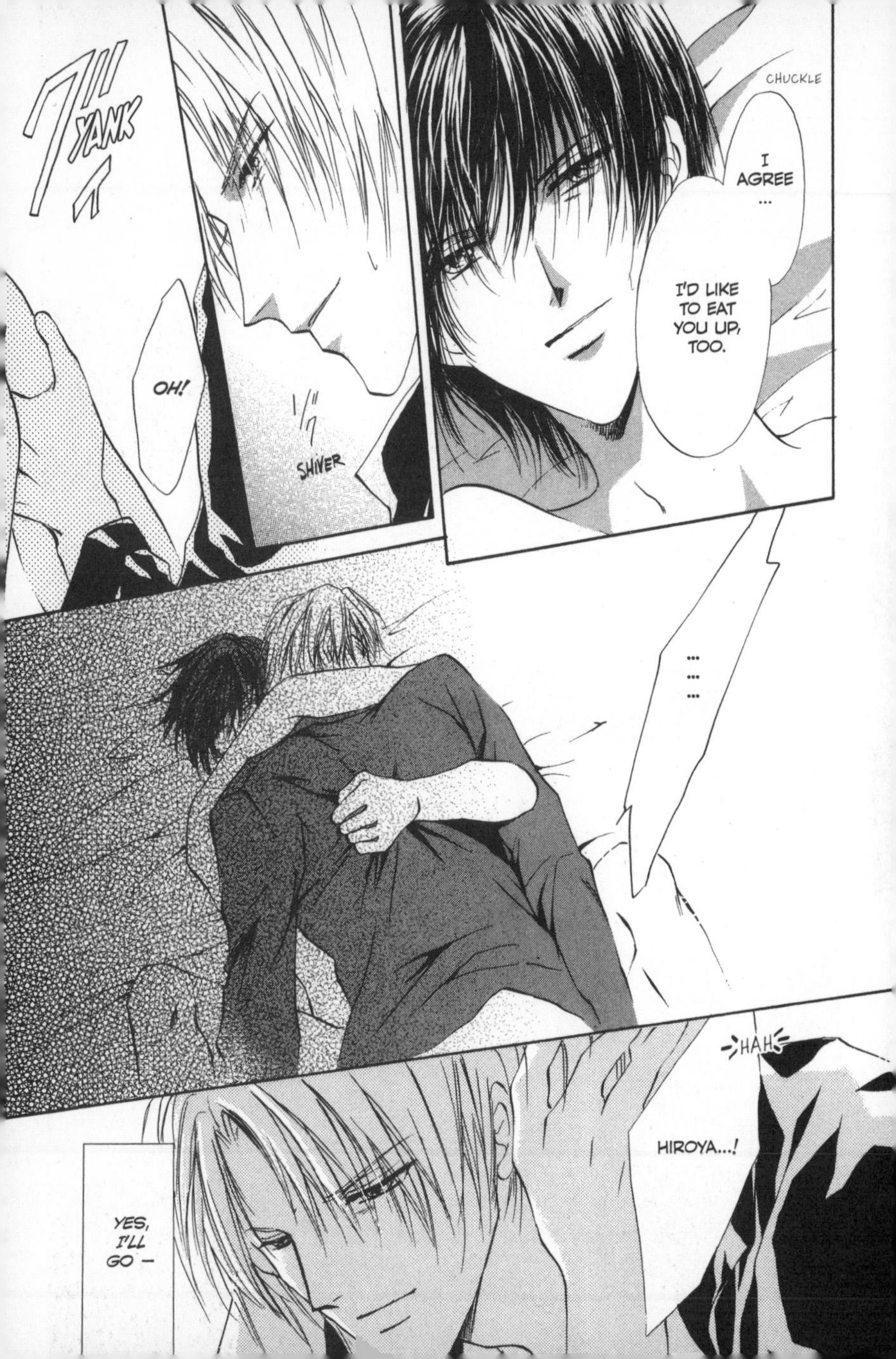
CHUCKLE
I AGREE ...
I'D LIKE TO EAT YOU UP, TOO.
SHIVER
YANK
OH!
... ...
HAH
HIROYA...!
YES, I'LL GO —

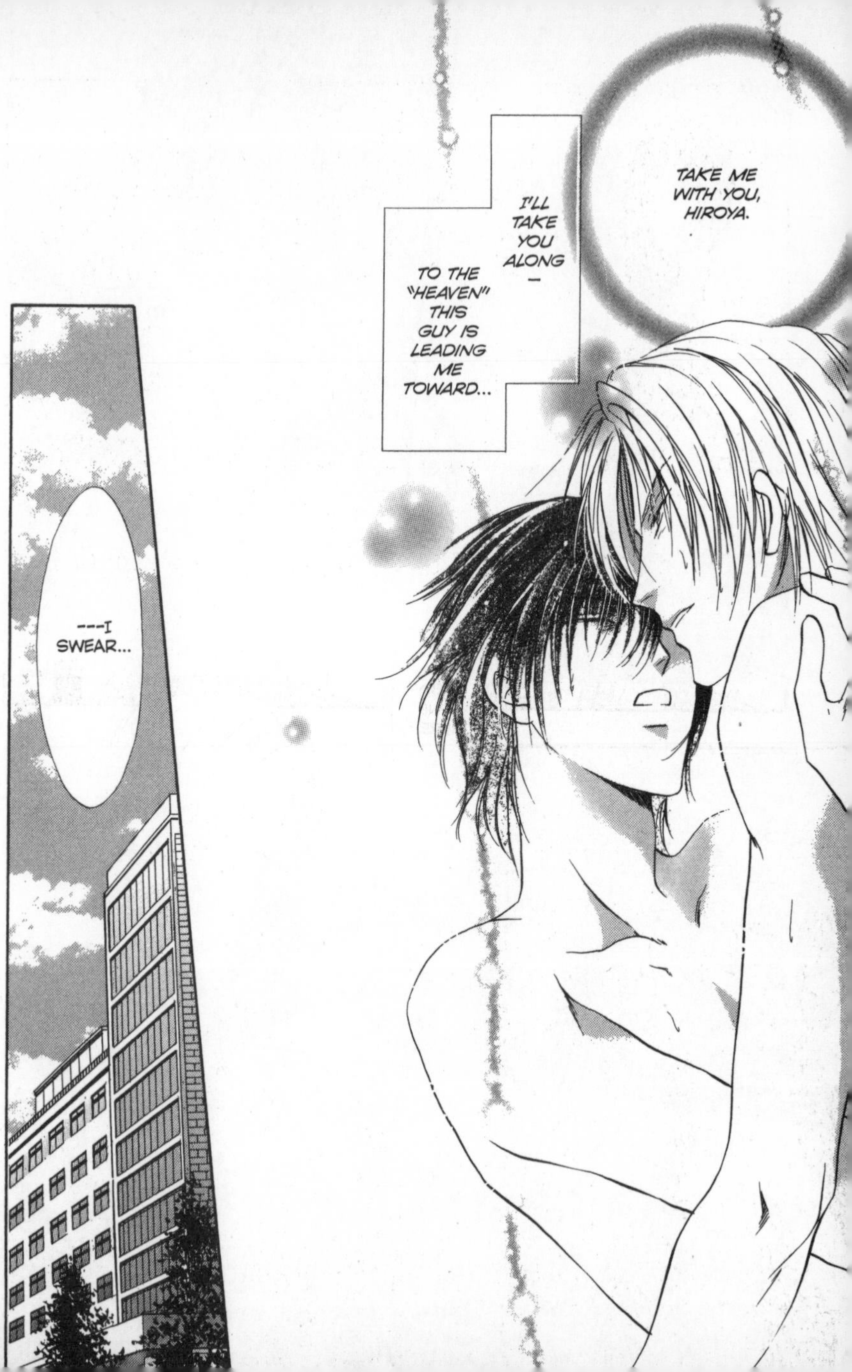
TAKE ME WITH YOU, HIROYA.
I'LL TAKE YOU ALONG —
TO THE "HEAVEN" THIS GUY IS LEADING ME TOWARD...
---I SWEAR...

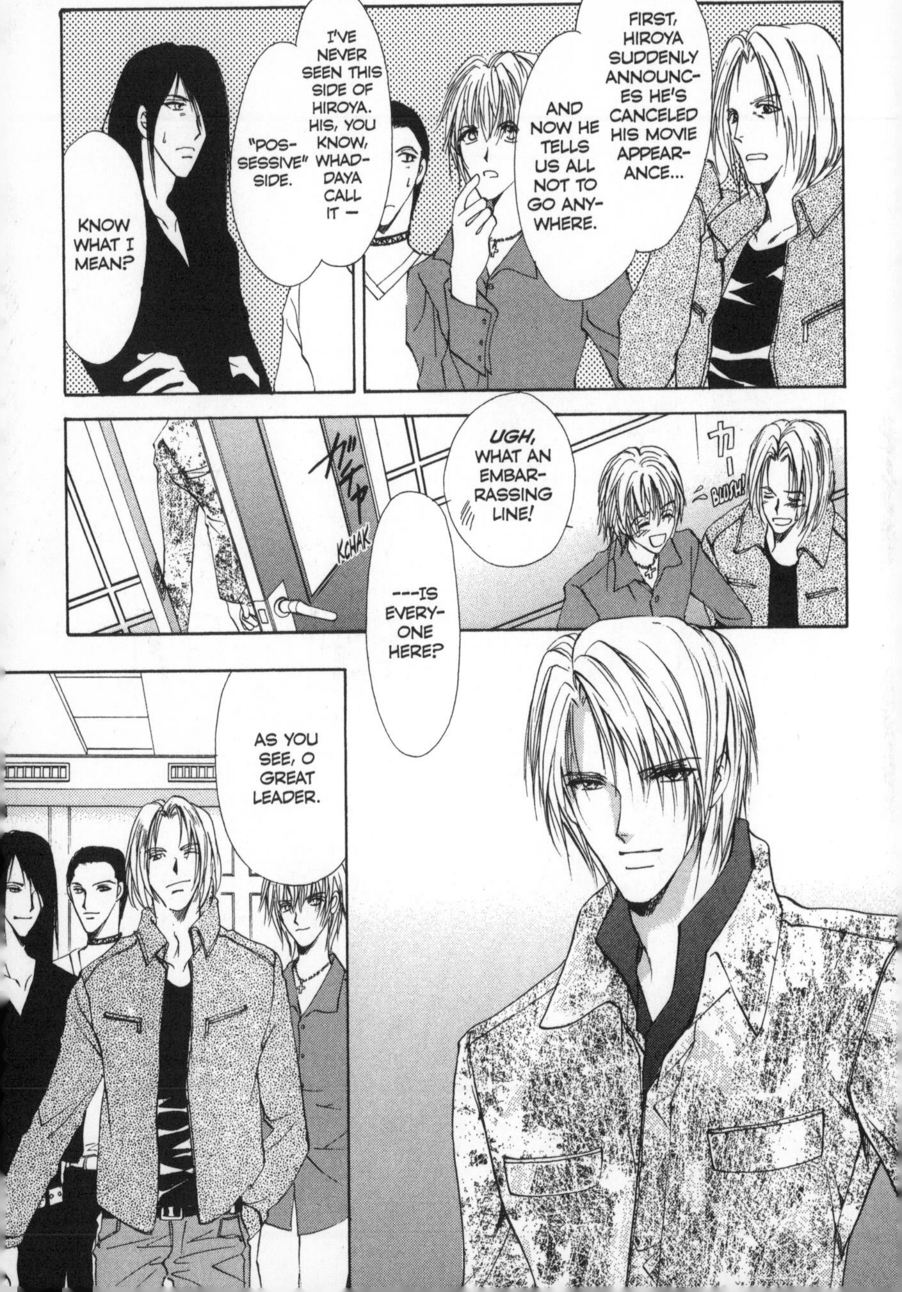
FIRST, HIROYA SUDDENLY ANNOUNCES HE'S CANCELED HIS MOVIE APPEARANCE...
AND NOW HE TELLS US ALL NOT TO GO ANYWHERE.
I'VE NEVER SEEN THIS SIDE OF HIROYA. HIS, YOU KNOW, WHADDAYA CALL IT —
"POSSESSIVE" SIDE.
KNOW WHAT I MEAN?
BLUSH!
UGH, WHAT AN EMBARRASSING LINE!
KCHAK
---IS EVERYONE HERE?
AS YOU SEE, O GREAT LEADER.

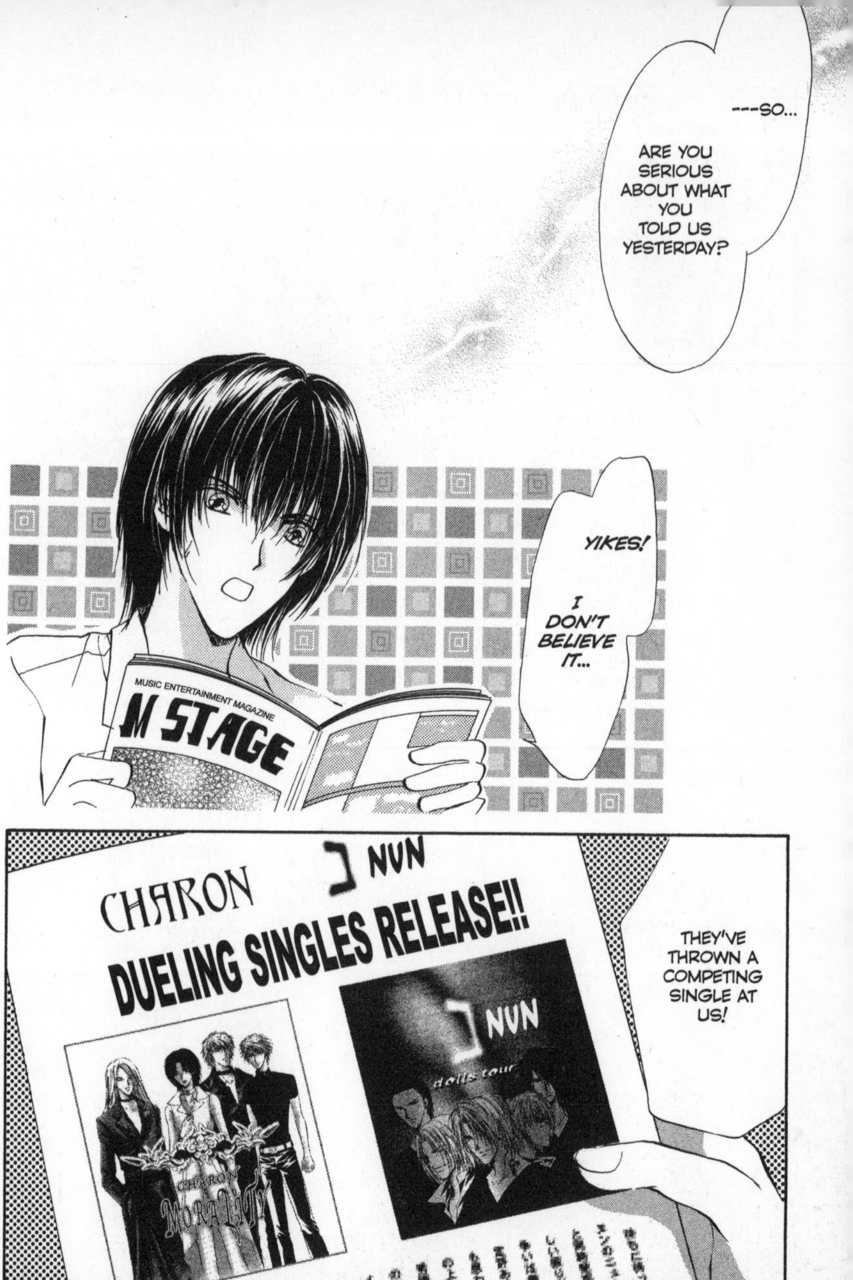
---SO...
ARE YOU SERIOUS ABOUT WHAT YOU TOLD US YESTERDAY?
YIKES!
I DON'T BELIEVE IT...
MUSIC ENTERTAINMENT MAGAZINE
M STAGE
THEY'VE THROWN A COMPETING SINGLE AT US!
CHARON
NUN
DUELING SINGLES RELEASE!!
NUN

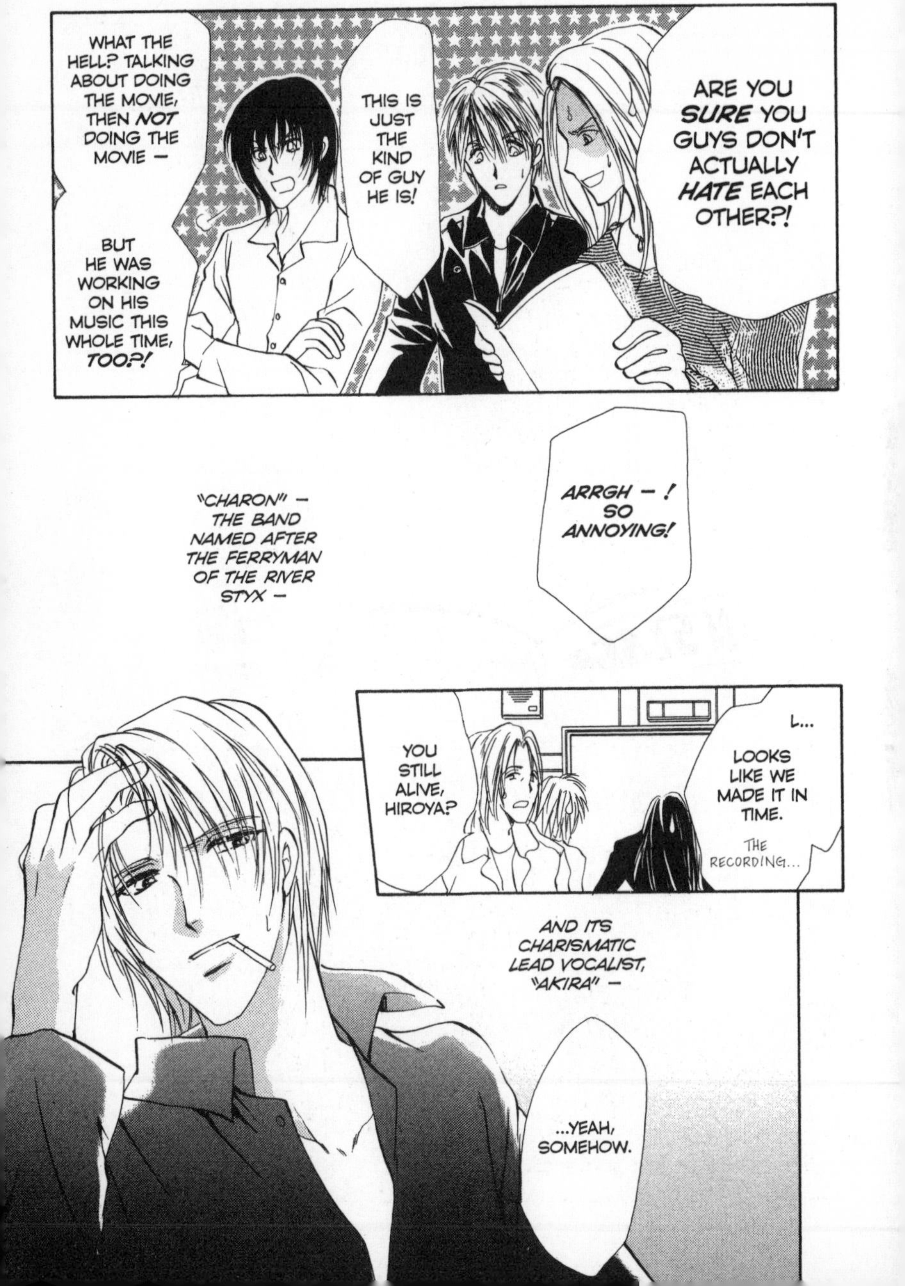
ARE YOU *SURE* YOU GUYS DON'T ACTUALLY *HATE* EACH OTHER?!
THIS IS JUST THE KIND OF GUY HE IS!
WHAT THE HELL? TALKING ABOUT DOING THE MOVIE, THEN *NOT* DOING THE MOVIE –
BUT HE WAS WORKING ON HIS MUSIC THIS WHOLE TIME, *TOO?!*
ARRGH – ! SO ANNOYING!
"CHARON" – THE BAND NAMED AFTER THE FERRYMAN OF THE RIVER STYX –
L...
LOOKS LIKE WE MADE IT IN TIME.
THE RECORDING...
YOU STILL ALIVE, HIROYA?
AND ITS CHARISMATIC LEAD VOCALIST, "AKIRA" –
...YEAH, SOMEHOW.

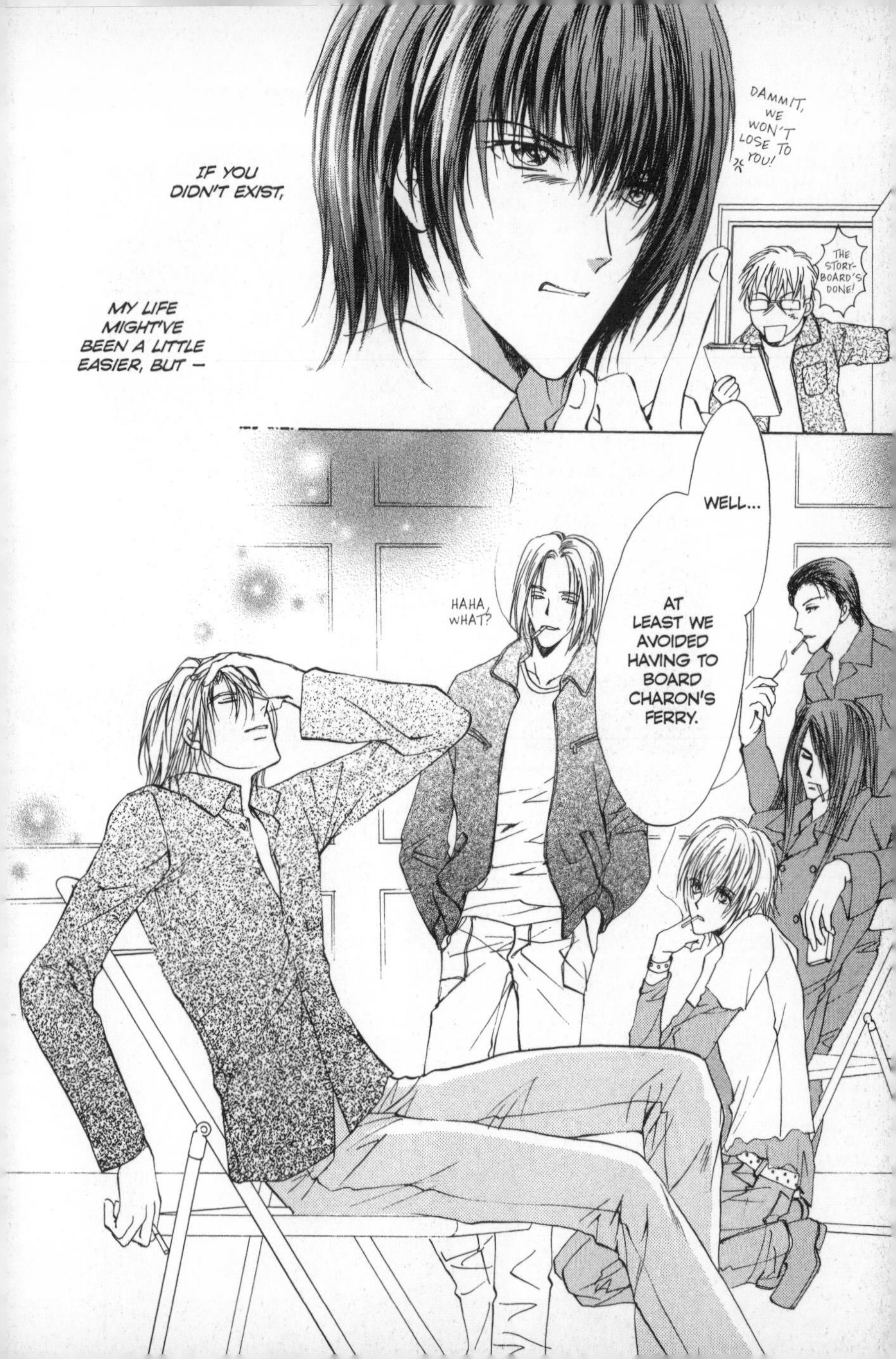
DAMMIT, WE WON'T LOSE TO YOU!
THE STORY-BOARD'S DONE!
IF YOU DIDN'T EXIST,
MY LIFE MIGHT'VE BEEN A LITTLE EASIER, BUT –
WELL...
AT LEAST WE AVOIDED HAVING TO BOARD CHARON'S FERRY.
HAHA, WHAT?

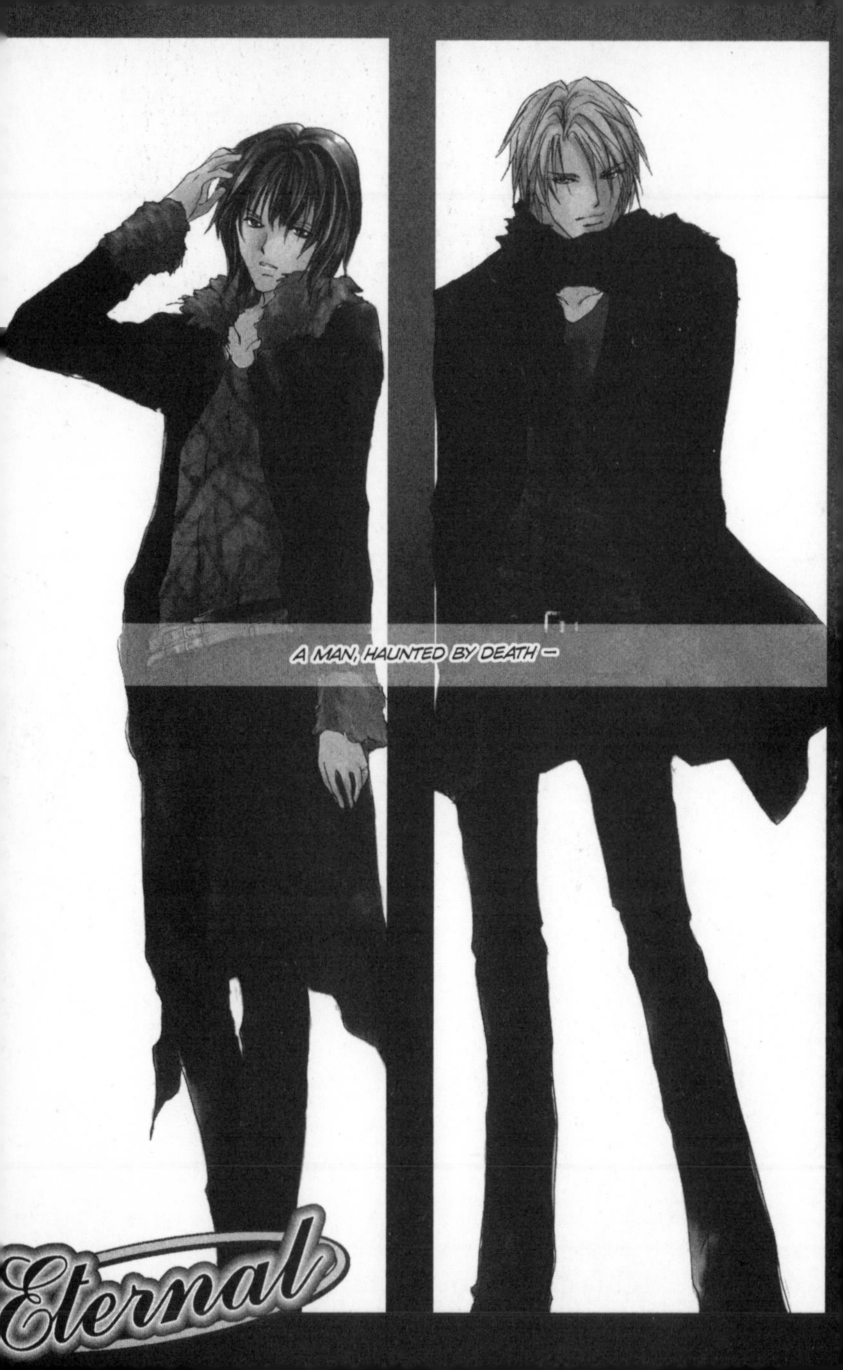
A MAN, HAUNTED BY DEATH –
Eternal

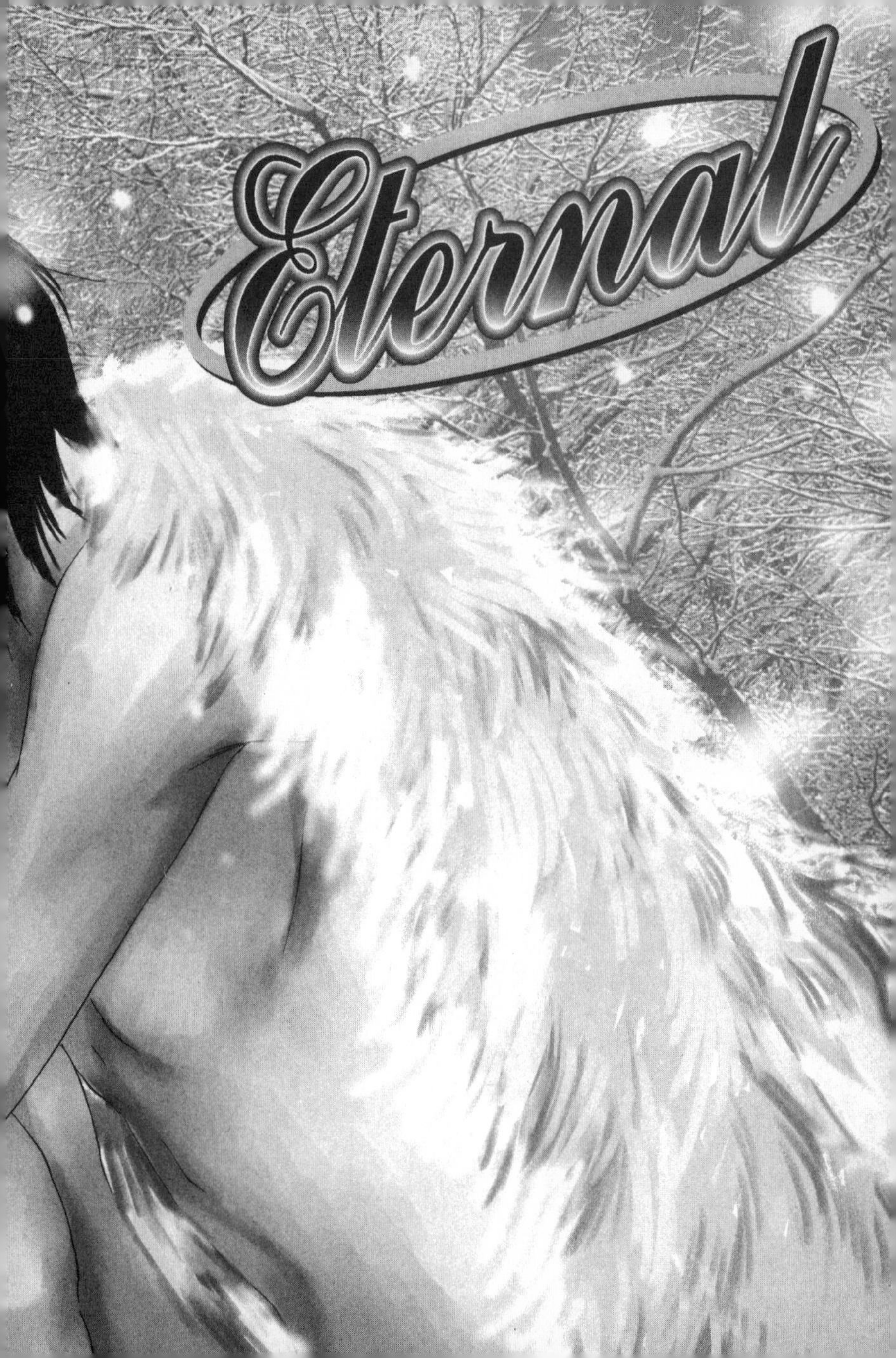
Eternal

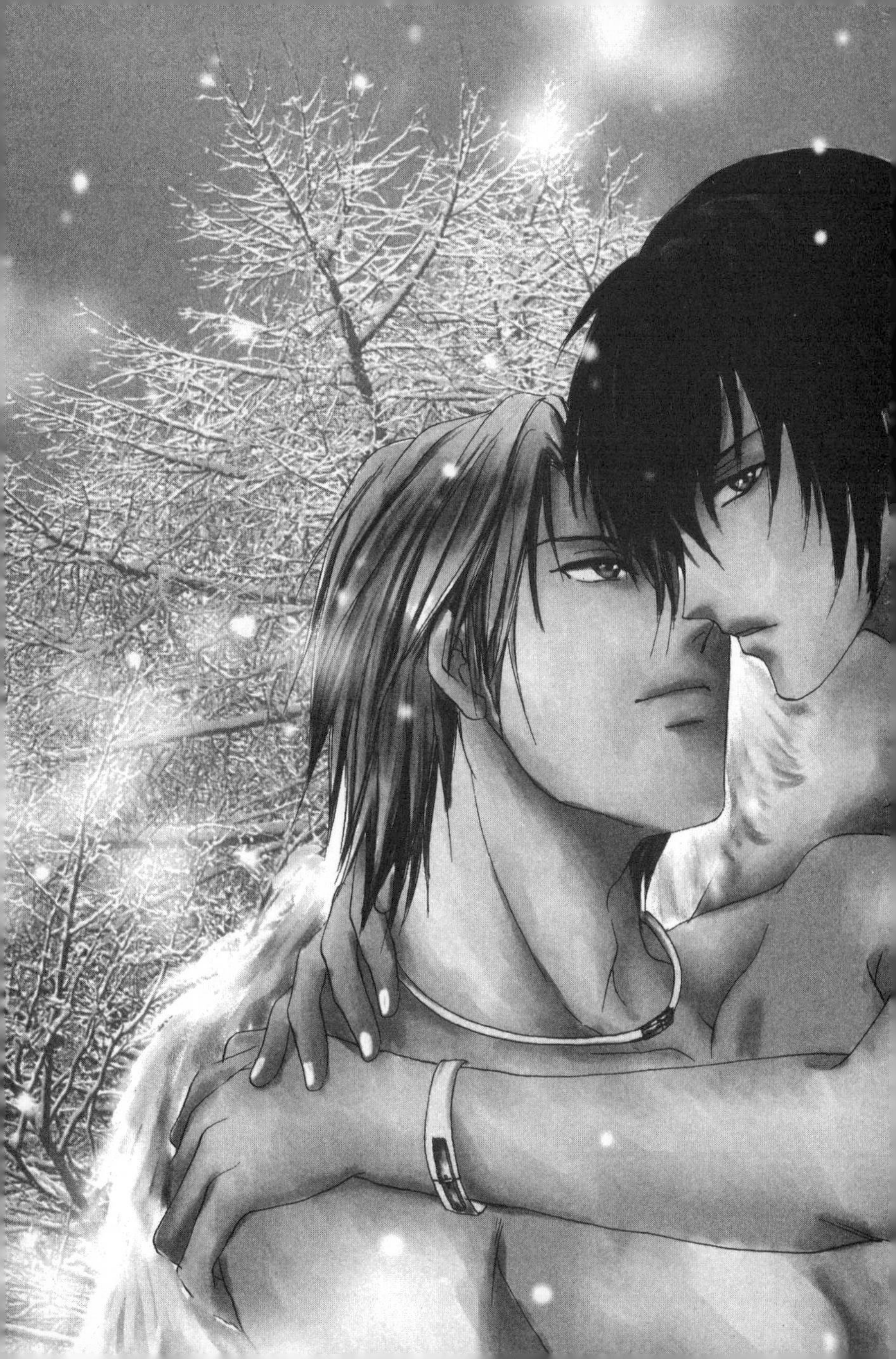

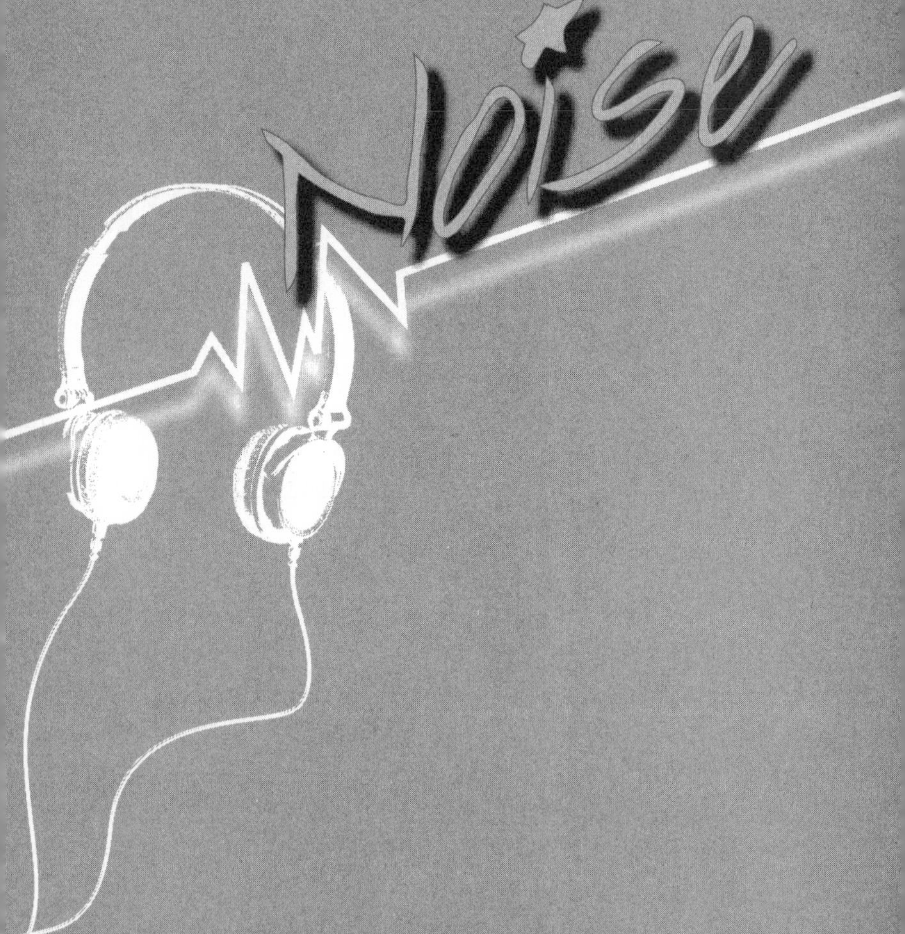
Noise

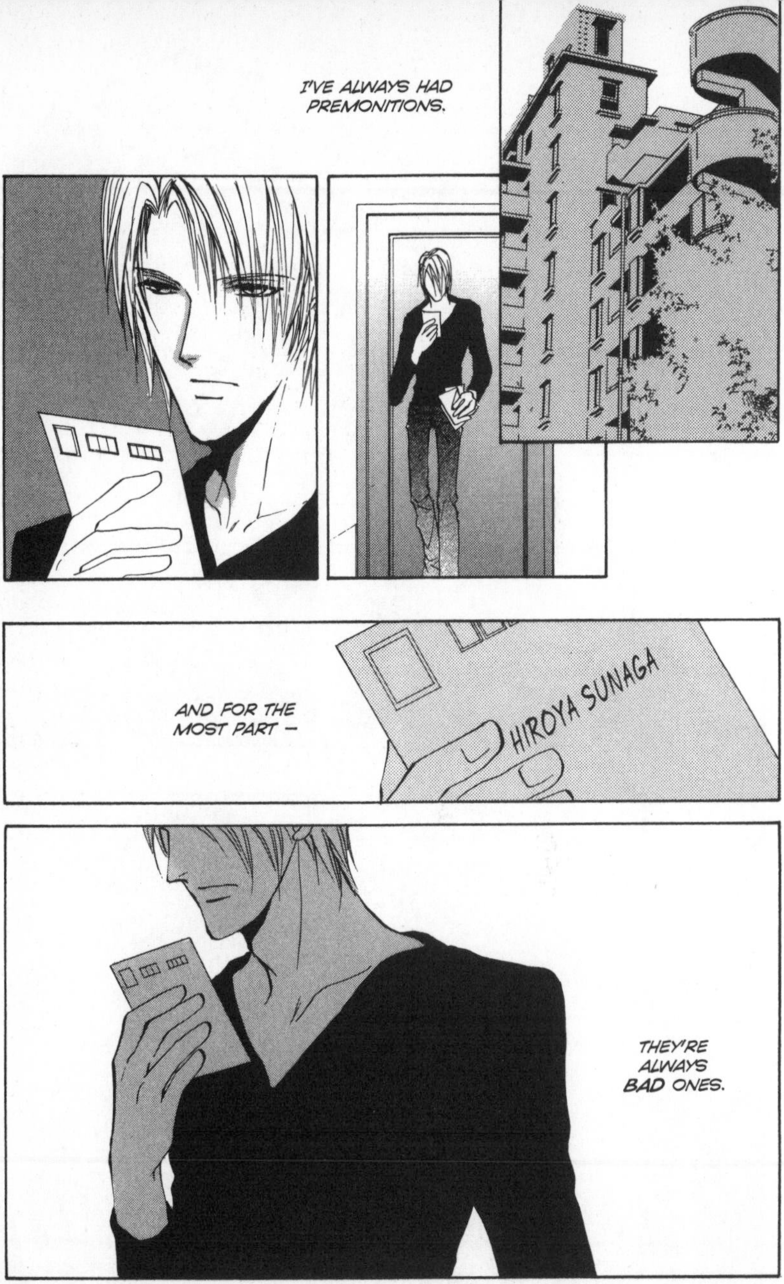
I'VE ALWAYS HAD PREMONITIONS.
HIROYA SUNAGA
AND FOR THE MOST PART –
THEY'RE ALWAYS BAD ONES.

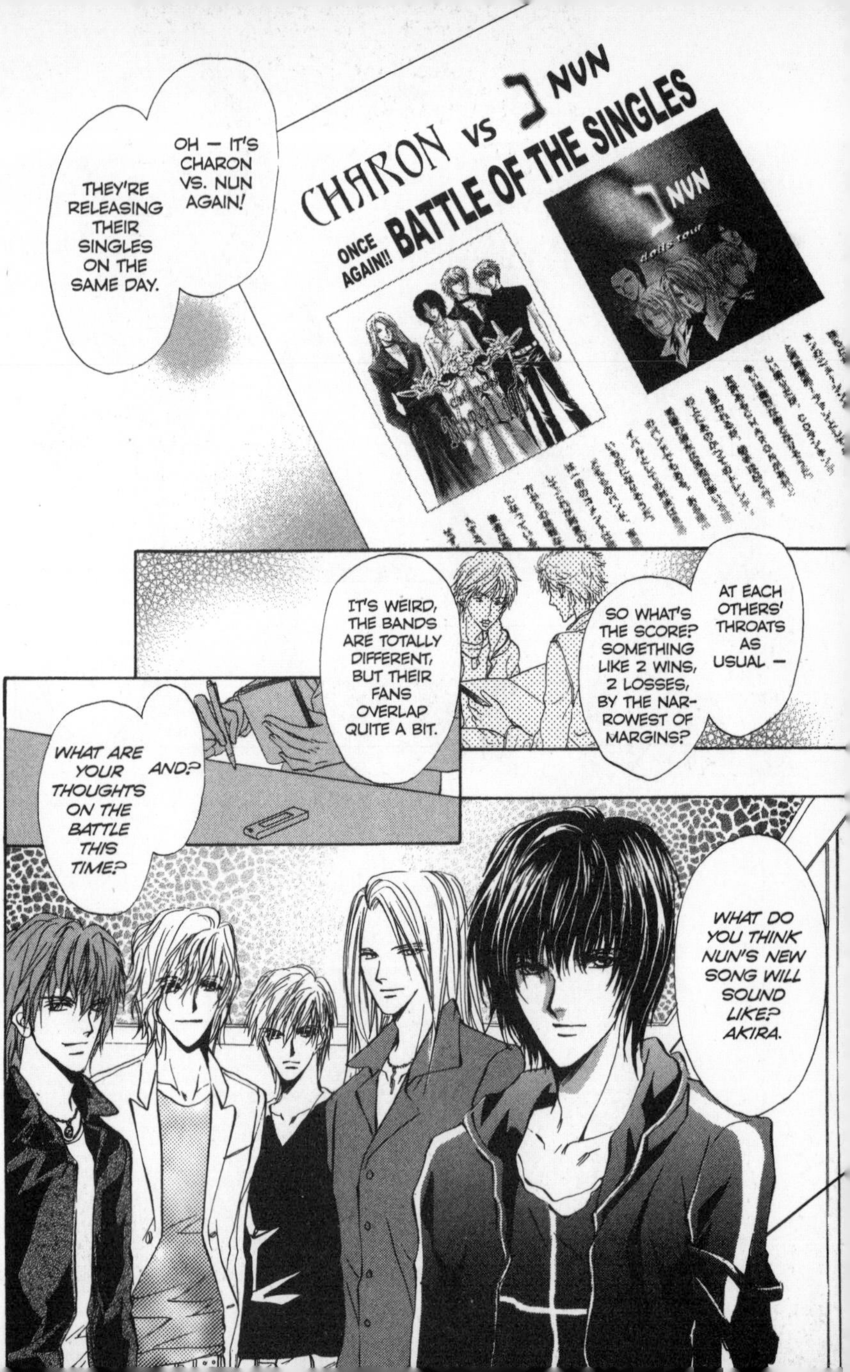
CHARON vs NUN
ONCE AGAIN!! BATTLE OF THE SINGLES
NUN
OH — IT'S CHARON VS. NUN AGAIN!
THEY'RE RELEASING THEIR SINGLES ON THE SAME DAY.
AT EACH OTHERS' THROATS AS USUAL —
SO WHAT'S THE SCORE? SOMETHING LIKE 2 WINS, 2 LOSSES, BY THE NAR-ROWEST OF MARGINS?
IT'S WEIRD, THE BANDS ARE TOTALLY DIFFERENT, BUT THEIR FANS OVERLAP QUITE A BIT.
AND?
WHAT ARE YOUR THOUGHTS ON THE BATTLE THIS TIME?
WHAT DO YOU THINK NUN'S NEW SONG WILL SOUND LIKE? AKIRA.

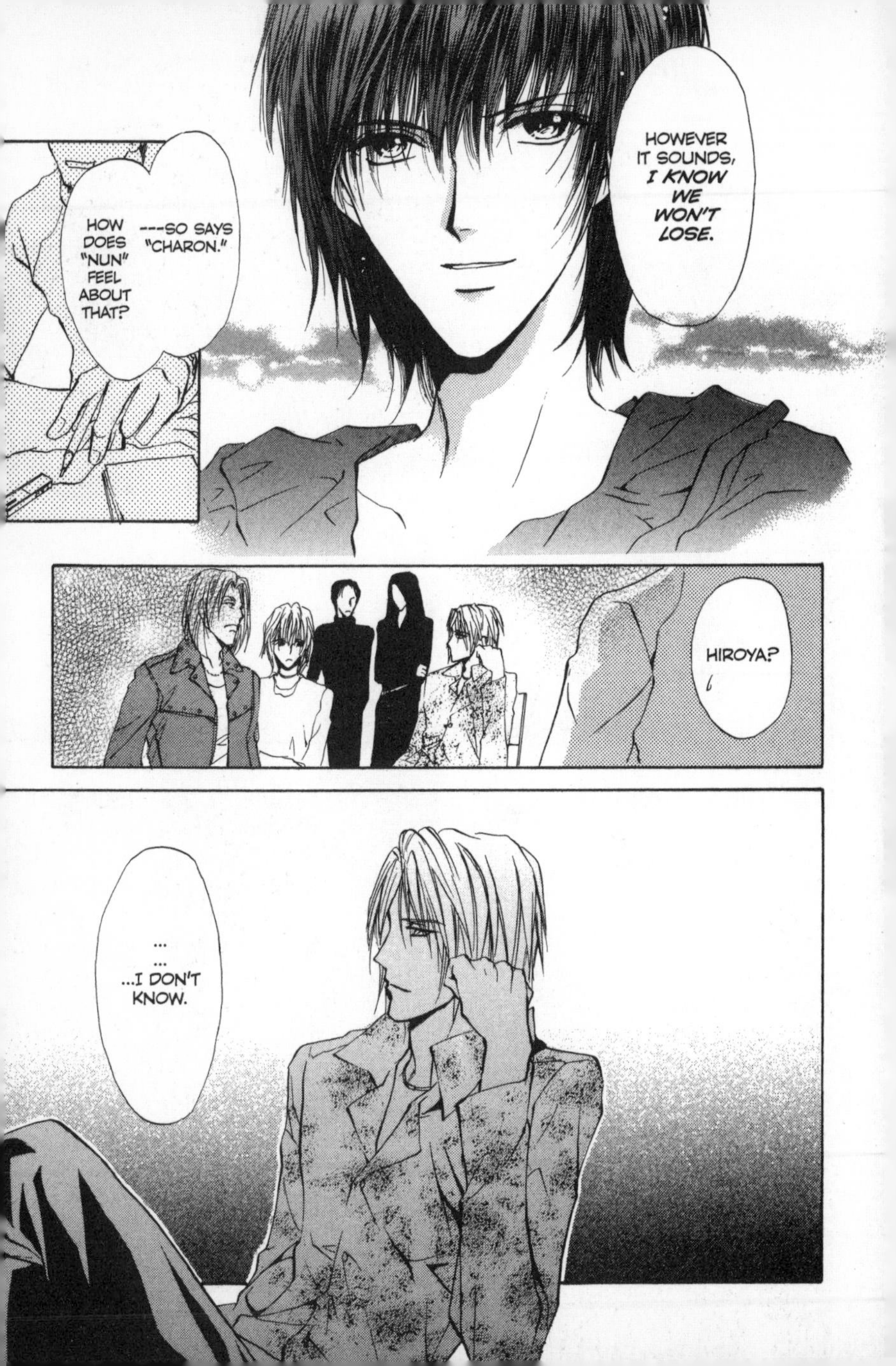
HOWEVER IT SOUNDS, *I KNOW WE WON'T LOSE.*
---SO SAYS "CHARON."
HOW DOES "NUN" FEEL ABOUT THAT?
HIROYA?
... ...I DON'T KNOW.

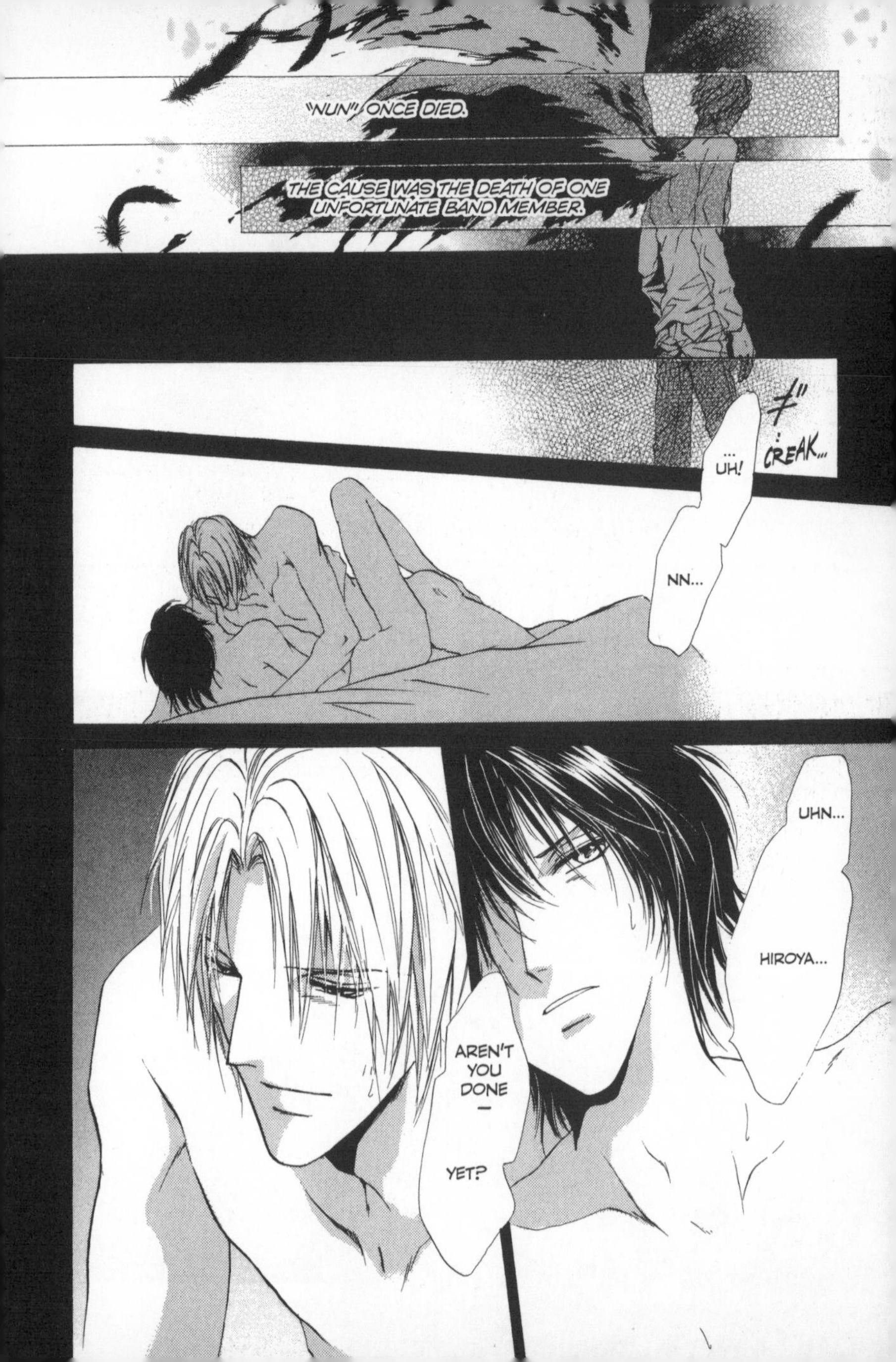
"NUN" ONCE DIED.
THE CAUSE WAS THE DEATH OF ONE UNFORTUNATE BAND MEMBER.
ギ
CREAK...
...UH!
NN...
UHN...
HIROYA...
AREN'T YOU DONE —
YET?

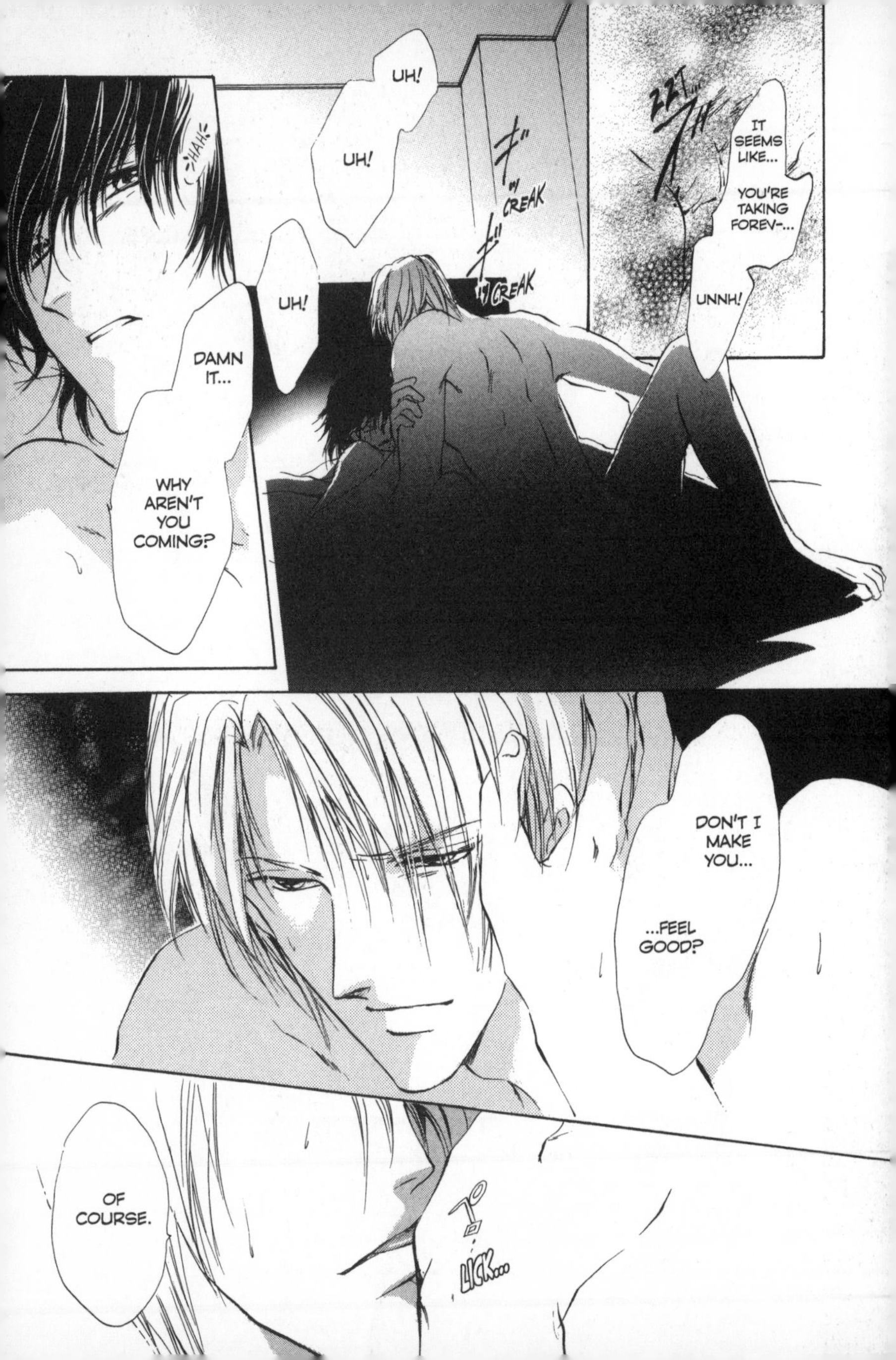
IT SEEMS LIKE...
YOU'RE TAKING FOREV-...
UNNH!
UH!
UH!
CREAK
CREAK
UH!
HAH
DAMN IT...
WHY AREN'T YOU COMING?
DON'T I MAKE YOU...
...FEEL GOOD?
OF COURSE.
LICK...

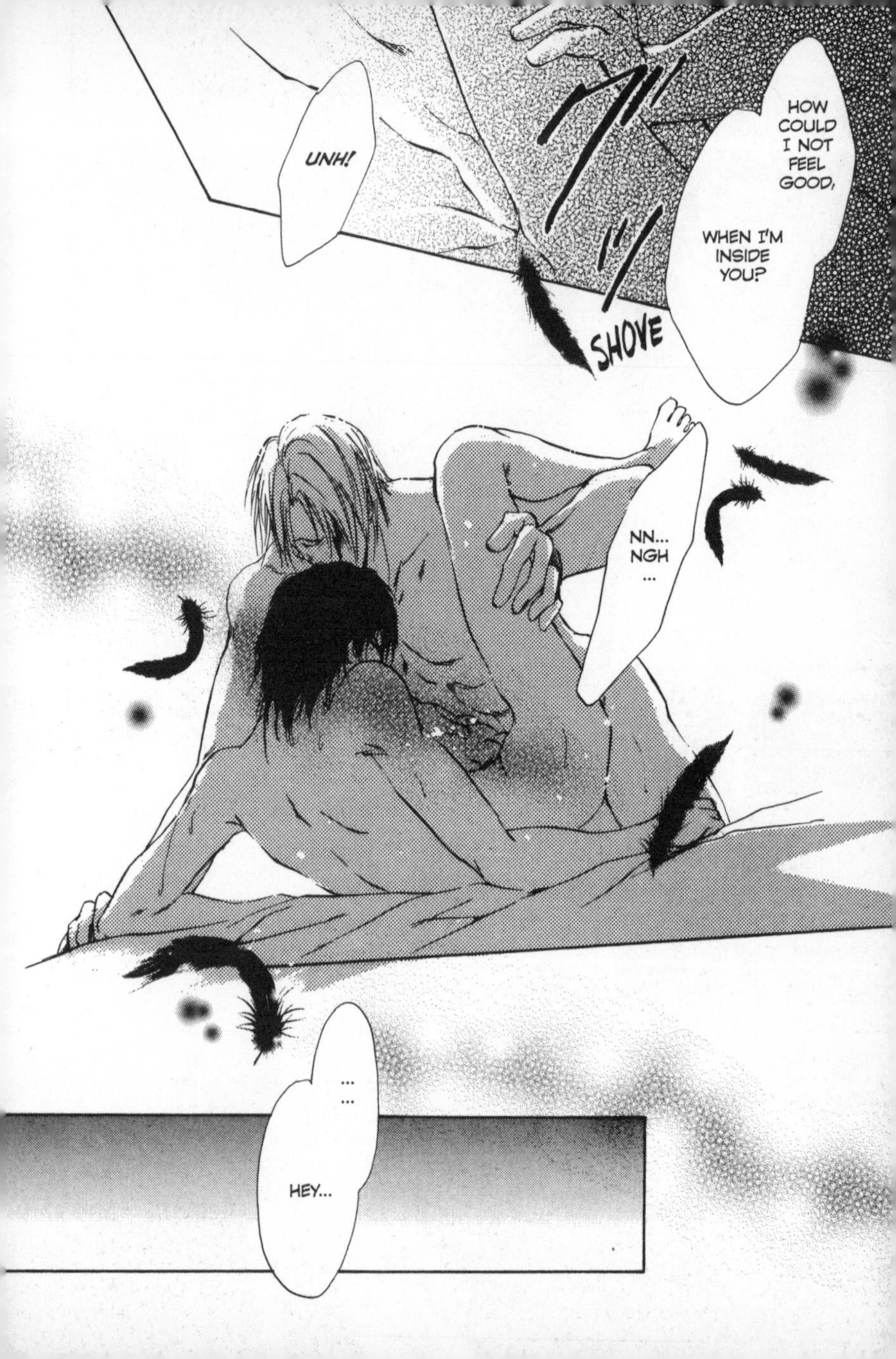
HOW COULD I NOT FEEL GOOD,
WHEN I'M INSIDE YOU?
SHOVE
UNH!
NN... NGH ...
... ...
HEY...

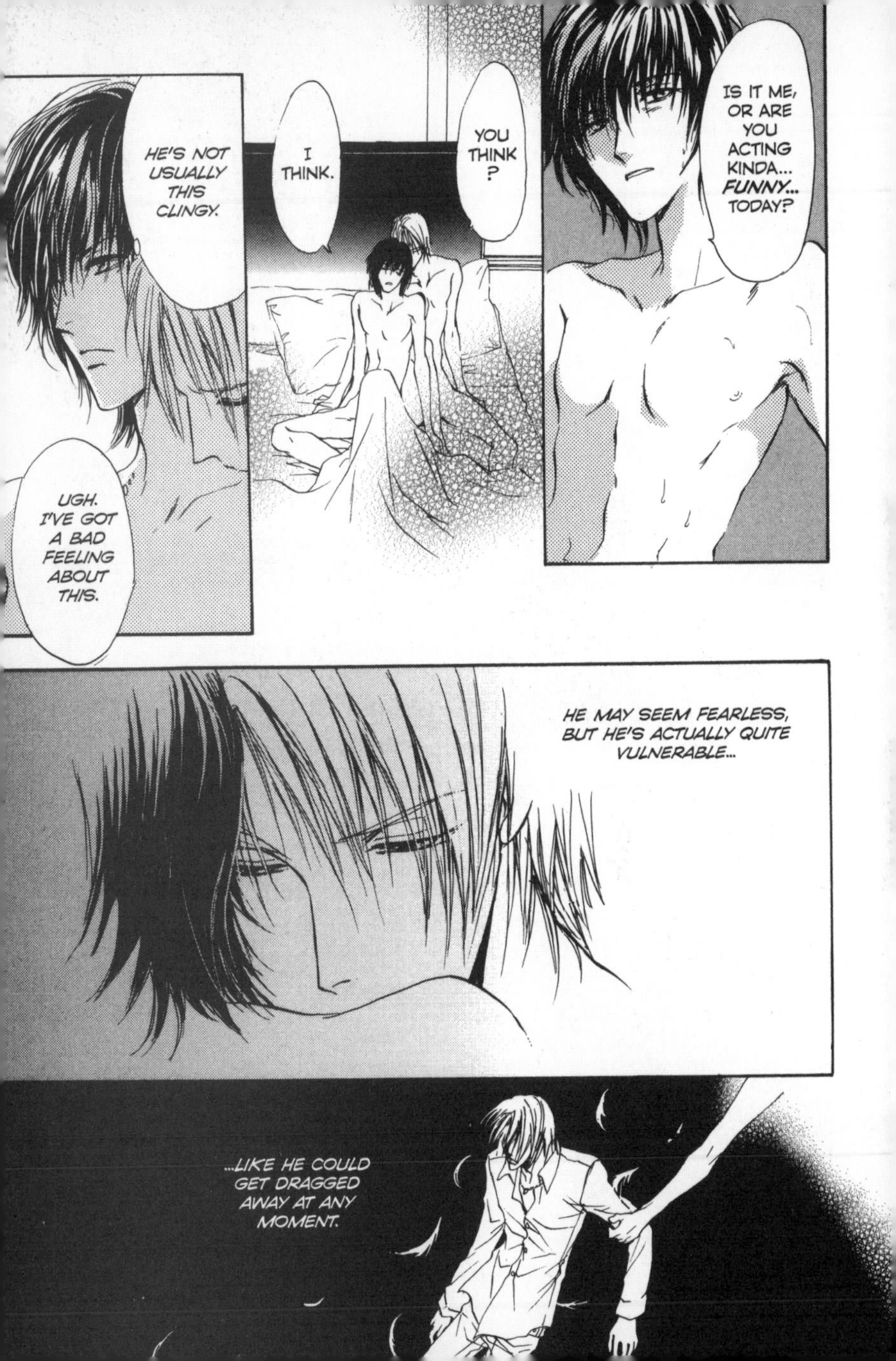
IS IT ME, OR ARE YOU ACTING KINDA... ***FUNNY...*** TODAY?
YOU THINK?
I THINK.
HE'S NOT USUALLY THIS CLINGY.
UGH. I'VE GOT A BAD FEELING ABOUT THIS.
HE MAY SEEM FEARLESS, BUT HE'S ACTUALLY QUITE VULNERABLE...
...LIKE HE COULD GET DRAGGED AWAY AT ANY MOMENT.

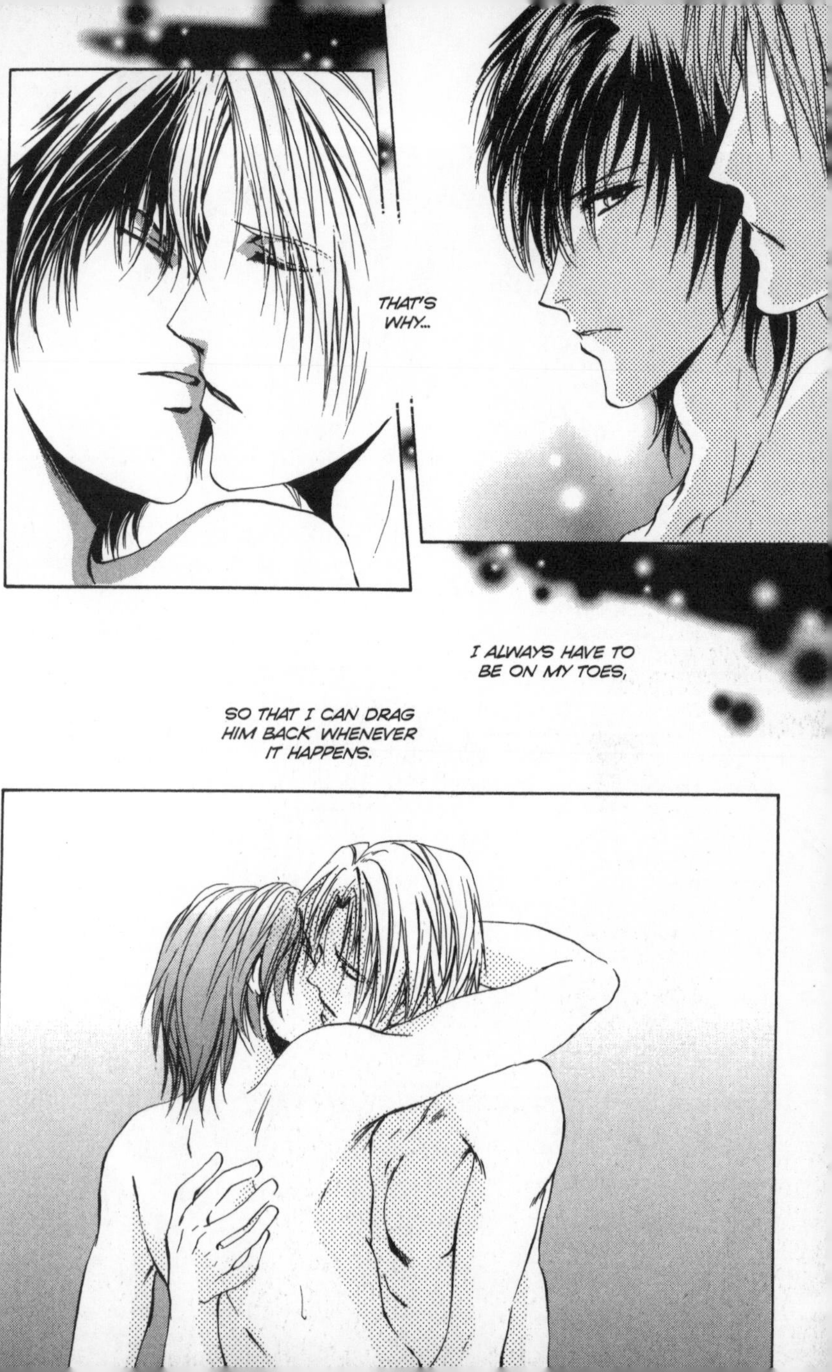
THAT'S WHY...
I ALWAYS HAVE TO BE ON MY TOES,
SO THAT I CAN DRAG HIM BACK WHENEVER IT HAPPENS.

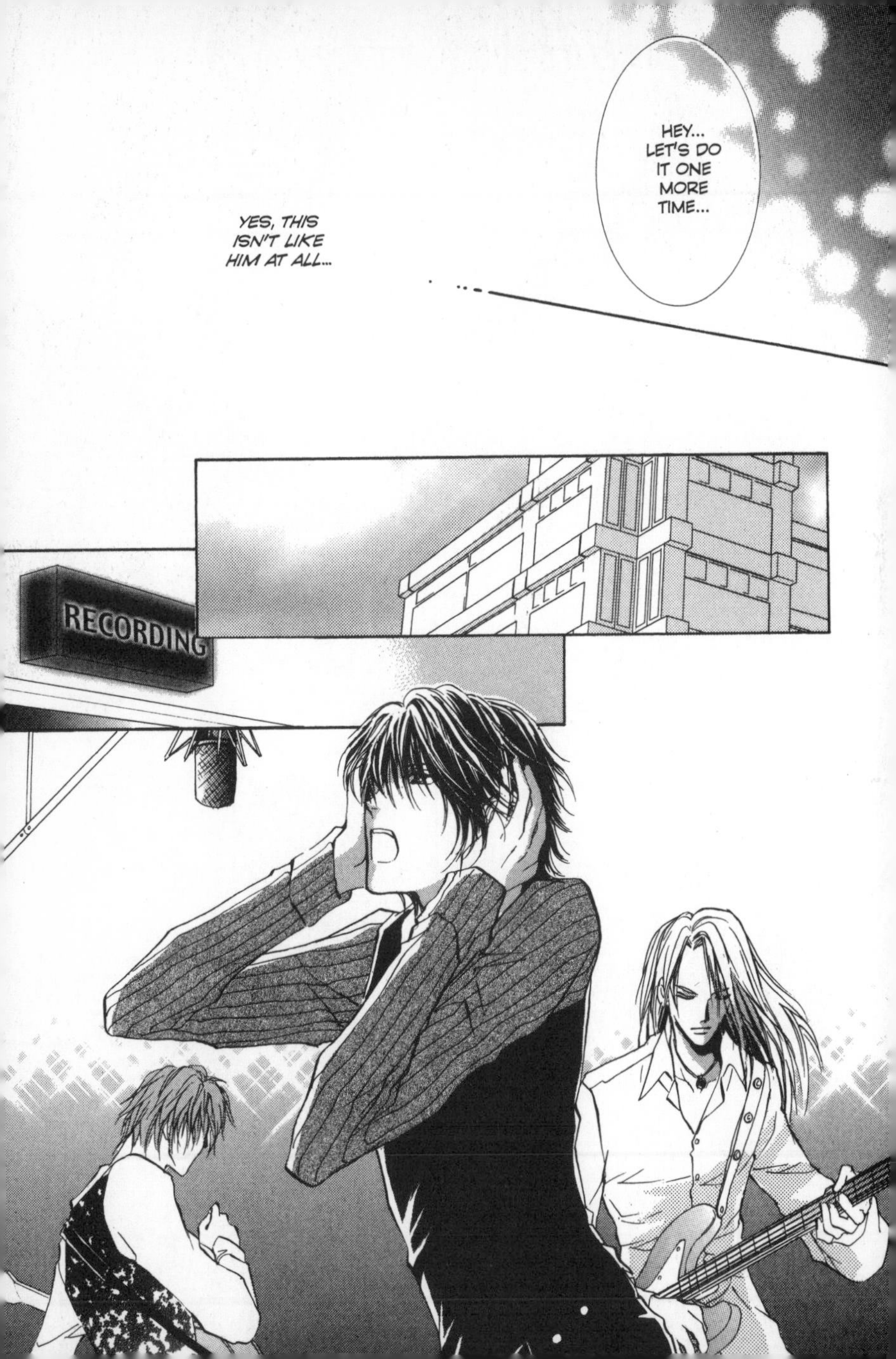
HEY... LET'S DO IT ONE MORE TIME...
YES, THIS ISN'T LIKE HIM AT ALL...
RECORDING

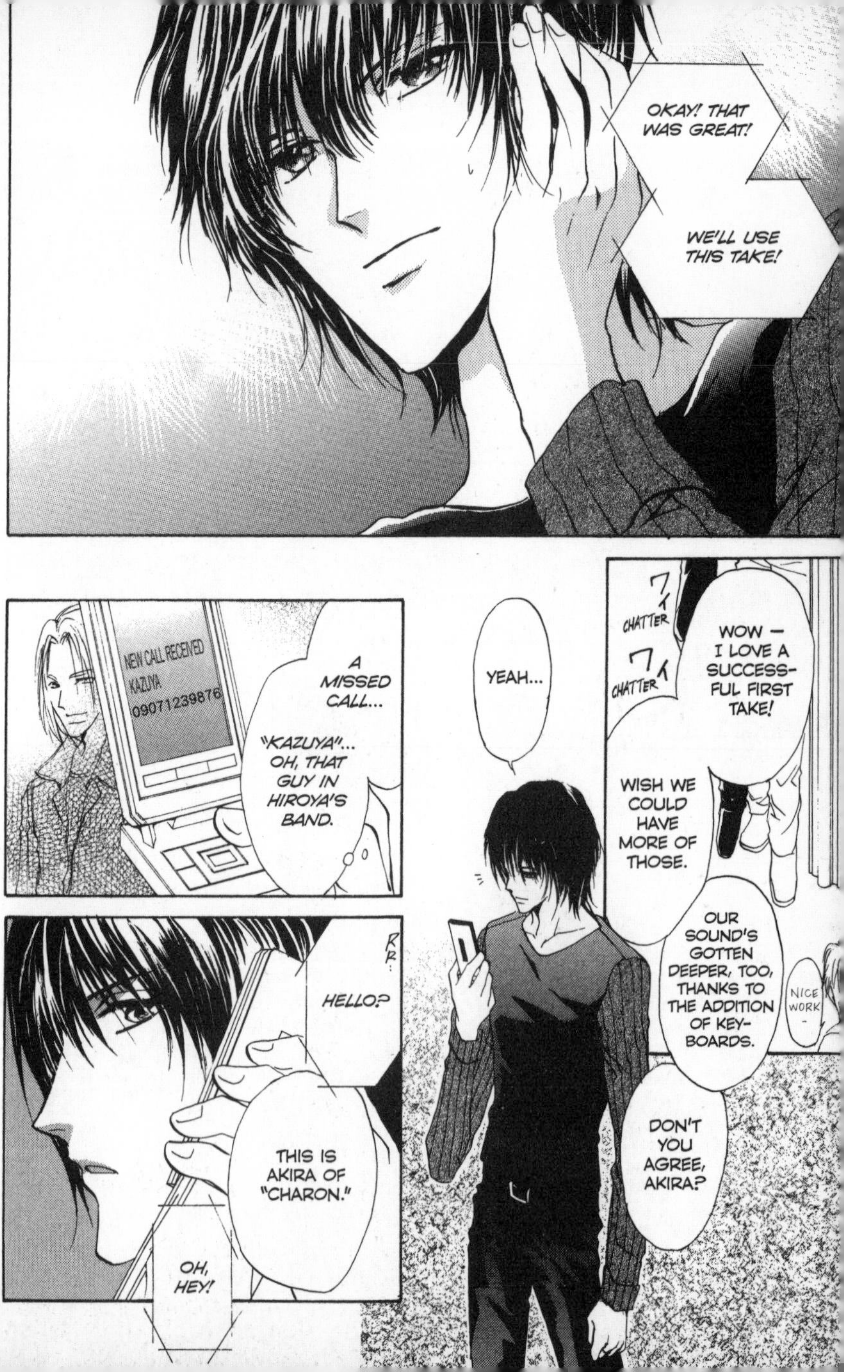
OKAY! THAT WAS GREAT!
WE'LL USE THIS TAKE!
ワイ CHATTER
ワイ CHATTER
WOW — I LOVE A SUCCESSFUL FIRST TAKE!
WISH WE COULD HAVE MORE OF THOSE.
OUR SOUND'S GOTTEN DEEPER, TOO, THANKS TO THE ADDITION OF KEYBOARDS.
NICE WORK —
DON'T YOU AGREE, AKIRA?
YEAH...
NEW CALL RECEIVED
KAZUYA
09071239876
A MISSED CALL...
"KAZUYA"... OH, THAT GUY IN HIROYA'S BAND.
RR
HELLO?
THIS IS AKIRA OF "CHARON."
OH, HEY!

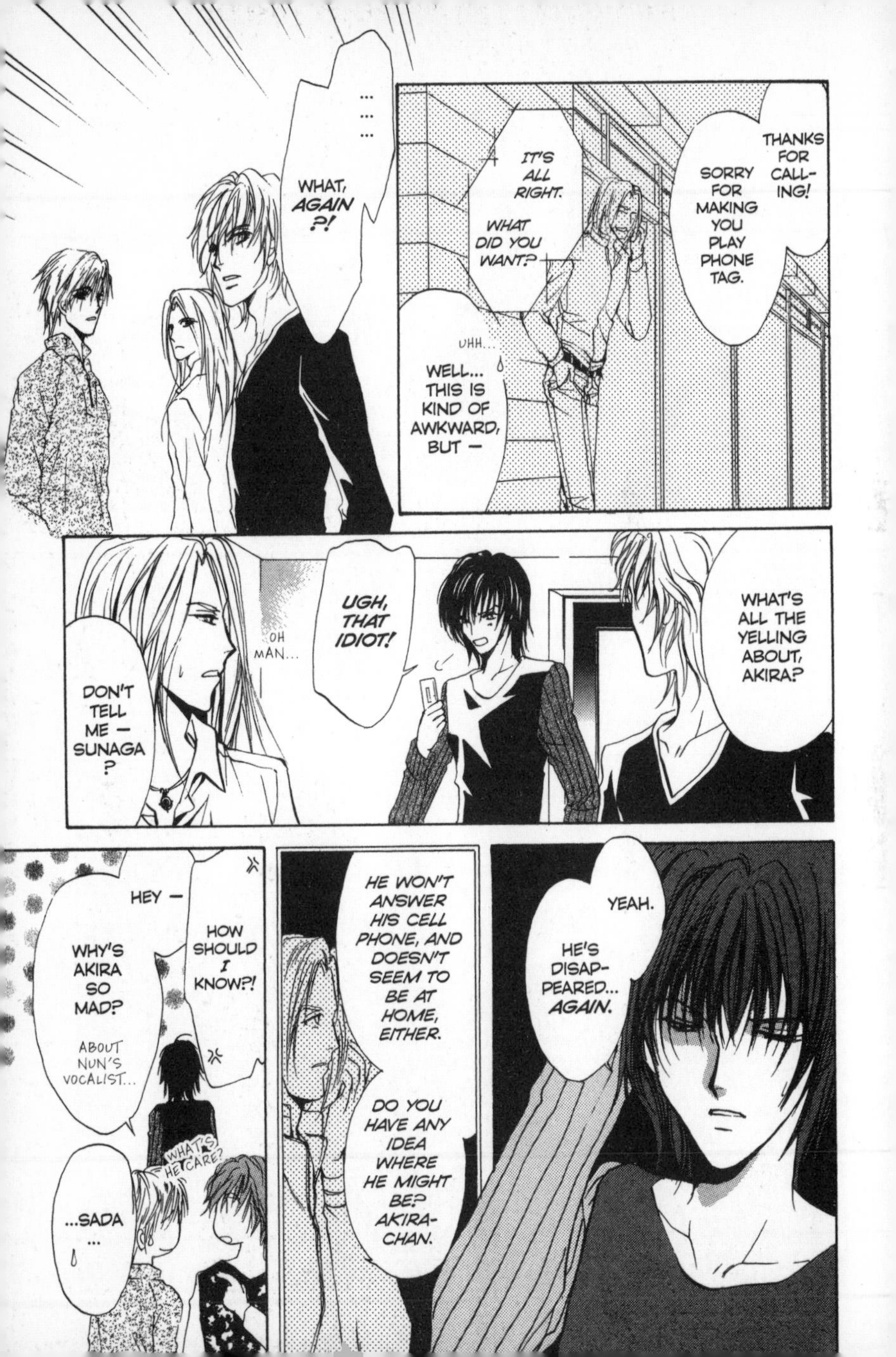
THANKS FOR CALLING!
SORRY FOR MAKING YOU PLAY PHONE TAG.
IT'S ALL RIGHT.
WHAT DID YOU WANT?
UHH...
WELL... THIS IS KIND OF AWKWARD, BUT —
....
WHAT, AGAIN?!
WHAT'S ALL THE YELLING ABOUT, AKIRA?
UGH, THAT IDIOT!
OH MAN...
DON'T TELL ME — SUNAGA?
YEAH.
HE'S DISAPPEARED... AGAIN.
HE WON'T ANSWER HIS CELL PHONE, AND DOESN'T SEEM TO BE AT HOME, EITHER.
DO YOU HAVE ANY IDEA WHERE HE MIGHT BE? AKIRA-CHAN.
HEY —
WHY'S AKIRA SO MAD?
HOW SHOULD I KNOW?!
ABOUT NUN'S VOCALIST...
WHAT'S HE CARE?
...SADA ...

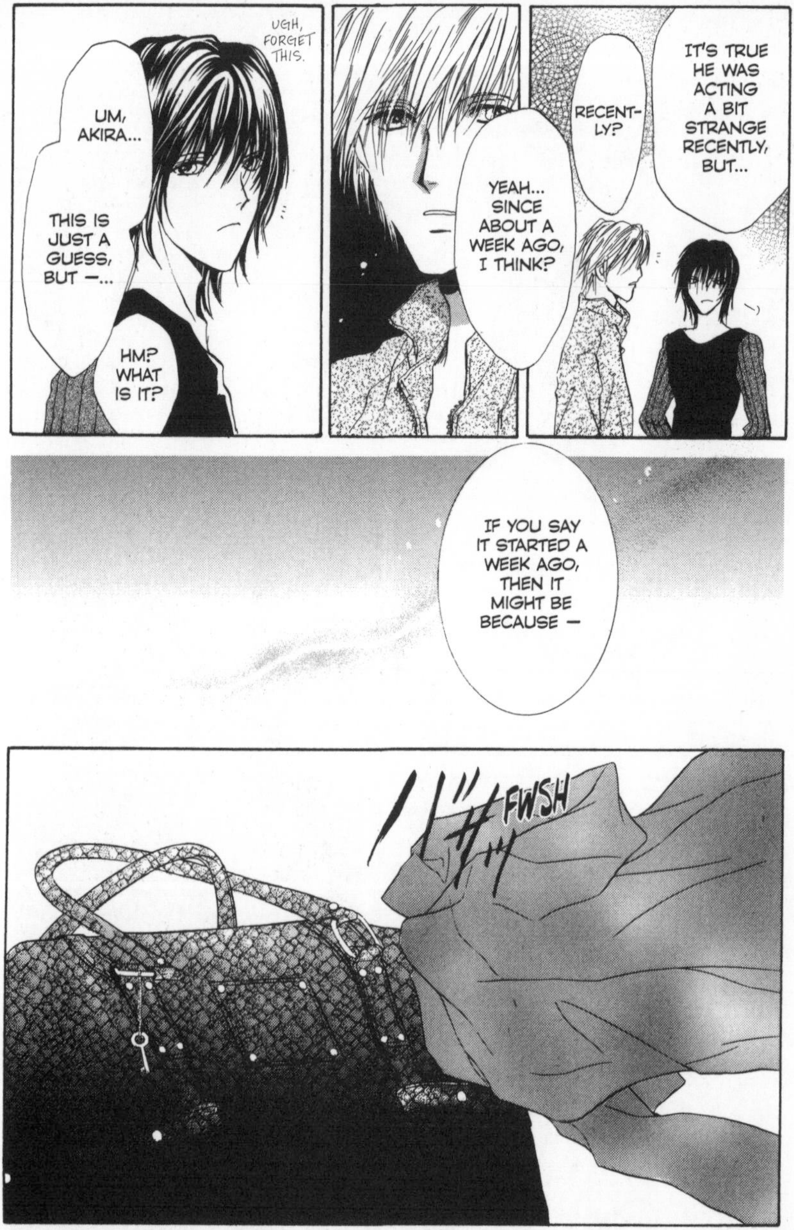
IT'S TRUE HE WAS ACTING A BIT STRANGE RECENTLY, BUT...
RECENT-LY?
YEAH... SINCE ABOUT A WEEK AGO, I THINK?
UGH, FORGET THIS.
UM, AKIRA...
THIS IS JUST A GUESS, BUT —...
HM? WHAT IS IT?
IF YOU SAY IT STARTED A WEEK AGO, THEN IT MIGHT BE BECAUSE —
FWSH

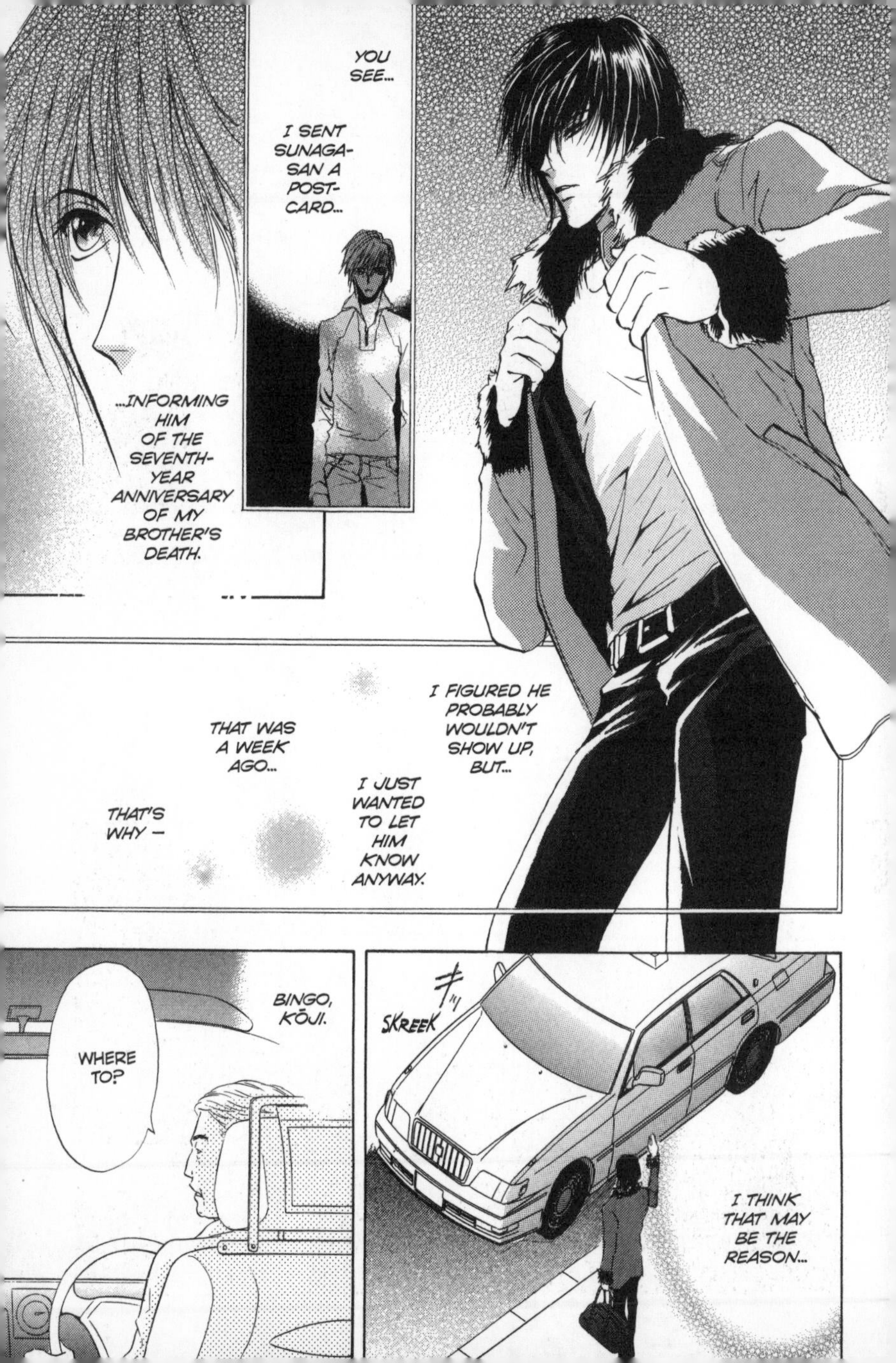
YOU SEE...
I SENT SUNAGA-SAN A POST-CARD...
...INFORMING HIM OF THE SEVENTH-YEAR ANNIVERSARY OF MY BROTHER'S DEATH.
I FIGURED HE PROBABLY WOULDN'T SHOW UP, BUT...
I JUST WANTED TO LET HIM KNOW ANYWAY.
THAT WAS A WEEK AGO...
THAT'S WHY –
SKREEK
I THINK THAT MAY BE THE REASON...
BINGO, KŌJI.
WHERE TO?

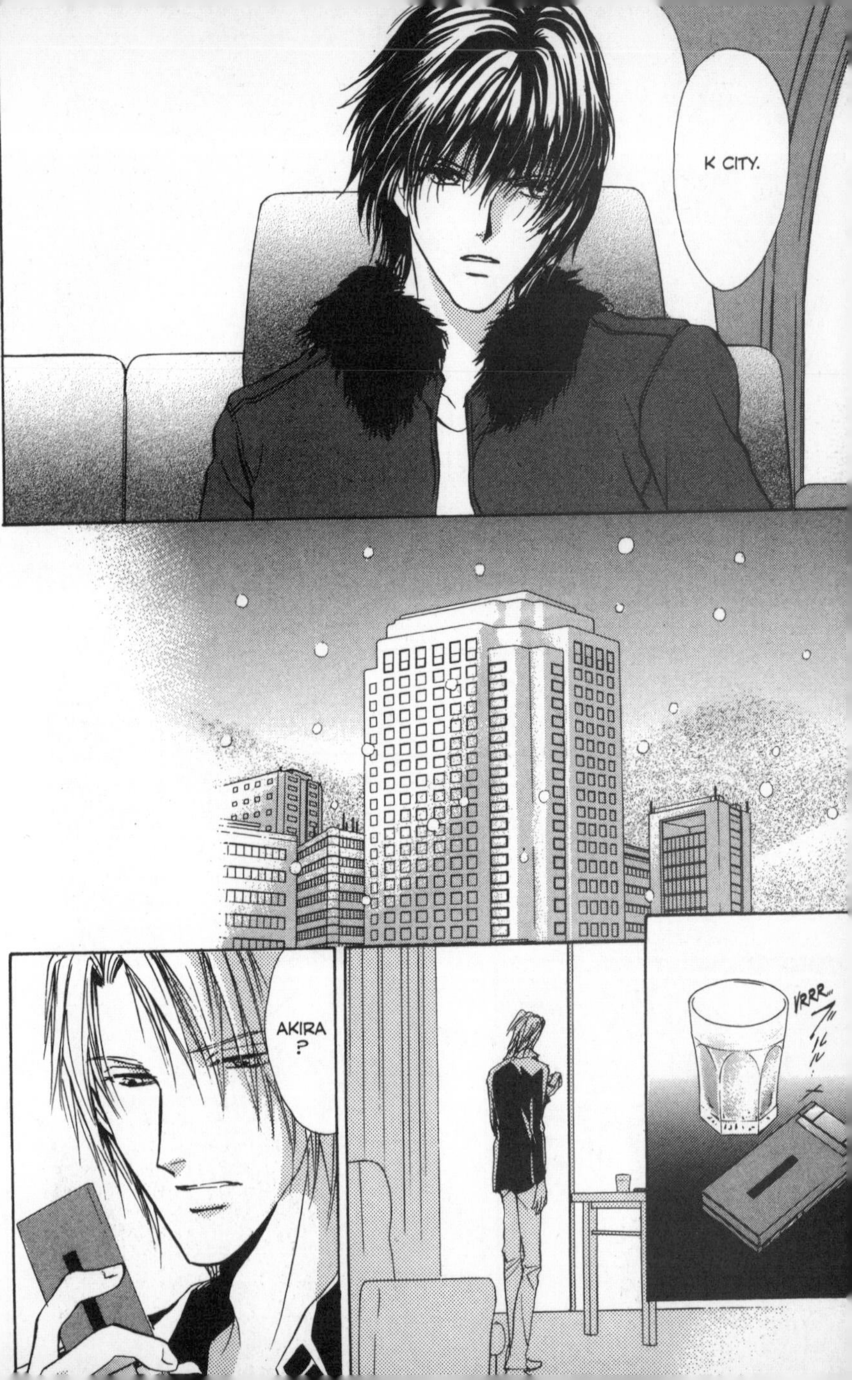
K CITY.
VRRR...
AKIRA?

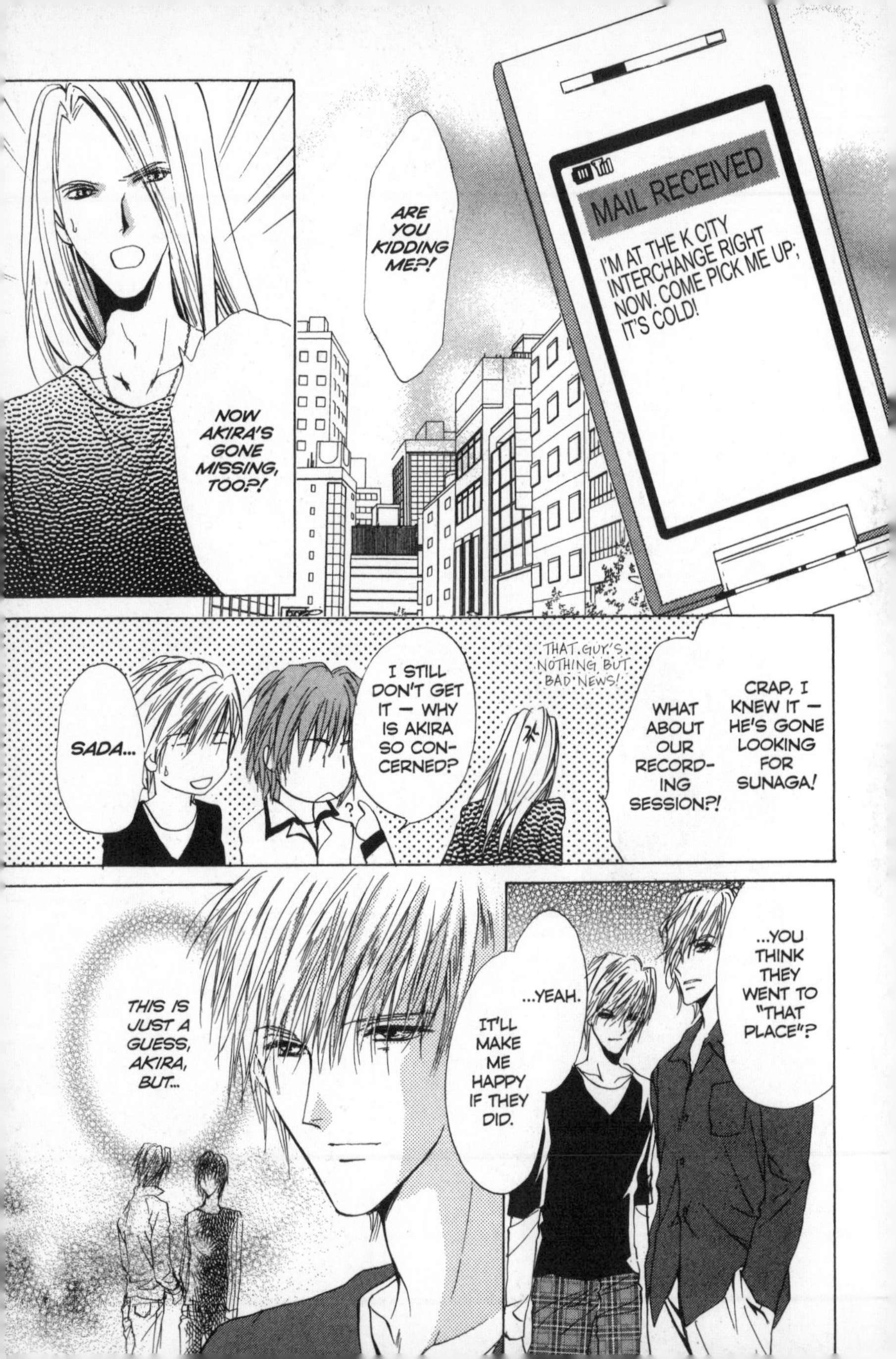
MAIL RECEIVED
I'M AT THE K CITY INTERCHANGE RIGHT NOW. COME PICK ME UP; IT'S COLD!
ARE YOU KIDDING ME?!
NOW AKIRA'S GONE MISSING, TOO?!
CRAP, I KNEW IT — HE'S GONE LOOKING FOR SUNAGA!
WHAT ABOUT OUR RECORDING SESSION?!
THAT GUY'S NOTHING BUT BAD NEWS!
I STILL DON'T GET IT — WHY IS AKIRA SO CONCERNED?
SADA...
...YOU THINK THEY WENT TO "THAT PLACE"?
...YEAH.
IT'LL MAKE ME HAPPY IF THEY DID.
THIS IS JUST A GUESS, AKIRA, BUT...

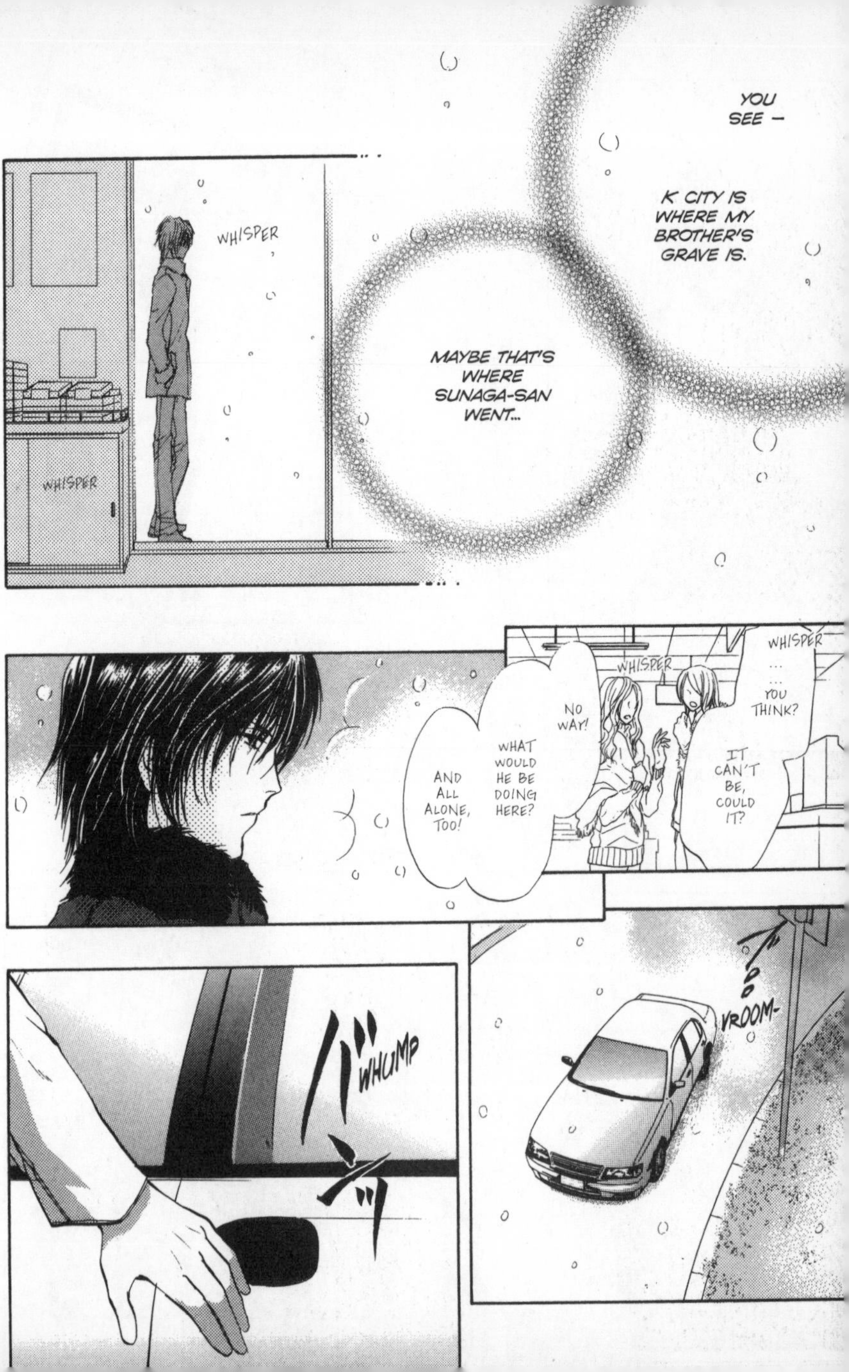
YOU SEE —
K CITY IS WHERE MY BROTHER'S GRAVE IS.
MAYBE THAT'S WHERE SUNAGA-SAN WENT...
WHISPER
WHISPER
WHISPER
... ... YOU THINK?
IT CAN'T BE, COULD IT?
WHISPER
NO WAY!
WHAT WOULD HE BE DOING HERE?
AND ALL ALONE, TOO!
VROOM-
WHUMP

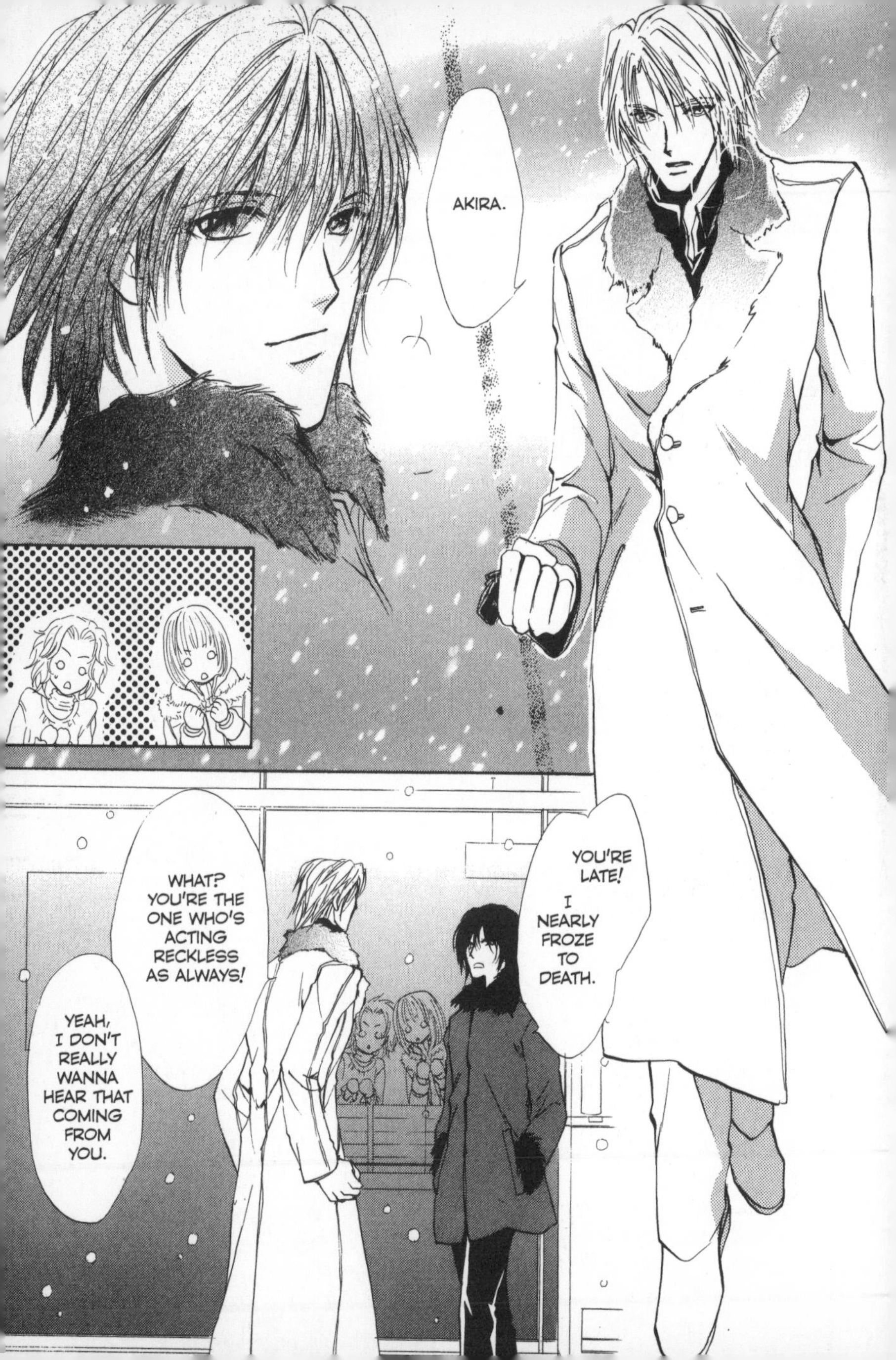
AKIRA.
YOU'RE LATE! I NEARLY FROZE TO DEATH.
WHAT? YOU'RE THE ONE WHO'S ACTING RECKLESS AS ALWAYS!
YEAH, I DON'T REALLY WANNA HEAR THAT COMING FROM YOU.

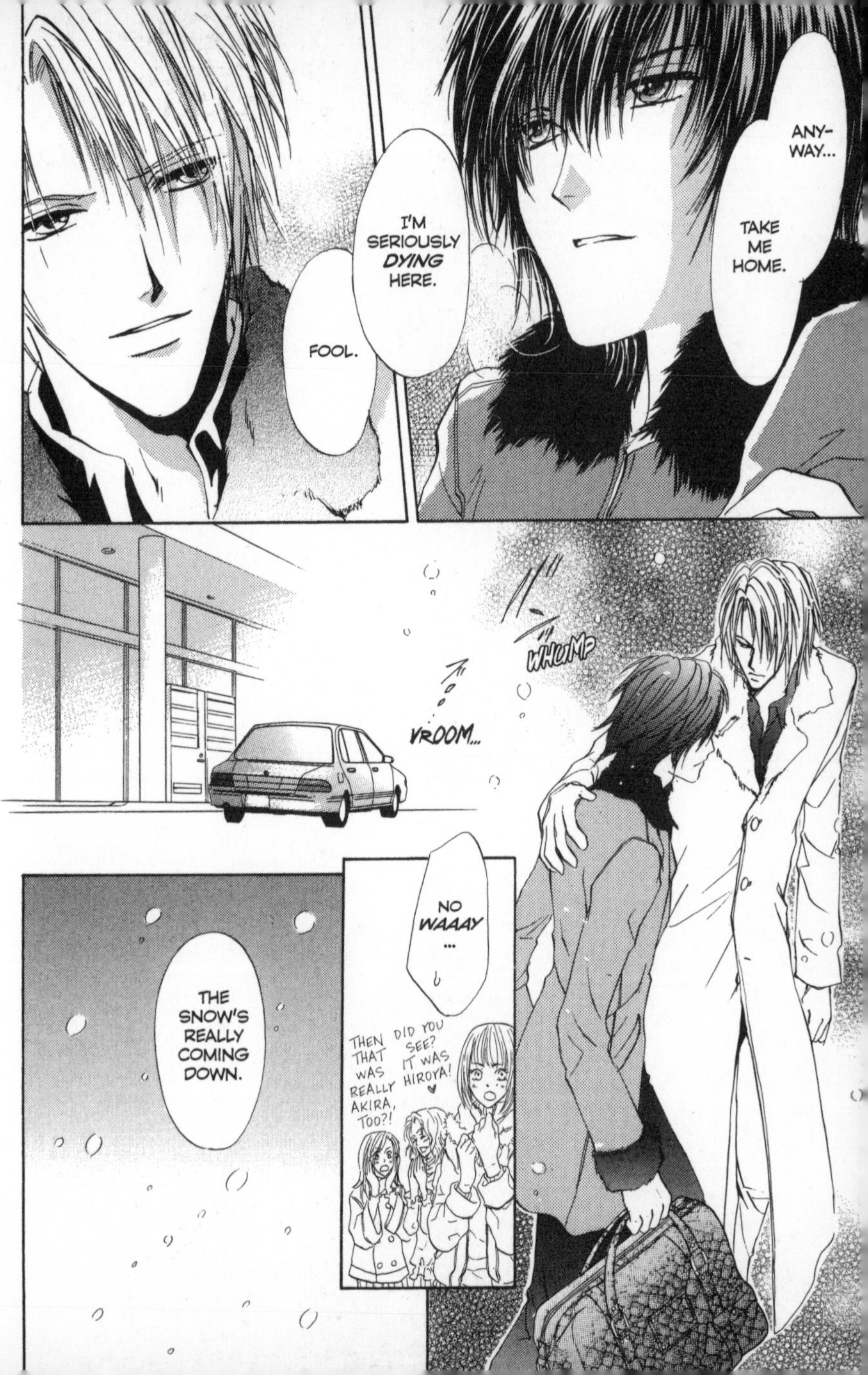
ANY-WAY...
TAKE ME HOME.
I'M SERIOUSLY DYING HERE.
FOOL.
WHUMP
VROOM...
NO WAAAY ...
DID YOU SEE? IT WAS HIROYA! ♥
THEN THAT WAS REALLY AKIRA, TOO?!
THE SNOW'S REALLY COMING DOWN.

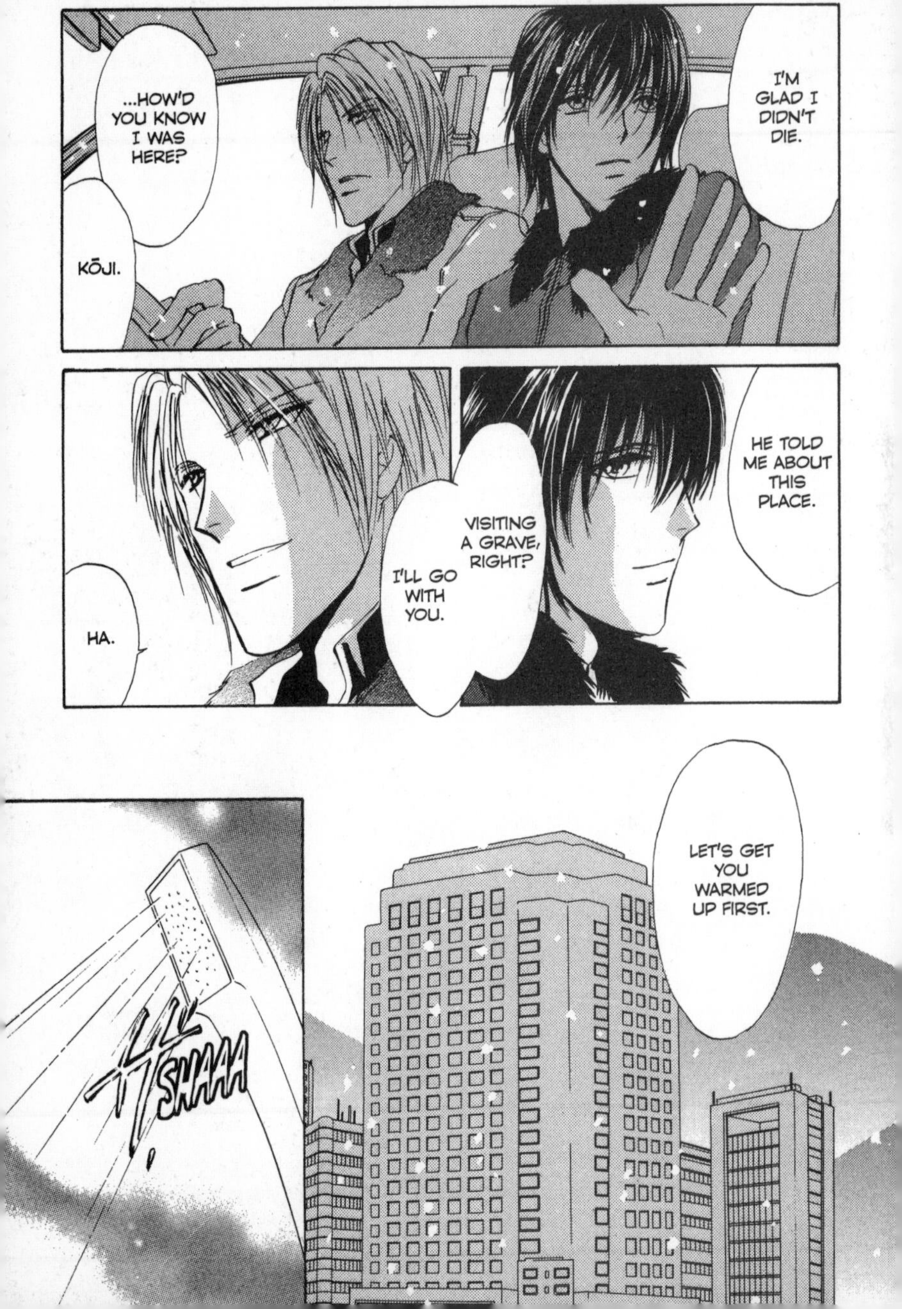
I'M GLAD I DIDN'T DIE.
...HOW'D YOU KNOW I WAS HERE?
KŌJI.
HE TOLD ME ABOUT THIS PLACE.
VISITING A GRAVE, RIGHT?
I'LL GO WITH YOU.
HA.
LET'S GET YOU WARMED UP FIRST.
SHAAA

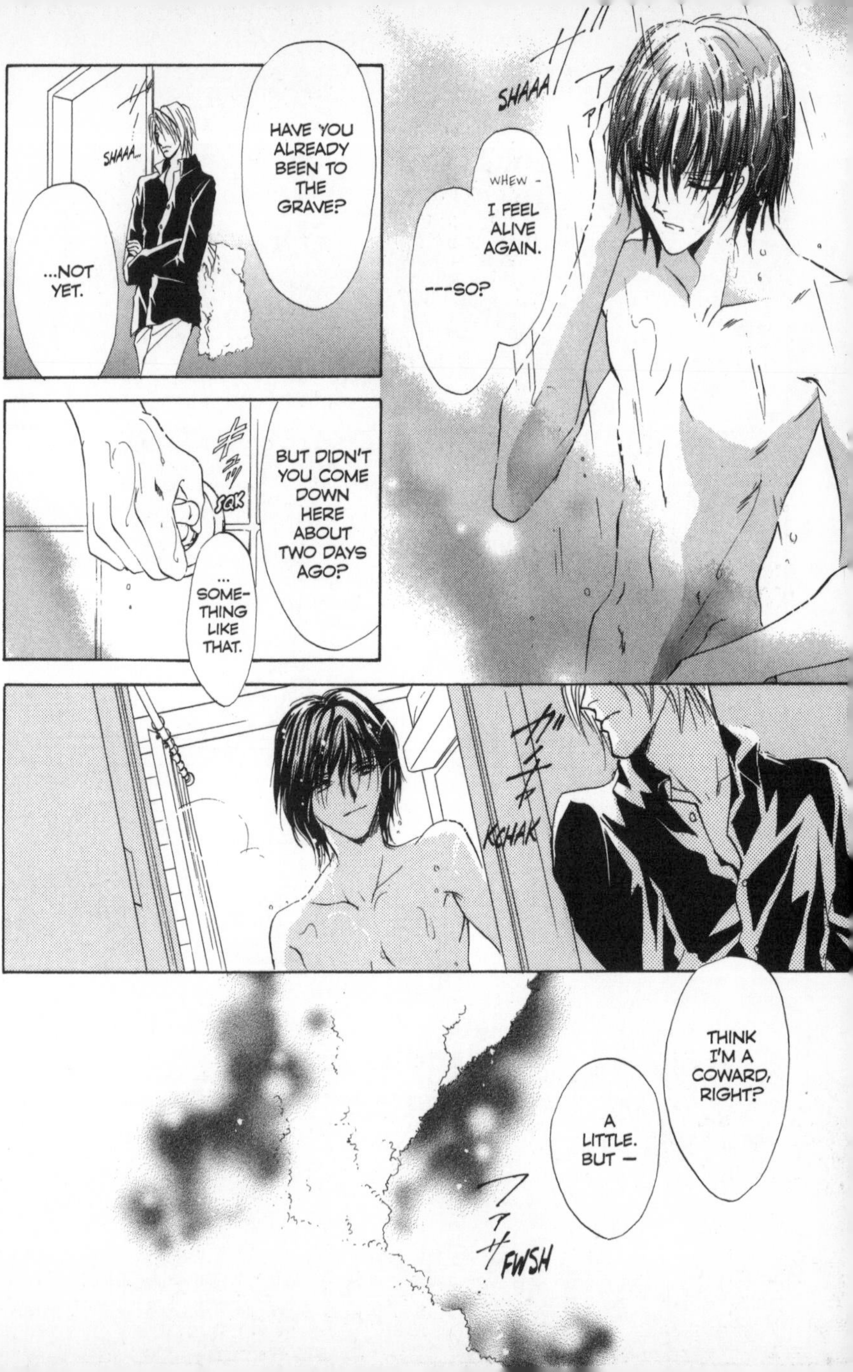
SHAAA
WHEW - I FEEL ALIVE AGAIN.
---SO?
HAVE YOU ALREADY BEEN TO THE GRAVE?
SHAAA...
...NOT YET.
SQK
BUT DIDN'T YOU COME DOWN HERE ABOUT TWO DAYS AGO?
... SOMETHING LIKE THAT.
KCHAK
THINK I'M A COWARD, RIGHT?
A LITTLE. BUT —
FWSH

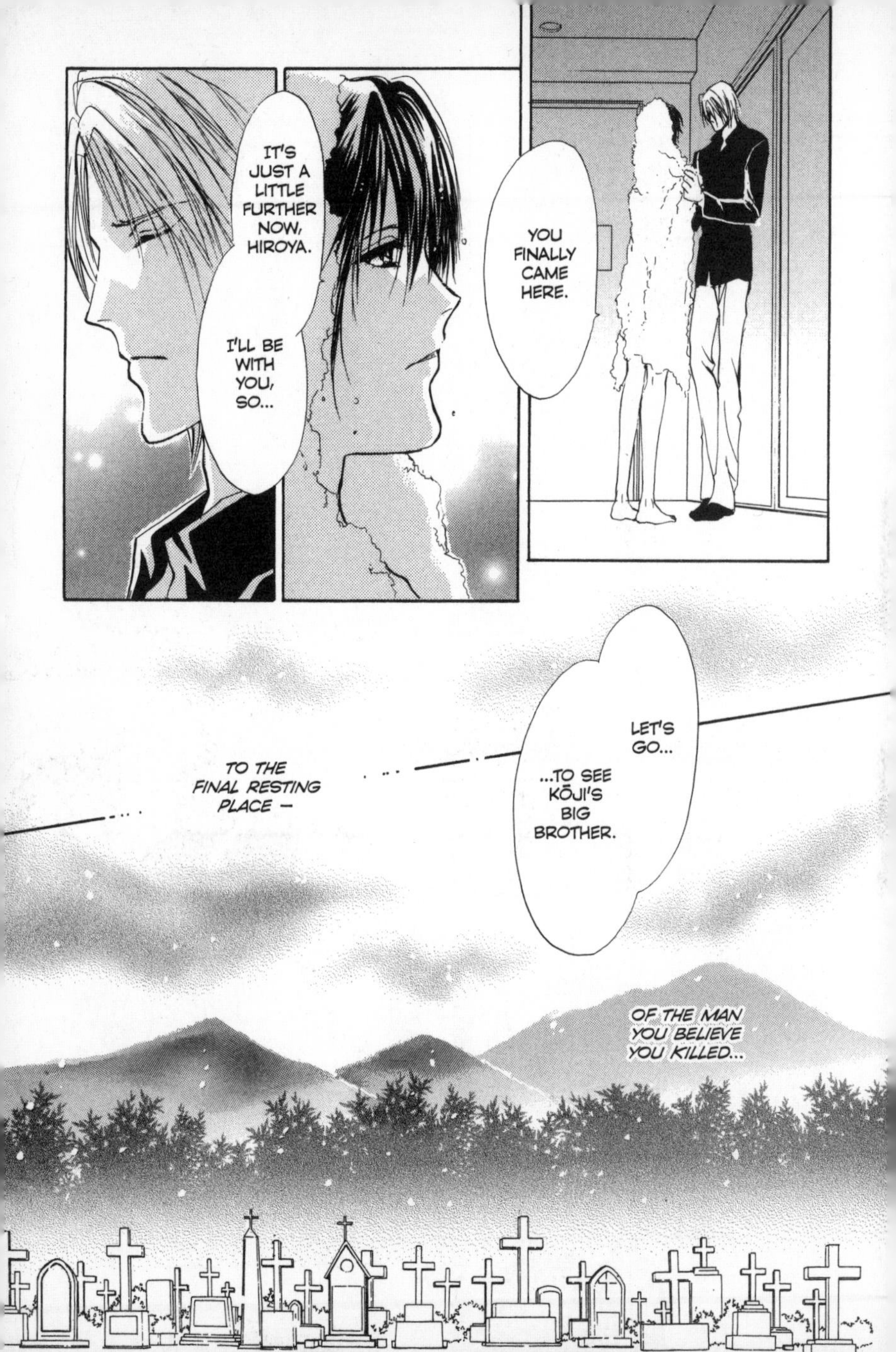
YOU FINALLY CAME HERE.
IT'S JUST A LITTLE FURTHER NOW, HIROYA.
I'LL BE WITH YOU, SO...
LET'S GO... ...TO SEE KŌJI'S BIG BROTHER.
TO THE FINAL RESTING PLACE —
OF THE MAN YOU BELIEVE YOU KILLED...

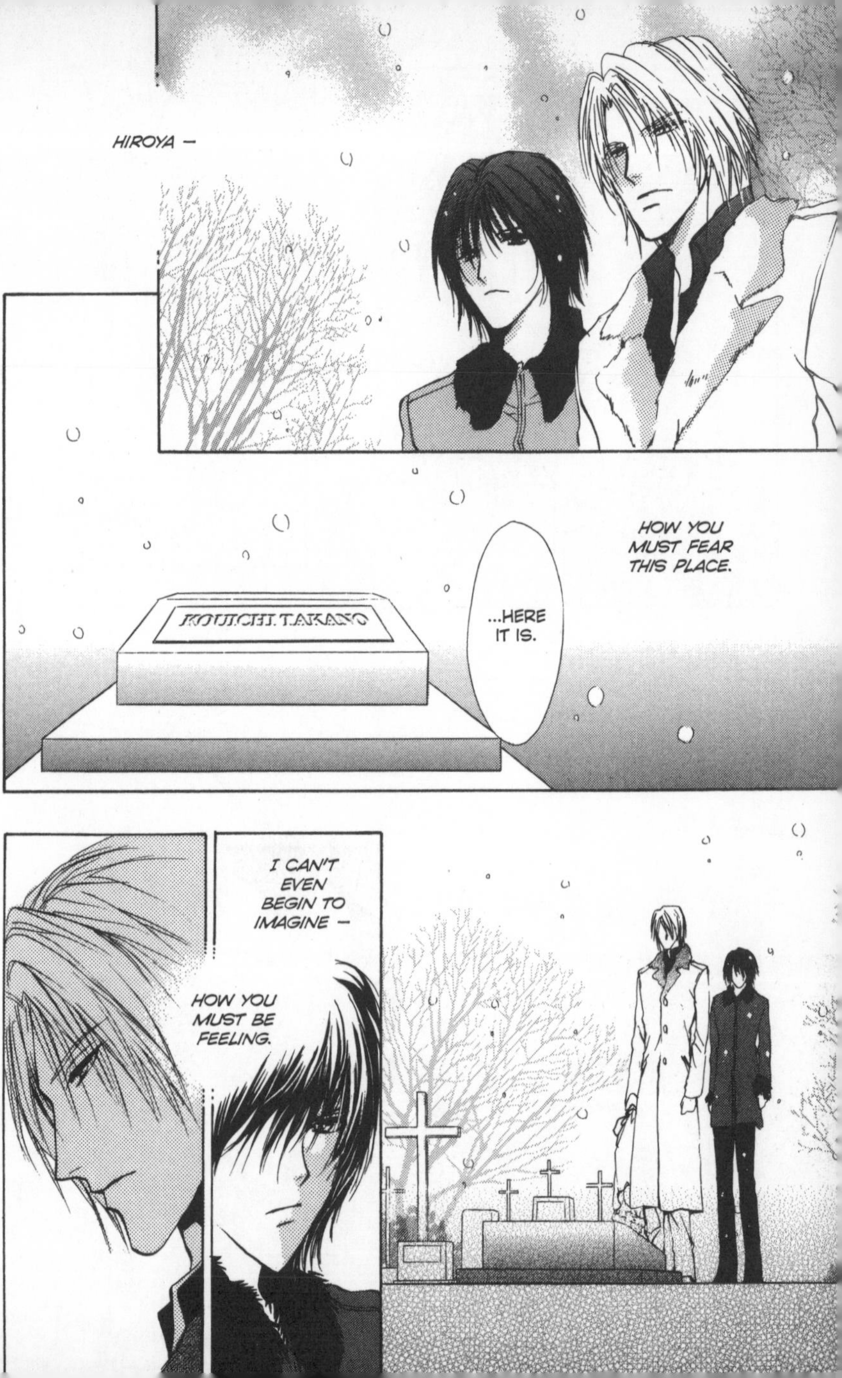

HIROYA —
HOW YOU MUST FEAR THIS PLACE.
...HERE IT IS.
KOUICHI TAKANO
I CAN'T EVEN BEGIN TO IMAGINE —
HOW YOU MUST BE FEELING.

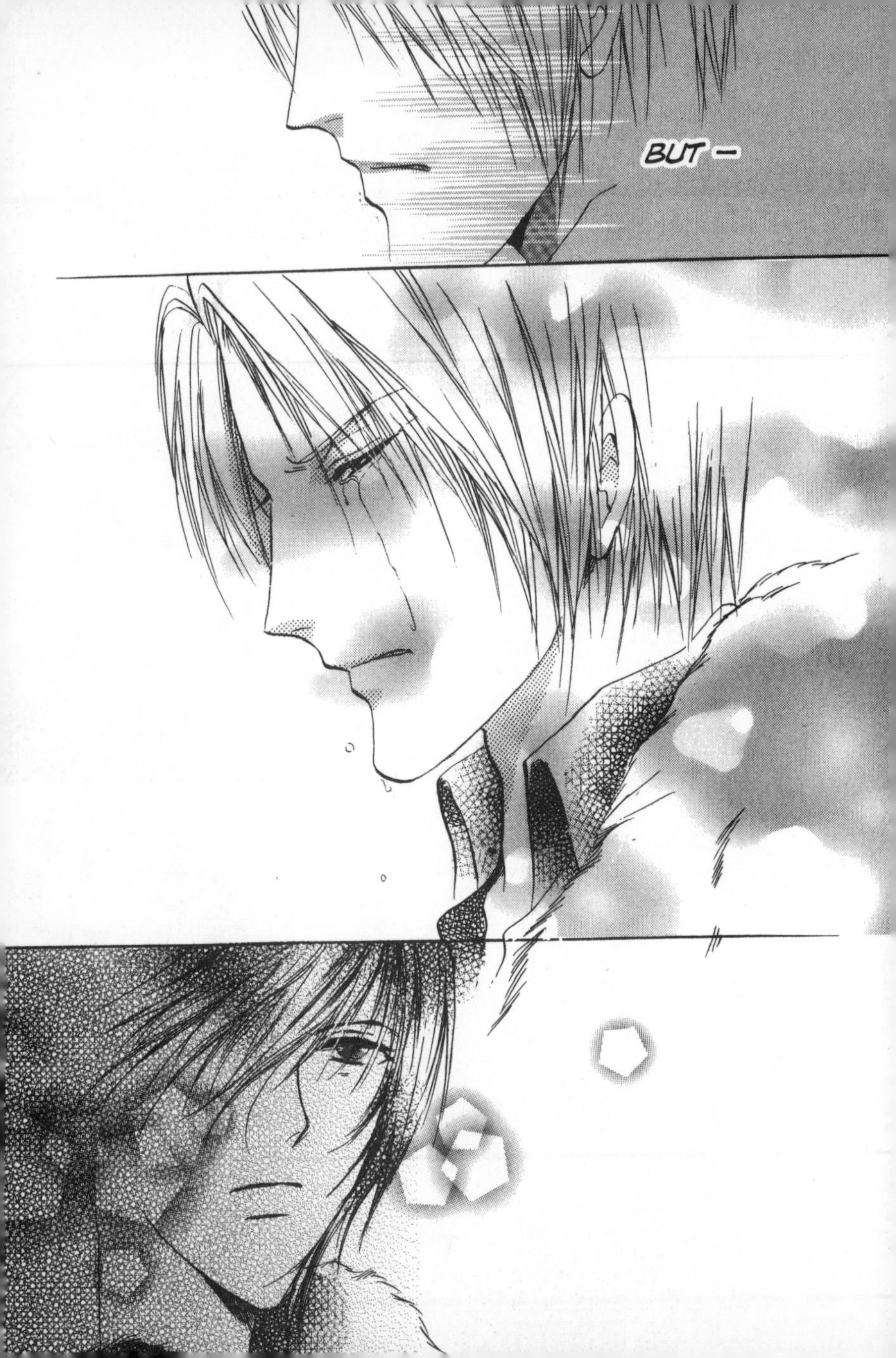
BUT –

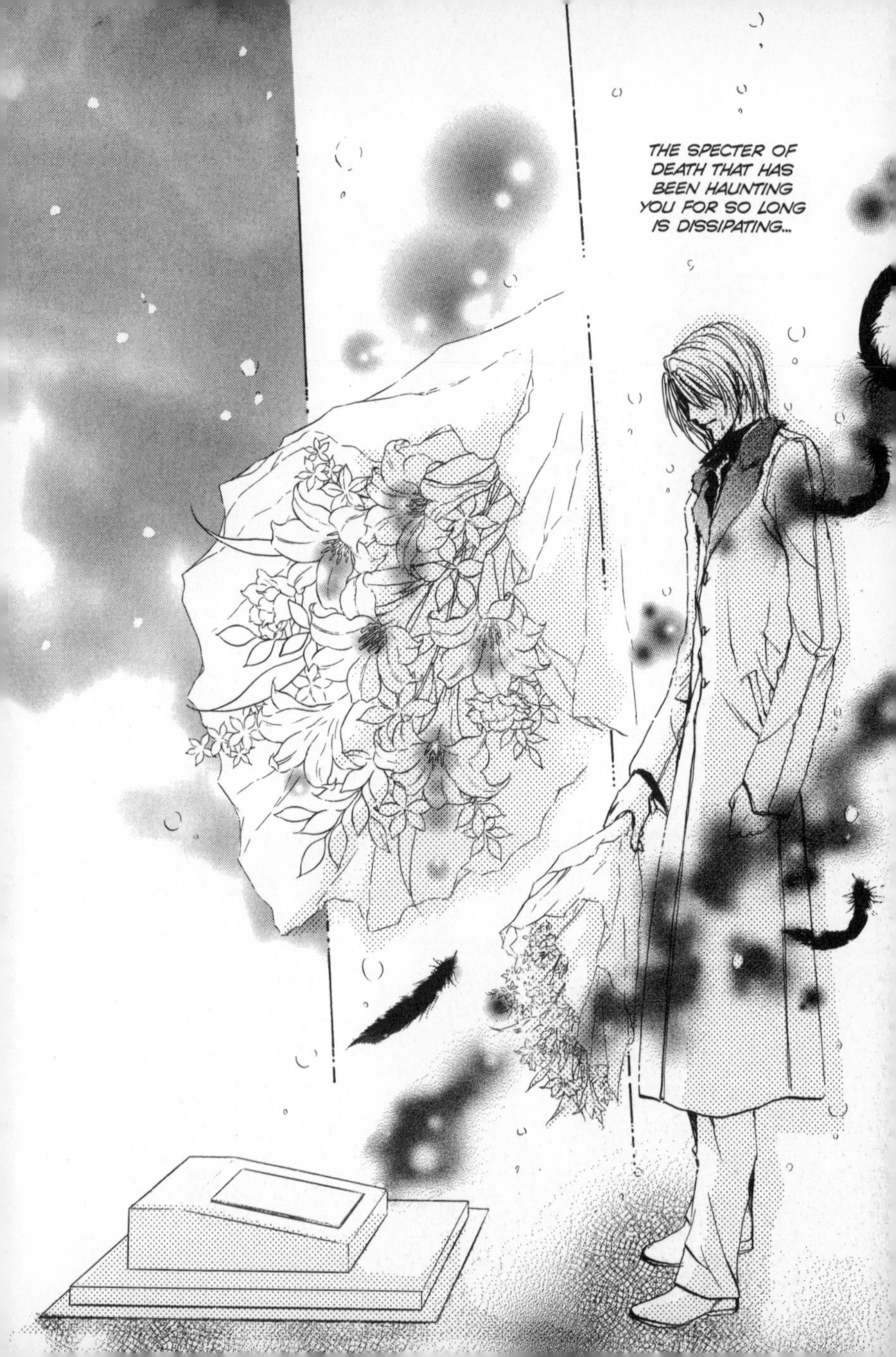
THE SPECTER OF DEATH THAT HAS BEEN HAUNTING YOU FOR SO LONG IS DISSIPATING...

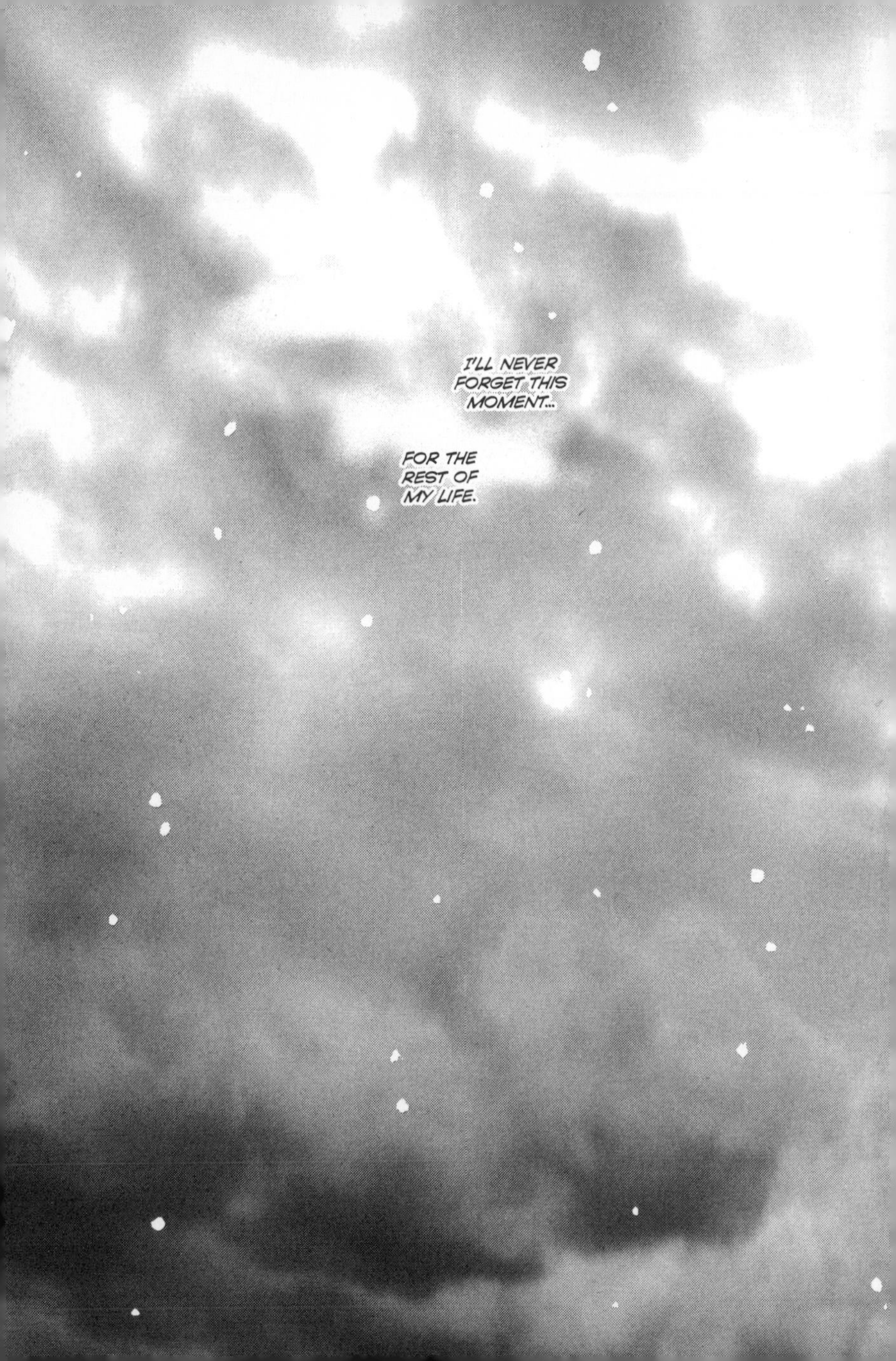
I'LL NEVER FORGET THIS MOMENT...
FOR THE REST OF MY LIFE.

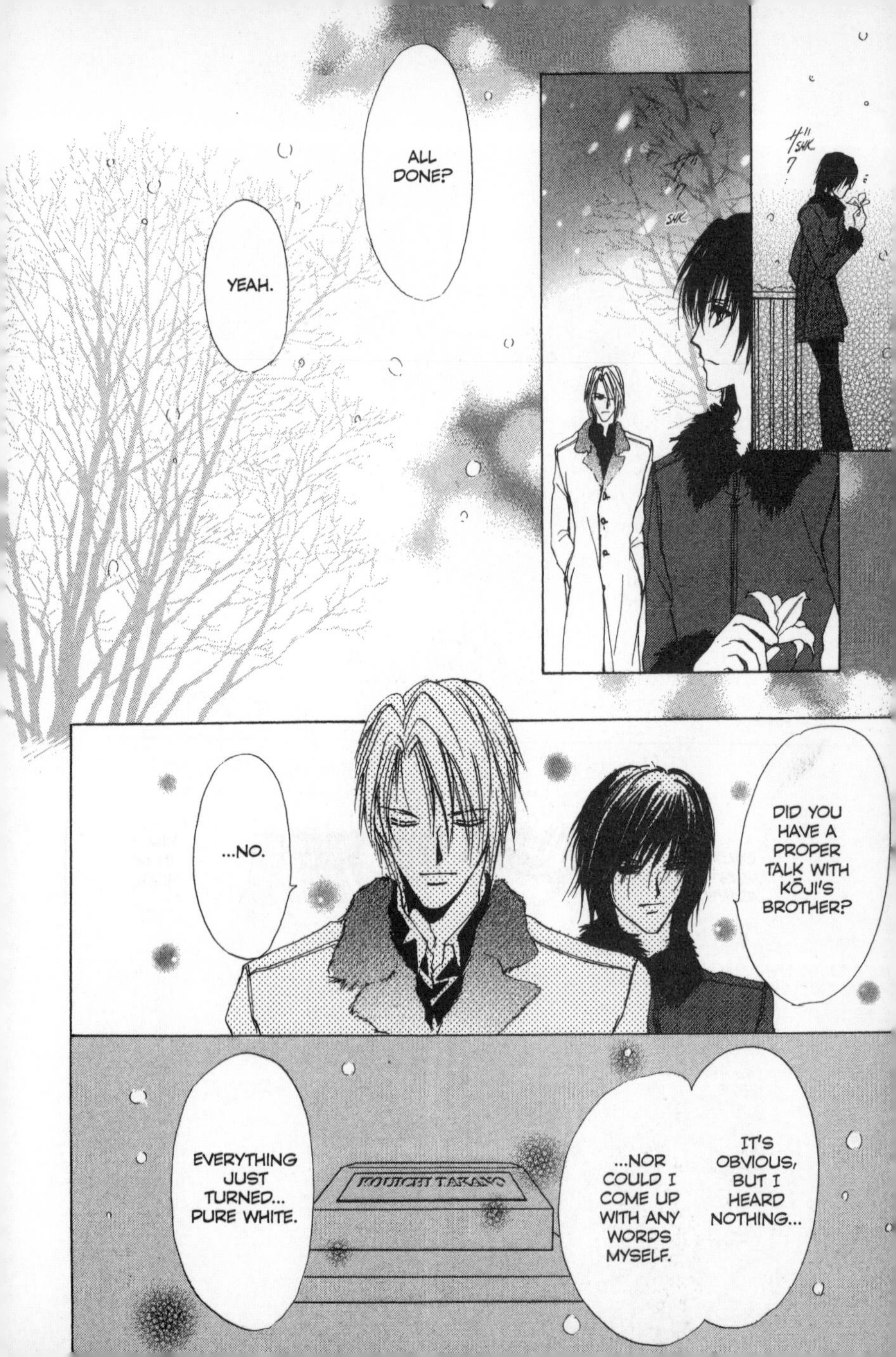
SHK
SHK
ALL DONE?
YEAH.
DID YOU HAVE A PROPER TALK WITH KŌJI'S BROTHER?
...NO.
IT'S OBVIOUS, BUT I HEARD NOTHING...
...NOR COULD I COME UP WITH ANY WORDS MYSELF.
KOUICHI TAKANO
EVERYTHING JUST TURNED... PURE WHITE.

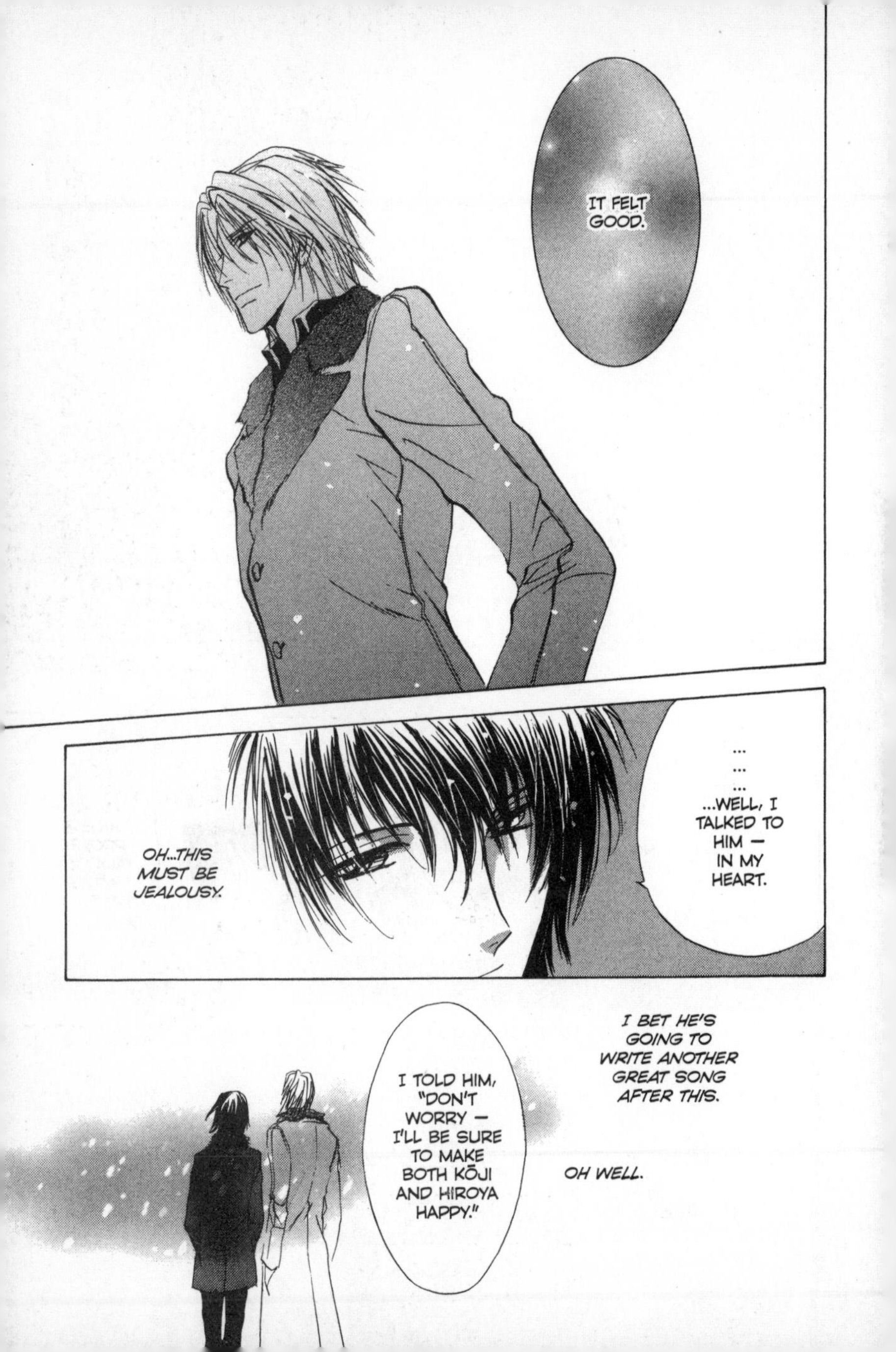
IT FELT GOOD.
...
...
...
...WELL, I TALKED TO HIM — IN MY HEART.
OH...THIS MUST BE JEALOUSY.
I BET HE'S GOING TO WRITE ANOTHER GREAT SONG AFTER THIS.
OH WELL.
I TOLD HIM, "DON'T WORRY — I'LL BE SURE TO MAKE BOTH KŌJI AND HIROYA HAPPY."

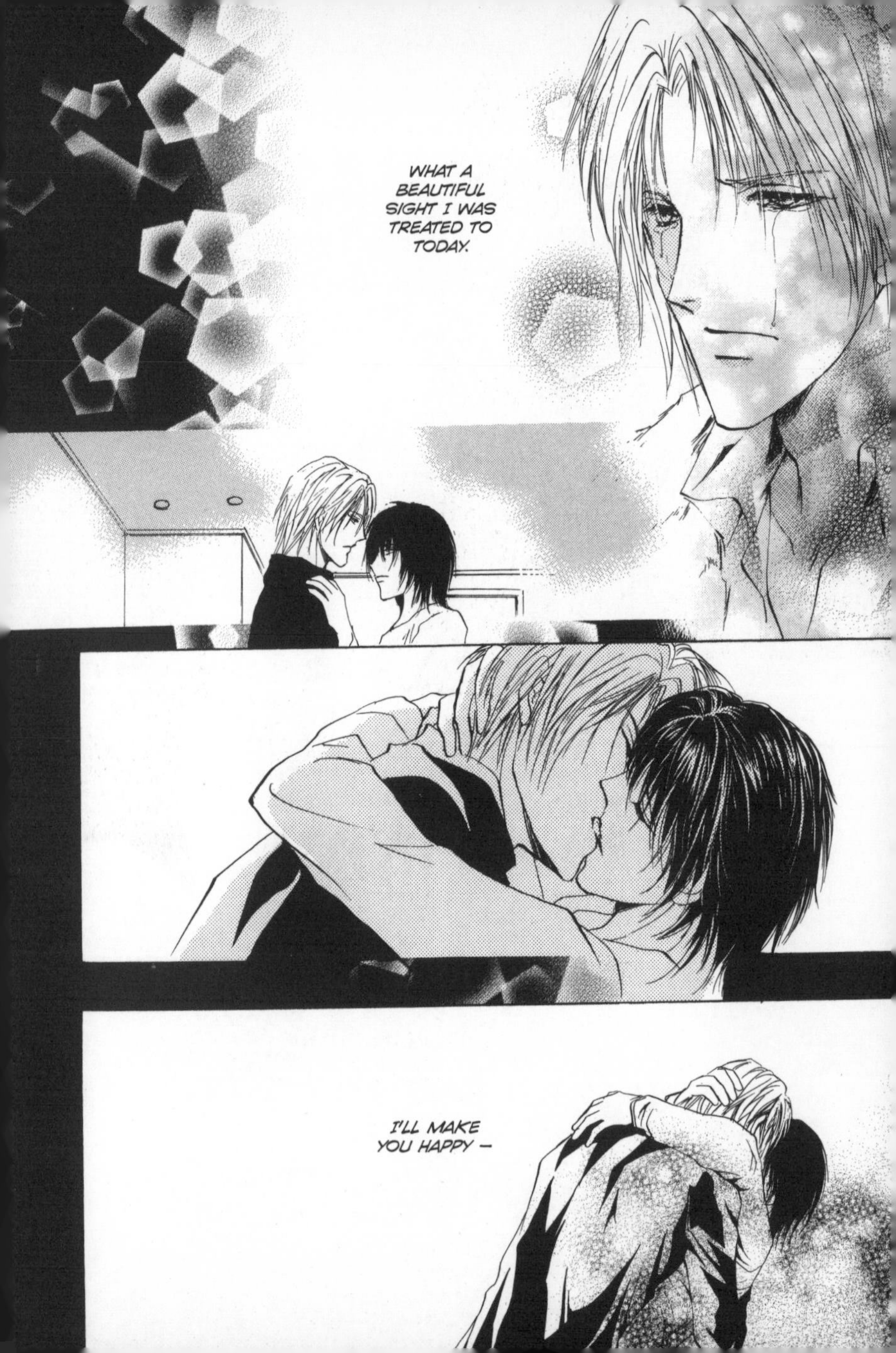
WHAT A BEAUTIFUL SIGHT I WAS TREATED TO TODAY.
I'LL MAKE YOU HAPPY –

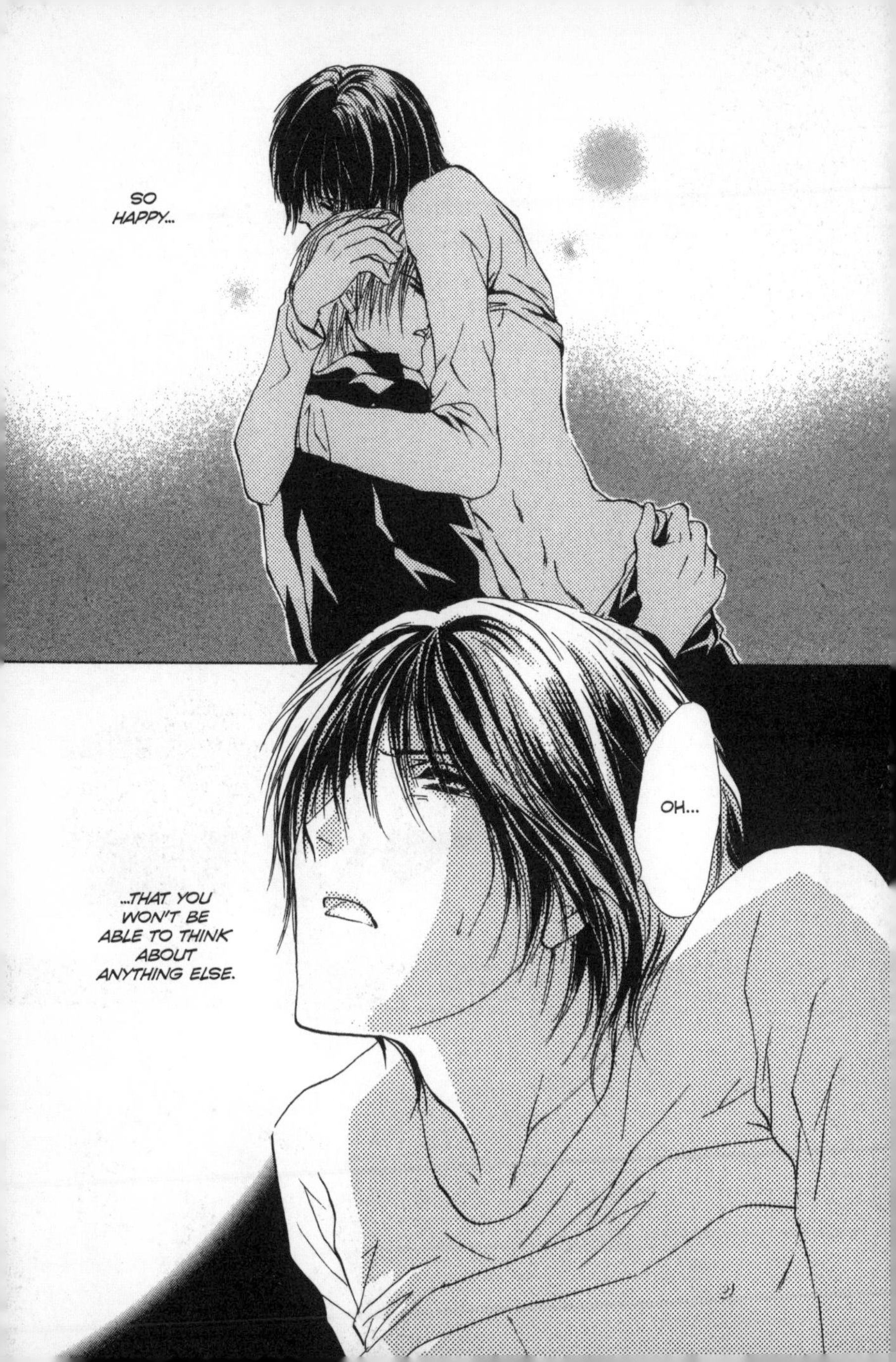
SO HAPPY...
OH...
...THAT YOU WON'T BE ABLE TO THINK ABOUT ANYTHING ELSE.

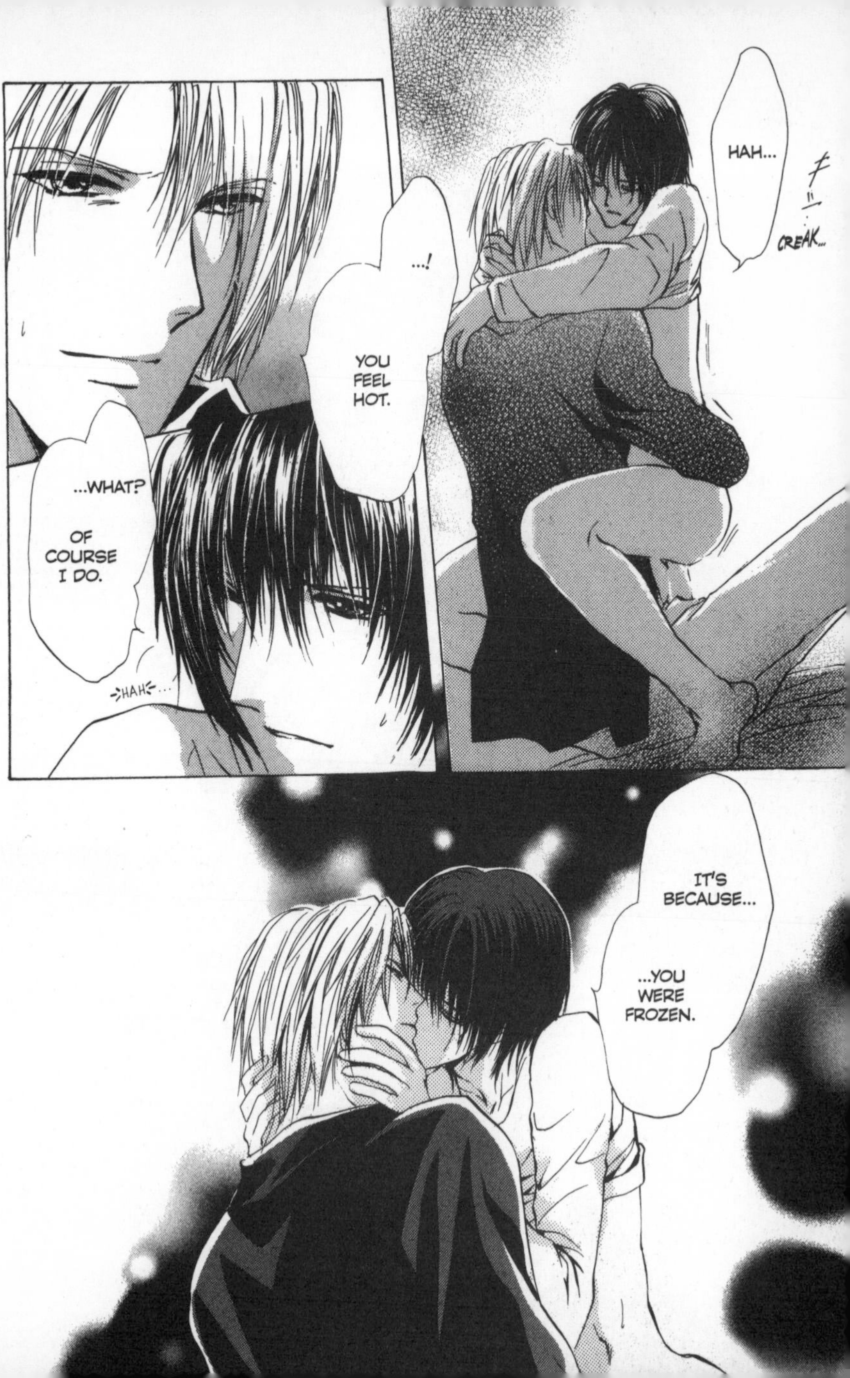
HAH...
CREAK...
...!
YOU FEEL HOT.
...WHAT?
OF COURSE I DO.
HAH...
IT'S BECAUSE...
...YOU WERE FROZEN.

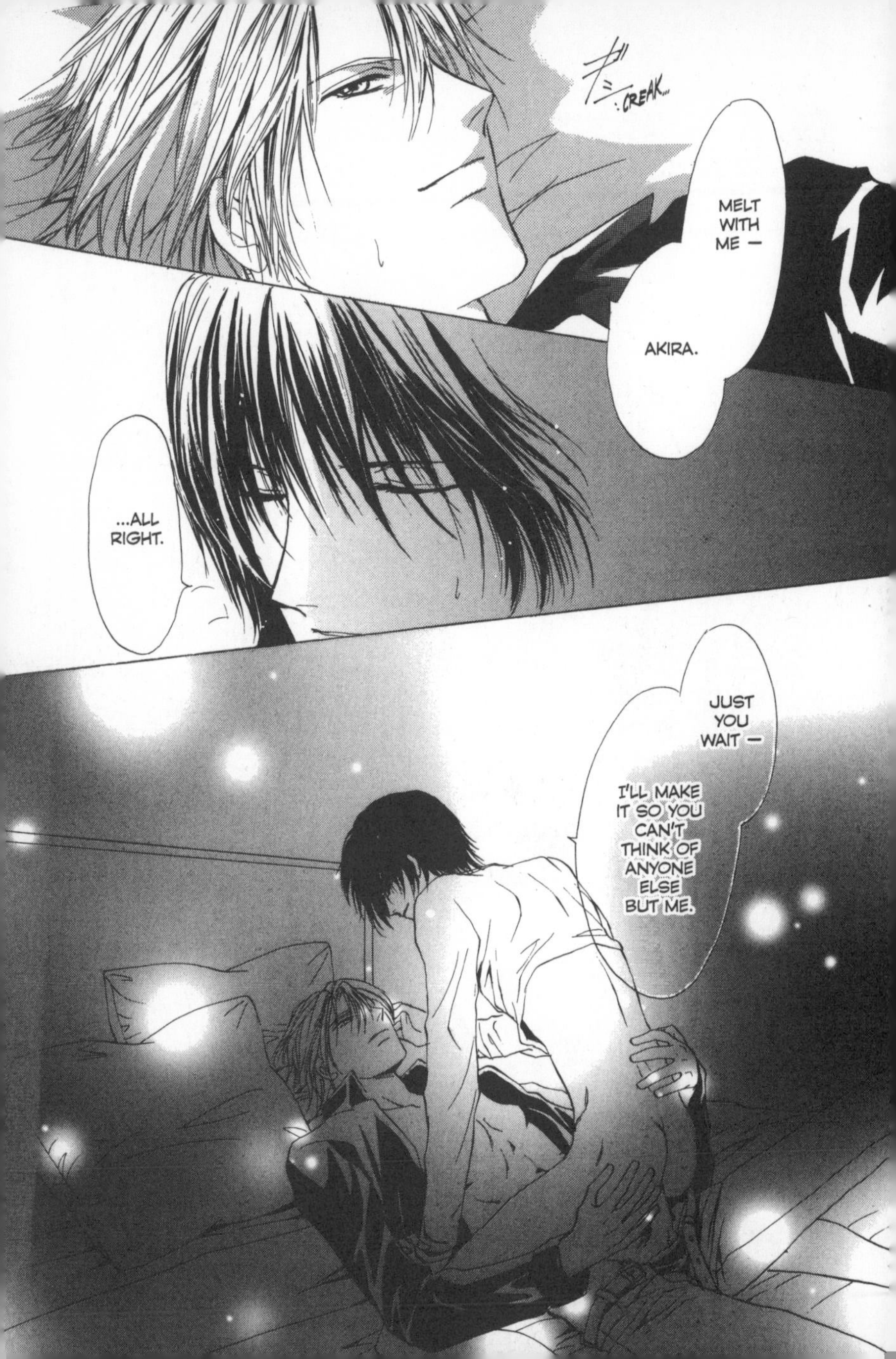
CREAK...
MELT WITH ME —
AKIRA.
...ALL RIGHT.
JUST YOU WAIT —
I'LL MAKE IT SO YOU CAN'T THINK OF ANYONE ELSE BUT ME.

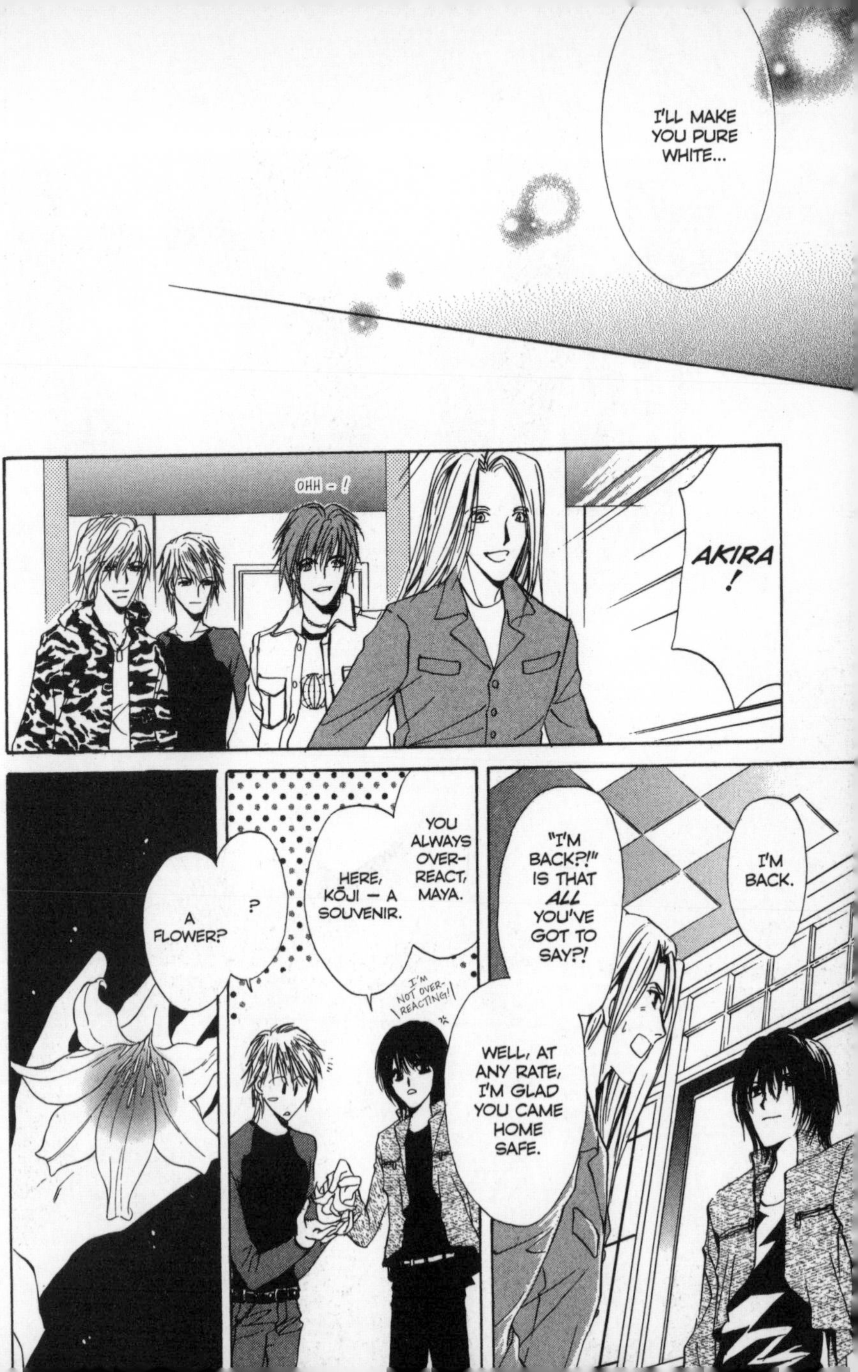
I'LL MAKE YOU PURE WHITE...
AKIRA!
OHH -!
I'M BACK.
"I'M BACK?!" IS THAT ALL YOU'VE GOT TO SAY?!
WELL, AT ANY RATE, I'M GLAD YOU CAME HOME SAFE.
YOU ALWAYS OVER-REACT, MAYA.
I'M NOT OVER-REACTING!
HERE, KŌJI — A SOUVENIR.
?
A FLOWER?

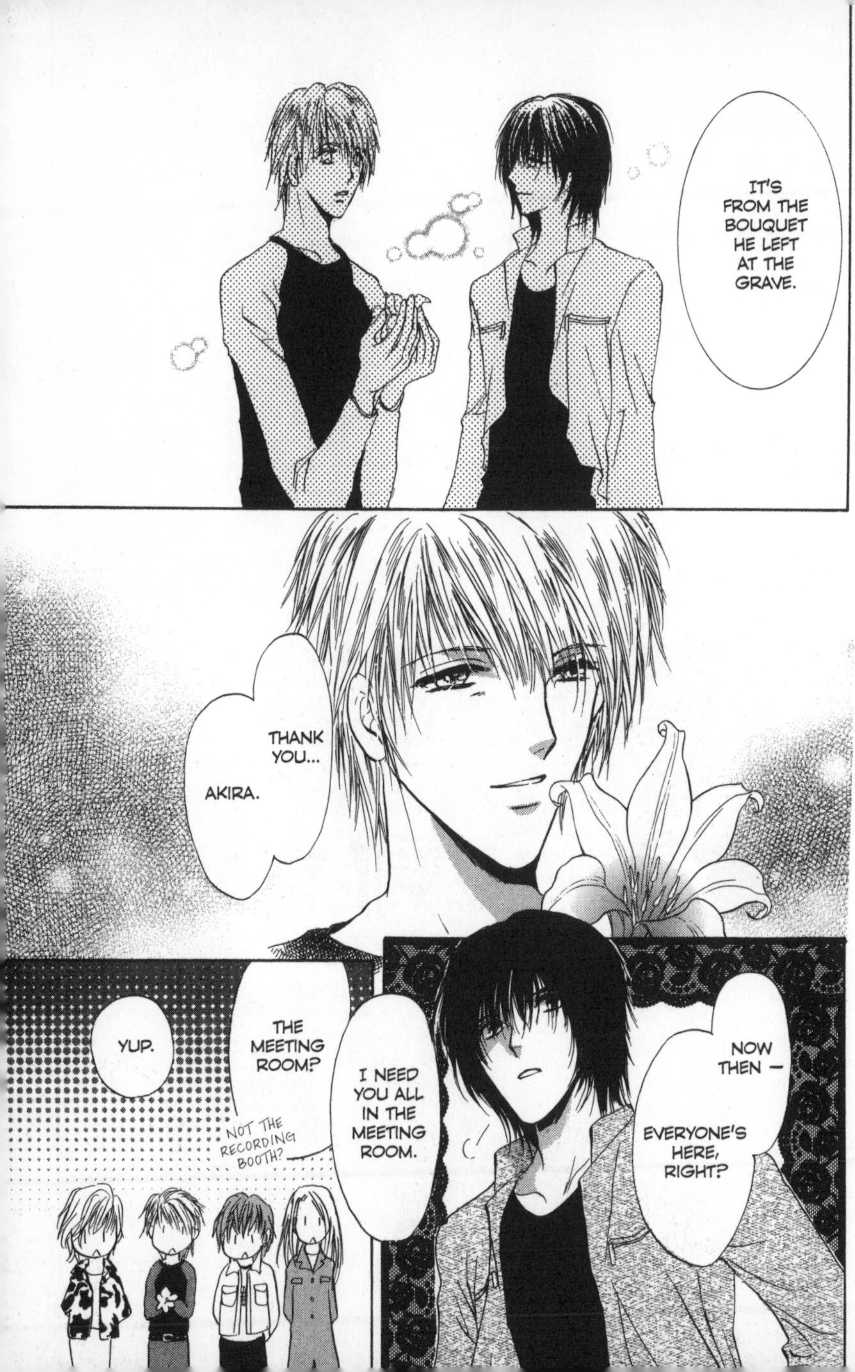
IT'S FROM THE BOUQUET HE LEFT AT THE GRAVE.
THANK YOU...
AKIRA.
NOW THEN —
EVERYONE'S HERE, RIGHT?
I NEED YOU ALL IN THE MEETING ROOM.
THE MEETING ROOM?
YUP.
NOT THE RECORDING BOOTH?

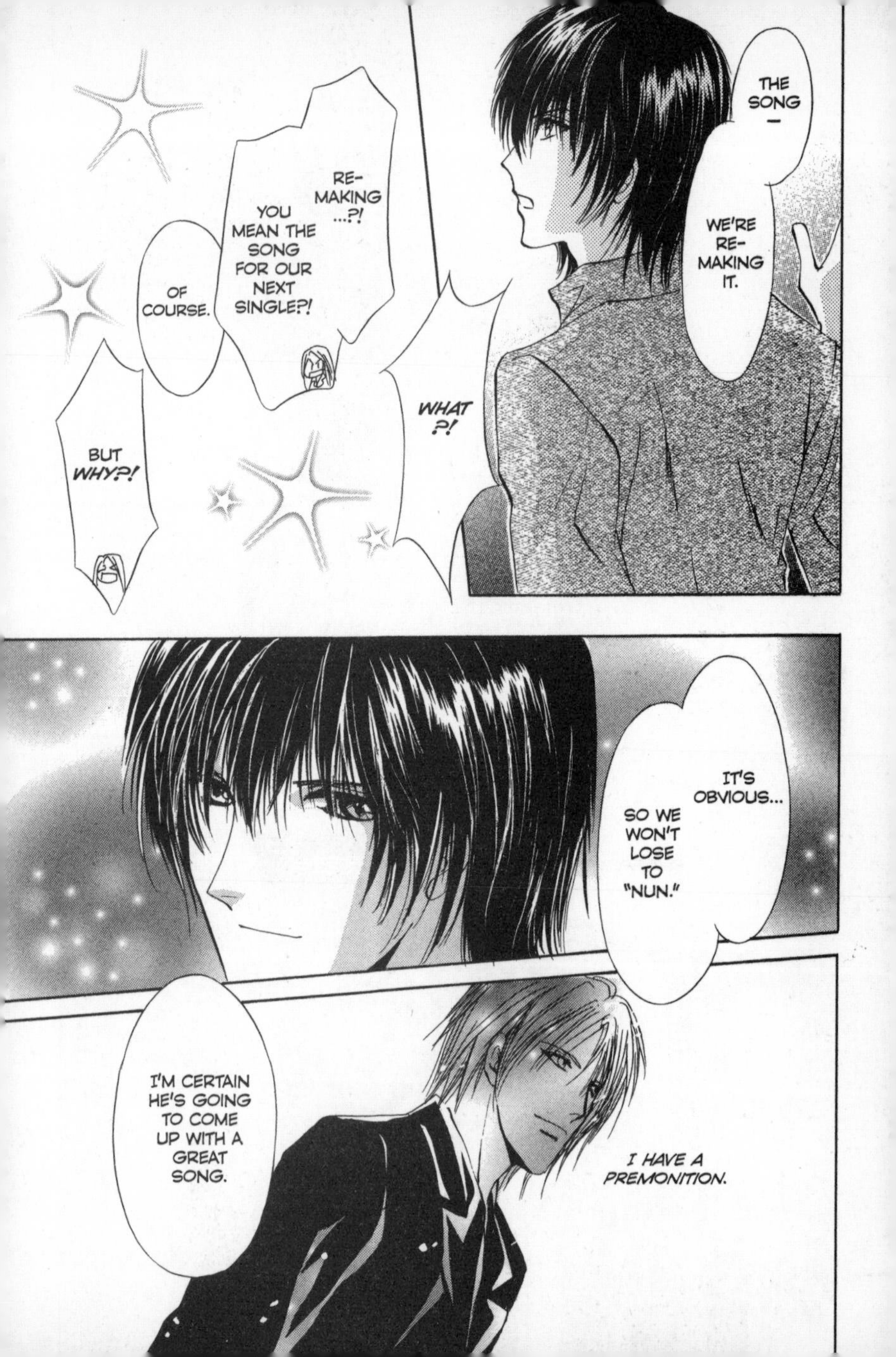
THE SONG —
WE'RE RE-MAKING IT.
WHAT?!
RE-MAKING...?!
YOU MEAN THE SONG FOR OUR NEXT SINGLE?!
OF COURSE.
BUT *WHY?!*
IT'S OBVIOUS...
SO WE WON'T LOSE TO "NUN."
I HAVE A PREMONITION.
I'M CERTAIN HE'S GOING TO COME UP WITH A GREAT SONG.

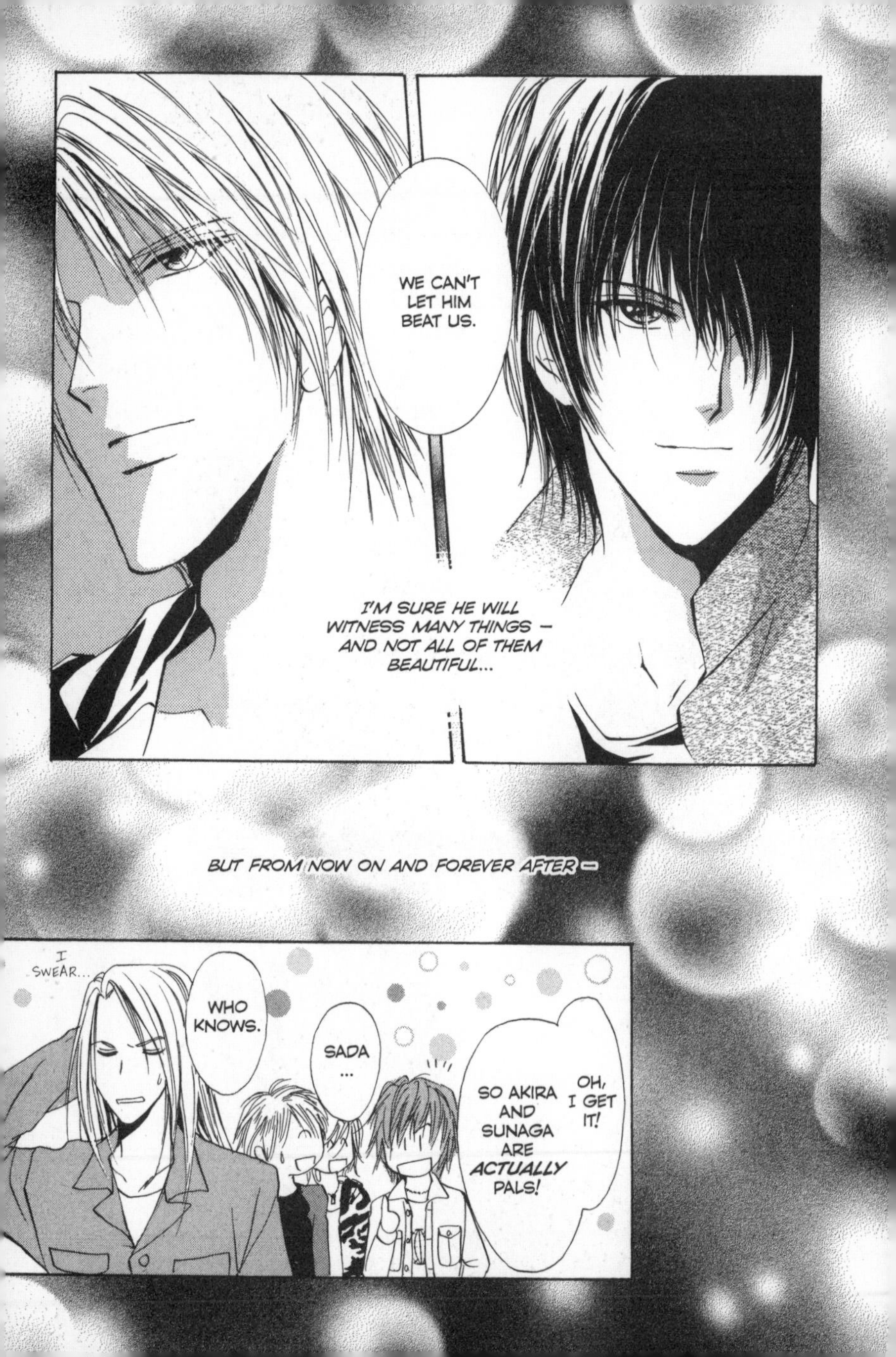
WE CAN'T LET HIM BEAT US.
I'M SURE HE WILL WITNESS MANY THINGS — AND NOT ALL OF THEM BEAUTIFUL...
BUT FROM NOW ON AND FOREVER AFTER —
OH, I GET IT!
SO AKIRA AND SUNAGA ARE ACTUALLY PALS!
SADA ...
WHO KNOWS.
I SWEAR...

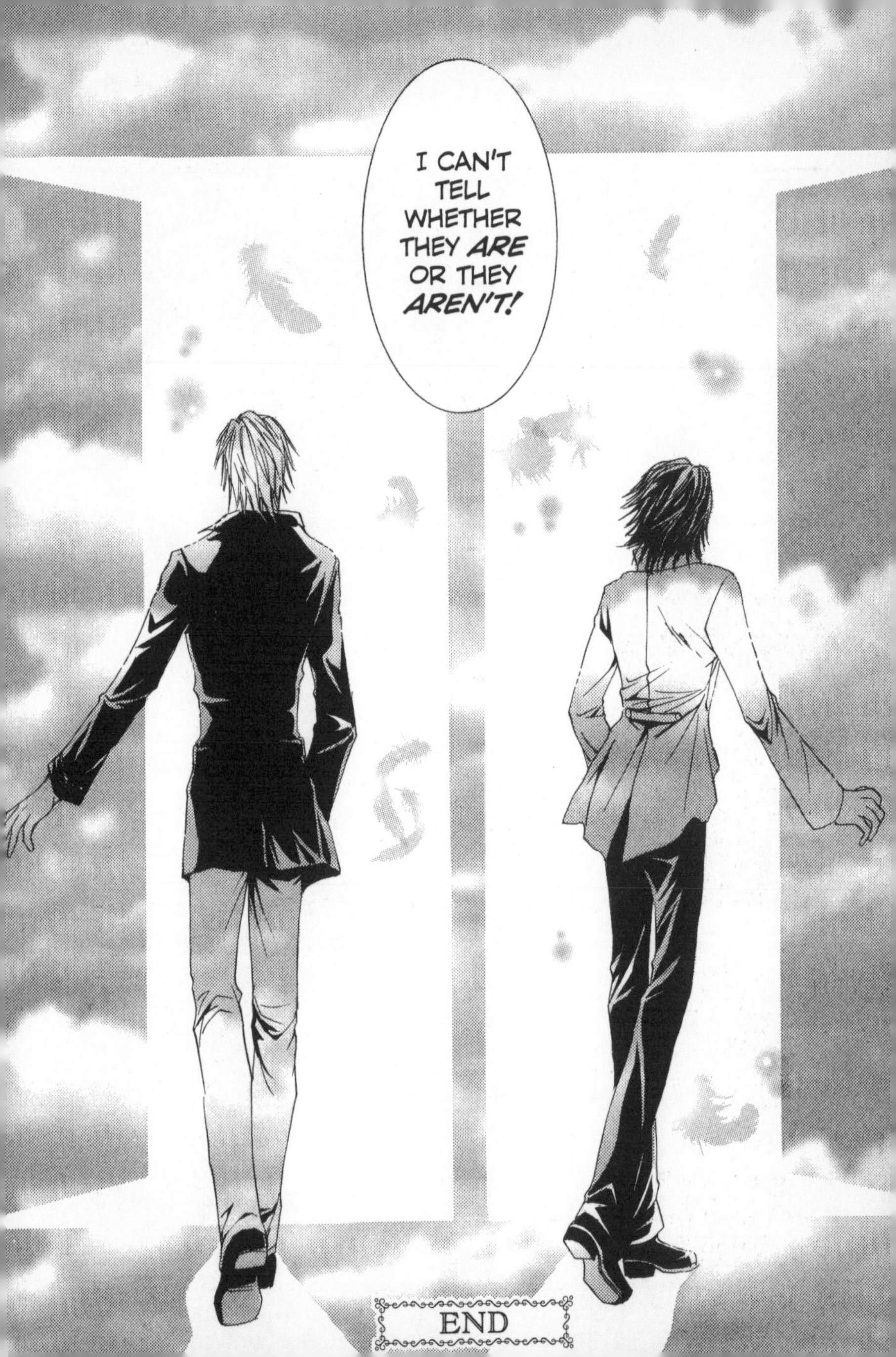
I CAN'T TELL WHETHER THEY *ARE* OR THEY *AREN'T!*
END

CHARON THEATER

カロン劇場

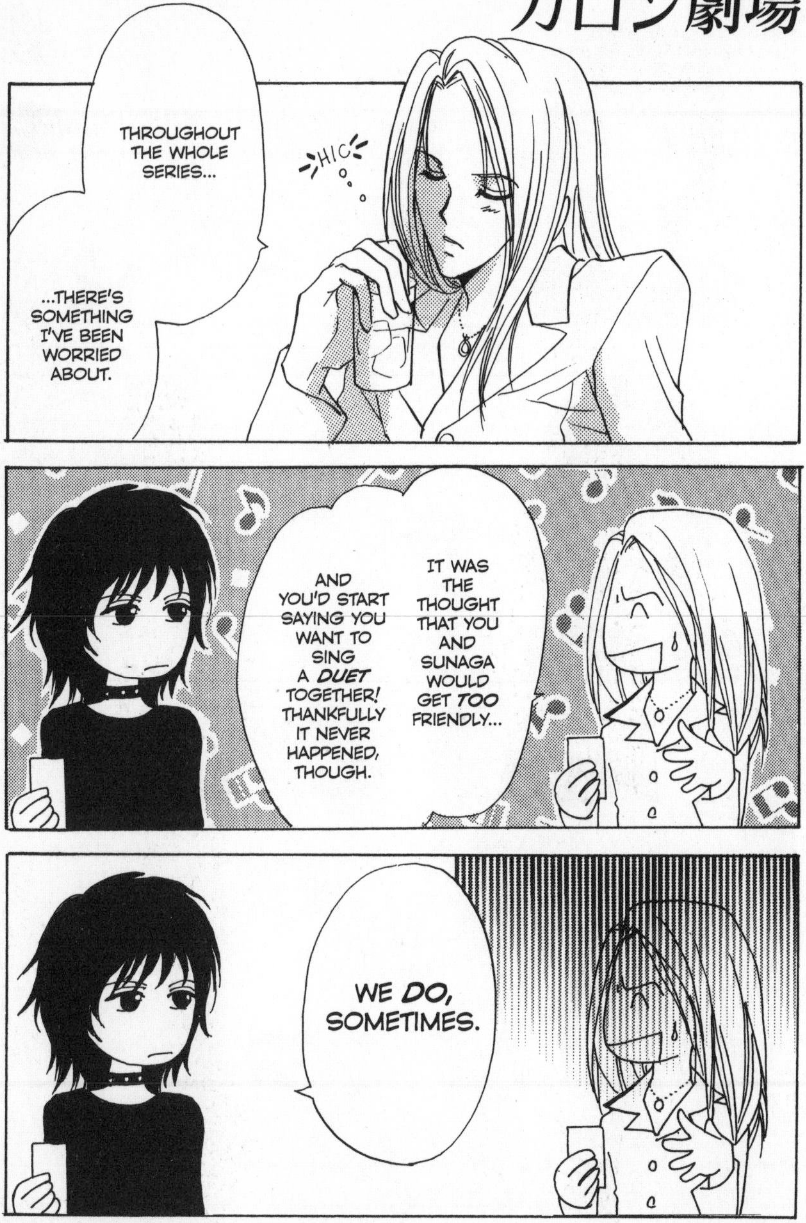
THROUGHOUT THE WHOLE SERIES... ...THERE'S SOMETHING I'VE BEEN WORRIED ABOUT.
HIC
IT WAS THE THOUGHT THAT YOU AND SUNAGA WOULD GET *TOO* FRIENDLY...
AND YOU'D START SAYING YOU WANT TO SING A *DUET* TOGETHER! THANKFULLY IT NEVER HAPPENED, THOUGH.
WE *DO*, SOMETIMES.

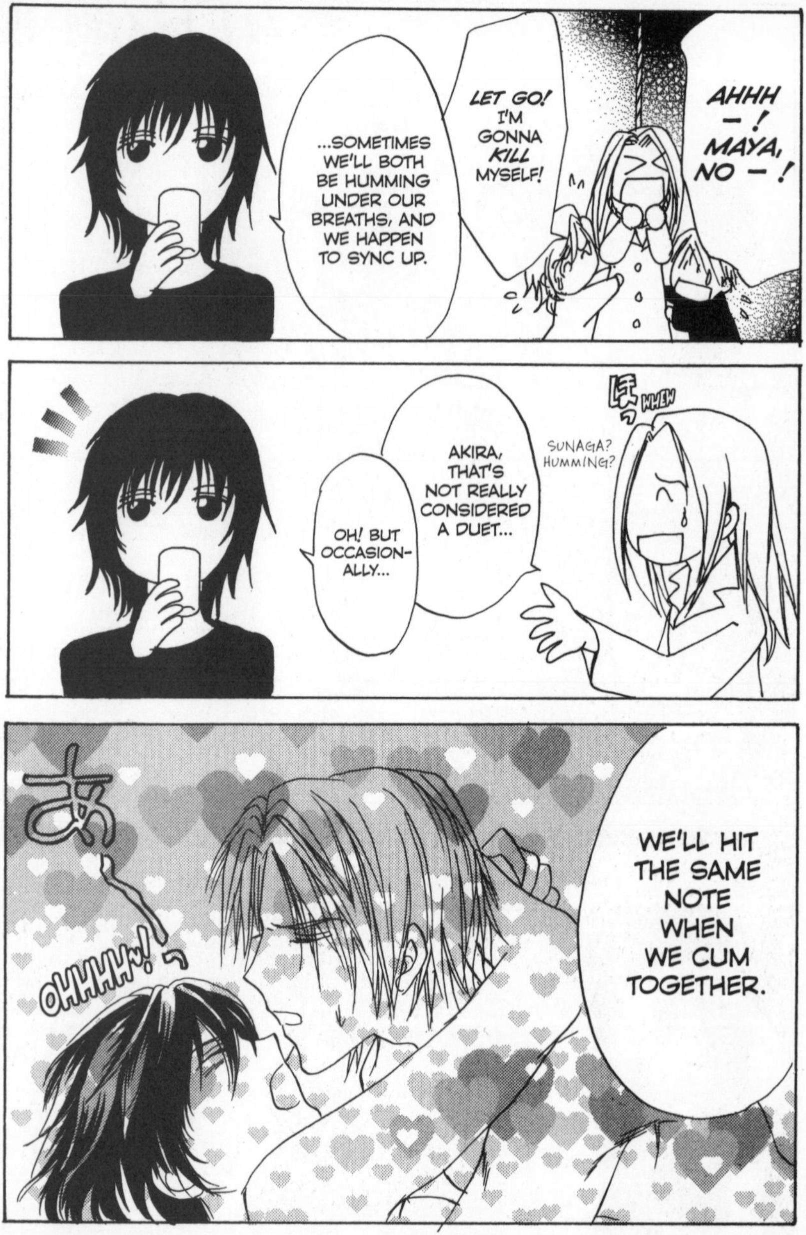
AHHH —! MAYA, NO —!
LET GO! I'M GONNA KILL MYSELF!
...SOMETIMES WE'LL BOTH BE HUMMING UNDER OUR BREATHS, AND WE HAPPEN TO SYNC UP.
ほっ WHEW
SUNAGA? HUMMING?
AKIRA, THAT'S NOT REALLY CONSIDERED A DUET...
OH! BUT OCCASION-ALLY...
WE'LL HIT THE SAME NOTE WHEN WE CUM TOGETHER.
あ〜
OHHHHH!

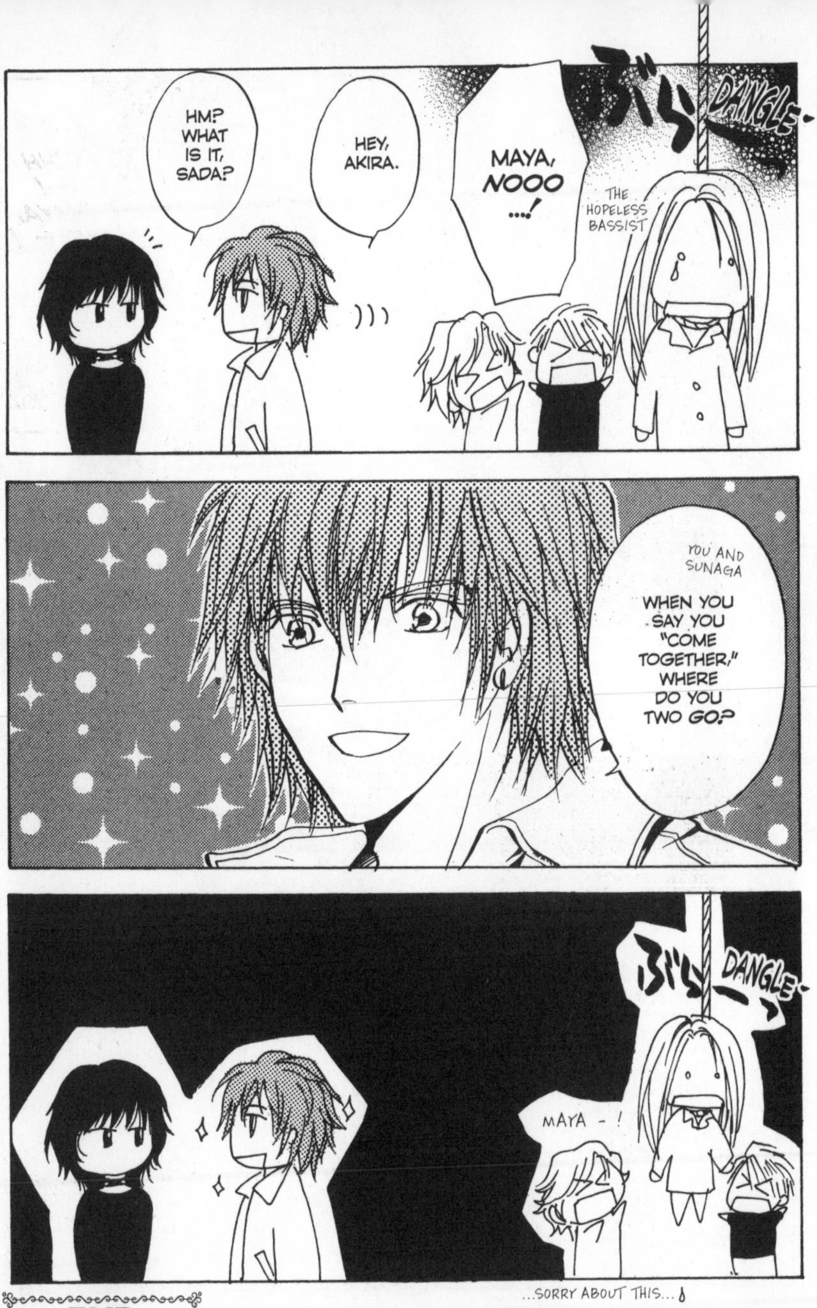
ぶらー
DANGLE
THE HOPELESS BASSIST
MAYA, NOOO ...!
HEY, AKIRA.
HM? WHAT IS IT, SADA?
YOU AND SUNAGA
WHEN YOU SAY YOU "COME TOGETHER," WHERE DO YOU TWO GO?
ぶらー
DANGLE
MAYA - !
...SORRY ABOUT THIS...
END

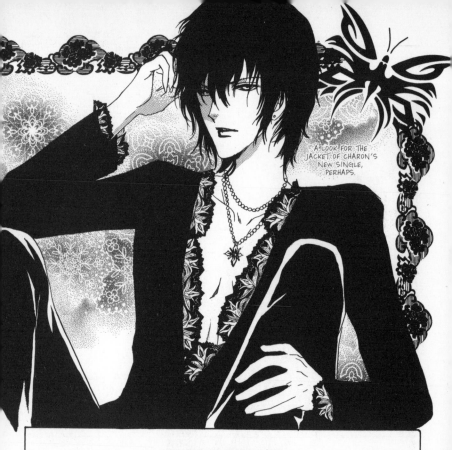

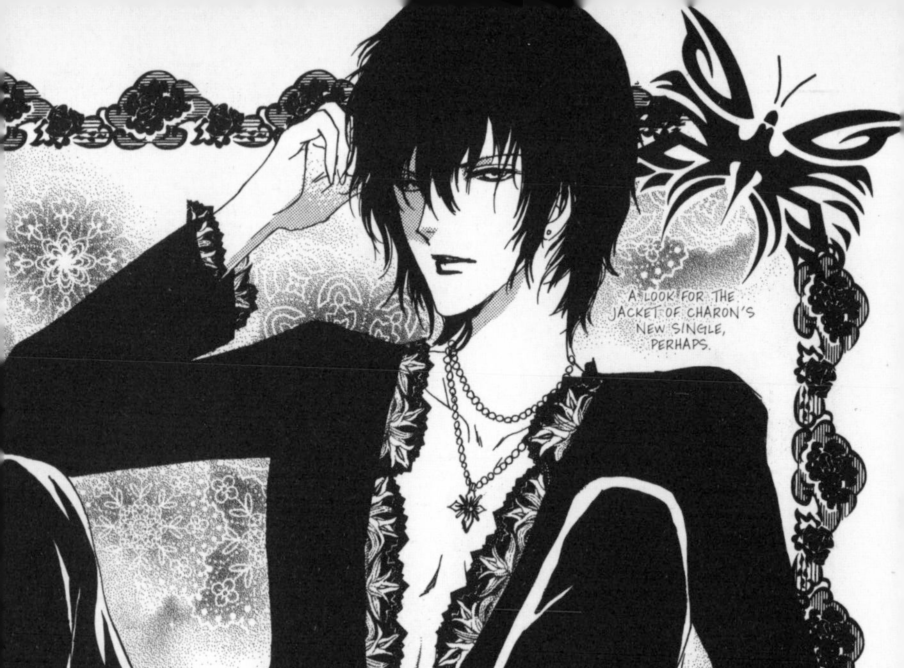
A LOOK FOR THE JACKET OF CHARON'S NEW SINGLE, PERHAPS.

AFTERWORD

YOU WHO HAVE READ THIS FAR! THANK YOU VERY MUCH!

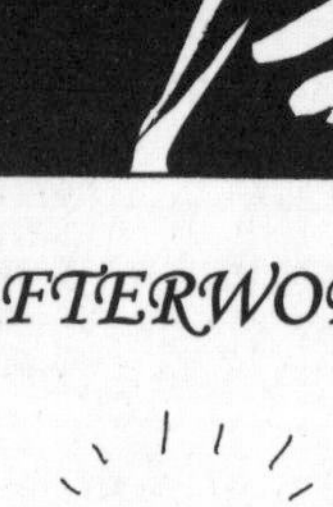
SORRY FOR THE WEIRDNESS OF THE BONUS ORIGINAL CONTENT.

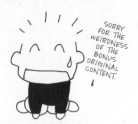

SOMEHOW, IT'S BEEN FIVE YEARS SINCE THE FIRST "YOKAN: PREMONITION" COMIC CAME OUT! THIS IS ITS SEQUEL, "NOISE."

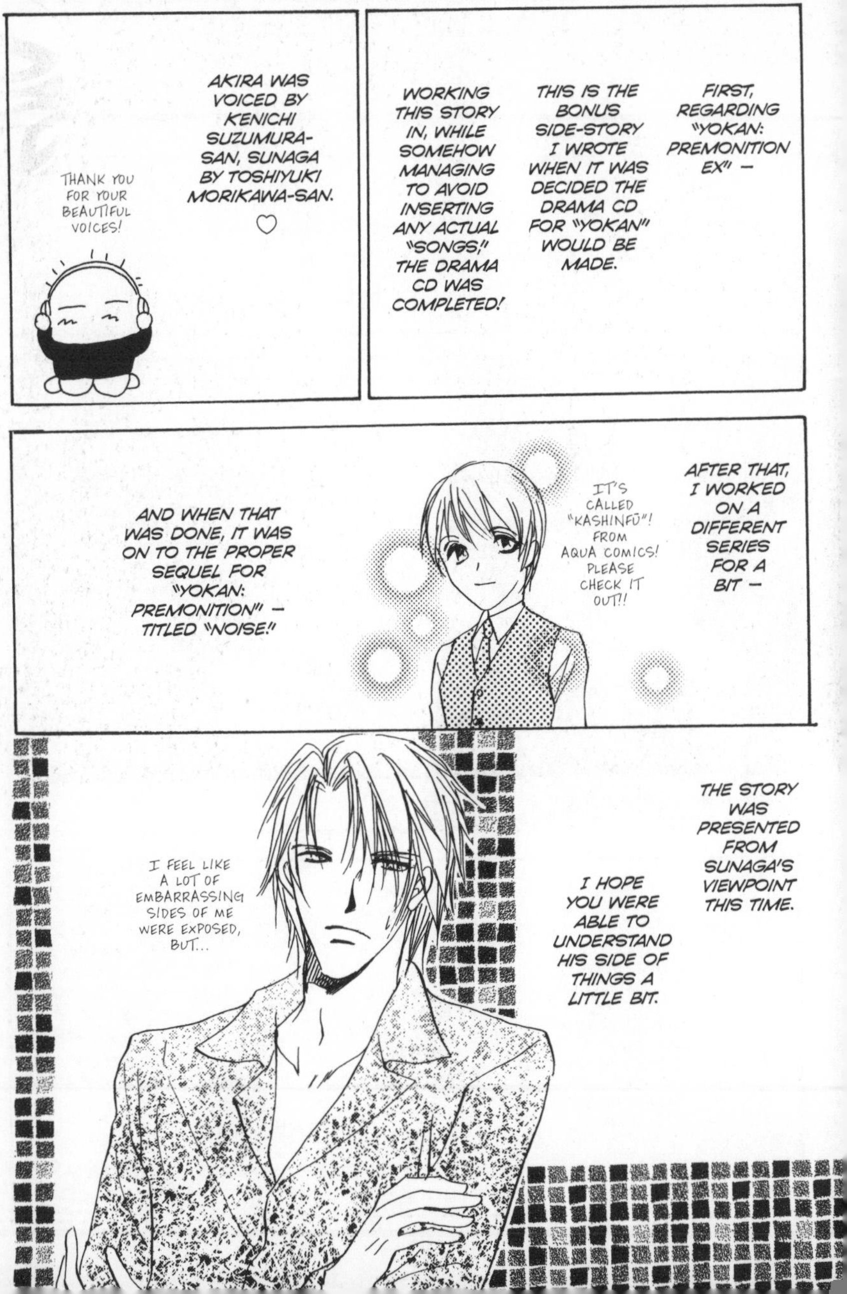
FIRST, REGARDING "YOKAN: PREMONITION EX" —
THIS IS THE BONUS SIDE-STORY I WROTE WHEN IT WAS DECIDED THE DRAMA CD FOR "YOKAN" WOULD BE MADE.
WORKING THIS STORY IN, WHILE SOMEHOW MANAGING TO AVOID INSERTING ANY ACTUAL "SONGS," THE DRAMA CD WAS COMPLETED!
AKIRA WAS VOICED BY KENICHI SUZUMURA-SAN, SUNAGA BY TOSHIYUKI MORIKAWA-SAN. ♡
THANK YOU FOR YOUR BEAUTIFUL VOICES!
AFTER THAT, I WORKED ON A DIFFERENT SERIES FOR A BIT —
IT'S CALLED "KASHINFŪ"! FROM AQUA COMICS! PLEASE CHECK IT OUT!!
AND WHEN THAT WAS DONE, IT WAS ON TO THE PROPER SEQUEL FOR "YOKAN: PREMONITION" — TITLED "NOISE."
THE STORY WAS PRESENTED FROM SUNAGA'S VIEWPOINT THIS TIME.
I HOPE YOU WERE ABLE TO UNDERSTAND HIS SIDE OF THINGS A LITTLE BIT.
I FEEL LIKE A LOT OF EMBARRASSING SIDES OF ME WERE EXPOSED, BUT...

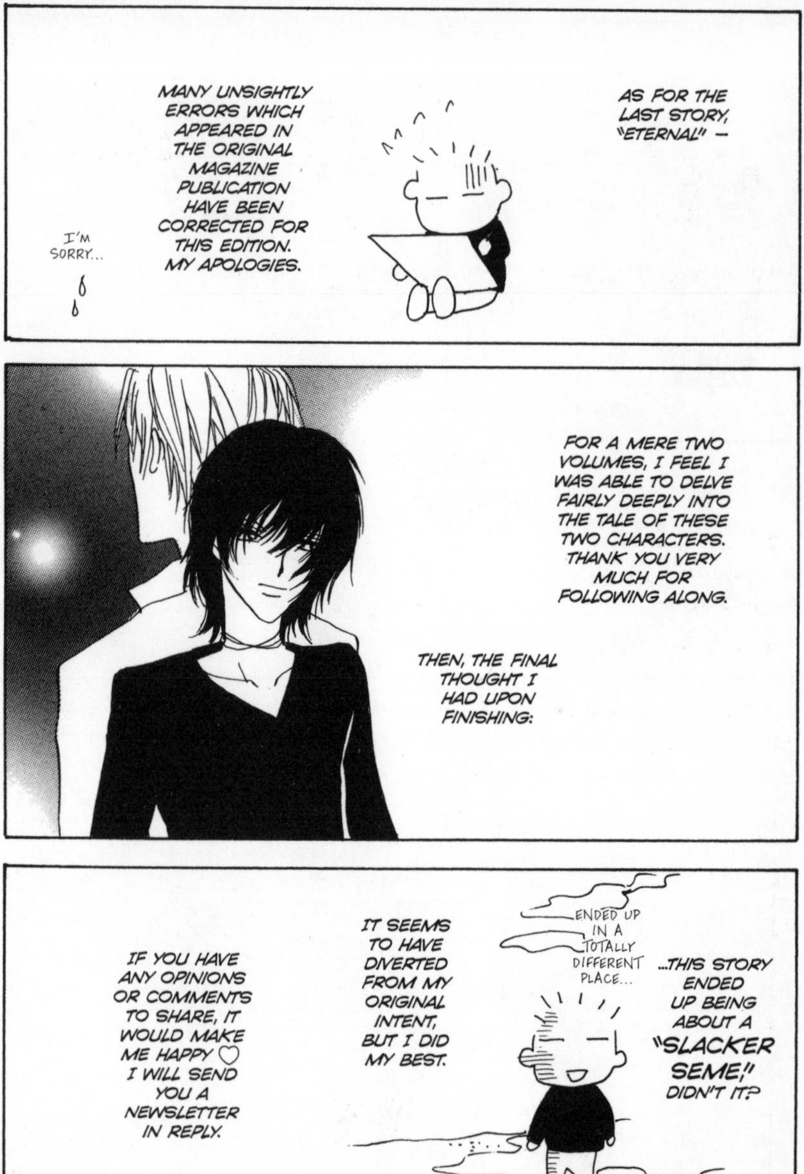
AS FOR THE LAST STORY, "ETERNAL" —
MANY UNSIGHTLY ERRORS WHICH APPEARED IN THE ORIGINAL MAGAZINE PUBLICATION HAVE BEEN CORRECTED FOR THIS EDITION. MY APOLOGIES.
I'M SORRY...
FOR A MERE TWO VOLUMES, I FEEL I WAS ABLE TO DELVE FAIRLY DEEPLY INTO THE TALE OF THESE TWO CHARACTERS. THANK YOU VERY MUCH FOR FOLLOWING ALONG.
THEN, THE FINAL THOUGHT I HAD UPON FINISHING:
...THIS STORY ENDED UP BEING ABOUT A "SLACKER SEME," DIDN'T IT?
ENDED UP IN A TOTALLY DIFFERENT PLACE...
IT SEEMS TO HAVE DIVERTED FROM MY ORIGINAL INTENT, BUT I DID MY BEST.
IF YOU HAVE ANY OPINIONS OR COMMENTS TO SHARE, IT WOULD MAKE ME HAPPY ♡ I WILL SEND YOU A NEWSLETTER IN REPLY.

OH, AND MY
HOMEPAGE
HAS CHANGED.

YOU WON'T BE
REDIRECTED TO IT
FROM THE OLD
HOMEPAGE (I'M
SORRY), BUT HERE
IS THE NEW URL
YOU CAN TYPE IN:

http://makoto-egg.com/

THERE'S A BBS, AS WELL
AS UPDATES ABOUT MY NEW WORKS.
PLEASE COME CHECK IT OUT ♥

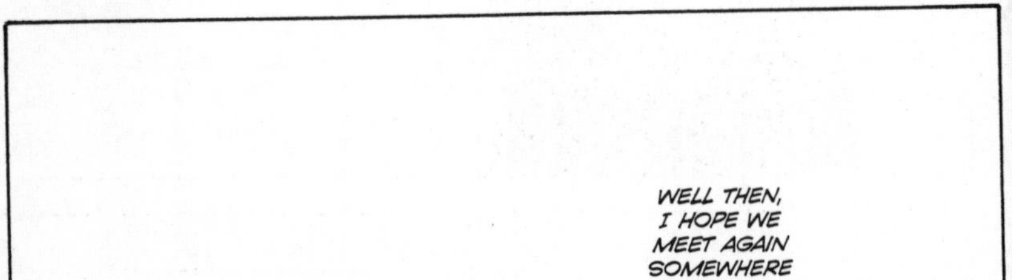

WELL THEN,
I HOPE WE
MEET AGAIN
SOMEWHERE
SOMEDAY.
♡

THIS
HAS BEEN
TATENO ~!

END

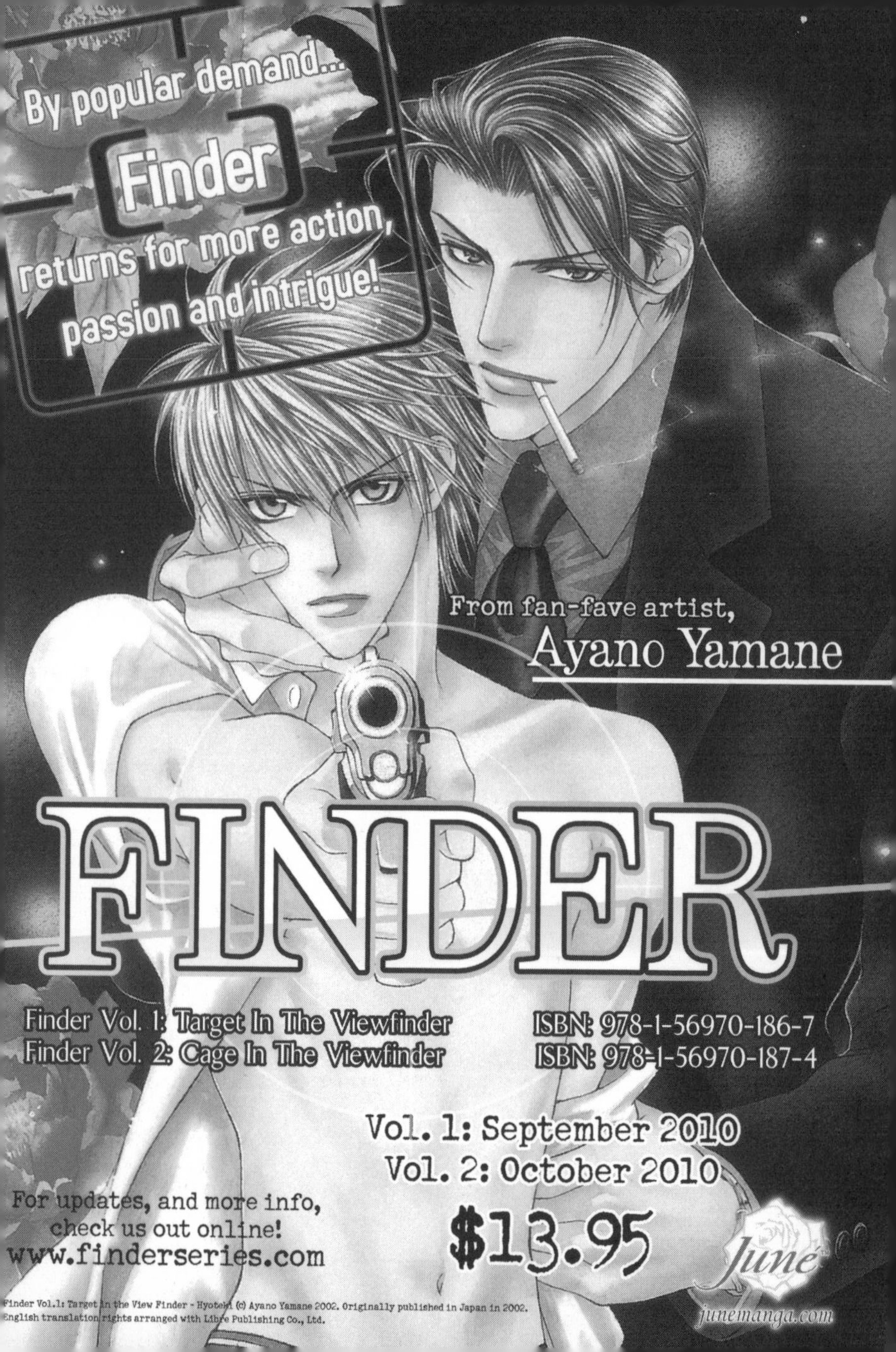
By popular demand...
Finder
returns for more action, passion and intrigue!
From fan-fave artist,
Ayano Yamane
FINDER
Finder Vol. 1: Target In The Viewfinder ISBN: 978-1-56970-186-7
Finder Vol. 2: Cage In The Viewfinder ISBN: 978-1-56970-187-4
Vol. 1: September 2010
Vol. 2: October 2010
For updates, and more info, check us out online!
www.finderseries.com
$13.95
June
junemanga.com
Finder Vol.1: Target in the View Finder - Hyoteki (c) Ayano Yamane 2002. Originally published in Japan in 2002.
English translation rights arranged with Libre Publishing Co., Ltd.

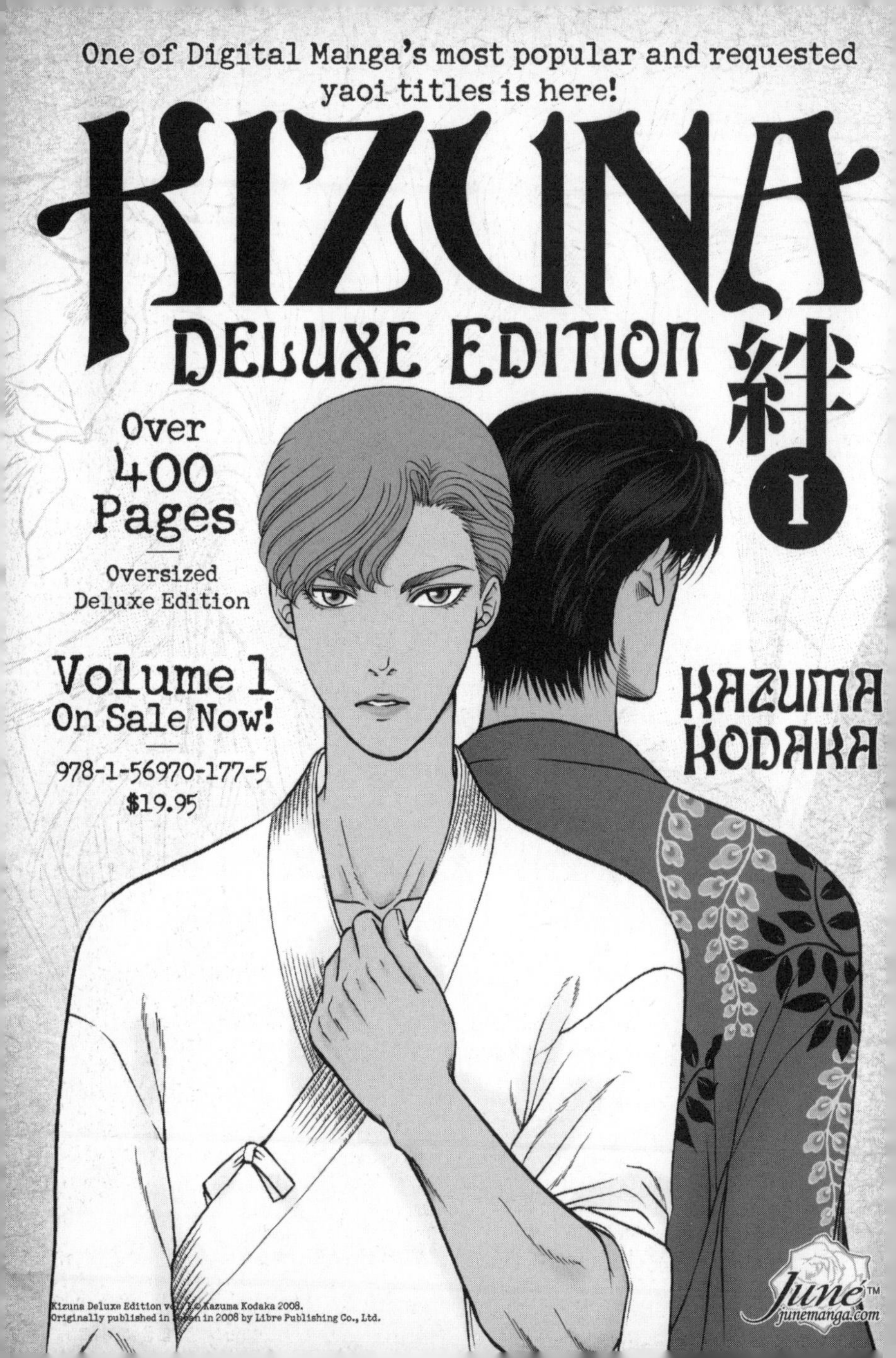
One of Digital Manga's most popular and requested yaoi titles is here!
KIZUNA
DELUXE EDITION
絆
I
Over 400 Pages
Oversized Deluxe Edition
Volume 1 On Sale Now!
978-1-56970-177-5
$19.95
KAZUMA KODAKA
Kizuna Deluxe Edition vol. 1 © Kazuma Kodaka 2008.
Originally published in Japan in 2008 by Libre Publishing Co., Ltd.
Juné™
junemanga.com

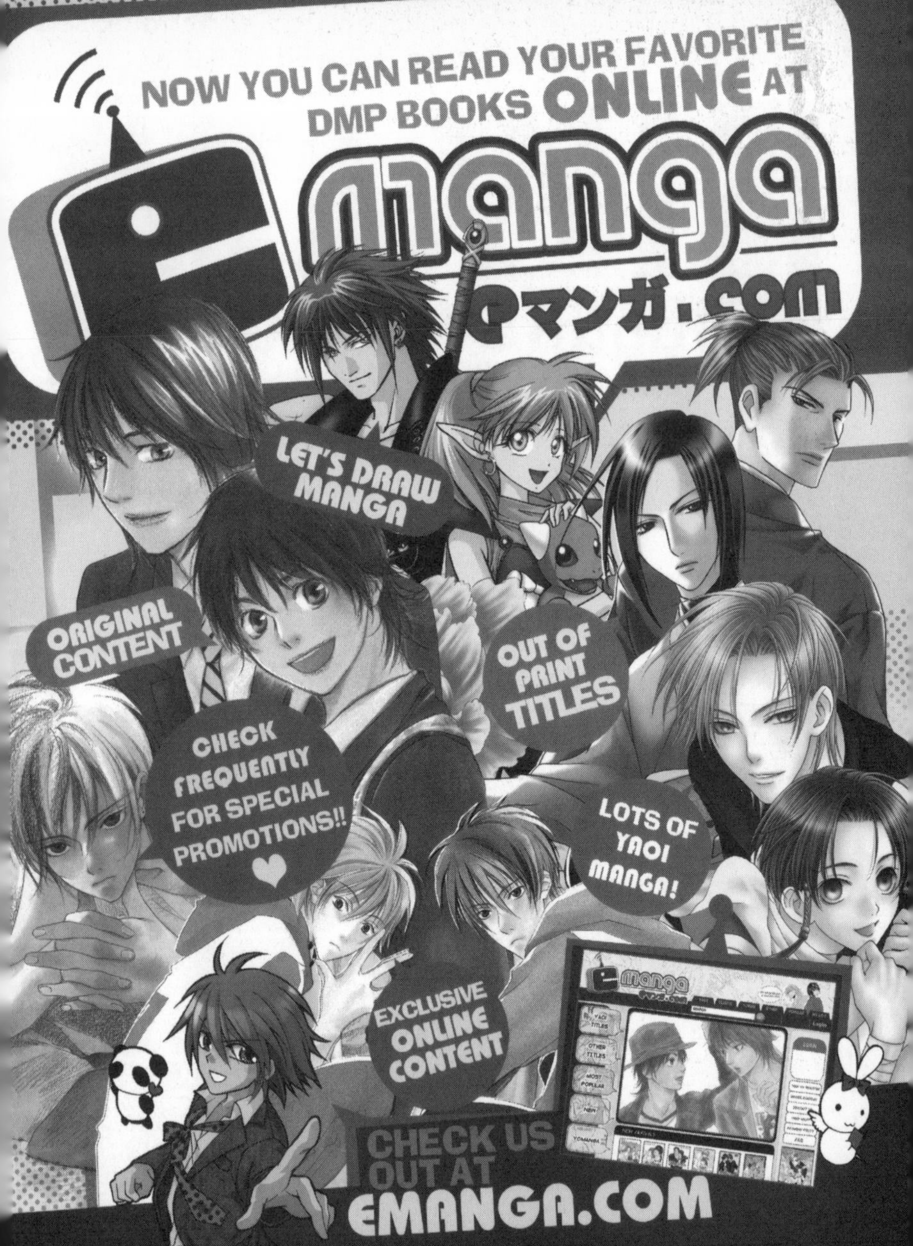
NOW YOU CAN READ YOUR FAVORITE DMP BOOKS ONLINE AT
emanga
eマンガ.com
LET'S DRAW MANGA
ORIGINAL CONTENT
OUT OF PRINT TITLES
CHECK FREQUENTLY FOR SPECIAL PROMOTIONS!!
LOTS OF YAOI MANGA!
EXCLUSIVE ONLINE CONTENT
CHECK US OUT AT
EMANGA.COM

STOP!

This is the back of the book!
Please start the book from the
other side...

Native manga readers read manga
from right to left to keep the manga
true to its original vision. To
enjoy, turn the book over and
start from the other side and read
right to left, top to bottom.

Follow the diagram to see how
it's done!

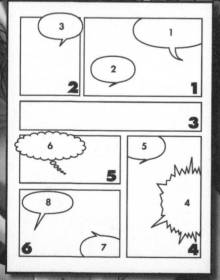

NATIVE MANGA

← **READ RIGHT
TO LEFT**

If you see the
logo above,
you'll know that this
book is published in
its original native
format.